MAIA

AND THE

R'ARMIMON GAMBIT

S. G. BASU

FOR MY SUPER FABULOUS BETA TEAM—BRENDA, DIANA, JOE

WITHOUT YOU, MAIA WOULD NOT BE MAIA

MAIA

AND THE

R'ARMIMON GAMBIT

GALACTIC MAP

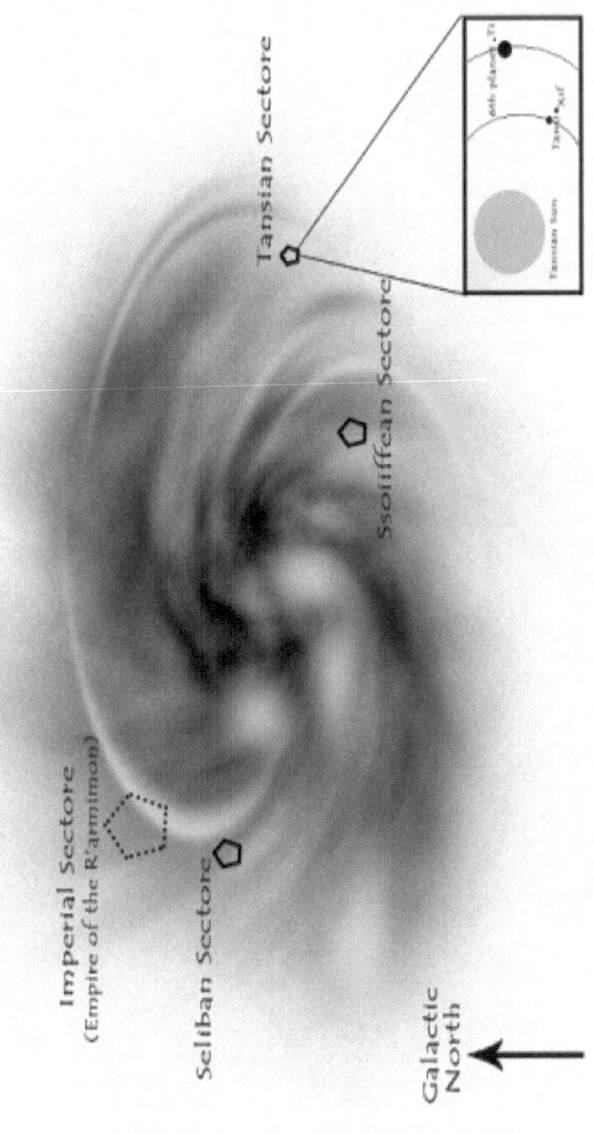

Imperial Sectore
(Empire of the R'armimon)

Seliban Sectore

Tansian Sectore

Ssoliffean Sectore

Galactic
North

Tansian Sun

Tansia XII

6th planet, TI

The Map of Tansi

Coloni Primei

Zagran ●

Coloni Vestei

The Third Continent

The Western Seas

The First Continent

ThulaSu ◎

The Eastern Seas

Dorgashian Folds

Miorie ◎

Shiloh ◎

Appian

The Second Continent

Coloni Aestei

The Fourth Continent

Tra ●

Coloni Centrei

Map Key

⬡ Jjord Settlement

◎ Solianese City

CHAPTER ONE

WAR GAMES

The Great Room was cold, even with crackling fires in two latticed grates desperately trying to spread warmth. The room was crammed. People stood in small huddles, talking in low voices. They seemed a nervous lot, frequently looking over their shoulders, cowering as they whispered some more. Quite often, they glanced at the closed entrance, as if they were expecting someone.

It was a while before the door finally opened and the crowd hushed immediately. A man wearing a black Gambrill, the uniform of the Scientific Defense Services or the SDS, rolled into the room in a chair fitted with wheels. He was covered from head to foot in bandages; tiny slits in the swaths revealed only his left eye, his nostrils, and his mouth.

Four people—two male and two female—followed him, all of them donning dark cloaks with hoods. The huddles disintegrated and quickly fell away toward the walls, heads bowing as the bandaged man made his way to the corner with the bigger fire.

"Thank you for making yourself available for this meeting," said one of the men who had followed the man in the chair. He pushed the hood off his head to reveal dark red hair. He was tall and his rounded nose was somewhat out of place on his otherwise bony face. "As you might have realized, this is not just a meeting of the Order of the Fyrstell . . . this is much more than that. We have been attacked. Our nation is under siege."

The crowd murmured, and the man waved to silence them. "Our Honorable Chairman Phocluus was grievously injured while trying to handle a threat that puts our existence in danger," he continued. "It is our immense fortune that the chairman has survived that vicious attack and he is recuperating well. Despite his condition, he insisted that he be present here today. He will sacrifice his life to save the future of his nation. He hopes that you, too, will meet this grave danger with a similar spirit."

Thunderous applause rolled throughout the room in jubilant waves. Someone shouted, "Chairman Phocluus," then another joined in, and then another, and soon the chants reverberated like drumbeats.

Chairman Phocluus slowly lifted his bandaged arms upward. When the room quieted, he beckoned the red-haired man. "Orano," he whispered through the slit of his mouth, "tell them . . . everything." Orano bowed.

"All of you know how the traitor ripped the heart of our Sedara to pieces," Orano started. "For years we have tried to put it back together, so we can leave this system. We have been looking for the Afterlight that was created when the heart was broken. For years, we searched in vain.

"Then, about a year ago, we traced one shard in the undersea territories and recovered it after much effort, only to discover that it contained no Afterlight. We realized it was either a fake or the Afterlight had morphed into something else. Once again, we were lost; we did not know how to proceed."

A collective sigh echoed across the chamber, like a desolate wind howling aimlessly through the forest.

"Since we discovered the identity of the traitor's offspring, we tried to have her cooperate with us. We pleaded that she help us out of this situation by sharing with us the memories of her mother. But just like her deceitful mother who stabbed us in the back, she refused to assist us. When we tried to secure her, she attacked."

"We lost some of our bravest soldiers and *almost* lost our esteemed chairman, but we gained in an unexpected way. This disgraceful attack revealed to us the location of what we have been seeking for so long. Just like we had suspected, the Afterlight has found a host for itself . . . the traitor's daughter."

A hush broke into a swell of murmurs. Then a woman's voice rose above the din and the room quietened once more. "That could only mean that she is a Shimugien."

"Yes, Lady Druuna," Orano said in an impatient tone.

Lady Druuna's cheeks looked flushed despite the chilly atmosphere. "And if that is true and she's still alive, then—"

"She could be as powerful as the princess, eventually," Orano interrupted. "But she is not there yet. It seems that she only recently became aware of her powers. We have to strike while she is still unprepared, before she can learn to use her powers with precision."

"But how?" Lady Druuna asked.

"Our forefathers dealt with the princess."

"And we have been paying the price since." The sharpness of Lady Druuna's voice cut through the residual hubbub. "I hope you're not suggesting that we tread the same path, Orano."

Orano pursed his lips and blinked. A tight silence hovered in the air. "Perhaps then, you can propose an alternative?" he responded bitterly.

"It's not my place to," Druuna replied. "This has to be taken up with the chancellor and the Custodians."

"We shall." Orano nodded. "In the meantime, there's no harm in assessing our options, is there?"

"I say we capture her right away," a man piped up.

Orano chuckled. "We cannot. First, we have to resurrect the chalice, the only thing powerful enough to restrain the Afterlight. And do not forget that the R'armimon are here. They will surely rush to protect her if they realize what she is."

"You think they do not know yet?" Lady Druuna asked.

Orano's shoulders sagged as he let out a long sigh. He shook his head, like the tired parent of a petulant child. "We hope not," he said. "Or they would have used her against us already."

"What do we do then?" asked another woman, her shrill voice piercing the taut air of the room.

Orano looked down at Chairman Phocluus, who nodded his bandaged head. "We stalk her, watch her every move," Orano replied firmly.

Lady Druuna gave a slight shake of her head. "How? Will you have spies tailing her?"

"It won't be very difficult to keep track of the girl as long as she's in that ludicrous contest," Orano said.

"You mean the Initiative?" Druuna asked, frowning. "But that's over. We decided to pull out when—"

"We can always change our mind," Orano said. A crooked smile twisted his lips. "We have to put on a show until we have readied the chalice. Then we make our move."

"How long will it take to get the chalice ready?" a man asked.

"We are working the miners hard to find the last of the Calbion on Ti. We are close," Orano said reassuringly, and the room broke out into cheers.

Chairman Phocluus raised a hand when the cheers had subsided a little. "Make no mistake, war is coming. Very . . . soon," he said. The broken words drifted out of his bandaged mouth and stilled the Great Room into a deathly quiet.

CHAPTER TWO

THE ROOF OF THE WORLD

Winter was a long and pitiless presence at ThulaSu. The cold, the darkness, and the swaths of snow that enveloped the ground in an icy, lifeless embrace never seemed to waver.

ThulaSu was far in the northern reaches of Tansi, perched high up above the craggy slopes of the Vesteran ranges. The mountains that surrounded the city shielded it somewhat against the blustery waves of cold that would have otherwise turned it into a barren wasteland, and in the shelter of the dark walls of the Vesteran, the city of ThulaSu thrived. To survive ThulaSu's dark and frigid winters, the mountain city's residents relied heavily on the notion of hope. There was an unmistakable grittiness about the place, something that made you push forth and keep on pushing and not give in.

Fifteen-year-old Maia—her fingers twirling a strand of dark-brown hair that ended a bit above her shoulder—looked out of the window of her room as the sun made its way above the peaks. The soft rays lit up her pensive face and made her hazel eyes glow. As

Maia watched the gold trickle down from the skies and spread across the expansive courtyard surrounding the Sun Temple, the frown grew deeper. Judging by the position of the sun, it was time for her daily control routines, and her best friend Dani was a little late.

It had been a few months since Maia and her friends arrived in ThulaSu. She had just escaped the Xifarians. They had almost captured her, but before they could haul her away to Xif, the light within her had revealed itself and burned them all.

The light saved her, but it was also unpredictable and hard to control, especially back then when it had just revealed itself. Every time Maia was angry or hurt, the energy of the light surged within her and tried to burst out. It was dangerous because if it broke free, it could scorch and kill anything near her. In other words, Maia was a living threat to anyone who came close.

Therefore, since arriving in ThulaSu, Maia had been assigned a stringent routine to control the power of the light. Each day started with exercises the Xinhagyi—the chief of the Order of the Sun, an armed league designated to protect ThulaSu—taught her to control the tumultuous powers raging within her.

Maia took breathing lessons, learned relaxation procedures and disengagement measures, and had long lessons in sparring. Even though Maia still felt the dreaded fiery rush inside her if she was agitated, no matter how little or for what silly reason, she could sense it quicker now and intervene to some degree of success. She practiced with devotion, never missing a moment of instruction with the Xinhagyi.

Dani was her companion during these exercises. Dani did not practice sparring along with Maia, but she had something else to work on. Dani was interested in learning the Solianese healing arts, and when she requested, the Xinhagyi had all too eagerly accepted her as a student. So, as Maia did her exercises, Dani went through her daily healing lessons. She took this opportunity with great seriousness and was never late.

This is not like Dani, Maia thought worriedly, as she pulled out her thick fur-lined boots and slipped a foot inside. A knock on the door sounded just then, and Maia rushed to open it.

Dani stormed in, out of breath and flushing. "We'll be late. Hurry up, you're dawdling like a Monkfish." The blue-eyed Jjord girl hastily tucked her short golden hair behind her ears and stomped in frustration.

This was new. Maia mused at her friend's demeanor. "Calm down, Dani," she said to the always-composed Dani. With a quick feel of her sword Bellator's hilt at her waist, Maia stepped outside. "We're not *that* late."

"We're plenty late. The Xinhagyi was going to show me how to scan for the nerve centers." Dani shook her head as they ran out into the corridor. "It's a long lesson. I've been trying to convince him to show it to me and he had finally consented. Now I blew it. You know how he hates lateness."

Maia sighed and stole a quick glance at her friend. The pensive frown that bunched Dani's forehead showed how much these lessons meant to her. Maia wondered how Dani would continue these lessons when the third and final stage of the Alliance Initiative started again. *If it started again,* Maia corrected herself quickly.

The sharp wind hit Maia's face with a thousand needles when the two girls stepped out into the courtyard. Gritting her teeth, Maia marched forward, forcing her mind away from the cold and into a sunny day two years ago in Appian.

The Alliance Initiative was how it had all begun. She had hated it when the Xifarians had forced her into the trinational competition after they had witnessed her expertly flying a glider, but it was not all that bad. Her team, Core 21, was almost like family. After having competed in numerous grueling challenges and been in several dangerous situations together, Maia and her teammates—Dani, Kusha, Nafi, and Ren—had grown into fast friends.

The Initiative was a competition between the nations of Xif, the Jjord, and the Solianese, in which kids between the ages of ten and sixteen participated. Touted to be a peace summit, it turned out to be a sham, a mere front set up by the Xifarians to gain access to the Tansian territories. The Solianese and the Jjord of Tansi barely agreed to it, almost to the point of suspending the project for about a year after the Jjordic phase of the competition. But now, if rumors around ThulaSu were to be believed, the Xifarians wanted to resume the Initiative.

For years, the Xifarians had been hunting for the broken heart of the Sedara — the artificial star inside the planet of Xif that enabled the planet-starship to fly across galaxies — that Maia's mother Sophie, had ripped. Recently though, they had become desperate to fix the Sedara, likely because the R'armimon, a shadowy foe of the Xifarians, had caught up with them. Since then, the Xifarians had grown more wily.

At first, the Xifarians used the cover of the Alliance Initiative to secure access to Tansian territories so they could search for the pieces of the Sedara. But now, things were different. The Xifarians now knew the location of the pieces they were seeking, that everything that was once inside the heart of the Sedara was now within Maia. They knew there was no way to resurrect the heart of the Sedara. Yet here they were, trying to resume the Initiative. And Maia could not fathom why.

"I only have a few days," Dani muttered under her breath as she wrapped her woolen scarf tighter around her neck. "The Xinhagyi will stop his daily lessons if that stupid Initiative starts up again. I hate myself for oversleeping."

"You overslept? What happened?" Maia asked. Dani was usually up long before sunrise, and she knocked on Maia's door precisely at the same time every day, like clockwork.

"Hans," Dani replied, sighing. "He was so upset last night about all that's going on. I kept talking to him, trying to cheer him up, and before I knew it, it was almost morning. Thought I would just make do with a nap, but I guess I should have just stayed up all night."

"What's Hans upset about?" Maia stopped for a moment to catch her breath as they neared the training arena behind the Sun Temple. Dani's older brother Hans worked closely with the Jjordic Leadership Council and often had information about the political maneuvering that happened behind the scenes. "It's about the Xifarians, isn't it? They must be forcing us to get the Initiative started, right?"

Dani did not answer, clearly distracted. She diverted her gaze toward the center of the open arena where the Xinhagyi sat meditating with a pile of scrolls to one side and some weapons on the other. "Ah, at least he's still here."

Something about Dani's avoidance of her question worried Maia. "What is it? What is Hans so concerned about?"

"Nothing, Maia," Dani said with a sidelong glance as she hastened to cover the distance between them and the Xinhagyi.

"Dani, wait." Maia grabbed Dani's arm, stopping her. "Is it about me then?"

"Patience is the greatest virtue." The voice seemed to float through the clear morning air, soft and calm, yet imposing in its crispness. Maia let go of Dani's arm and they slowly stepped toward the Xinhagyi. The old man's shriveled face had puckered even more from frowning. "Punctuality is a great virtue as well. Since you have failed to uphold the latter, today I shall test your respect for the former. Please, pick up your weapons, and let us try a Palonkian Contact, degree fifth."

Maia's mouth fell open as the Xinhagyi's words sunk in. Degree fifth? That was practically impossible.

"Have we decided to spend all day pretending to be statues?" the Xinhagyi said.

"Wish that was a choice," Maia muttered glumly. She took a deep breath and stepped into the training ring.

CHAPTER THREE

THE PALONKIAN CONTACT, DEGREE 5ᵀᴴ

The sun had coursed up the sky and spread its warmth a little when Maia and Dani had finished preparing their weapons. The Palonkian Contact was a difficult combat maneuver, and degree 5th meant it was almost near impossible. Butterflies danced in Maia's stomach at the thought of failing . . . again.

The Palonkians were natives of the South Seas, one of the few indigenous tribes that refused to become a part of the Solianese Empire after Tansi was colonized. For the most part, the Solianese left the Palonkians alone; they were too few anyway to make a difference in the political games. However, they were quick to adapt the Palonkians' combat techniques.

The Palonkians' preferred weapon were discs that resembled chakras broken in half, their jagged circumference shaped into various combinations of blade orientations. In the middle was a rectangular slot to be used as a handle. Degree 1st required only one disc in each hand, the serrated edges forming a sharp extension over the knuckles.

The Palonkian Contact was mostly a fistfight, but instead of using bare fists, now one had to contend with fists covered with saw-toothed blades and spines. Degree 5th meant holding five discs in each hand in which the combatant's fists resembled a porcupine of sorts.

The training blades were quite harmless though, only made of palm fronds and they lacked any sharp edges. However, their rims were laced with a red dye that left its mark on the opponent's body.

The Xinhagyi's voice cut through the cold. "Ready?"

"What a stupid mess," Dani grumbled, struggling to arrange five discs in her right hand. "All because of my—"

"Are we ready yet?" the Xinhagyi's voice came again, persistent and thoroughly vexing.

"I hate all this combat training," Dani muttered. "All this senseless fighting and trying to hurt each other."

Maia sighed. While Dani had never been too aggressive, she had not always shied away from combat either. But lately, she seemed to despise all sorts of combat training. Maia wondered if the transformation had been triggered by her friend's dedication to the art of healing. Whatever the reason, Maia did not think it mattered. Dani had to fight if she wanted her healing lesson from the Xinhagyi.

Maia, on the other hand, enjoyed the training sessions. She was far from being in control of the powers within her, but it was getting better every day. Now she could wield the power to some extent, summon the light inside her by simply saying 'Yoteh'—the invocation chant the Xinhagyi had taught her. The light did not always respond to her call but when it did, Maia could manipulate the energy somewhat.

Smiling to herself, Maia walked over to the center of the arena with cautious steps, clutching the discs tightly in both hands so their formation would not be messed up, and took her stance. Dani followed shortly after, her face scrunched, lips puckered, and brows knit in a deep frown.

"Begin!"

Maia took her first swipe at Dani. Dani sprang back, but not fast enough. Maia's right hand had made contact and a red streak of dye left a mark across Dani's right shoulder. The Xinhagyi chuckled loudly and rose to his feet, circling the warring duo as he spoke.

"Healers have an inclination to shy away from combat. We often find it difficult to indulge in a sport that harms the bodies that we strive to heal, but you cannot give in to such urges."

Maia tried to land a blow on Dani's shoulder but missed.

The Xinhagyi continued. "Our experience in combat teaches us how wounds come to be. Knowing how we can hurt each other is critical in understanding how to heal the body from such injuries. Moreover, you always need to learn to defend yourself."

Dani seemed to have taken the Xinhagyi's words to heart. She came in fast, her fist dazzling in the bright sunlight as it grazed past Maia's forehead. Maia jumped to the left and lunged, planting a blow on Dani's stomach. Dani's armor took the brunt of the assault, but the force of the strike knocked the girl off her feet and she fell onto the ground, heaving.

"Not good." The Xinhagyi strode over to Dani and frowned. "You might feel a sharp pain when you inhale. Your friend got you right above the Halcyionic nerve center. It is named after a famous warrior of the Lower Houses, Tenki Halcyion, who was also a healer. He was injured in a battle and paralyzed from the waist down for the rest of his life. His life-changing injury came from a blow to the Halcyionic. Remember that location—it is a particularly sensitive seat of nerves."

Dani slowly rose to her feet and soon they were punching, swiping, and ducking once again. The Xinhagyi circled them, observing their moves, explaining techniques, and admonishing them or praising them from time to time.

Palonkian Contact was one of the most exhausting combat exercises. Maia's fists throbbed, her grip on the discs slipping as sweat collected on her palms. Even in the cold, Maia was drenched. Her heart beat furiously, and her feet started to drag. There was no sign of the worrisome searing sensation of a blast furnace inside her, no indication of the endless energy that had once been the heart of the

Sedara trying to break out of her.

That's a good sign, Maia thought. She swerved wildly to dodge Dani's jab and failed. The hit left a lingering sting on her left jaw. Dani was good, but she needed to be better.

Maia sidestepped to avoid a vicious hook. She swerved and brought down both hands on Dani's shoulder before the girl could regain her balance completely. Dani fell forward but recovered quickly. She came fast at Maia, showering punches on her body as she closed in.

Maia retreated, her thoughts dithering for a moment. The Xifarians had taken everything from her. First, they killed her mother, and then, about a year ago, they murdered Dada, her grandfather. She had been on the run since. Maia's fists tightened, nails digging painfully into her palms. The Xifarians were going to pay for it all. She was going to make them pay.

Dani closed in faster than Maia had expected. She tried to duck, but Dani kicked, her left foot landing on Maia's chest with a ringing thud.

Maia's insides crumpled as the air left her lungs. She saw the Xinhagyi's eyes widen and the blue skies swirl as her body flew backward and landed on the ground with a dull thump. Her back erupted in pain, her sight turned hazy.

As Maia struggled to breathe, a dazzling curtain of fire drifted over her senses and wrapped around her. Beyond the curtain, a dark shadow hovered to life, and the figure crept toward her.

"It is not only my Xif, it is yours as well, as it should have been your mother's," a man's voice said, steady and cold. Even though it felt like she had known that voice all her life, Maia could not remember to whom it belonged.

"Don't you dare speak of my mother," her own reply drifted to her ears. Scorching flames burned her insides. Maia yearned for a breath of cold air but found none.

"Your mother was a traitor. And you will *always* be the traitor's daughter."

Maia shuddered. She knew that voice and she had heard those words before, but why couldn't she place them?

"Stop," she screamed. A volley of fire broke out from her palms and hit the shadowy man, flinging him backward through the air.

Cold hands grabbed her face.

"Miir?" Maia blurted.

Someone slapped her cheeks. Voices called her name and the curtain of fire dimmed.

"No," Maia screamed, "don't go." She wished for the curtain to stay. She needed to find out what happened to that man. Who was he? Why did he remind her of Miir?

"Maia, wake up." The Xinhagyi's voice tinkled through her senses and the last traces of fire died down inside her.

She was sprawled on the ground; the Xinhagyi was bent over her while Dani stood to her side, watching, her crumpled face stained with tears. Maia noticed the smoke rising from her fists. The palm fronds were gone; she had burned them completely.

"What happened?" she asked, propping up on her elbows. "I didn't hurt you, did I?"

Dani broke into a sob. "No. I hurt you bad. You went into one of your . . . fits. I shouldn't have—"

"Dani," the Xinhagyi interrupted sharply. "One of the most important lessons in being a healer is being able to have your emotions in check. Serve with your heart, but act with your brain. This is *not* your fault, so do not blame yourself for it."

Dani nodded as she wiped the tears from her cheek, then kneeled next to Maia. "Did you see something, Maia? You were mumbling."

"I heard voices. I saw someone . . ."

"Miir?" Dani asked almost apologetically. "You called his name."

"I don't know who I saw, but the voice was familiar." Even though she did not know a moment ago, now Maia had no doubt that it *was* Miir. She knew that voice, one that had insulted and mocked her so much over the years.

Three years ago, during the Xifarian leg of the Alliance Initiative, the Xifarian chancellor's son, Miir, was Maia's team mentor. Once, he had saved her from an assassin of the R'armimon. They had drifted apart since, mostly due to differences in loyalties.

But what did this vision mean? It felt as if she had heard those words before, said those words before. But when? The last time she had spoken to Miir was at the pier on Lupitiali before he had thrown her into the poisoned waters below. Then he went on to murder her Dada. And Herc and Emmy.

Maia stifled a groan and turned toward the Xinhagyi. Perhaps he would know what it meant. "Why did I see this?" she asked. "I haven't had a vision in a long time."

The Xinhagyi's lips thinned into a line, and his eyes glinted with hardness.

"What's wrong?" Maia asked hesitantly.

"Do you remember our first lesson, Maia?" he said.

Maia nodded, her spirit collapsing like a pricked balloon. She found her voice after a quiet struggle. "Do not dwell on thoughts of vengeance."

"Yes," he said grimly. "The power inside you is no plaything, Maia. It can be dangerous, to you and to everyone around you. If you try to use it for petty purposes without understanding its capabilities or repercussions, you bring a grave danger upon everyone. You have to let go of thoughts of revenge."

Maia tore her gaze away from those clear gray eyes.

"I'm sorry. I won't—"

"Let go of your anger. Those who have left us cannot be brought back by acts of revenge."

Maia nodded hastily. She wanted to vanish, crumble into the dust under her feet.

"Go now. Come back when you've thought enough about it."

The Xinhagyi turned and walked away, leaving Maia cold, shamed, and miserable on that bright morning.

CHAPTER FOUR

THE DORERS

The chilly air felt colder than usual as Maia trudged back toward her room with Dani. The Xinhagyi was right; she was basking in her newfound powers a bit too much. No one knew what went on behind closed doors. She was working on a plan for revenge, a plan to make people pay for their crimes, for robbing Maia of her family. They were tiny dolls, stone replicas clad in rags, of all the Xifarians who had hurt her, ones who had ruthlessly slaughtered her family and friends—Chairman Phocluus of the SDS, the chancellor of Xif, his wife Asiyaah, the chancellor's sons Remii and Miir, their friend Amanii, and a few nameless ones. Every night, Maia lined them up and summoned her powers to burn them. Every night, she practiced and prepared for the time she would encounter them in person.

Dani nudged her arm. "Do you want to walk to the ramparts for a bit? I don't feel so good. I need some air."

"All right."

It was not a good thing to play with the light inside her room, especially since she had very little control over it. But the need was overwhelming. *It's not safe; I have to give it up.*

Maia's cold fingers reached for the broken pendant around her neck, the one her mother Sophie had passed down to her, the one she always wore. She traced the filigreed lines of the half-circle, finger desperately seeking the touch of the mother she had never known.

"I've become obsessed with the healing arts," Dani chattered next to her. "That's not good either."

She could not just let the Xifarians walk free. No, that was not an option. But how could she exact her revenge? Without her powers she was nothing. Nothing compared to her powerful enemies anyway. How then?

Maybe . . . she had to wait.

Yes, that's it!

She had to wait until she had mastered the light within and then—

"You know what, Maia? I wish the Initiative would start soon," Dani said. "That would take our minds off these things."

"I'd rather not take part in that fake competition anymore," Maia said, frowning.

Although, being part of the Initiative was the safest thing for her. She was still an enemy of the Xifarians. She was still in their crosshairs. There was little to protect her from them. There were her newfound powers, of course, but she could hardly use them right. She could go into hiding, but the Xifarians always caught up.

The Initiative, however, was a perfect shield. It would protect her as well as her friends. She recalled what the Xifarian chancellor had told her years ago. They would not harm her while she was participating in the Initiative—its sanctity was supreme. But he had also said, when she was out of it, all bets were off. The chancellor had kept his word. The Xifarians had only come to get her when the Initiative had been called off after the Jjordic phase.

"On second thoughts, I can't wait either," Maia said, sighing.

Dani did not seem to hear her. "I wish I could take it easy like everyone else," she complained. "Look at Kusha. He just eats and sleeps and sleeps and eats, all day long. He could just hibernate and no one would notice."

Dani and Kusha had been officially seeing each other for the last two months. Maia had thought it would be awkward when her closest friends turned into a couple, but it was not bad at all. Dani, like everything else she did, kept her cool. Other than personal comments like the one she just made, their relationship was placid in public. But Maia only had to look at Dani and Kusha's sparkling eyes when they were near each other to appreciate the deep and thriving bond between the two.

"Look at Ren," Dani continued. "I mean, just look at him. Showing off to his devout dorers. He has even more girls today."

Ren's friend Karhann, another Xifarian boy who was also part of the Alliance Initiative, was visiting and every morning the two boys sparred on the ramparts. Today was no different. A few paces ahead on the rampart, Ren and Karhann were practicing swordplay surrounded by a throng of Solianese kids. These kids were all students at the universities at ThulaSu and it seemed like they had never seen people as thrilling in their lives. Their eyes were wide, postures alert and stiff, a beguiled expression painted on their faces as they watched Ren and Karhann spar.

Maia shook her head, a bit annoyed. Sure, she understood the amazement at seeing two Xifarians so closely, but it was annoying when these stupefied throngs followed Ren and Karhann around like a swarm of bees following a stick doused in honey. They oohed and aahed, they fought among themselves to win a chance of running errands for the boys, and they collected memorabilia. If Ren picked up a twig to use for his practice, some kid would pick it up as soon as it was discarded. If Karhann used telekinetics, or TEK waves, to make a pyramid of leaves, the kids would fall over each other to collect one from the pile. Nafi said they were all put into personal scrapbooks, and each addition was revered. Such was the culture of dorers in ThulaSu.

In the last few days, Ren seemed to be gathering the attention of one particular section of dorers, a bevy of swooning girls. They were always dressed at their best, their hair perfectly made, and Maia suspected they even put kohl around their eyes. Giggling merrily among themselves, they followed Ren around ThulaSu in small groups, and always from a distance. Ren sometimes waved at them, at which they giggled more. Nafi rolled her eyes and shook her head at the sight of these girls, Kusha and Dani always chuckled, but Maia found herself quite annoyed by the spectacle. It was idiotic, she decided, all this fawning. And it was particularly disgusting how thoroughly Ren seemed to enjoy this following. Things were no different this morning.

"Maia, what's wrong?" Dani was staring.

"What?" Maia tried to shoo the scowl that had spread across her face. "Nothing."

"You look angry," Dani said, chuckling loudly. "Sure it's nothing?"

Maia groaned as she noticed a curly-haired girl batting her eyelashes at Ren. "I guess I don't get these . . . admirers or—"

"Dorers, Maia," Dani corrected, chuckling. "Shortened from 'adorers.'"

"Adorers . . . dorers, whatever. Don't they have anything better to do?"

"They're just harmless fans, Maia. Besides, it's their Solstice break," Dani remarked. "What else would they do?"

"I don't know." Maia shrugged. "Read a book, learn something new, do something more useful than watching a pair of boys show off."

"They're good cheer though. And their presence seems to be helpful for our friend." Dani nodded at a particularly exuberant Ren who pranced around a purple scarf that Karhann swished through a ripple of TEK waves. Every time Ren's sword made contact with the swiftly moving scarf, the crowd of dorers cheered.

"They're like monkeys in a circus," Maia said after watching

Ren's antics for a bit. "Let's get out of here. It's tiring."

Dani agreed and followed Maia as she strode away from the crowd. They had barely taken a couple of steps when a loud shout made them stop and turn around.

A boy ran up to them. "Maia?" he said, panting. The breeze ruffled his sandy hair and threw it across his forehead in a tussle. The morning sun shone on his bright blue eyes, making them sparkle. He smiled, left cheek dimpling. He looked just like Maia remembered him from last summer, only taller.

"Maks?" Maia felt her throat tighten. Maks, short for Maksim, was from her village Appian, and seeing him here brought back memories of the rolling hills surrounding her home.

"Don't tell me you forgot?" Maks crossed his arms and fixed a mock glare on Maia. "Really? You forgot that I came to ThulaSu? It's been that long already?"

Maks, a year older than Maia, was the village baker's son. He had befriended Maia the previous year in Appian. They had grown close until Maks was sent back to ThulaSu.

"I . . ." Maia stopped, unable to explain. So much had happened. Dada was gone forever. The Xifarians had chased her all across Tansi. Maks probably did not know; news did not travel that fast among the Solianese continents anymore. She would tell him, but not now. "I'm sorry. I'm just kind of tired after all the travel."

"Oh, of course. You're part of the Initiative," Maks chuckled and pointed at the crowd behind them. "Are those your friends?" Maia nodded. "Wow, this is crazy."

"Crazy?" Maia asked.

"I just never imagined I'd meet you here. You're a celebrity, right?"

"No, I'm not," Maia protested vehemently. "Believe me, I'm no such thing. I—"

"Don't believe her, Maks," Dani chimed in. She shot a sidelong glance at Maia. "She's quite a hero. I'm sure she will tell you all about it herself. I'm Dani by the way."

Dani was right. Her secrets were not hers anymore. For the past couple of months, her presence in ThulaSu had been kept under wraps over concerns of safety, but with rumors of the Initiative starting again, the clampdown had slackened. And very soon, everyone in ThulaSu would know about her. They would know of her story as well. Maks would find out anyway and it would only be fair if he heard it all from his friend.

"I'm no hero, but . . ." Maia took a moment and braced herself. "I've had quite an adventure since last summer. It'll take a while to tell you everything."

"It's Solstice break, Maia. I've got all the time in the world," Maks replied.

"I should let you two catch up—"

"Maia, Dani," a frantic scream erupted behind them. Nafi, her auburn hair lit up by the low sunlight, stood at the front end of the rampart waving frantically and yelling. "Come here, quick!"

Maia exchanged a look with Dani, then muttered a quick apology to Maks. "Sorry. We'll get together soon."

Maks flashed a dimpled smile before waving goodbye. "I'll find you later."

"He's quite charming," Dani said in a singsong voice as the duo strode toward Nafi. "Well done, Maia."

Maia frowned and shot a suspicious glance at her friend. "He's a friend."

"Did I ever say he's not?"

"Dani—"

Maia's protests were cut off as Nafi grabbed the two girls by their arms and dragged them in the direction of the Garaha Gates.

CHAPTER FIVE

AT THE GARAHA GATES

The university town of ThulaSu was built in the shape of a ring with concentric circles that formed the various buildings. At the center of that ring was the Sun Temple. The residential buildings and the refectories were arranged on the western side. Along the eastern periphery of ThulaSu were a series of nine large structures; four of them housed the classrooms and teaching areas, and the rest were used by the local government officials.

The Garaha Gates was a set of seven massive gates that formed the eastern entrance into ThulaSu. The arches of the gates stood like a bridge between the ramparts on the south and the east of ThulaSu. Nafi was leading them toward the bridge.

"Nafi, what's going on?" Maia asked as soon as they had fallen into a steady pace.

"You'll see," Nafi replied, green eyes twinkling. "Who was the boy? You have a dorer too, huh?"

Maia grunted noisily when Dani burst into loud, unnecessary chuckles. "He's from Appian. Got to know him last summer," Maia said.

Nafi flashed a curious look. "*Know* him, huh?"

Maia shook her head and looked away. No answer from her was going to satisfy Dani and Nafi, who were clearly bent on making her friendship with Maks into something more than it was, so there was no point trying. It would only frustrate her more.

Thankfully, Nafi decided to give up on the topic. "How did the morning exercises go?" she asked.

Maia did not feel like discussing her latest debacle. She left the talking to Dani and let the beauty of the vista soak into her. The sun had barely cleared the eastern peaks and the light was still soft and faded. The paving on the rampart was moist from the previous night's frost. The gray stones appeared darker and more imposing at this hour of the day. The mountain ranges surrounding ThulaSu were imposing. Rising into the sky, about four times the elevation of ThulaSu's highest point, they looked like a sparkling white crown around the city. Clouds hung around the glistening snowclad slopes, as early sunlight colored their peaks in shades of gold, red, and pink.

"Maia."

She could have ignored Nafi's yell, but Nafi grabbed her arm and shook her out of the lightness. "What?" Maia asked, a bit annoyed at the disruption.

"You had a vision? Miir was in it?"

There it was, Nafi's inquisition, the part Maia was dreading. Nafi was a fierce supporter of the team's erstwhile mentor. Hers was a loyalty that Maia did not quite understand. It was not a crush but deep, profound admiration for Miir. Although devastated that Miir had had a hand in the murder of Maia's grandfather, Nafi still held out hope for him. Maia did not understand why. How could a merciless murderer be redeemed?

Nafi tugged her arm. "Well, did you?"

"I didn't see him," Maia replied. "I might've heard his voice."

"And?"

"And what?"

"What did he say?"

He had said things that she did not want to hear, let alone repeat to Nafi. He had said spiteful things about her mother, Sophie, and about her.

"I can't remember," Maia lied coldly. She was not ready to go down that path yet. Perhaps later, alone in her room, she would mull over every word, but not now.

"Hmm," Nafi said simply.

They walked the rest of the way to the Garaha Gates in uncomfortable silence, slowing as they drew close. Outside the gates, a serpentine road tumbled down toward the valley far below. Within the walls of ThulaSu, the road flattened and divided into multiple branches, the widest of which led to ThulaSu's administrative buildings. It was next to one of these buildings that the Raptor—short for Onclioraptor, a state-of-the-art Xifarian spacecraft—sat like an eagle surveying its hunting grounds.

"The Xifarians are here already?" Dani said breathlessly. Maia was stunned as well. She knew the Initiative was about to resume and soon, but she did not expect it to be right now.

Nafi nodded. "Kusha asked me to come over to the Gathering House if we wanted to view the proceedings. He said we're starting the final phase of the Initiative in a day or two."

"Kusha asked you to come?" Dani said.

"Of course. How else would I have found out?"

It made sense that Kusha would know matters of the state, particularly here in ThulaSu. He was the heir of the House of the Sun, the ruling family of ThulaSu. Since Kusha was underage at sixteen, his father acted as the steward. However, he still knew more about the internal goings-on than any regular person.

"Ren would have liked to be here," Maia said. "Why didn't you tell him?"

Nafi scoffed. "He was busy showing off his skills to those stupid dorers. Didn't want to disturb him. Besides, if I told him, Karhann would come along and I don't quite like him."

Maia and Dani shook their heads in unison, but Nafi simply rolled her blazing green eyes. Nafi—the youngest of the team—could be stubborn. The girl harbored a strong dislike for Karhann since the first phase of the Initiative and she still held on to it after all these years.

"So, are you coming or not?" Nafi asked, raising a quizzical eyebrow at her friends.

Dani nodded and followed. Maia stepped after them a moment later, her feet dragging a little at the thought of leaving Ren behind.

CHAPTER SIX

A PROMISE RENEWED

Kusha was waiting for them at the front door of the Gathering House, a domed building made of orange-red bricks.

Kusha had put on some weight, Maia noted. The mop of unruly hair was the same though, and his prized inheritance—a red headband with the golden sigil of the sun—fought a losing battle with his curly locks as always.

"Kusha, you're up early today," Dani said, nudging Kusha's arm playfully.

A crimson flush spread across Kusha's face. "I'm up because I need to," he replied with a shrug. Then he turned to Nafi. "What took you so long?"

Nafi rolled her eyes. "Takes time to find everyone."

"Everyone?" Kusha looked behind them and frowned. "I'd say you're missing one. Didn't Ren want to come?"

"She didn't want to ask him because Karhann was around," Maia said snippily. Nafi shrugged.

Kusha shook his head. "Nafi—"

"All right, all right," Dani interrupted, just the way she always did. She was the peacekeeper of the team. "No harm done. We'll fill Ren in later. Now tell us what's going on here."

Kusha scowled at Nafi one last time before thumbing at the closed doors behind him. "They're all in there—people from Xif, the Jjord envoys, my father, and other Solianese house leaders. They're discussing the Alliance Initiative."

"Can we get in?" Maia asked. She was desperate to see what was going on.

"Yes, that's why I called you. I have access to the viewing gallery. This way."

He led them to a side door, nearly half the size and nowhere near as showy as the main door that was deep amber-hued and bolstered with sculpted brass panels. A flight of wooden stairs led them to a small viewing gallery with two rows of seating.

"Hey!" someone called as soon as they entered. It was Dani's older brother, Hans. He had been traveling back and forth between Zagran and ThulaSu, spending quite some time in the mountain city. He had always been close to the team, but since risking his career to help Maia when she was on the run from the Xifarians, he had become even more attached to them.

"Hans! Didn't expect you here," Dani said. "I thought you were leaving for Zagran first thing in the morning."

"I was, but I wanted to hear this before I left," Hans said. Below the viewing gallery was a meeting room where twenty high-backed chairs formed a large circle at the center. Farther behind them were rows of regular seating that Maia presumed was for viewers. A sizeable group of people clustered together in small groups, speaking animatedly among themselves. Maia noted the Jjord, clad in white, their abalone talismans gleaming. She did not recognize any of them.

"The premier didn't come?" Maia asked Hans as she settled into a chair behind him. During their stay in Zagran, Maia and her teammates had met with the Jjord Premier, Oliena. She was a forceful and effective leader, and Maia had hoped to see her face the Xifarians.

"I don't know any of the people here."

Hans turned and scanned her face with his bright blue eyes. "The Premier has sent her envoys to speak for her." He smiled. "Don't worry, Maia. I know the people Oliena has sent. They're good."

Kusha had sat down next to Maia and patted her hand. "What's there to worry about, Maia? With the power of the light in you, you don't need to fear the Xifarians anymore. Besides, they've learned their lesson. I don't think they'll try capturing you ever again."

"Unless they terribly miss being roasted alive," Nafi quipped.

Dani and Hans broke into chuckles, but Maia could not. Something, a thought she could not pin down, needled her. "I don't know. It just seems weird that the Xifarians would want the Initiative to continue after they failed to capture me, and after knowing the light has morphed into me and there's no way of fixing the heart of the Sedara. They have nothing to gain by this farce anymore."

Kusha squeezed her shoulder and flashed a bright smile. "Perhaps they just want to play nice. Since everything is out in the open now, they want to cooperate and . . . coexist in peace."

Maia scoffed. Coexist in peace? That was the last thing the Xifarians would do. She had made plenty of mistakes in the past in judging people, but there could be no mistake about the Xifarians' intentions. They could be up to nothing good.

"Besides," Kusha continued, "my father is down there. Sahiiraan Tsininio is there also. They know what the Xifarians have been up to. They'll take care of things."

Maia caught a glimpse of Kusha's father, the portly Steward Lok, mingling with the Jjord. With him was Sahiiraan Tsininio, the leader of another Solianese house who had known Maia and her teammates for a long time. Sahiiraan Tsininio had helped Nafi's father, Aihnswothe Feirah, whisk Maia away from Miorie when Xifarian agents were trying to capture her.

"The Aihnswothe isn't here either," Maia said, missing the stalwart's steady presence.

"Maia, you worry too much," Nafi piped up from her other side.

"My father can't be at every meeting with the Xifarians. Besides, he's not a Sahiiraan; he doesn't get invited to all meetings anyway." Maia suppressed a sigh and scanned the Xifarians. Dressed in dark Gambrills, they stood in a tight huddle on one side. She did not find a single familiar face among them either.

"What are we waiting for, Steward Lok?" said a brash, boisterous voice. "Shouldn't we get started?"

"Not that horrid guy," Nafi hissed.

It was indeed the horrid and unmistakable Sahiiraan Leeam, the leader of the House of the Broken Seas and a Xifarian supporter through and through. His son, Lex, an utterly spoiled brat, had been part of the Initiative until his team was eliminated in the first phase.

Maia sank further back into her chair, fighting the chills invading the tips of her fingers and toes. Something inside her said over and over that this was not going to go well.

In the chamber below, the participants took their seats. There were few people in the viewers' section, mostly locals who had come out of curiosity.

When everyone was seated, Steward Lok ran his fingers through his unruly mop of hair and cleared his throat. He bowed hastily and started. "On behalf of the principality of ThulaSu, I welcome the envoys of the Xif and Jjordic nations. I'm grateful that you could join us today. We're here to discuss whether we want to continue with the Alliance Ini—"

"Don't let the stewardship go to your head, Lok," Leeam interrupted. He waved—his pale gold, ponytailed hair swishing—dismissively at a red-faced Lok and continued. "There's nothing to discuss here. We've simply gathered to officially restart the contest after certain short-sighted people"—he shot a blistering glance at Tsininio—"disrupted our long-standing collaboration with Xif."

"How dare he interrupt my father?" Kusha whispered, his voice trembling with rage.

Maia placed a hand over Kusha's curled fist. This was why Nafi's father, the Aihnswothe Feirah, needed to be here. Leeam and his cronies were rotten to the core, and they did not care for decorum.

Thankfully, Tsininio jumped to the steward's defense. He strode over to Lok and glared at Leeam. "Sahiiraan Leeam, you've been the leader of a . . . sufficiently prominent house for a while now, is that correct? Long enough to learn about the proprieties of a council like this? In case you've forgotten, let me remind you, Sahiiraan, that we do not interrupt anyone during a council, and we wait our turn to speak. And we never interrupt the host during his opening address. If you forget that etiquette again, I'm afraid that I shall have to disinvite you from future proceedings."

"Yes," Nafi whispered, throwing her fisted arms in the air jubilantly. "Take that, you brainless Leeam."

Leeam and Tsininio locked stares for a moment or two before Leeam slinked back into his seat. Tsininio smiled and nodded at Lok. "Please continue, Steward Lok."

"W-we . . ." Lok stammered to a start and continued, "we are here to discuss if the Alliance Initiative needs to be restarted. I leave the floor open to debate."

"Come on, Father," Kusha whispered agitatedly as Lok stumbled back into his seat. "Tell them about the heart of the Sedara already."

Dani looked over her shoulder at Kusha. "It'll be all right, Kusha. Wait and see."

Maia held her breath. They were going to discuss her mother and her . . . again. She wrapped her arms around her torso, trying to make the feeling of bareness go away. It hardly helped.

On the floor of the council, Tsininio rose from his seat, then bowed and glanced at everyone around him. "I will start if you all permit. It has been nearly a year since the last phase of the Alliance Initiative concluded. A lot has transpired since. A most important truth has come to light in the past few months.

"For a while, the Xifarians have been accusing the people of Tansi of stealing an artifact that is crucial to the functioning of their planet. We had no idea what that artifact was . . . until now. I won't go into that much detail because I'm afraid certain far-sighted friends will grow too impatient, but I will just say this: We know that artifact could have destroyed our sun, and as an aftermath, destroyed Tansi."

Tsininio paused and turned toward the Xifarian envoys. "If our destruction is your intent, why should we have any relations with your nation, let alone have a peace initiative with you?"

The room was silent. Maia had not realized that she was clenching her fists until she felt a stabbing pain in her palms. Just as one of the Xifarian envoys rose to his feet, the door of the viewing gallery fell open with a loud thud and everyone jumped.

Ren careened in. Behind him was a staff-bearing Rayan, the girl from Korobieltes whom Sophie's friend Zaara had assigned to shadow and protect Maia. Rayan shot a frustrated look at Maia before propping her staff against the wall and taking a seat next to Dani. Rayan was upset because Maia had been slipping out of her watch. She wanted to shadow Maia just like she had been instructed by Zaara, but the Xinhagyi poured cold water over her plans.

"Maia needs some freedom," the Xinhagyi had said. "You can watch over her, but only from a distance. If you keep following her all the time, she cannot get back to being normal. So, please, Rayan, give her some room to breathe." Since then, and not happily, Rayan kept her distance. Maia had breathed a little easy, but Rayan still watched. And the sense of being watched all day was not the least bit uplifting.

Ren stomped over, crossed his arms, and glared at his teammates. "Why didn't anyone tell me about this?" he demanded. "If it hadn't been for Rayan—"

"Ren, be quiet," Dani whispered.

"I'll be quiet when you answer me," he retorted. "What, you didn't think I'd be interested in this? You didn't think I'd care?"

Nafi snorted loudly. "It doesn't seem like you care. All you're interested in is flirting with those feather-brains, and hanging around with that good-for-nothing Karhann."

"Like it or not, Karhann's my friend," Ren snapped. "Just like you are. Or I thought you were."

Nafi was about to retort, but Maia grabbed her arm before she could utter a sound. "You can fight later, Nafi. Now let's do what we're here to do," Maia said, then flashed Ren an apologetic smile. "Sorry, Ren. I should've gone back to get you. Won't happen again. Sit down, please."

Ren sat down reluctantly. Maia turned her attention back to the floor below. A Xifarian with dark red hair and a rounded nose that stood out prominently on his gaunt face had taken the floor.

"Steward Lok, thank you for inviting us. We are honored . . . and grateful," he said with a quick nod toward Lok before smiling at Tsininio. "You have leveled a substantial accusation at us. All I have to say is that you are wrong."

Maia sat up, anger swirling like a twister inside her. The heart of the Sedara would destroy Tansi's sun, her mother Sophie had said that herself. At the cost of her life, Sophie had broken the heart of the Sedara, a mechanism that propelled the Xifarian planet-spaceship. If she had not broken the Sedara, it would have consumed Tansi's star and doomed Tansi.

The red-haired Xifarian envoy continued. "The artifact we lost— the heart of the Sedara—does not harm anyone. It does not destroy stars as you claim. It only provides our nation the energy that it needs to survive."

"That's a lie," Maia said, seething at how easily the Xifarian was spurting untruths.

"All we wanted was some cooperation from you," the Xifarian continued harshly, "but instead of helping us, you attacked us viciously."

Maia was sure he was talking about her face-off with Chairman Phocluus of the Scientific Defense Services three months ago. But he had it all wrong. The Xifarians, led by the chairman, had come to capture her and kill her to find information about the heart of the Sedara. She had only reacted, defended herself. Besides, she did not even know then that the light was inside her, let alone how powerful it was or that it would strike back at her attackers.

"Liar," Maia muttered.

The man went on, "That attack, entirely unprovoked if I may add, killed nine Xifarian soldiers and grievously injured the chairman of the SDS."

Maia's fists clenched. Chairman Phocluus was still alive?

"He should be dead." Words skidded out of her mouth, scorching her insides as they came out. "He doesn't deserve to live."

Dani leaned over and grabbed Maia's arm. "Maia, breathe. Push the anger away, like the Xinhagyi taught you. You cannot get angry at them. You can't take his words to heart."

Maia sucked the cold air in with all her might. It did nothing to help calm the anger that had already spread its wings inside her. The searing heat was trying to break free. She could not let it. She had to control herself, get over her emotions, or she would hurt someone unintentionally.

"Deep breaths, Maia," Dani instructed, her hand tightly clamped on Maia's arm.

Tsininio was on his feet again. "You attacked a defenseless child, not knowing she was powerful enough to thwart you. And now, because you've been so utterly defeated, you put the blame on her? Why didn't you call for a council so we could talk about it? Why did you have to resort to petty abduction?"

"No one abducted anyone," Leeam growled. "Aren't you placing too much trust on a bunch of stupid and irresponsible kids?"

"There you go again, Sahiiraan Leeam. Speaking out of turn seems to be your thing," Tsininio said. "But I shall answer you: I have faith in those kids. And I also believe Aihnswothe Feirah's testimony on the matter. You, on the other hand, I have trouble trusting."

The Xifarian chuckled and held his arms up. "My apologies, Sahiiraan Tsininio, Sahiiraan Leeam. I do not mean to accuse anyone of anything. All I want to say is that this is the gravest of misunderstandings that should not have happened at all. But since it has, we are here to fix it. Give us a chance to show our good intentions. Let us complete the Initiative together."

The room quieted. Tsininio looked questioningly at the other

Solianese leaders. Some of them nodded, some shook their heads. It seemed to Maia that most of them were in favor of resuming the contest. The Jjord did not raise any objections either.

"Let us do a show of hands," Steward Lok suggested.

The Xifarian cleared his throat and hurried to the center. "Before you cast your votes, allow me a few more words. Our chancellor has a message for the council. To show our good faith, we shall bring back all of the miners from Ti, just like you have always wanted. They will return before the Initiative ends, that is our promise. I only hope you will show some faith in us."

"By the stars!" Nafi blurted. "Did he just say they'll return the miners? All of them?"

Maia struggled to find her voice. "He did say that."

For years, the Xifarians had been forcibly recruiting Solianese miners to work in their deadly mining camps on Ti, a distant frozen moon. No one ever came back. Why did they suddenly want to let the miners go now? Why did they want the Initiative so badly?

Ren frowned at Nafi. "I know it's a problem when someone does bad things. But why is it a problem when they do something good?"

Nafi huffed. "Because it's so unlike them, that's why."

That was true. It was so unlike the Xifarians to concede anything, much less the miners who worked on Ti. The Solianese had demanded their return for years and for years the Xifarians had turned a deaf ear. And now . . .

On the council floor, hands went up in favor. Almost everyone, except for Tsininio, Lok, and a couple of others, was in favor of the Initiative.

The red-haired Xifarian envoy smiled and bowed low. "Our eternal gratitude," he said. "You will be proud of your decision."

That Maia doubted. It appeared that she was not the only one who had doubts, as the viewing gallery stayed quiet even when the participants of the council applauded each other raucously on the floor below.

CHAPTER SEVEN

THE ARBITRATION COMMITTEE

The next two days went by in a haze. A winter storm covered ThulaSu in a blanket of snow and everyone was trapped indoors. On the second day, around evening, Maia secretly nursed a grouchy mood.

The Xifarians' keenness to continue the Initiative had startled her and still worried her to no end. Being cooped up did not help matters. She suppressed her anxiety and kept her thoughts to herself, fearful that Ren would be offended if she aired her continued suspicions about the Xifarians.

That afternoon, she got an unexpected visit from Kusha's father, Steward Lok. Lok smiled and pulled her into a warm embrace as soon as he arrived.

"Maia, I'm so sorry we don't meet more often than this. We have to arrange for a gathering when your mother returns, Kusha," he said, running his fingers through his unruly mop of hair. Maia smiled a little, noting his similarity with Kusha.

Kusha who had accompanied his father nodded. Kusha's mother, along with his younger brother and sisters were away visiting family on the Second Continent.

"Anyhow, I'm here to talk to you about another matter today," Lok said. "As you know, the Alliance Initiative begins soon. I was not in favor of restarting it, mostly because there are concerns about your safety. I could not stop it anyway. However, I wrote to the Xifarian chancellor and expressed my concerns. He has assured me that the sanctity of the Initiative is paramount. You have nothing to fear as long as you're part of the competition."

A long sigh of relief coursed out of Maia. Part of the anxiety sitting squarely on her chest lifted in an instant.

"He had once said the same to me," Maia said to Lok. "And he sort of kept his promise. He didn't come for me until the Initiative was stalled."

Lok smiled. "Well then, I'm relieved."

"Do you know why they are so eager to restart the Initiative?" Maia asked. "They don't need access to Tansi anymore. They've promised my safety. Why then?"

"Perhaps they just want to mend the relationship," Kusha said. He chuckled seeing Maia's indignant face. "We can hope, right?"

They could hope, but certain things hardly ever changed.

"Anyhow, I came here to assure you," Steward Lok said as he rose to his feet.

"Thank you. I'm honored that you personally came to tell me this," Maia said, bowing.

Even though Lok had brought a mighty assurance, Maia could not drive away worrisome thoughts from her head. There was something else going on, something she did not understand. Maia was sure the Xifarians were not out to make peace with everyone.

Her bedroom was chilly, but Maia wanted air. She opened the window wide and perched on the sill. The town looked deserted. The Sun Temple sat in a field of white, alone and unmoved. The last rays of the sun lingered in the sky and tinged the peaks of the Vesteran ranges in orange and purple hues. The world was at peace. Maia closed her eyes and breathed in deep, letting the icy air settle inside her and calm her fears. She had to believe in peace, Maia reminded herself. She had to believe that there was a chance the Xifarians had good in them.

Down below, she noticed a black-cloaked figure who stood out against the white snow. The figure walked down the eastern ramparts and started across waist-deep snow toward the Sun Temple.

"What in the world is wrong with you?" Maia muttered, squinting hard to observe the person's movements.

No one had ventured into the courtyard in two days. ThulaSu was built and managed to sustain its population in case storms like this blew in. No one needed to go outside of the residential buildings until paths were cleared, and usually, they were not cleared until a few days after the storm. Maia knew the Xinhagyi and his Kausaka guards had vacated the temple two days ago.

The person—Maia assumed it was a man from his gait—continued across the courtyard at a steady pace. There was something odd about how he moved through the pile of snow. It was as if he was out on a stroll on a perfectly normal day. He did not seem to struggle at all but glided through it. The light outside was dimming by the moment, but Maia could have sworn the snow was parting to make way for him. There was something else, something Maia could sense but could not clearly make out from the distance.

She sucked in a breath. His cloak reminded her of the Order of the Fyrstell, the whip-wielding, hooded, and masked Xifarian brutes they had confronted time and again. They had almost broken the Stabilator on Xif and sabotaged the Jjordic energy fields in Zagran. Had the Order of the Fyrstell found a way to break into ThulaSu as well?

Just then, a loud rap sounded on her door and Maia almost fell off the windowsill, her heart thrashing wildly. Another impatient rap sounded.

"Maia, open up. It's Nafi."

Nafi barged in—auburn hair flying—as soon as the door parted.

"Why do you have the window open in this freezing cold?" Nafi demanded as she wrapped her arms around her torso. "Close it, close it now," she yelled.

"All right, all right. It's not that cold anyway." Maia tugged at the window shutters, her eyes searching for the strange cloaked man in the courtyard, but he was gone.

Nafi strode over to the window and peeked outside. She stared for a moment and then looked at Maia questioningly. "What are you looking at?"

"There was a man, Nafi. He walked all the way from the ramparts there to the Sun Temple."

Nafi's brows crept up her forehead. "A man? Walking? In *that* snow?"

Maia nodded. It was indeed unbelievable, but she had seen him.

"You must be imagining things, Maia." Nafi waved dismissively and shook her head. She pointed outside at the snow-covered courtyard. "Look at the snow. If someone walked through it, he'd leave a track, right? But there's nothing . . . not a mark."

The snow did look undisturbed, but how could that happen? Then it dawned on Maia. The man must have been using telekinesis to move the snow. But telekinesis was not something just anyone could do. He had to be Xifarian.

Can it really be the Order of the Fyrstell? No, that was a ridiculous thought. The Order's thugs would not just walk into ThulaSu like that. Besides, this person's cape seemed different; it shimmered slightly even in the dim light as if something silvery was painted over it.

Maia massaged the bridge of her nose. Was she imagining things like Nafi said? She had often had strange dreams and even visions once in a while, then she had discovered this fountainhead of destructive energy inside her, and now . . . seeing things with her eyes wide open? What sort of a freak had she turned into?

"I'll close the window," Nafi said, pulling the shutters in and locking them in place while Maia stood lost in thought. Nafi tugged her by the elbow. "Hey, Maia. What's wrong?"

"But I saw him, Nafi," Maia whispered. Suddenly, she knew what had felt odd about the man; it was the familiarity of his gait. His walk reminded her of . . . Miir.

Nafi squinted at her for a moment. "The light's very dim outside, Maia. And you're sort of tired from being indoors. You could've dozed off or something and had a dream."

Maia could not stop the chuckle. Nafi was no Dani; consoling people did not come naturally to her. Truth be told, it hardly came to her at all.

"That's all right," Maia said, forcing her swirling thoughts away. "What's going on? Something you wanted to say?" She settled into her bed and Nafi plonked down on the opposite end.

"Yes," Nafi said. She pulled out a piece of paper from her pocket. "Look at this. They handed it to us downstairs."

"They?"

"A couple of ThulaSuian monks. Kusha said they teach at the university."

The paper was nothing fancy, a simple yellow-hued parchment. On it was a handwritten note.

The Alliance Initiative

Chief Arbitrator: Monk Hilledunn

Arbitration Committee: Master Kehorkjin (XDA), Supervisor Aerika (UAAS)

As one of the teams that qualified for the third and final phase of the Alliance

Initiative, you are hereby invited to ThulaSu to participate.

Wish you well.

Maia read it over a few times, her eyes lingering on familiar names. Master Kehorkjin had supervised the first phase of the Initiative on Xif and Aerika had supervised the second in Zagran. Her team had not had a good relationship with either of the supervisors, but at least they had parted on better terms with Aerika.

"So . . . Master K is back," Maia said, shuddering as she recalled the man's mirthless gray-blue eyes and cold demeanor.

"Yes, he is."

"And Aerika."

Nafi nodded wisely. "Yes, her too."

"And this Monk Hilledunn? He'll be our—"

"Chief supervisor of the Solianese phase," Nafi said. "And from what Kusha could gather, he's the nicest teacher in ThulaSu."

For a moment or two, Maia lost her words. "T-that would be nice," she stuttered back to life. "The supervisors have all been far too kind to us until now."

Nafi chuckled. "And that was even before anyone knew us," she said. "Now we're famous. So, I'll be glad if Hilledunn turns out nice and friendly."

Maia agreed. They were famous indeed. Infamous actually, all thanks to her. While Maia's friends had rallied around her voluntarily as more and more of her past came to light, Maia still felt guilty about pulling them into the dangers that swirled around her. A tight knot grew larger in her gut and made her insides shrivel. It was all her fault. Because of her, all her friends had been marked forever.

"I'd rather not participate at all," Maia said, sighing. She knew that was an impossible wish, her participation was bound by the pledges made by her nation and her wishes did not matter.

Nafi shrugged. Then she chirped in an excited voice that yanked Maia out of misery. "I hope our mentor is not someone as flaky as Joolsae."

Joolsae, their team mentor during the Jjordic phase, had been worthless. Even Maia had to agree that the rude and arrogant Miir from the Xifarian phase was a far better mentor than Joolsae.

"Guess we'll find out soon," Maia said. Nafi nodded as she got off the bed and headed toward the door. "Did they say when we start?"

"Next week," Nafi replied. She stopped at the threshold, her emerald eyes blazing. "We're one of the last ten teams, Maia. You think we could win this?"

Maia replied even before Nafi could blink. "We will win this, Nafi. We have to."

It was even more important this time to win. She could not afford to lose the protection of the Initiative, not until she had mastered the power inside her completely.

CHAPTER EIGHT

ALMOST FAMOUS

Over the next few days, the cleaning crews cut out enough paths through the snow for most activities to resume. Mountainous piles of snow remained heaped on the sides of the treacherous and slippery pathways.

Maia and her teammates did not have too much to do in the days leading up to the third phase of the Initiative, so they simply lounged around and relaxed. Karhann had left for Xif to be with his family before the third phase began, so even Ren gave up his early morning showing-off sessions for the dorers.

The team was sitting at a wooden table with built-in benches on all four sides. A large bowl of stew of carrots, onions, and succulent pieces of meat that poked out of the thick, smoking broth, sat in the center. Next to it was a basketful of braided loaves sprinkled with spices and baked to shiny brown perfection.

"There's going to be a huge meeting tomorrow," Kusha announced as the crew munched on a delicious lunch. "It's about the Damoclian Connector."

"That's why Hans said he'd be here. He didn't tell me what for." Dani shook her head morosely. "He's been very quiet since he went back to Zagran. He hardly tells me anything."

Nafi raised an eyebrow. "Why do you sound like that's unexpected?"

"What do you mean?" Dani asked.

Nafi rolled her eyes. "How can you not get it? He misses Rayan. He's depressed."

"I know he does," Dani replied. "But still . . ."

Hans and Rayan were not a couple . . . yet. Clearly, Hans had feelings for the girl from Korobieltes, but it was hard to fathom Rayan. Nafi could be partly right, Maia thought, but Dani was right too. Even if he were missing Rayan, it would not explain Hans's aloofness from the sister he adored.

Nafi frowned and was about to retort when Maia leaned over and nudged Kusha's arm. "So, what's going on with the Damoclian Connector?"

"Remember, the Jjord agreed to rebuild the Connector?" Kusha asked.

Maia remembered it well. Years ago, the Solianese and the Jjord worked together to build the Damoclian Connector, which was a channel of energy between Zagran and ThulaSu. It would have been a step toward solidarity between the two nations, but Xifarian saboteurs destroyed it before it was completed. In the aftermath, a section of Zagran blew up, killing thousands, including Dani's parents. Kusha's family, the House of the Sun, the appointed protectors of the Connector, was accused of treason.

The Damoclian incident had been the reason for the biggest fallout between the Solianese and the Jjord in recent times. But when Maia and her teammates foiled the Xifarian attempt to damage Jjordic power installations, the Jjord decided to aid the Solianese once again and rebuild the Damoclian Connector.

"The Connector is almost complete," Kusha continued. "This council will discuss security issues. You know, since the Connector was sabotaged—"

"I know," Ren said hastily.

A stiff silence would have fallen over the table had it not been for the munching and the slurping.

"Perhaps my father will be here," Nafi said thoughtfully.

"He has been invited," Kusha informed. "Tsininio will be there obviously. Even some parliamentarians are traveling from Miorie, I hear."

Maia's heart did a wild flip. She put her spoon down and gulped the large chunk of potato she had been chewing. Could that mean that her uncle Alasdair was on the way?

"Do you know which parliamentarians, Kusha?" Maia asked.

Kusha shrugged. "No. They're expecting a sizable contingent though."

The thought of seeing family made Maia smile. Her uncle Alasdair and her cousin Sana had risked their lives to get Maia away from Xifarian agents in Miorie. With her grandfather's passing, they were the only family she had left and her heart wrenched just thinking about them.

Dani leaned over and bumped Maia's shoulder with hers. "I think your uncle won't miss a chance to visit you, Maia. Who knows, he might bring your cousin along too."

Nafi snorted. "Seriously, Dani? Maia is upset with everything as is, and now you're giving her false hope?"

"False?" Dani retorted. "Why would you say that? It's natural for them to want to come and see Maia." Kusha and Ren nodded in agreement.

Nafi stared at Dani incredulously for a while before raising both her arms. "All right. Whatever keeps you happy."

Maia turned her attention back to the meal. Nafi was undoubtedly not good at mincing words and Maia knew she had a point. Getting her hopes up was not good, and hoping that Uncle Alasdair and Sana would visit was an unrealistic dream. Aunt Rowyena would not approve of such a long trip, not when Sana had school to attend and Uncle Alasdair was partially handicapped. Maia unhappily chewed on her meat.

Just then, an excited scream rang out. Everyone spun around to see.

"There," a girl shouted. She was no more than thirteen. Her red hair was tied into a ponytail, and her eyes were wide as she stared at Maia's table. Behind her was a group of seven or eight kids, all about the same age. The girl pointed and shouted, "That's her. That's Maia."

Before Maia could fathom what was happening, she was surrounded. Boys and girls formed a circle around her and thrust their notebooks in her face.

The red-haired girl grinned toothily and waved a feather-topped pen at her. "I'm Lela. I'm a big fan of how you fought those nasty Xifarians when they came to capture you. I mean, *biiiiigg* . . . fan. Would you mind signing my autograph book? I'd really, really, really love it if you do."

"Mine too," said a dimpled-cheeked girl.

"And mine," a curly-haired boy with large brown eyes said.

Maia would have sat there stunned into silence if it had not been for Dani's nudge. "You got dorers, Maia," she whispered. "Go on, sign their books."

So she did. Scribbling her name across colorful little pages, dazed by the squeals of delight and questions about her adventures, Maia did not know what to make of it. Both the Aihnswothe and the Xinhagyi had told them to lay low out of fear of drawing unwanted attention, and they had. No one knew who Maia or her friends were until now. With the Initiative resuming, that anonymity would vanish anyway, but this sudden and overwhelming attention was not something Maia wanted or liked. She wondered how they found out. Someone had to have told them. But who?

As soon as the excited mob of fans left, Maia turned to her teammates. Nafi chortled to her heart's content. "So, Maia," she said between cackles, "you've got an army of dorers now."

The fact hardly amused Maia. "Yes, but how do they know?" she demanded. She looked each of her friends in the eye. "We were supposed to lie low for as long as we could, remember?"

Nafi stopped laughing and Maia realized her tone had been rather harsh. But this was serious stuff.

"Someone must have told someone," Maia said again. "Which of you did it?"

"Not me," Nafi said.

Kusha shrugged. Dani shook her head. Ren, on the other hand, busily poured himself some more stew.

"Ren?" Maia asked. "Don't tell me —"

"What?" he said, looking up cautiously. Then he stirred his stew with utmost attention attentively. "Well, I have nothing to do with those screaming little creatures. I didn't tell *them* anything."

"Who did you tell?" Maia asked.

"I . . . might've told this guy . . . and this girl . . . and this other guy," Ren said. "Hey, they said they knew you from way back in Appian. I thought they knew everything already."

Nafi crossed her arms and glared at him. "Seriously, Ren?"

"Maks? Was his name Maks?" Maia asked.

"Yes, that's his name."

"You said another guy and a girl." Nafi shoved Ren, making him wince. "Who are the other two?"

Maia guessed who the other two were. "Aman and Nisa," she said.

Nafi widened her eyes. "Who-man and who-sa?"

"They're also from Appian," Maia explained. The four of them had spent a good summer together. It was not all laugh and play and there were plenty of arguments, but together they had stopped some nasty tree poachers. The memory of it brought a smile to Maia's lips as she stood up and gathered her bowl and plate.

"Where are you off to?" Kusha asked.

"I'm going to go look for my friends from Appian," Maia said. "I need to tell them to go easy on the publicity."

Dani left the table and followed Maia. "Do you know where to find them?"

"I do." Ren jumped to his feet. "They usually hang around the southern ramparts now. Near the garden gates. I'll come with you."

"No, thank you," Maia said firmly. Even though her heart drooped a little when Dani and Ren's faces dimmed, she held on to her decision. "I need to talk to them alone."

"We could walk with you," Dani said.

"I'll be fine, Dani. No one will risk kidnapping me again."

She walked away hastily. Maia was worried Dani would follow her, and immensely thankful when she did not. She was yearning for some alone time, which she got very little of nowadays.

Maia made her way through the shrinking mounds of snow and up the stone stairs to the top of the southern ramparts. The garden gates Ren had mentioned were in the middle of the section. They were not much of a gate but an opening into a good-sized and well-designed garden outside the walls. The monks maintained it beautifully and it was pretty even in winter. Even if she did not come across the trio from Appian, this would be a good time to check out the garden, as she had only ventured outside ThulaSu's walls once since she arrived.

She found them right where Ren said they would be, near the garden gates. Maks was leaning against the wall, and Nisa and Aman were sitting atop it, all of them immersed in animated chitchat. Nisa noticed her first.

"Maia," she yelled before jumping down from the wall and rushing toward her. Aman and Maks followed. "So good to see you again. And in ThulaSu of all places."

Maia smiled and waved at the trio. Nisa had no idea how glad she was on seeing them again. They reminded her of Appian, of times when she had a grandfather to run to whenever she needed. "Hey, guys," she said, pushing away the lump of pain in her throat that always formed when she thought of home.

"You never told us anything about anything, Maia," Aman accused, swiping at the silky locks that had a habit of falling across his forehead. "You never told us you were such a hero."

Warmth flooded Maia's face at his words. It was weird how awkward her laughter sounded to her own ears. "No, no, Aman. I'm not a hero. Not at all. I just . . . fought back so they wouldn't kill me."

Aman brought his hands together in a resounding clap. "And that's what makes a hero."

"All right," Maia said. A strange jitter swept over her on seeing Aman's enthused face. "But we can't have every kid in ThulaSu running after me. It could get them into trouble."

"Who said anything to anyone?" Maks crossed his arms and looked at Nisa to Aman.

Nisa held up her arms. "Not me. I didn't say anything."

Aman smiled sheepishly when Maks frowned at him. "I . . . didn't know I wasn't supposed to. You aren't mad at us, are you, Maia?"

Maia shook her head vigorously. She was more worried about it than angry. She did not want to be portrayed as a hero. She did not like the adulation nor needed it. More importantly, too much of a spotlight on her could rile the Xifarians.

"I'm not," she said, not wanting to scare them by discussing all the issues. "Let's just keep things normal until it's all resolved."

"All right," Aman said, poking the stone paving with his feet. "I'm sorry, I —"

"It's no big deal."

An awkward and nervous silence drifted around them until Aman spoke again.

"I have some schoolwork to complete," he said hastily. "I'll see you later?"

Before Maia could nod, Nisa also muttered something, then she took off with Aman.

"Don't *you* have any schoolwork?" Maia asked Maks.

"No."

"I see. All the time in the world, huh?"

Maks chuckled. "Yes, something like that."

"Then perhaps you could show me around the garden. I've

always wanted to see it."

"Of course. Come on," Maks said, ushering her in the direction of the gates.

Much snow was still piled in the garden, although some of the pathways were trodden down to the paved walkway under their feet. Maks led the way down the meandering path through the Darkwoods. Trees rose tall, forming a shady canopy overhead. Areas on the forest floor were cleared to make room for sculptured gardens of shrubs. Maks slowed after they crossed one such clearing that he said was the garden of roses.

"You should come here in summer. This place smells like heaven."

"I can imagine," Maia said. Hundreds of rose bushes were arranged in eye-pleasing patterns over the area.

"And here," Maks said, tugging her by the arm, "is my favorite place in the world — the bowers."

Maks pointed at a nook between the edge of the rose garden and the towering conifers beyond. The creeping vines of the thistle roses climbed over short pergolas and formed a series of arched canopies. The vines were bare now, but Maia could imagine how there would be a cluster of bowers in the warmer months.

Maia walked into the closest one and ran her hand over the vines. "It's nice. Wish it were summer now."

Maks smiled. He seemed to want to say something but hesitated.

"What?" Maia asked.

"Nothing," he said as he stared awkwardly at the ground. "I . . . was just thinking . . . what are you going to do after the Initiative is over? I mean, will you go back to Appian?"

His question was like an unexpected blast of scorching air that left her breathless and shaking inside. Since Dada's death, she had only thought of surviving, one day at a time, and even now, her thoughts were occupied by the Xifarians. She had not even thought about where she would live after the Initiative was over, or what she would do then. To be honest, she did not want to think of it.

"I'm sorry," Maks blurted. "I didn't mean to upset you. I was only wondering if you'd stay on here at ThulaSu or go live with your uncle in Miorie."

She could not live with Uncle Alasdair. No doubt he would welcome her and so would Sana, but Aunt Rowyena would not approve. That was all too clear from the last time Maia had visited them.

"I have no idea, Maks. I know I'm not wanted very much in Miorie," she said truthfully. "And there's no one left in Appian."

"You could come and live with us," Maks said. That he was earnest was clear, and it lifted Maia's spirits in an instant. "Really, my parents would love to have you. Honestly, we'd be honored," he said.

They had barely known each other for a month the previous summer, but the friendship had stuck. "No, Maks. I'm the one who's honored that you'd even ask. That's so sweet of you . . . and kind. But I don't think I can ever go back to Appian after what happened."

Maks nodded gravely. "How did this all happen, Maia? Ren told us things, but I wish you could tell me." A worried look clouded his eyes the moment the words left his mouth and Maks hastily raised his hands. "You don't have to tell me if you don't want to. I won't be mad at you."

"I'll tell you," Maia said. Lots of people knew about what had happened, and in a few days, even more would know. "But it's a long story. Let's find a place to sit."

They talked until the sun had dropped low in the sky. Maia did not leave out a single thing. It was funny how light she felt after she was done talking. A load that had sat on her chest forever flitted away. Maks did not say much, but his silence gave Maia support she did not even know she was seeking. It was a release that had taken a long time coming. After spending years in Appian trying to hide her past, someone from the village finally knew her true story.

Chapter Nine

Forsaken

I t was the day before the Initiative was set to resume. Maia woke up late and headed straight to the refectory for lunch hoping to find the rest of the team there. She only found Kusha running out of the room with a boxful of bread. On seeing Maia, he flashed an awkward smile of someone who had been caught doing something improper.

"Hey, Kusha," she called. He waved and ran out even faster.

"Wait!" Maia rushed after Kusha, barely managing to grab his shirt. "You didn't even say hello. What's going on? Where are you off to?"

"Outside," Kusha replied, thumbing at the door vaguely. "We're outside. Come out when you're done having lunch."

"All right." Maia tentatively let go of him. He slinked back a couple of steps, then took off like a mouse with a two-headed cat on its tail.

"That's odd," Maia muttered, watching him disappear.

Maia rushed through her meal, barely paying the stuffed

leavened bread the attention it deserved. Before long, she was out in the courtyard looking for her friends, but other than students and teachers of ThulaSu going about their daily routines, she saw no one.

It was weird. They never left her behind. They never left anyone behind. One person or another would find time to round up stragglers.

That's a lie! We'd left Ren behind when we went to watch the council at the Gathering House. A sudden emptiness, a hollow feeling, enveloped her insides. Perhaps, this was how it would be from now on. Perhaps they had all grown too old to keep being the loyal friends they used to be.

The wristband, Maia remembered suddenly. It was a gift from the Xifarian Tierremorphe, Mahswa Tabrin, for their courageous stand at the Seliban Temple during the first phase of the Initiative. The firestone wristbands were instant communicators. The only problem was that they seemed to have a mind of their own. Maia had not been able to use hers since the light inside her had grown stronger. Still, she decided to give it a try.

She tapped it once and tried to focus on a thought code to trigger the communicator the way Kusha had taught her. She cycled through all of her friends' names and even "bread" because Kusha had been carrying some the last time she saw him.

Nothing happened.

"This is ridiculous," Maia muttered angrily to herself.

With no way of knowing what her friends were up to and nothing much to do, Maia headed toward her room. Even though the bright sunshine was streaming through the large open windows of the corridor, the place felt dim and cold. The dark stone floor seemed intent on sucking warmth away from her feet. It felt like she had been walking forever until someone ran up to her.

"Maia," called a breathless voice. Maia whirled around smiling. She had expected to see all of her friends, but it was only Ren.

"Ren! Where's everyone else?"

"You tell me. Are they at the Damoclian council already?"

That was it. They were at the council of Solianese and Jjord leaders discussing the Damoclian Connector. But why would they leave her behind? Or Ren?

"I don't know where they are," Maia said, trying to hide the disappointment in her voice. Kusha had lied to her. "Why didn't *you* go with them?"

"Karhann was supposed to be back this morning, along with this team," he explained. "I went to look for them."

"His team is here already?"

Karhann, Loriine, Baecca, and another Xifarian boy whose name Maia could never remember made up Core 7, an all-Xifarian team that was always in fierce competition with Maia's team, Core 21. It did not help that the relationship between the two teams had been hostile to begin with, mostly because of the animosity between Nafi and her cousin Loriine.

"Not yet. But it's about time they were. The Initiative starts tomorrow, remember?" Ren said.

"That's right." Usually, contestants arrived a day or two before the competition started. "But where are our friends?"

Ren scratched his chin as he thought. "Where do you think a council would happen?"

"The Gathering House perhaps?"

"Let's go look."

They took off along the rampart, hurrying across the slippery pathways, hardly speaking on the way. Maia was lost in thought. She did not understand why Kusha would lie to her about the council. His behavior was simply mind-boggling.

"Oh, great," Ren exclaimed as they neared the red brick building. "They have guards on duty today."

There were four guards, armed with broadswords, each wearing red vests with a large emblem of the sun across their chests. They belonged to Kusha's house, the House of the Sun. It made sense that a council discussing security for the Damoclian Connector would be guarded, but it also meant they were in trouble. Kusha had been the ticket to getting past all closed doors in ThulaSu thus far and without him, there was little chance they would be let in.

"At least we know the council is here," Maia said, sighing.

"I guess that's one good thing," Ren replied. "But that's probably the only good thing. I don't think they'll let us in, Maia. Not with this face." He pointed to his face and Maia chuckled.

Even though Ren, a Xifarian, had taken to wearing the ThulaSuian style of clothing, he still looked nothing like anyone from Tansi. His spiky black-and-white hair and his dark pupils that had a spattering of white dots were as alien as ever.

"Let's try anyway," she suggested, unwilling to give up.

The guards blocked their path as soon as they approached the stairs leading up to the door.

"You need a permit to get inside," one guard said, eyeing Ren suspiciously. "Do you have one?"

"No, we don't. Our friend Kusha is inside. We were supposed to meet here," Maia said, looking the man squarely in the eye. "Kusha is the—"

"We know who he is," the guard interrupted. "But we don't know who you are unless you show us a permit in your name."

As Maia shook her head in exasperation, Ren grabbed her arm and tugged. "Maia, let's go. They won't let us in."

It did not seem likely that the stony-faced guard would yield and Maia would have heeded Ren's suggestion if it were not for a group of youngsters sauntering out of the building. Three boys, about sixteen or a bit older, laughed and hollered as they walked out the door. The one in the middle was strikingly handsome, with bright eyes and a sharp nose accentuated by gold hair that was pulled into a ponytail. His companions were burly, their faces twisted in weird and grotesque ways when they smiled as if they had a bitter pill in their mouths.

"Lex?" Ren's surprised voice reached Maia's ears before she could recoil.

The handsome Lex spotted them. "Maia, it is you," he shouted, his guffaws making the guards turn around to look. "I'm so lucky to meet the heroine of the saga and her loyal sidekick, Ren," he bellowed. "What are you doing out here? You should be inside, at the center of the ring."

"You're always charming, Lex," Maia snapped. "Why don't you mind your own business and leave us be."

"How can that be?" Lex crooned. "How can I not acknowledge you? They're looking for you inside."

"Maia, let's get out of here," Ren said, nudging Maia's arm. "Come on."

"Oh no." Lex stepped closer. "You shouldn't. You ought to come inside. Really. The council's getting nowhere without you."

Maia looked at Ren, puzzled. What did Lex mean?

"You don't know, do you?" Lex chuckled, a mocking glint shining in his pretty eyes. "The Jjord are debating if they should revoke their promise on the Damoclian Connector."

"What? They can't do that," Maia blurted.

"Of course, they can, and they're going to," Lex said, chuckling throatily. "Given that we, the Solianese, have chosen to harbor you after you tangled with the Xifarians and roasted their chairman alive, they have a right to be worried."

Maia scoffed. "I tangled with the Xifarians? *They* came after me."

Lex let out a mighty sigh. "So we hear. Not directly from you though, but from your friends who won't let you testify in front of the council. Why would the council believe a second-hand account of what happened out there? The Xifarians say they're innocent. What's wrong with believing them?"

Maia could not believe her ears. It took a while until she found the words. "My friends won't let me testify?"

"Yes. Didn't you know? Your friends said you're not in a stable state." Lex smirked, tapped his forehead, and winked.

It was infuriating to watch him taunt her, but Maia vowed that she was not going to lose her temper.

"Really?" she said, forcing a smile.

"Yes," Lex said, and turning to his two imp-like companions, asked, "Isn't that true, boys?"

The imps nodded gleefully.

"Maia, let's go," Ren said again.

"Yes, let's," Maia said.

If she had not been invited to the council, she could not just barge in. There were protocols to be followed with such things. She turned away, lost in thought.

"You're still the loser you always were," Lex yelled. "A loser and a freak."

Maia turned around and glared at Lex. He could call her names; he could call her mother names for all she cared. She just had to stay in control of her emotions . . . she had to . . . for the sake of everyone around her. She could not let the anger take over.

"What a waste of time on the Connector," Lex said, his cronies joined in laughing. "Years of work go down the drain because of the freak's antics."

Maia stopped. Her nation had suffered enough in the hands of the Xifarians, all because of their dependence on Xif for energy. The Connector could set them free and get them out of slavery. If her testimony was the one thing that was needed to make it happen, she *had* to find the strength to face the council. She could not dash her nation's hopes, she could not let all that work go to waste. She was not going to run away. "Ren, I need to get in there."

"Maia, you can't," Ren protested vehemently. "Don't you see? He's trying to bait you into it."

"I know. But what if the Jjord are really breaking their promise? We need the Damoclian Connector. What if my testimony is the only thing that's standing in its way?"

"But, Maia —"

"I can handle it, Ren," she insisted. She was done with standing idly by while things came crashing down around her.

"You're not ready for this, Maia. Just the other day you said the Xinhagyi is worried about your control over the light."

"That was just the one time Dani and I had combat training."

"So you did lose control at least once."

"That was physical combat, Ren. I don't think people are going to beat me up with cudgels in a council."

Ren looked away and scanned the building behind them, his face rigid. He slowly thumbed at the Gathering House. "There are lots of people in there, Maia. They can get hurt if you were to lose control. And you could lose it because there will be people in there who'll do their best to make you."

"I know I can do this, Ren," Maia said with every bit of conviction she could muster. She *had* to do this. She had to make things right with the Damoclian Connector. She was sure she could.

Lex, who had been watching them intently from near the entrance, raised an eyebrow when they walked over to him. He smirked when Maia asked him to escort her inside. Chuckling happily behind them, Lex and his imps led Maia and Ren into the main floor of the Gathering House.

Chapter Ten

Center of the Ring

Maia's heart missed a few beats when her eyes adjusted to the dimness inside the building. The place was packed to the brim. It seemed as if all of ThulaSu was there to watch, which was understandable. The Damoclian Connector was far more important to the people of ThulaSu than the Alliance Initiative.

Ren drew closer to whisper. "Maia, are you sure? There's still time to get out of here."

A part of her wanted to run away, but the rest of her wanted to make sure that she was not the roadblock between the Solianese and their future. She reached for Ren's hand, finding it as cold as her own. His fingers curled around hers tightly nonetheless.

The walk to the center of the room where the ring of chairs stood took forever. Maia only had a vague impression of heads turning to look at her, some gasps, people in the ring rising as she approached. She saw Sahiiraan Leeam's gloating face and Tsininio's worried one, and there was a dull drone of people speaking. All Maia was sure of was Ren's steady grip on her hand and the conviction in her heart. She was not going to give in to fear or anger.

Someone dark and towering strode up to her as she neared the ring. "Maia," he said, bending a little to look into her eyes. It was Aihnswothe Feirah, Nafi's father. Her sight cleared a bit. If the Aihnswothe was here, there was nothing to fear.

"Aihnswothe Feirah," she gushed happily. "So glad to see you."

"Glad to see you also, Maia. But why are you here? I told them you shouldn't be here, it's —"

"We didn't know," Ren blurted.

"That's all right," the Aihnswothe said. "I can still get you excused."

"Is it true the Jjord want to rescind because they haven't heard directly from me?" Maia said.

The Aihnswothe closed his eyes and sighed. "That may be, but you shouldn't be here. You're not ready for Leeam's interrogation."

"I am," Maia insisted. "I can't let the work on the Connector stop. This needs to be finished so we can stop depending on Xif. Anyway, I've seen Leeam before. I can handle him."

As if on cue, the handsome and sneering face of Sahiiraan Leeam peeped from behind the Aihnswothe.

"Aihnswothe Feirah, didn't I tell you? These children are very capable. You're worried for no reason. Besides, it's only a few simple questions. We simply need to hear from Maia about what happened with the Xifarians so we can know how much we need to commit to the security of the Connector. It has blown up on us once and we can't let it happen again, can we? The Jjord have lost enough for us, and we can't ask them to write off lives not knowing the situation fully."

The sniveling snake! Just the other day, Leeam called them stupid kids, and now suddenly they were capable? Leeam and his cronies were behind all the scheming, Maia was sure.

"My statements on her behalf should be enough," the Aihnswothe said. "You don't need to drag a child through this. She's been through a lot already."

Maia wanted to say she could handle it but held her tongue. Ren tugged on her hand and nodded, his eyes fixed on a woman in white who rose from her chair and walked toward where the Aihnswothe and Leeam argued.

Maia gasped. "Premier Oliena."

Premier Oliena was the leader of the Jjordic nation. Maia recalled how supportive she had been to the Solianese cause. Even resurrecting the Damoclian Connector was primarily her initiative.

Oliena smiled at Maia and Ren as she neared the group. "Oh, dear, both of you have grown so tall," she said, eyes flitting from Ren to Maia. "Maia, I'm sorry to hear what you've been through. My condolences for your loss," she said, lightly placing a hand over her heart. "Any other time I wouldn't ask you but . . . we are in a quandary here. It would really help our cause if we could hear your account of what happened between you and the Xifarians."

Maia nodded. She could tell them everything . . . all that she knew anyway. Talking about Sophie did not hurt as much anymore. She could do it.

Oliena turned toward the Aihnswothe. "Aihnswothe Feirah, I promise you, I shall not allow unnecessary questioning."

Aihnswothe Feirah shook his head in despair. "I mean no disrespect, Premier, but if Maia is rattled, she might—"

"Explode?" Leeam guffawed.

Aihnswothe Feirah glared at Leeam and Maia did not miss the way veins on his temple stuck out. "Believe it or not, yes. You'd be dead before you knew it."

Leeam froze for a moment before his eyes scooted down to Maia. There was a flicker of fear in his mocking eyes.

"She'll be fine, Aihnswothe," Oliena said. "I give you my word. I'll be the one questioning her, not Sahiiraan Leeam. Is that good, Maia?"

Maia nodded. With a quick glance at Ren who flashed a nervous smile, Maia followed the premier into the ring.

Oliena led her to an empty chair. "Have a seat, Maia. And don't worry, we shall keep it simple."

The questioning began right after. Oliena kept her promise, not letting Leeam utter a single word. She took the chair next to Maia and requested her to start with everything she knew about her mother.

Maia vaguely saw the Aihnswothe's face tighten, and Tsininio and Steward Lok's heads came together as they worriedly discussed something. She could not see the viewing gallery upstairs because of the spotlights glaring on her face, but she knew her friends were up there watching and praying for her.

She began from the time she was in Miorie, when she believed her mother, Sophie, was a traitor who had betrayed her nation. She told them about how Sophie was actually a hero, who had sacrificed her life to tear apart Xif's Sedara. It felt easy, as her lips moved almost on their own, her voice a stream of its own consciousness. As if, she had this chore before. Maia realized that she had indeed. She had been retelling her mother's story and hers many times over.

How long would she have to keep doing this? How long before they believed?

Leeam's face scrunched up with laughter when Maia explained that the heart of the Sedara would have destroyed Tansi's sun if Sophie had not destroyed it. The portly Aloysus, a prominent Jjord and Leeam's friend, smirked when she said the Xifarians were trying to put the Sedara back together by finding its broken pieces Sophie had left behind.

Strangely, Maia felt nothing. No anger, no frustration . . . nothing but a vagueness that surrounded her like a cocoon.

"So, where are they now?" Oliena asked. "I mean those broken pieces of the Sedara's heart . . . the shards, as the Xifarians like to call them."

Maia braced for the mockery that was sure to follow.

"There are no shards. The light that made up the heart of the Sedara is inside me. When Sophie touched the light, it found a host inside her unborn child . . . me."

Leeam burst into laughter, and even Oliena's stern look failed to stop him. "You mean to say," he said between chortles, "that this all-powerful heart of the Sedara that can hold the energy of stars is inside of you? So, pray tell me, how are you still alive? You said your mother died because she touched the light. Why not you?"

That was something Maia had thought about a lot. How did she survive? Like her, Sophie was also a Shimugien—one born with the natural ability to absorb the energy soaking L'miere crystals that made up the Sedara—yet Sophie had not survived the light.

"I don't know," Maia replied.

A sharp pain twisted in her heart. Even though she had been telling everyone Sophie's story, the truth was, she knew precious little about her mother, about her own heritage. She hardly even knew the basics. How did Sophie rip the Sedara? Who helped her do it? Miir's mother Asiyaah? But why? And did Asiyaah betray Sophie in the end like Zaara believed?

"All right. So—"

"Sahiiraan Leeam"—Oliena's sharp voice cut Leeam off—"you're not allowed to question."

"Please, Premier," Leeam bowed, his hands folded. "This is the last one. Please." Oliena took a moment too long to respond and Leeam jumped in. "So, Maia. You've been . . . throwing fireworks since you were a baby then, is that true?" Leeam said.

Although unkindly put, it seemed like a harmless question. "No, I didn't," Maia replied. "I didn't come to know of it until a few months ago. I had no idea—"

She stopped and bit the inside of her cheek, suddenly realizing how potent the question really was. Although it would serve the interrogation well, she could not tell them the reason her powers had come alive. She did not know for sure, but it had something to do with the massive trauma of losing her family and . . . Ruche!

Ruche was a strange man who Maia bumped into every so often, and always when she was at her most vulnerable. He never said so, but her friends suspected he was R'armimon. She had last met him while fleeing across the Dorgashians after Dada was killed. He had done something—chanted strange, foreign words—that changed something inside her. Ren believed Ruche had somehow awakened the dormant energy within.

Leeam drummed his fingers and circled Maia's chair, a predatory smile on his lips. "So you suddenly found this endless energy of the stars right when Chairman Phocluus was begging you to help him? Mighty convenient, don't you think?"

"That's enough, Sahiiraan Leeam," Oliena snapped.

As much as Maia wished she could explain, she knew it would be a mistake to tell Leeam about their theories of Ruche. One, these were only assumptions. And then, he would only twist her words unrecognizable.

A loud cackle tore through her thoughts and Maia blinked to clear her vision. Leeam was laughing. He turned his palms up and rolled his eyes. "I don't know about you, Premier, but this sounds like a tall tale to me. I think she tried to feed the Xifarians the same lies, and when they refused to believe, she used some sort of weapon on them. What it was, I don't know, but I don't believe she burst spontaneously into this wave of energy. This —"

"Sahiiraan Leeam, please stop," Oliena said.

Leeam ignored her and continued his tirade, pointing an accusing finger at Maia. "This is a dishonest, hateful, and utterly devious creature. By her own account, her mother was a double-crossing cheat. Why should the daughter be any different?"

"Sahiiraan Leeam, you'll please be quiet."

"Why should I?" Leeam growled. "I think this girl knows where the shards are and she's hiding them. We should give her away to the Xifarians for questioning — let them find what they need and leave us Tansians in peace."

The Aihnswothe and Tsininio unanimously protested Leeam's suggestion and Premier Oliena tried to quieten them but with no success. Everyone in the room — on the council and in the viewing area — erupted into agitated discussions among themselves.

Maia felt frustration stir deep in her gut. It was small, but it made her twitch nonetheless and her fists curled into balls. She had done well so far, and she had to keep it that way. She had to play it safe.

Yet, this futile and humiliating discussion over her fate was prodding her in the wrong direction. And as hard as she tried, she could not get past Leeam's suggestion of giving her away to the Xifarians. What was she? A toy? A piece of furniture? And when would he understand that the Xifarians cared nothing about Tansi or its people? All they cared about was fixing the Sedara so they could get away from here no matter the cost.

The flicker inside her twitched again and Maia jumped up from her chair. She had done what she could have done and now she had to leave.

She had barely taken one step when Leeam yelled, "Where are you off to?"

The ring fell silent as if by magic and within a moment or two, the entire room was quiet enough for Maia to hear herself breathe.

"I'm leaving, Sahiiraan Leeam," she said, her voice as cold and firm as the frozen grounds of ThulaSu. Maia could hardly believe the stoniness of her tone. "I came here to tell you what had happened because I thought my statement could clarify things. I wanted to do everything I could to help finish the Damoclian Connector. I believe I have now done everything in my power. What you choose to do next is up to you."

She paused a moment to take in Leeam's reddening face and quivering lips. Her firmness had stunned him enough, Maia thought happily. But she was not done yet.

"A few more things, Sahiiraan Leeam," Maia continued. "You can't give me away to anyone because I'm not yours to give. Don't try to take me by force, or you'd bring upon yourself the fate of your Xifarian friends. That light inside me, the one you mock, is more powerful than anything you've seen. So, I'd be careful if I were you."

Leeam's brows knotted and his mouth puckered. The color on his face deepened into a vivid shade of pink.

"The Xifarians can't get their hands on the shards because it's all inside of me, Sahiiraan Leeam. But if they find another way to fix the heart of their Sedara, then we'll all be dead. If I were you, I'd stop heckling kids and look into the real danger that's upon us."

Maia turned toward Premier Oliena and bowed hurriedly. "I hope you'll excuse me, Premier. I don't think it's safe for me to be here any longer."

Maia turned away, breathing fast and deep to keep the flame inside her from growing. Ren took her arm as soon as she had stepped out of the ring and the room seemed to hold its breath while Maia walked across it.

CHAPTER ELEVEN

INSULTS AND APOLOGIES

As soon as Maia and Ren stepped outside, they were surrounded by the rest of the team.

Dani pulled Maia into a tight embrace. "Are you all right?" she whispered.

Maia nodded. She had left at the perfect time. Now the heat inside was dying down fast.

Dani smiled and patted her shoulder. "You did great. I'm so proud of you."

"You shouldn't have come, Maia," Nafi burst out. "This was dangerous. You risked—"

Kusha placed a hand on Nafi's arm. "Not now, Nafi. Not here."

Maia cringed a little at the sight of Nafi's indignant face, but she quickly steeled herself. True, she had taken a huge risk, but she had known she could handle it. And she did.

"Can we get out of here, please?" Ren said.

"Yes, let's," Dani said hastily. She slipped an arm over Maia's shoulders and together they started down the stairs.

They had reached the bottom of the stairs when a gentle voice rang out behind them. "Maia."

Maia spun around, grinning widely at the woman in brown robes. Mahswa Tabrin was a Xifarian Tierremorphe, one with the power to morph terrains at her will. She had given them their firestone wristbands during the Seliban Challenge on Xif. The Mahswa had also been the one to tell Maia she was a Shimugien and had comforted her when she was scared out of her wits.

"Mahswa Tabrin," she cried, rushing to the woman's side. Her friends followed. "I didn't expect to see you here."

"Well, I fully expected to see you all," Tabrin replied with her usual reassuring smile. "You all look so much older . . . and wiser."

Her gentle voice was calming as always, and the last bit of unease inside Maia vanished as she spoke.

"Are you here for the Damoclian Council, Mahswa?" Kusha asked.

Tabrin shook her head. "No, I'm here as an arbitrator . . . a special judge for the Initiative."

"Wow, that's awesome," Ren said. "We didn't know that. They didn't have your name on the leaflet."

"Ah, that," Tabrin replied, nodding. "It was a last-moment decision."

"At least we'll have one judge who's not upset with us to begin with," Nafi said making Mahswa Tabrin chuckle.

"Why would anyone be upset with you, Nafi?" she said, still chuckling.

Nafi's brows came together in a petulant frown. "Don't you see how they love us? Didn't you hear how Leeam jeered at Maia?"

The Mahswa's face darkened. "Yes, Maia, about that . . ." The way her words trailed off made Maia's spine tingle. "I have to caution you, Maia. Do not get into thinking you're invincible." She paused again as hesitation rippled across her face.

"What do you mean, Mahswa Tabrin?" Maia asked hesitantly. What was the woman afraid to tell her?

The Mahswa shook her head as if she were driving a terrible thought away. She smiled, but unlike her usual smile, there was no peace in this one.

"It won't come to that, I hope," she muttered under her breath. She looked at Maia and smiled that lifeless smile again. "Just be careful."

Maia wanted to probe some more but she hesitated on seeing the Mahswa's distracted and troubled face. Before the Mahswa could recover, a different thought invaded Maia's head with gusto. "I wanted to ask you something. Leeam mentioned it today and I've been wondering too. How did I survive the light when my mother couldn't? She was a Shimugien just like me, so . . ."

The Mahswa's face froze as if a whip had been flicked across it. She stared, her eyes narrowing slowly into slits. Her lips parted a little, but before she could utter a word, a group of men, all clad in black cloaks, their hoods drawn so low that almost no face showed, emerged from the Gathering House. The back of their cloaks had the imprint of an enormous silvery-gray skull that shimmered slightly. Maia's heart skipped a few beats.

The man she had seen gliding through the snowdrifts in the courtyard had been wearing the same attire. It was not the hooded cloak of the Order of the Fyrstell, but something else. Who were these people?

Whoever they were, they marched away fast and without a glance at Maia and her teammates. When Maia looked over at the Mahswa, the woman's face had paled. Her worried gaze was fixed on the group that was walking away rapidly.

"Mahswa," Maia called.

Mahswa Tabrin put her hand up. "Wait," she said. She took a few faltering steps toward the group of men. "I'll speak with you later, Maia," she said and hurried away after the cloaked men.

Maia and her friends watched her disappear between the buildings up north, all of them somewhat taken aback by the Mahswa's rushed departure.

"Who were those people dressed in black?" Maia asked.

Kusha gave a listless shrug and no one else seemed to have answers either.

Nafi cocked an eyebrow. "Anyone else find the Mahswa's manner weird?" She continued when no one replied. "I always thought Mahswa Tabrin was the sanest Xifarian I've met. But now . . ."

Ren crossed his arms and glared at Nafi. "So all Xifarians are crazy, huh?"

Nafi scrunched her face as if she had been hit with a fly swatter. "What? I didn't say that."

"Of course you did," Ren snapped.

"All right, that's enough," Dani chimed in. "Let's leave this place now. I don't want to see Leeam and his cronies one more time today. So you two hold on to your anger, fight somewhere else away from here."

"Suits me," Nafi muttered before striding off toward the ramparts. Ren shook his head angrily, but when Maia hooked her arm through his, he too relented and they started walking back together to their living quarters.

They were about to turn the final bend in the rampart when Nafi, who had been walking a few paces ahead of them, screeched to a halt.

"What is that?" she said, pointing ahead.

The reason for Nafi's outburst became clear as soon as they reached the bend. An imposing Xifarian fighter craft, although half the size of an Onclioraptor, sat in the courtyard, its wings spreading menacingly over the snow-covered grounds. Maia held her breath as Ren whooped, throwing his fists into the air.

"Yes! It's here!"

When Maia looked questioningly at Ren, he grinned. "It's our racing craft."

"It looks awesome," Maia said.

Nafi's brow shot up. "Our?"

"Karhann and I race together," Ren said, then sprinted toward the craft. "Didn't I tell you?" he shouted.

Nafi glared at Kusha. "Is that allowed? Your father allowed a Xifarian fighter craft to land on the Sun Temple's courtyard? Has he lost it?"

"Nafi!" Dani's sharp voice of caution silenced the girl, and Kusha let her rude words slide, so they trooped down in silence. Ren was talking animatedly to a group of boys and girls who stood next to the craft.

"Not those jokers again," Nafi grumbled. The "jokers" were Karhann's teammates and members of Core 7—Loriine, Baecca, and the pasty-faced boy.

Maia braced for more fireworks. Encounters with Core 7 were never peaceful, and with Nafi in a crabby mood, this one could not be pleasing.

Karhann smiled and waved at the group. "Hey, guys," he said genially.

Maia waved back and walked closer to the craft, admiring its contoured nose that hung mid-air above their heads. "That's one impressive craft, you two," she said to Karhann and Ren. Both boys beamed, and Karhann ran a hand over the stout landing gear.

"Thanks, Maia," he said. "We love our Viperine."

"Viperine?" Maia asked. She touched the craft's pale underbelly, enjoying the smooth feel of metal under her palm. "That's a nifty name."

"They are pretty cool," Karhann said. "Even if they aren't as fearsome as the Raptors, they're good for navigating through tight places."

"Besides, they're affordable," Ren said with a loud chuckle. "A Raptor is a zillion times more expensive than this."

Karhann thumped Ren on the shoulder. "Someday, Ren, we'll have a Raptor of our own."

Ren nodded and sighed wistfully. "Yes, someday."

"You boys are so lucky," Nafi started rather demurely. "Look at us. We play with rag dolls and sticks and stones. And you? Playing with aircraft and dreaming of even bigger ones. But you know, you kids have to start big. You have huge shoes to fill."

"Whatever do you mean, dear cousin?" Loriine, who had been observing them quietly, simpered in her usual irritating way.

"Well, you have to train to be like your fathers and mothers, don't you? And graduate to destroying stars and planets in a few years," Nafi said caustically.

"Nafi!" Dani chided. "That's not nice."

"What?" Nafi shot back. "You don't like me telling the truth, Dani?"

"I don't mind the truth," Dani replied coolly. "But you shouldn't be bringing parents into this."

"Why not?" Placing her arms on her hips, Nafi glared at Dani. "All of their parents are on the list of the Xifarian 'who's who.' Do you see any of them standing up against the chairman and his SDS? Do you see anyone coming to help Maia or Tansi? No, you don't. That's because they're all busy planning how to destroy our sun. They are the real villains here, Dani, not me for calling them out."

Dani looked away but Maia placed a hand on Nafi's shoulder supportively. Maybe Nafi was rude, but she was telling the truth. A fleeting silence fell. It hovered tentatively around them until Loriine stomped over to the girls.

"That is a lie," she hissed into Nafi's face. "No one wants to destroy your pathetic little sun and your broken-down planet. We just want to get out of here and leave you wretched beggars alone with your sticks and stones."

"You're either stupid or the biggest liar alive, and I think I'll go with the liar," Nafi hissed back. "Your planet flies after it sucks all the energy from our star, but you knew that already. It's nothing new; Xif has been doing it for hundreds of years now, ever since it left its original orbit."

"Stop spreading these lies," Loriine shouted. Baecca and the pasty-faced boy had joined Loriine, flanking her sides like staunch bodyguards. Loriine pointed accusingly at Maia. "Your friend is a liar and you are too. All of you."

"If anyone's lying, it's you," Nafi shouted back.

They stood glaring at each other, fists curled and nostrils flared. For a moment, it felt like they would hurl themselves at each other. Dani grabbed Nafi's arm, and Maia tried to push the warring cousins apart.

"We should leave," Maia said, dragging Nafi away from Loriine. "Your screaming at people won't change a thing," she chided as they pulled a reluctant Nafi into the building.

"How can they just keep on denying it?" Nafi fumed.

"Because they don't know the Sedara would destroy your sun. Or that for as long Xif has been flying across the galaxy, it has been destroying stars," Ren said softly. "If Maia didn't tell me how the heart of the Sedara makes Xif fly, I wouldn't have known, and neither do they."

Nafi's face drooped a little and her pace slowed. "Guess you're right," she admitted and stole a quick glance at Dani. "Stop. I think I owe them an apology."

Maia stared wide-eyed at Nafi. Nafi hardly ever apologized. And the thought of her saying sorry to Loriine and Karhann was simply . . . dumbfounding.

"Um . . . are you sure?" she stammered.

"Yes," Nafi said firmly. Pushing aside Ren and Kusha, she marched back toward the courtyard.

"I'll go with her," Dani said before rushing after Nafi.

Maia did not have to think long to decide what she wanted to do. Nafi had taken a bold step, and she had to be by Nafi's side. She yelled, "Wait, I'm coming too."

"Good luck," Ren shouted.

As they approached the courtyard, they heard Loriine's loud voice. She sounded hysterical. The girls slowed and came to a stop.

"I can't believe you stayed quiet, Karhann," Loriine shouted. "What is it? Has hanging around with Ren turned you into a minion of those down-planet scum or what?"

Karhann muttered something, but Maia could not hear what it

was.

"No, I won't be quiet. I don't care if anyone hears. Scum is scum, and I'm not afraid to call it that," Loriine continued.

Maia's insides tightened. She stole a glance at Nafi and noted her fisted hands.

"Let's go back," Dani whispered. Maia was worried herself, but Nafi did not budge.

"She made that false allegation to our face. That we're about to kill them all, destroy their system and whatnot," Loriine said, "and you just sat there and took it? Do you have a thing for that stupid girl or something?"

"Shut up, Loriine. I don't have a thing for anyone," Karhann retorted.

"What is it then? Why would you let them call our nation, our people, our parents, names?"

For a moment, there was quiet and Maia felt a wave of sadness. She knew what it was like to learn about deep, dark secrets, and in the case of the Xifarians, they had a lot of them.

"Because I know what they say is true," Karhann said morosely.

"You know?" Loriine shouted. "What do you mean? How?"

"Because my lineage won't let me forget," Karhann continued in a sad tone. "Other than the higher-ups who obviously know everything, it's us, the unfortunate ones from the Seliban system, who know the whole truth. Well, we and the Origin Scrolls in the Chancery Archives."

"What?" Loriine blurted. "Wh-what are you talking about?"

Karhann and his teammates huddled together and started talking in hushed voices.

Maia held her breath. She did not fully understand the meaning of what Karhann had just said, but she did not know if this was an appropriate time to intrude upon Karhann and his teammates.

"I can apologize later," Nafi declared suddenly and no one disagreed.

They walked back in silence to where Ren and Kusha had been

waiting. Ren flipped his hands on hearing about Karhann.

"We all know of his Seliban heritage. That's nothing new," Ren said. "No idea about the other stuff though."

The topic was forgotten in a while, but a strange memory from a long time ago crept up from long-forgotten depths. Maia did not know why she thought of that large engraving she had seen in the Seliban Temple on Xif nearly two years ago. Or why she remembered every detail in it so clearly—the tattooed man on a platform cradling an orb, a throng of people behind him with their hands outstretched as if to stop the man with the orb, and that other man in a Xifarian Gambrill reaching for the orb. She did not know what it was, but she was sure there was something about that engraving. If only she could find out what it was.

CHAPTER TWELVE

THE INITIATIVE RESUMES

Maia woke up to a cold and cloudy morning. She rolled out of bed with difficulty, wishing she could stay under the covers longer, but she had no choice. She had to get up and get out. It was the first day of the third phase of the Alliance Initiative.

By the time Maia's sluggish steps took her to the refectory, her teammates were already attacking breakfast. One look at what they were eating—gray crushed cereal mixed with milk and boiled into a gooey slush, a favorite in ThulaSu called milk-pottage—made Maia's spirits dip further. She grabbed a bowl and reluctantly scooped some of the grub into it.

"Eat up, everyone," Dani said from across the table. "The first day is always long. We'll have a late lunch most likely."

"Yes, Mother," Nafi muttered under her breath.

Maia forced some of the pottage down her throat. There could not have been a worse start of the Initiative than this.

"Hey, guys," a bright voice propped up her drooping mood

somewhat. A wiry boy was waving from a nearby table.

"Hey, Jiri," Ren waved back.

Jiri was part of Core 13, another group that had made it to the final phase. He and his teammates—Anja, Luem, Corin, and Nair—were good friends with Core 21. Maia knew Anja more than the others since she was from Shiloh, the big town next to Maia's village Appian, and also because Anja had shared a dorm with them during the second phase in Zagran. The dark-haired girl waved happily at them.

"It's good to see those guys," Kusha said. "It's been so long. I can hardly recall the other teams that made it here."

"How can you forget?" Nafi said between gulps of pottage. "Jiri and team are Core 13, all right? They got top honors in the Jjordic phase. Core 34 . . . Kenan and his mates came in second. Those Core 7 brats were third and the fourth place was that all-Jjord team . . ."

"Core 10," Dani completed. "I remember Core 45 came in fifth."

"I know Core 45," Ren said cheerily. "Vyessa's in it."

Nafi scrunched her nose. "Vyessa? Who's that?"

It was weird that they knew so few of their fellow contestants. That was partly because there was little time to hang out with people during the contest and partly because Maia and her teammates always ended up entangled in crazy adventures. Maia knew most of the other contestants by their faces, but it was hard to remember their names.

"Long curly brown hair, big brown eyes, taller than Kusha," Ren described as the rest of the team tried to recall. "How could you forget her? She's mind-blowing."

Nafi's mouth fell open and her eyes grew large. "Mind-blowing? That's what you say when you talk about your Viperine."

Ren chuckled. "What can I say? She's super pretty."

Nafi scoffed and rolled her eyes before concentrating on her food once more.

"I know she's from Zagran, that's all," Dani said. "I hardly recall the rest of the teams. We barely scraped through, remember?"

Maia did remember. The final challenge at Zagran had been a big mess. They were penalized for not being able to reach the final destination together as a team because they had to respond to a cry for help from Hans and ended up fighting Xifarian saboteurs. Kusha had been wounded and people had died, including Bikele, a close friend of her mother. Core 21 had come in ninth place.

"You must be the marvelous Core 21," a croaky voice interrupted Maia's drifting thoughts. "I've been looking all over for you."

Maia could barely stifle a gasp when she looked up. He had to be seventeen or eighteen, and he reminded her of a toad, the golden ones with bulging green eyes that used to live by the hundreds in their pond in Appian. He was squat and had a large round nose that seemed like it would pop at any moment.

"Who are you?" Nafi demanded.

The toad laughed, but it sounded more like a horse clearing its throat. "I'm your team mentor, of course." He bowed a little. "Everrol Dernmooth at your service."

"Oh, hello. I'm Dani," Dani rose to her feet and bowed with elegance. Kusha waved and introduced the team. Maia did not have the energy or interest to rise or bow or talk so she simply smiled. She did not care much about mentors anymore anyway, they were either useless like Joolsae or backstabbers like Miir.

"I'm here to assist you during the Initiative," Everrol said. "Anything you need, anything at all, you tell me, all right? I shall now escort you to the room where Monk Hilledunn will give the welcoming address.

"Thanks, but you don't need to wait on us," Kusha said. "It's at the Reception Gallery, yes? We can get there ourselves."

Everrol laughed as if Kusha had just said the silliest of things. He rubbed his hands together and croaked heartily. "You're *my* kids now. I can't let you trouble yourselves finding your way through these cold, dark hallways of ThulaSu. I shall always be with you. Always. Forever."

Maia realized her surprise at Everrol's rather passionate declaration was not just her own. The rest of the team was staring open-mouthed at Everrol as well.

"Seriously, Everrol," Kusha insisted, "it's no trouble. You see, I'm from around here."

Everrol closed his enormous eyes and croaked. Pulling a chair from the next table, he sat down and crossed his arms. "I know you, Kusha. I know all about you. Who doesn't? But you've been placed under my wings, see?" Everrol stretched his arms to his sides and flapped them like a bird. "You're my brood. And Papa bird will take good care of you."

"Doesn't Papa bird have classes to attend or something?" Nafi's biting voice came hurtling across the table.

Everrol rubbed his hands together again and rocked back and forth as if he had heard the funniest joke. "They told me you were funny," he said between hoarse chuckles. He wiped the corners of his eyes with his meaty fingers. "No. No classes. Papa bird has been excused from all classes today so he can take care of you."

Maia did not know if that was supposed to make her happy. Everrol seemed strange and something about him made her uneasy. Perhaps it was because his gaze seemed to linger on her longer than on anyone else, but then that was expected now that everyone knew about her.

She forced another spoon of pottage into her mouth and chided herself for her suspicions. Being distrustful had not always done her good. She had to take her time. Even if Everrol looked weird and behaved funny, she was going to take the time to judge him.

***

They sat in a dim room lined with rows of worn-out wooden chairs. Since the teams were arranged based on their ranks at the end of the last phase, Core 21 was in the ninth row. Everrol sat at the center of the bench. Maia, Dani, and Ren were huddled to his right and Nafi and Kusha sat on his left. The teams were filing in slowly and Maia hoped the address would begin soon, but there was no sign of Monk Hilledunn or the arbitration committee.

"How are you liking ThulaSu?" Everrol whispered to Maia.

"It's nice," she replied curtly. She was not very happy with the way Everrol was practically sticking to them, and the rest of her teammates seemed to agree based on the grimaces that donned their faces.

Jiri's team, Core 13, sat way up front. Their mentor—a girl with a long brown braid—was chatting with a few other mentors at another corner of the room. Everrol was the only mentor who was sitting with the brood.

"And you, Ren?" Everrol leaned forward to look at Ren.

"I love it," Ren replied. To Maia's surprise, he continued the conversation eagerly. "So, Everrol, how long have *you* been at ThulaSu?"

From the corner of her eye, Maia noticed Nafi throw a fearsome glare at Ren, but Ren barely even noticed. Everrol, on the other hand, seemed pleased beyond belief.

"I've been here, for like, forever," he said, giggling like a child. "ThulaSu is my home."

"So . . . you live here? All year?" Ren asked.

"Yes, sorta. My parents passed when I was a wee Lil thing, and I've been here since I was six, raised by the monks."

A sense of guilt twitched inside Maia. The poor guy was an orphan, just like her. He was probably just a simpleton craving for the company and that was why he stuck to them.

"There's never been so much excitement around here before," Everrol said, rocking back and forth on the bench. "I wish the Initiative could go on forever. Did you know there's a fighter craft in the courtyard? Never thought I'd see one of those up close."

Ren and Maia exchanged a quick glance.

"That's a Viperine," Ren explained. "Belongs to my buddy Karhann and me."

Everrol turned sideways to face Ren. His eyes had grown so large that Maia was almost worried they would pop off his head. "You don't say!" he said. Ren nodded solemnly. "Can you . . . please . . .

consider giving me a ride on it . . . sometime? Anytime," Everrol said, his words coming in broken spurts.

"Of course, Everrol," Ren replied. "We can—"

"Can you go easy on the chitchat please?" Nafi's annoyed voice stopped Ren midway. "I'd rather hear the welcome address."

Maia had not noticed when the front of the room had filled up. She looked over the heads of the rows of contestants to the front of the room. A man in muted yellow robes and long hair that ended a little above his shoulders stood on a dais, smiling. His face was oval and slightly pudgy, and every time he smiled, his chin jutted out. Maia deduced he was Monk Hilledunn, the chief arbitrator.

Next to him were the other members of the Arbitration Committee for the Solianese phase of the Initiative, three people whom Maia knew very well. The severe-looking gray-haired man dressed in a Gambrill was Master Kehorkjin of the Xifarian Defense Academy. Next to him was the white-suited and skeletal form of Aerika from the University of Arts and Sciences in Zagran. The third person was Mahswa Tabrin, back to her usual serene persona in her flowing brown gown.

"Welcome to ThulaSu, young friends," Monk Hilledunn said in a cheery tone. "And welcome to the third and final phase of the Alliance Initiative. I have heard many great stories about you—your bravery, your persistence, and your intellect—from these capable masters who have worked with you before. Now I expect to be awed by you also. Do you think I'll get to see some of this awesomeness?"

The room broke into loud cheers. Hilledunn seemed like a nice person just like Kusha had said. Maia joined in the cheer until Hilledunn smiled and raised his hands above his head to urge the room to quiet down.

"As has been the practice, this phase will also be split into two segments, each ending with a challenge. After the first challenge, five teams will be eliminated. That'll leave us with the final five teams that will move on to the last challenge of all. The victors of that will be crowned winners of the Alliance Initiative."

Maia could not believe they were so close to the end. Years ago, she never would have even thought about competing in the Alliance Initiative, and here she was, at the final stage. After everything that had gone on, and how on alert she had been, it felt good to get lost in the excitement.

"Now, since this is the final phase, we will stretch its duration a little. Instead of the six months you usually get to complete two challenges, you'll get close to a year to train and complete the Solianese phase."

"Hmm. That means we're stuck here with our mentor for a year," Ren whispered into Maia's ear, making her chuckle.

"Each team will have their own mentor, who will work closely with you, assist you, and advise you," Hilledunn continued. "Today they will show you to the rooms where most of your training sessions will be held, as well as introduce you to the teachers."

Everrol clapped his hands excitedly. "Yes, yes, yes. Can't wait to introduce you to my favorite teacher."

As much as Maia did not want to admit it, she found his excitement endearing. He reminded her of Kusha during the first phase when they rode in the Fahrbot into Xif.

Monk Hilledunn paced in front of the room and clasped his hands together. "I do not want to keep you here any longer and make you listen to my boring talk," he said. "Instead, I shall let you walk around the university and get used to your new surroundings."

The contestants stirred, clearly eager to head outside and explore, but Hilledunn raised his arms and urged the youngsters to calm down.

"I have one last thing to say before I dismiss you." The room fell silent. Hilledunn held out his right hand and beckoned. "Maia of Core 21, please come and join us here."

Maia felt a hot wave charge through her, and it was not the surge of her powers. Instead, it was a flash of embarrassment and being put on the spot.

"What in the name of the stars?" Ren blurted.

Maia forgot to breathe. She simply stared at Hilledunn's outstretched arm. Everyone whipped their heads around and stared at her, their eyes judging. Maia's heart pounded wildly. What did he want with her?

"Come on out," Hilledunn called again, smirking at her in an odd, vulturine way. The three people standing next to Hilledunn shifted uncomfortably.

This can't be good.

Her legs were numb as she stood and Maia feared they would buckle under her when she walked. She had barely taken a step when Nafi shot up on the other side of Everrol.

"I'm coming with you, Maia," Nafi declared, and before Maia knew what was happening, there was shuffling and movement and all of her teammates had surrounded her.

Together they walked to the front of the room, her friends on each side. Her heart thudded, but not as fiercely. Tears pricked Maia's eyes at the thought that she had ever gotten mad at them. They were her friends through thick and thin. She felt prepared for whatever Hilledunn could throw at her.

When they reached the front of the room, Hilledunn cleared his throat. "I only called Maia and you're all here. You're quite a team." Kehorkjin grunted and Mahswa Tabrin smiled.

Nafi grinned. "That's what we're supposed to learn from the Initiative, right?"

"Together we're stronger than we'll ever be alone," said Ren.

Hilledunn's face darkened a tad, but Aerika's lip curled into a smile before she turned away to look at the ceiling. Maia smirked.

"Sounds splendid," Hilledunn said. His eyes roamed over the five faces and came to rest on Maia. She could have been mistaken, but Maia thought she saw a glint of anger in his dark eyes.

With a smile, Hilledunn turned to the audience. "I'm not sure how much you have heard about recent developments, but I'm sure you will catch up quickly. News travels fast within ThulaSu, so you will know things happened with one of your fellow contestants." He looked over at Maia and patted her on the shoulder.

"Maia, for no fault of her own, is . . . somewhat unstable and a threat to your safety. I'm asking you . . . everyone . . . to be cautious with her and around her. Your life is at stake here, remember that." He looked down at Maia one more time and flashed a chin-jutting smile. "And you, Maia, put some distance between you and the rest."

Maia's heart thumped wildly once more. *Unstable? A threat to your safety? Your life is at stake?* His words cut her like a knife. As she saw the rows of faces turn grim and fearful, a bottomless pit opened up inside her. Pairs of curious eyes looked at her as if she were a circus exhibit. Maia wished she could turn invisible, or the ground would part and suck her in, or she could simply run away far from here. But none of that happened. Even though her teammates held on tightly to her arms, even though she knew this would be over soon, Maia could not push down the misery.

Hilledunn smiled at Maia again. "I hope you understand. This had to be said. For everyone's safety."

Maia nodded. "I understand," she said, gazing into his deep, dark eyes. She felt something in its depths and it was not pretty. He was not the nice person he was pretending to be. He was enjoying hurting and embarrassing her. Maia came to one conclusion: She had to put him in place.

Maia gritted her teeth. "With all due respect, Monk Hilledunn, but if I'm such a danger to those around me, do you think you've made anyone safer by calling me up here? I can tell you that right now I'm hardly as calm as the Xinhagyi would like me to be," she said, watching the fear course up his pale face and making it paler still.

Hilledunn turned away from her as if he had been slapped. "All right, everyone," he yelled. "You're dismissed."

The walk back to the long stone corridor outside took forever. Maia knew this was going to be a very long year.

Chapter Thirteen

The Glass House

All the way down the damp and winding corridor, Maia barely heard the chatter around her or felt the frigid floor under her feet. Most of the other groups shrunk away from them as if they were diseased, and Maia focused on nothing but the patterns of the stones on the ground.

Nafi fell back to her side and nudged her arm. "Maia," she whispered sharply. "Stop looking like you've done something wrong."

She had not done anything wrong, yet everything was wrong with her. She had to admit, even if it was only to herself, that she was not at the place the Xinhagyi wanted her to be. She could lose control. And if she lost control, she could be a threat to the others, that was undeniably true.

"You have nothing to be ashamed about, do you understand?" Nafi's fingers dug into Maia's arm. "What that stupid Hilledunn did was . . . mean and stupid. You can't let that upset you."

"But, he's right, Nafi," Maia whispered. "Maybe he could've done it in a nicer way, but it's the truth. I'm not very stable, and if I were to—"

"You're not." Nafi's eyes blazed with anger. "You're not going to explode into a ball of fire just like that. Even when you didn't know of the light inside you, it took a lot to get you to . . . explode, didn't it? And now you're training with the Xinhagyi. There's no way you're a threat."

Maia wished she could believe her, but she felt uneasy. Maybe her participation in the Initiative was a mistake. She did not have good control over her powers . . . What if something upset her badly? What if the light surged out of her? What if she hurt or . . . killed someone?

Nafi sighed loudly. "Come on, Maia. You've got to believe in yourself and not what they tell you."

"I'm trying, Nafi."

"Not hard enough," Nafi grumbled.

Ahead of them, Everrol and the others slowed. The narrow corridor had opened into an airy hallway. Talking to Nafi had helped; Maia felt a little lighter and her thoughts had cleared.

"Come on in," Everrol said. He was motioning toward a pair of large wooden doors that were partially open.

"Wow," Nafi exclaimed as they stepped inside.

The room was beautiful. It was made entirely out of glass. All of the walls, the roof, and even parts of the translucent floor let light stream inside. The walls were crisscrossed by metal frames that ran up and down and across the length of the room. Large tables—fifteen in total—were placed in rows along the room. Plants of various sizes were set on the tables with pots and pitchers of all shapes.

"What is this place?" Ren said, his voice brimming with awe.

"This"—Everrol raised his arms—"is ThulaSu's famous Glass House."

Nafi leaned toward Maia and whispered, "House? It's more like a room. And how can it be famous if I've never heard of it?"

Everrol looked at Nafi, the corners of his lips twitching. "That's because ThulaSu likes to keep its secrets. We don't go about broadcasting our treasures."

"So . . . no one knows, which means it's not famous," Nafi reiterated caustically.

Everrol grimaced before beckoning them. "Follow me, I'll show you to your table."

Dani fell back a little as they walked. "Why do you have to cross him all the time?" she asked Nafi.

"Because he's annoying?"

"Maybe he is, but he's our mentor. We'll need his help."

Nafi rolled her eyes and scoffed. She clearly did not see any value in appeasing Everrol, and, like always, she was not shy about making her opinion known. Dani shook her head and strode away from them. Everrol led the group to a table that was set up against the far wall and quite a distance away from the rest of the tables. There was a metal plaque set at the center that said "21."

"This is where you'll work," Everrol said. A large potted plant with bulky and flat pink leaves sat at its center. The plant was pretty aside from the serrated edges of the bright leaves that looked downright vicious. "You've already been given some lovely Pink Pantheronicas to study. You're really lucky to have those. And one for each table too. We've always had just one in a class to share."

"Hey, guys! Just look at the view from up here." Ren's excited shouts made them forget Everrol and the Pantheronicas. People from other groups also flocked around Ren in an instant.

"Fantastic," said someone.

"I don't believe this," someone else said.

"Oh, my goodness," said another. "This is too scary."

Maia held her breath as she walked up to Ren. It was indeed breathtaking and scary at the same time. The floor of the Glass House was a projection out of the mountain range that formed ThulaSu's foundation. Instead of being carved into the walls of the range like the rest of the university, this room jutted out of the rocky wall and practically hung in the air. They could see the whole city below them. The Vesteran ranges seemed close from here, and the valley with the

Sun Temple at its center was scarily distant. Slightly dizzy, Maia turned away from the stunning panorama.

"See?" Everrol raised an eyebrow at Nafi. "Have you ever seen such a view?"

Nafi gave him a blank look and walked back to the table. She pulled out a chair, sat down, and reached for the pink-leaved plant.

"No!" Everrol yelled. He threw himself at Nafi's outstretched arm and slapped it away, almost knocking Nafi down to the floor. The pink leaves snapped together with a mighty clap. The room gasped.

"Good save, Everrol. Chopped or chewed fingers wouldn't have been an auspicious beginning at all." The voice—low and nasal—sounded from near the door. Maia spotted a dwarf of a man with a protruding belly that made a rounded tent of his muted yellow robe. "But you should've warned them as soon as you brought them in and avoided this altogether. That's why you've been selected as mentors."

He walked—almost glided—over to the Core 21 table and looked up intently at Nafi.

"Curiosity is good," he said, every word ending in a deep nasal twang, "but sometimes it's also good to be cautious. ThulaSu is full of surprises. Tread with care, Miss Nafi."

Nafi scrambled off her chair and nodded vigorously. "Yes, sir," she said. Maia detected a faint tremble in her voice, which was unusual. "I'm sorry."

The man waved off her apology. "No big deal," he said jovially before clapping his hands. "Mentors, you can all leave now."

"Can I stay, Monk Tessio?" Everrol said immediately.

"No, you cannot, Everrol," Tessio replied just as quickly as if he had been expecting Everrol to ask that question.

With a loud sigh, Everrol departed along with the other mentors. Maia observed the interaction curiously and wondered how Tessio would turn out to be, but overall, she liked him. As soon as the doors closed behind them, Tessio scrambled onto a high platform near one end of the room. Clearing his throat noisily a couple of times, Tessio addressed the groups.

"So, boys and girls," he started in a clear, loud voice, "what have we learned today?"

When the room remained silent, Tessio looked pointedly at Nafi and asked, "Miss Nafi? Care to illuminate us?"

Nafi's face turned a shade of crimson but she managed a clear reply regardless. "We need to be careful with things we haven't seen before?"

Tessio raised his stubby hands upward and rocked from side to side, almost comically. "Yes, dear. Never fear the unknown but always proceed with caution. Right, children?"

Every head in the room nodded wisely.

"So, what are we going to learn here?" Tessio asked next. He seemed to like starting with questions. "Any ideas?"

A hand shot up near the back of the room. Maia recognized the bushy-haired boy with his hand raised as Kenan from Core 34.

"Hand-to-hand combat with man-eating plants?"

Monk Tessio burst into chuckles. Holding up his arms in the air he said, "No, no, no. No combat training here. In here, we shall learn about certain medicinal plants that have such strange and miraculous properties they could even be called magical."

"And murderous," Nafi muttered under her breath.

"This beautiful plant in front of you" — Tessio pointed at the Pantheronicas — "is one such miracle. Can you guess what its special property might be?"

"What's there to guess? We saw it already. It bites people," Nafi piped up.

Clutching his little potbelly, Tessio broke into laughter again. "No, no, no," he said. "This plant, this delicate-looking plant, grows in the dead of winter. Can you believe it? When nothing else but the Darkwoods are left standing, these fragile little things start blooming. So, tell me, other than being ferocious, what else about the Pantheronicas might we be interested in?"

Ren's arm shot up in the air. "That it's cold-proof," he said.

"Nothing is cold-proof, my boy," Tessio said. "But this plant does have the ability to resist the cold to a great degree. How do you think it does that?"

The room remained silent.

"Feel its stem," Tessio said. As everyone in the room stared at him aghast at the instruction, Tessio clutched his belly and laughed. "All right. I was just checking if you had learned to be careful yet. Before we feel the stem of a Pantheronicas, we do this."

He jumped off his dais and walked to a nearby table strewn with various instruments and books. Tessio rummaged through the pile and picked up a long stick with a feather stuck at its tip and marched over to where Karhann and his team were sitting. Waving the feather-tipped stick like a wand, Tessio deftly tapped the stem of the Pantheronicas right where it met the soil. In an instant, the plant drooped, its leaves curling into balls. It was as if Tessio had put it to sleep.

"See that? It's harmless now," Tessio said with a reassuring smile. "Now feel the stem while I help the others."

Tessio went from table to table putting the Pantheronicas to sleep. Nafi sprung on the plant as soon as it crumpled.

"Gentle, please," Tessio said, raising a sharp brow at the girl. "They are rare plants, so please treat them with care."

Maia touched the waxy stem as gently as she could, quickly feeling the ribs that rose from the base of the stem to the tips of the leaves.

"Don't they feel warm to you?" she whispered to Dani, who nodded in response.

"They have built-in heaters," Ren whispered.

Tessio was hovering near them, observing the contestants. He leaned closer to Maia's table. "They sure do. These plants produce a special chemical called 'calorfine' that's key to their survival. This substance nudges every cell in these plants to produce heat—ramping the production up and down as needed. Those ribs are pipelines or plumbing to distribute that heat. Those ribs are also nerve-rich, so when I struck the base of the stem where all the nerves come together, it immobilizes the plant. Temporarily, of course."

His description suddenly reminded Maia of a day long past. It was their second day on Xif and the first time the team had met their mentor, Miir. He had tested their skills using a strange beetle pod, the Raap beetle. Vicious and deadly once out of the pod, the only clean way to kill the Raap beetle was to disable the nerve center of the pod. Maia shifted uncomfortably in her seat as she remembered her own attempt to disable the Raap pod. She had set a few beetles free on purpose, and even though she had tackled them all before they harmed anyone, Miir had not been pleased.

It was odd that she remembered Miir's words so clearly even after all this time. "Can't help showing off, can you?" he had said, his dark eyes glinting with disapproval.

Maia shifted again and Dani leaned closer. "What's wrong? You look . . . sadder. Are you still thinking about Hilledunn?"

Maia was about to wave Dani's concern away but then thought otherwise. "Tessio's description reminded me of the Raap beetle. Remember that?"

Dani's eyes grew a tad wider before she broke into a grin. "You're right. That had a nerve center we had to disable. What a day it was. We had met Miir for the first time and he was not a friendly soul."

"He was fine," Nafi, a forever fan of their erstwhile mentor, commented sharply from the other side.

"Agreed. Way better than the useless Joolsae and the sticky Everrol," Ren said.

Maia bit her lip so hard it hurt. The pain was good though, as it helped push away the memories of Miir's betrayal. But some memories were strong and impossible to fight away, Maia quickly realized. Miir had murdered her grandfather, and Herc and Emmy as well. He could have been a better mentor than the others Ren mentioned, but everything else about him was rotten. She did not need her friends praising him around her.

"Can we stop discussing him, please?" she said. Her voice must've been sharp because everyone looked at her curiously and a little worriedly.

"Of course, Maia," Dani said in a reassuring voice. "Sorry."

"You're the one who brought it up," Nafi commented wryly.

"And why do we have to stop discussing him?" Ren asked from across the table. His brows had furrowed deeply. "He was harsh, I'll give you that. But he was good to us also."

Maia seethed at Ren. What was wrong with him? Didn't he know Miir was responsible for Dada's death?

"You know he killed my Dada, don't you?" she said. "And Herc. And Emmy."

"You *think* he killed your Dada?" Ren retorted. "You don't have proof of it, do you?"

"What did you say?" Maia could feel her voice grow sharper. "You need proof of his involvement? Remember *Shadow*? His Onclioraptor? *Shadow* was there when they set fire to our farm. And if *Shadow* was there, Miir had to be there also. What other proof do you need?"

Ren continued to poke the patterned pot of the Pantheronicas without looking up at her. His lips were pursed stubbornly and his face a little flushed.

Frustration grew rapidly inside Maia. Why was Ren defending Miir? Was it because he was a Xifarian and needed to defend one of his own no matter what?

Maia turned away. For a moment, she just wanted to run—out of ThulaSu and into the woods, away from Ren and his biased arguments. In the next moment, she just wanted to shake some sense into her friend. She knew neither was an option, so bracing herself, she look into Ren's mottled eyes.

"Don't you remember what his mother did to mine? Maybe you don't, Ren. But Asiyaah left Sophie in prison and used her to buy her family the chancellor's office. I can never trust Miir or his family, don't you understand?" More words created a painful lump in Maia's throat, and somehow she pushed them out. "Never thought you'd side with him over me, Ren."

Ren looked up, his accusing and strangely sad eyes boring into Maia's. He was just about to say something when Tessio walked over.

"Move away from the Pantheronicas now, people. It's about to wake up." Sure enough, barely a moment later, the plant's pretty pink leaves stirred and the stem stiffened.

Tessio walked over to his high dais and held up a tiny transparent vial that held something shiny inside. "This is an extract from the Pantheronicas, and what do you think it contains? Ren?"

Ren, who had been sulking since the argument with Maia, jumped up. "Plant juice?" he said, shrugging.

One more time Tessio doubled over and laughed. "Yes, yes," he said, "but what does that juice contain?"

"Calorfine?" Karhann said.

"Yes," Tessio exclaimed. "This is full of calorfine. Put a drop of it on your skin and you can brave a blizzard in a bed shirt."

"Why just a drop?" Loriine asked in her usual lazy drawl. "I'd use the whole bottle and never have to worry about winter coats."

"No, no, no." Tessio wagged a finger at the girl. "You can never use more than a drop or two at a time. And you can never use the calorfine extract more than twice a month. You know why?"

Loriine shrugged listlessly. The room did not make a sound.

"That's because our cells can only handle that much. Use more calorfine than advised, you risk destroying your cells forever. You could die."

Maia drew a long breath. The calorfine extract was, in short, deadly. Why was Tessio showing such a dangerous thing to them? It had to tie into one of the challenges. She wondered what sort of a challenge it would be.

"Anyway, we don't need to worry about it at the moment." Tessio put the vial away and reached for a stack of paper. "Right now, we shall study the Pantheronicas. Here's some paper for taking notes."

The session went on and on—listening to Tessio's description and explanation of the Pantheronicas physiology, drawing pictures of the plant and its complex cellular structure—until the sun had moved past the highest mark in the sky. At that point, Tessio excused them, and together they trooped out of the Glass House.

CHAPTER FOURTEEN

DOWN IN THE DUNGEONS

E verrol was waiting on a bench right next to the doors. He sprung to his feet and grinned as soon as the team stepped out.

"How was it?" he asked, eyes shining.

"Good," Kusha replied curtly. "What are you doing here? None of the other mentors are around."

It was a bit strange. All the teams were walking back to the refectory for the afternoon meal, all without a chaperone.

"I take my duties very seriously. Others obviously don't," Everrol said. "Now let's go. We have to finish lunch and head to the next session."

"Really, Everrol, we can do on our own just fine," Kusha insisted.

"In case you haven't noticed, we're not little kids," Nafi added.

Everrol simply grinned sheepishly. "I like being with you. Am I that much of a burden for you?"

Everrol's piteous words had an immediate effect. Dani shifted uncomfortably next to Maia and even Nafi looked away in haste. But a thought flowed into Maia's mind, nagging at her.

"Were you instructed to follow us all day?" she asked, watching Everrol's face intently. There had to be a reason as to why he insisted on being with them every moment, and Maia had started to think it was because of her.

He stiffened and blinked, clearly taken by surprise at the question. He laughed and it sounded a little nervous to Maia.

"Why would anyone do that?" Everrol asked.

"Monk Hilledunn would like to keep an eye on me," Maia said. "Or it could be someone else. I don't know. But I know this: You can't be the only mentor who loves this mentoring chore so much."

Everrol chuckled loudly. "Oh, come on. Look at me. Do I seem like a spy to you?"

"That you don't," Ren said, tenderly patting his belly as he threw a beseeching look at Maia. "I'm hungry."

"Let's go then." Everrol started down the corridor at a brisk pace.

Maia followed grudgingly with the rest of the team. There was no doubt Everrol was sticking to them for a reason, and the more she thought about it, the more she thought it was because of her. She could not force the truth out of Everrol, but she had to find out whose spy he was, and fast.

They finished eating quickly and without much conversation if one discounted Everrol's never-ending stories of ThulaSu. Some of his tales were fairly entertaining, but ever since the thought of him being a spy had made its way into Maia's brain, she found it hard to tolerate his presence. She could not lose her patience, so she held her tongue and stuffed herself with as much of the meat-buns as she could before they headed to their next session.

Everrol led them down a flight of damp stairs that seemed to have never seen the light of day. Dilapidated lamps hung on the walls, their light feeble at best. The smell of moisture hovered steadily in the air. About ten steps down Nafi hollered.

"All right, someone please tell me we're going the right way."

"We are. Of course, we are," Everrol replied. "I'm taking you to your Metaphysical Studies session."

"More like you're taking us to a dungeon," Nafi retorted.

"This is where Rizweendur Sottekaja lives."

"Who's that?" Ren asked.

"The guru of metaphysics," Everrol replied. His bulging eyes became the size of pigeon eggs as he leaned toward Ren and whispered, "He can separate his spirit from his body at will. Every night he's said to hover around ThulaSu like a ghost."

"What nonsense," Maia blurted. "That's not possible."

"Says the one who claims there's the light of the stars inside her," Everrol snapped back, making Maia stiffen. The way Everrol had replied, with such vehemence and indignation, was unexpected. As if he had been waiting all along to snap at her like that.

"You're saying we'll be taught to pull our spirits out of our bodies?" Dani asked.

"Nah," Everrol replied, chuckling heartily. "That's not something anyone could do. You'll learn some beginner's stuff I think, like studying people's auras."

Maia could not rein in the excitement. "Really? We will?" she said. She had wanted to learn more about auras since she had heard about them from Sophie's friend Zaara in Korobieltes. This seemed like a dream come true.

Everrol turned his palms up and shrugged. "Well, I don't know for sure, but since that's one of the first lessons of metaphysics . . ."

"Yes!" Maia squealed, her fists shooting up in the air.

Just then, Karhann and his team came careening down the stairs, chortling loudly, and at that precise moment, someone yelled, "That's a disgrace. I won't stand such behavior in my sanctum."

The voice was human but imbibed with a roar of a wild beast, amplified as it blasted through the tight space of the staircase. Maia jumped and shrunk backward as did everyone else. Everrol had paled considerably.

"Shhh," Everrol said. He placed a trembling finger on his lips. "Keep your voices down."

Together they tiptoed down the rest of the stairs. The lower they went, the dimmer the lights grew, until when they reached a cavernous room at the end of the staircase. There was barely any light at all. Many of the other teams were already there, and as soon as Everrol and his brood entered, all eyes turned on them.

Maia quickly scanned the room. All the contestants of the Initiative were seated in chairs arranged in semicircular rows around a roaring fire. Next to the fire stood a figure who Maia knew from the first glance was the owner of the terrifying voice. And at the moment his large, smoldering eyes were fixed on Everrol.

"You was the one in charge of showing them way, true?" the man bellowed at Everrol.

Everrol nodded so fast that Maia almost thought his head could come off his shoulders.

"You has done enough. Now leave," the man said. Maia noted how strangely he spoke, his words mismatched and sometimes missing altogether.

Everrol took a step back, and then another, and then he scooted out of the room.

The man raised his arms and beckoned Maia and her friends. His dark curly hair, like a lion's mane, framed his face. His eyes, large and intense, burned below a pair of long, arched brows. High up on his forehead was a carelessly dabbed red mark.

"What be the reason for your amusement?" he asked in a boisterous voice, yet his lips hardly parted. It was as if the man was an amplifier of sounds; even a whisper escaping his lips would probably sound like thunder.

"Um . . ." Nafi stammered. "I . . . we were—"

Kusha looked back angrily at Karhann and his teammates. They did not say a word, but Maia knew it was not their fault. Her shout of glee was the reason the master was peeved.

"They didn't have anything to do with it," Maia said. "I'm the one who laughed. Please excuse everyone else."

The man's eyes came to rest on Maia and she froze. "So be it. Your friends be free to take their seats."

Karhann and his buddies slinked away, but from her immediate vicinity, no one moved. Maia fidgeted. While she appreciated the support of her friends, this protective swarming routine was getting a bit too much, especially now. It was almost as annoying as Everrol refusing to leave. Maia braced herself as the towering man's eyes narrowed.

"Please take your seats," she whispered through gritted teeth. "I can handle myself."

The knot around her shifted slightly.

"What be the meaning of this?" the man said, his brows furrowing.

"We're together," Nafi squeaked.

"There be no need for drama in my sanctum. Take seats. Now," the man growled, and the crowd around Maia dispersed like a bunch of scattered flies. Even though Maia was thankful they left, her stomach churned a wave of cold.

"Your name?" the man asked.

"Maia, sir."

The man lifted his arms in the air and brought them down in slow circular motion to show the room. "What be this place?"

"Your sanctum, sir."

"Who be I?"

"Master Sottekaja, the guru of metaphysics?" Maia offered cautiously, recalling Everrol's description.

"No, not master. Revsi Sottekaja. But that not be all," he replied. "I be the keeper of the spirits of ThulaSu, and what do spirits seek?"

This was bordering on crazy, but staring into the glowering eyes of Revsi Rizweendur Sottekaja, Maia did her best to maintain her composure.

"I don't know," she muttered as she searched blindly for a suitable answer. "Quiet . . . maybe?"

"Close," he said, "but not exact." He threw his arms up in the air and yelled, "They seek respect."

Maia shuddered and nodded vigorously. "Yes, of course."

"So you understand," he said. "Good. Take seat."

He whirled away toward the fire pit as Maia scooted.

"Remember," his brassy voice shook the chamber before Maia sat down between Ren and Dani, "spirits here not like levity. If you want place in this sanctum, carry yourself with seriousness. You need do that for your sake more than anyone else's. Would you know why?"

It was funny that both their teachers had a thing about starting with questions. No one answered though. No one even moved. It was so quiet in the room that Maia was sure everyone was holding their breath.

"That because you need spirits in this chamber to aid you in your search for spirit within you. You insult them, you lose chance of seeing auras."

Maia took in a deep, long breath and her fists curled. *Yes! Yes! Yes!* They were going to learn to look at auras after all.

Not everyone was as happy. Loriine, muttered behind her, "Some hack! I doubt if any of us will see anything."

Baecca, Loriine's fast friend and teammate, scoffed in reply, "It's a bunch of mumbo-jumbo. I'd rather not come to this dump and waste a year of my life. I wish they didn't force us to keep going."

Revsi Sottekaja began handing out chunky balls to everyone. Before long, Maia had a purple one in her hands and realized it was not a ball but a glass sphere with an intricate pattern inscribed within. The room was full of murmurs now and Sottekaja did not seem to mind.

Dani leaned over and whispered, "What have you got? Mine looks like the ocean."

It was curious, to say the least. Within Dani's sphere was a beautiful pattern of aquamarine waves, complete with crests of white spray.

"Mine looks just like a Viperine," Ren said. "Don't you think so?"

Whatever was inside the sphere did look like a small version of the Xifarian craft Ren and Karhann owned.

"What's yours, Maia?" Ren asked.

"I don't know," Maia replied. She really could not tell what the blob inside the sphere meant. It was a mix of red, blue, and green, and Maia thought she could see a tree, some water, and a lot of fire. But nothing stood out the way Dani's and Ren's did. It was a murky mix of colors at best.

"Hmm, I can't tell anything from it either," Dani said thoughtfully. "Perhaps it's not supposed to mean anything."

Revsi Sottekaja's blaring voice interrupted them. "Everyone received gazing crystals? Excellent! Now, we learn to meditate. Hold your crystal in your palms and look at pattern you see inside, then close your eyes and try see it in your mind. Clear your thoughts. Focus on every detail inside those crystals. When you think you recollect every detail, come to me."

With that, Sottekaja sat down next to the fire pit, clasped his hands over his lap, and closed his eyes.

"What's he doing?" Ren asked.

"Meditating," Dani said.

That seemed to be true, but the roomful of curious youngsters stared and whispered nonstop.

"Do not look at me," Sottekaja bellowed after a moment or two. "Your crystal is not on my head; it is in your hand."

Maia turned her attention to her crystal as he had asked. She tried to memorize the littlest turns of paint and the smallest curves and swells, but soon realized how difficult of a task it was. First of all, it was hard to keep her thoughts on one thing; they darted around from Appian to Xif to ThulaSu and everywhere in between. For a brief moment or two that she could focus, her memory of the crystal barely matched the real one.

Maia was frustrated and she realized that she was not alone. People around her had started fidgeting restlessly. Sharp sighs and grunts and impatient shuffling filled the air soon after. Next to the fire pit, Sottekaja hardly stirred.

"I hate this," Loriine declared. "What a waste of time."

"Told you so," Baecca piped up. "I'm going to write to my mother. They need to get us out of this dump."

"Quiet, you two," Ren hissed at the two girls. "I can't concentrate if you keep chattering."

Maia was about to chuckle but the thought of insulting the spirits made her rein in her mirth. Loriine kept muttering angrily. Thankfully, Ren did not hear what she said and Maia was relieved to see Sottekaja stir at the same time. He opened his eyes and scanned the room in a slow, sweeping motion.

"You," he growled at a girl sitting in the row nearest to him. "What be your name?"

"Vyessa."

Maia recalled that name, the Jjord girl Ren liked.

"You mighty pleased about something. I assume you able to recreate your crystal in your thoughts."

"No, it was hard. I couldn't."

"Hmm. Then what is you so pleased about?"

"Um . . . nothing. I . . . nothing," Vyessa said.

"Let's find out what that nothing be then," Sottekaja said. He closed his eyes again and Vyessa immediately clasped her head as if in pain.

"What's he doing?" Dani sounded alarmed. "Is he reading her mind?"

"I see you thinking of someone," Sottekaja said. "I see it be a boy."

Someone giggled behind them and Maia was sure it was Baecca. She stole a quick look at Ren. He seemed anxious, his eyes wide as he held his breath.

"This boy," Sottekaja kept on speaking, "he part of this group. What be his name?"

"Please don't," Vyessa wailed, her hands still clutching her head as if she wanted to shield her thoughts.

"Ren? That be the boy you can't stop thinking of? One who makes you smile when you should be trying to concentrate?" Sottekaja said.

Next to Maia, Ren sat up like an uncoiled spring. "What? She likes me?"

"Oooh," Loriine crooned. "Someone has a thing for Ren. And it's not a squid."

Baecca broke into hushed giggles at Loriine's jab and Maia fumed. They were referring to Chylomyhrra the squid, Ren's riding partner in the Jjordic phase. Not only was Chylomyhrra the smartest animal Maia knew, but she was also the reason Maia survived Zagran.

She spun around and glared at Loriine and Baecca. "Shut up, you two," she hissed.

Up near the fire pit, Vyessa was sniffling. Sottekaja's eyes were wide open now and they flashed at the faces around him.

"You see, there be no secrets from me. You come to my sanctum, you respect its rules. There be no other way."

That was clearly a warning. He would punish anyone who was not following his instructions by revealing their secrets. What he had said about Vyessa's thoughts was harmless enough, but Maia could not bear to think how ruthless he could have been with them.

"This is scary," Dani whispered.

Sottekaja rose to his feet and brushed off invisible dust from his flowing red robe. "Go now," he said. "Take your crystals and exercise your minds tonight. I see you tomorrow."

It was funny how quickly nearly fifty people scrambled out of their seats and rushed toward the exit. As if, they were fleeing a dragon's lair. Kusha and Nafi were seated on the opposite side of the room and they now ran up to Maia, Dani, and Ren, Nafi giggling silently as she punched Ren in the shoulder.

"She likes you," Nafi whispered. "She really, really likes you."

"Nafi," Maia cautioned. "He warned us not to take this lightly. Be serious unless you want your thoughts read out."

"Oh, come on, Maia," Nafi said with a casual wave, "aren't you happy for Ren? I am." She jabbed Ren in the chest and gave him a teasing look. "Hey, aren't you going to talk to her?"

"I might," Ren said in a distracted voice.

"You might?" Nafi said. She threw a quick look behind them. "The poor girl is so embarrassed; she'd feel much better if she knew you've always liked her too."

"You're right." Ren nodded. "I'll go talk to her."

"At least wait until you're out of the sanctum," Maia reminded. They had just walked out of the room and had not reached the base of the stairs yet.

Nafi frowned and shook her head. "We're enough out already. What's with you, Maia? Stop being so chicken all the time."

Chicken? Maia had to stop and douse Nafi in the best glare she could muster. She was not chicken. She never was chicken. She was simply trying to be careful.

Sottekaja could be dangerous and Maia simply did not want her teammates to be humiliated like Vyessa. "I'm only trying to keep all of us safe. He called me up once already. And you saw how he treated Vyessa," Maia said in a stern voice.

Nafi rolled her eyes and Dani placed herself firmly between her and Maia. Ren fell back a step and whispered, "See you guys later." Then he was gone.

The rest headed straight to the refectory to finish a mostly quiet dinner. Maia was thankful that at least Everrol did not show up. She was still upset with Nafi and made it a point not to speak with her or even look at her. The girl was arguing too much and becoming too much of an annoyance, she thought angrily. Ren did not show up for dinner and he was nowhere to be seen even when the team retired to their rooms that evening.

That night Maia placed her crystal on the bedside table and tried to practice remembering the patterns within. She failed every time. She felt lost. While everyone else had spotted concrete scenes and images, her crystal confused her. Hopeless and sad, her shoulders feeling like boulders were sitting on them, Maia slipped under the covers. She knew she could not put too much emphasis on it, but it somehow felt symbolic that her crystal was murky, with no beginning or ending, with no place to settle down and just be.

Chapter Fifteen

Fractured Paths

The beginning of the third phase should have been an indication enough of the dreadful times that were coming. Within the first week, Kusha had been bitten in the arm by a Pantheronicas and he had to be sent to the infirmary when his wounded arm turned purple and swelled to twice its normal size. Thankfully, the healer monks were used to treating Pantheronicas bites and seemed completely in control of things. The very next day Dani got herself a nasty scratch, also courtesy of the Pantheronicas. Hers was a surface wound though, so she did not lose mobility of her arm as Kusha did. But still, sporting a swollen and purple hand was no fun.

It was not just Kusha and Dani. Every other team was bruised and battered and missing a team member or two, all thanks to the dreadful Pantheronicas. Monk Tessio kept promising experiments with the calorfine, but all he did day after day was discuss the physiology and habitat of the murderous plant. By the second week, Maia was tired of studying the same diagrams over and over. But there was no way of getting past Monk Tessio, who seemed to be in the habit of springing surprise tests on the teams.

Revsi Sottekaja's sessions were no more cheerful either. Jiri was punished in the second week and his secret wish of trying out the colorful dresses the women of ThulaSu wore was revealed to a largely snickering audience. Jiri refused to come out of his room for a day and a half until Hilledunn and his assistants coaxed, cajoled, and finally threatened him. It did not end with Jiri; every few days someone or the other would be humiliated by Sottekaja and secrets revealed.

Maia and her teammates kept their mouths shut in that room. It did not help that none of them were making much headway with the gazing crystal. Karhann was the only person who had successfully remembered his crystal, much to the joy of his teammates. That did not please Sottekaja too much who was disappointed with the overall lack of progress.

"If you cannot master gazing crystal, I cannot teach you auras," he bellowed about three weeks since the training had started. "And if you know no auras, you know nothing. You be worthless."

That evening, Maia sat with Nafi, Kusha, and Dani in the refectory with her gazing crystal next to her plate of food. The colors of the jumbled-up pattern looked even more mixed up to Maia.

"Maia, can you please put that thing away?" Nafi said, scowling at the gazing crystal. "I just can't stand it."

Maia was in no great mood either. "Why don't you look somewhere else? I want to keep trying."

Nafi's brows shot up and her lips curled in a mocking smile. "Really? You can't focus enough when you're doing nothing, but you're trying to focus while eating? The food's going to make some miracle happen or what?"

"Whatever, Nafi." Maia waved her away dismissively. "I don't want to talk."

Nafi let out a long sigh and counted the rafters for a while, her mouth pursed. "Aren't you guys missing Ren?"

Maia squinted at Nafi. Was that what was bothering the youngest of their team? Ren had been missing meals with the team and everything else they did for that matter. He only showed up at the training sessions, and even then he was constantly distracted. Maia saw him every so often though, mostly with Vyessa with whom he seemed to be growing a relationship, and sometimes with Karhann. Maia did miss having the lively boy around.

But this was not the time to be emotional about people's absence. They had to commune with that blasted piece of crystal.

Maia took in a deep breath before replying to Nafi. "No, I'm not."

Nafi rolled her eyes and started chewing a piece of bread with vigor. "You've been touchy lately." She leaned sideways to nudge Dani who sat next to her. "Isn't she touchy, Dani?"

Dani threw a sidelong glance at Nafi and then looked hastily at Maia before shaking her head. "We're all tired with this stupid mind exercise, that's all."

"You're too chicken to tell the truth, Dani," Nafi declared and turned toward Kusha who had been absent-mindedly stirring a bowl of vegetables. "What's with you, Kusha?"

"Hmm?" Kusha looked up, his gaze blank. He was clearly thinking of something else altogether.

Nafi stared at him for a bit before looking away. "Never mind," she muttered.

A grudging silence fell over the table for a while and Maia was thankful for the quiet. The cold, the sunless days, the fruitless tasks they had been wrangling, it all added up to a spirit-sucking existence and no one seemed to fare well. Shoving a sizable piece of bread into her mouth Maia stared once again at her gazing crystal, trying to etch every speck of color inside it in her brain.

"Maia," a cheerful voice said. Maia looked up and her heart flitted. Maks was heading toward her with Aman in tow. Big grins stretched their faces. "Haven't seen you in a while," Maia said. "Where did you disappear?"

"Lots of work," Aman replied while Maks pulled a couple of chairs up to the table. "We have advance class work, and this crazy woman is training us in combat this year. She works us so hard that we can barely make it back to our rooms after sparring practice."

"Wish we could have some sparring practice," Nafi chimed in. "Who's this awesome teacher?"

"She's new at ThulaSu," Maks informed. "Calls herself Monk Konnae. They say she's from the far side of the Second Continent."

Maia sat up. "Really? She's from the west?"

Maks nodded. Stories had it that on the Second Continent everything west of Appian had turned into a desert wasteland since the fall of the Solianese Empire a century ago. Millions had perished and now only a few pockets of life—all of them dusty hellholes full of outlaws, smugglers, and the like—remained in the massive Second Continent. This woman had come from one of those hellholes. Maia wanted to see this woman, the combat trainer Konnae.

"She's tough," Aman said, drawing abstract patterns on the dining table with his gloved fingers.

"Yes, she is. We've been dog tired," Maks said, sighing deeply. He pointed at Maia's gazing crystal next. "Looks like you're having fun as well. The spirit herder of ThulaSu giving you a hard time?"

Maia ran a hand over her tired eyes and shook her head. "Don't get me started on that. None of us can get past this gazing ball exercise. And if we can't, he won't teach us about auras. We think our first challenge will have something to do with auras, so if we can't learn that, we're toast."

Maks chuckled. He exchanged a quick look with Aman before looking back at Maia again. "Well, sorry to disappoint, but there are very few people who can get as far as seeing auras, Maia. Both of us failed his class. We got past the gazing though, but that was it."

"I still think it's a sham. There are no auras anywhere," Aman said.

"I support that idea," Nafi piped up. "This gazing thing is just a waste of time."

"Oh, come on," Maia retorted. "Zaara could see it, remember, Dani?" Maia would never forget visiting her mother's best friend,

Zaara, in the ruins of Korobieltes, the burned-down capital of the Solianese.

"You said yourself, Zaara was crazy," Nafi snapped back. "This guy is crazy too. Maybe they simply hallucinate or something."

"Nisa said she saw one," Maks countered. "She isn't crazy."

"She bluffed," Aman said, scoffing. "But don't tell her I said that."

"All right, guys," Dani held her hands up. "Can we do without the arguments? I'm so tired I can't take it anymore."

Maks stiffened and folded his arms into his lap. "Sorry," he said. "We didn't mean to bother you. We came over to ask you if you'd be interested in working on the Damoclian Connector."

Maia's ears perked up and everyone sat up eagerly.

"Tell us more," Maia said.

"Well, you know the last stage of work is going on in ThulaSu. The plan is to get the Connector up and running as soon as possible. But there's a lot to be done. The Jjord engineers are doing final checks on the hardware, setting up the control system and the pipelines, servicing the channels to the power grid, and all that. Needs a lot of hands. So we're helping out in our free time."

"And?" Nafi asked.

"And you could too. If you want."

"Of course, we want to help," Maia said. She looked around the table at the eager faces of her teammates. Even Kusha seemed to have shaken off his earlier stupor. "Don't we, guys?"

Heads nodded in unison.

"Great. I'll get you in then," Maks said, springing to his feet. "See you later, Maia," he said before rushing away with Aman.

***

Two days later, Maia and her teammates had something new to do. Aman came by and handed them a daily routine of sorts. They had all been assigned to various sections of the Damoclian Connector. Maia was particularly happy with her assignment at the distribution room at the mouth of ThulaSu's power grid. Even better was the fact that she had been paired with Dani. Kusha and Nafi were sent to assist the engineers in calibrating the flow controllers in the Coronation Chamber. Ren was assigned the task of cleaning and organizing the gazillion tools needed daily for the construction.

Maia and Dani rushed to the mouth of the power grid right after Sottekaja had released them after yet another unproductive training session. The entrance to the grid was near the Garaha Gates, and the large bolstered doors were guarded by a group of Kausakas.

"What do you want?" the leader of the group demanded when Maia walked up the stairs.

"We're volunteering," Maia replied, panting. "For the Connector."

It took a while before the guard had checked their credentials with the engineers inside and let them past the door. Maia walked in expecting the depressing darkness and the suffocating smell of damp and dust she had experienced when she had walked into Appian's control room years ago. She was pleasantly surprised.

The room was bright, lit up by at least a dozen Jjord LumTorches in addition to the old and yellowed Solianese wall lamps. The inside was also far from the charred and miserable entryway to the power grid in Appian. About twenty people worked in small groups; most wore white overalls and the others were students of ThulaSu who had come to help. Soft, uplifting music wafted through the air.

"This is nice," Dani said appreciatively.

"Yes, I hadn't expected anything half as cheerful," Maia replied. "Whenever I hear power grid, I think of Appian's. That's in a sorry state."

Maia swallowed the lump in her throat as she thought about the night she had lost her grandfather along with Herc and Emmy. The Xifarians—Miir, his brother Remii, and Amanii—had attacked her in Shiloh, the town next to Appian and she had fallen into the lake Lupitiali. She would have drowned that night if she had not been sucked into a crevice that led to the power grid. She had somehow made it back to Appian through the grid only to find that the Xifarians had struck. They had wiped out a part of Appian and killed her family.

"Maia, are you all right?" Dani asked, shaking her gently by the shoulder. Dani never missed a thing.

"I'll be fine," Maia replied, forcing cheer into her voice. The Xifarians had destroyed her life, but she had to push the thoughts away. She had to get in control of her powers first. Then, only then, she could get even with the ones that had wronged her.

Dani slipped an arm over her shoulder and squeezed lightly. "It's all right to be upset, Maia," she said reassuringly. "You keep holding it inside you, and that's not good."

Maia knew Dani meant well, but she did not want to keep talking about that night. When a Jjord engineer in white overalls with the Jjordic emblem of a mermaid splashed across its middle walked over to them, she breathed in relief.

"You're here to help, right?" the brown-haired man with smiling brown eyes asked. "I'm Rudi. Come on over here, we have some gearboxes to fix."

They were quickly sucked into the repairs and Maia had no idea how much time had passed until Rudi the engineer stopped by.

"It's past sundown, girls," he said, nodding appreciatively at their handiwork. "Good work here. But you have to go back now. We don't keep volunteers around so late. Come back tomorrow though. We have plenty to work on."

Maia and Dani trooped back to the main building chattering happily as they walked along the ramparts. It seemed like they had done something truly useful. They had neared the staircase that led down from the ramparts to the grounds below when they heard Ren's voice.

"Admit it, Nafi, this is biased," he shouted.

Maia turned questioningly at Dani only to be met by her puzzled gaze. They rushed as quickly as they could along the slippery path. They found Ren, Nafi, and Kusha standing near the parked Viperine.

Ren stood with his arms on his hips while Nafi paced back and forth. Kusha stood a step or two away, rubbing his chin intently.

As soon as Maia and Dani neared, Ren took a step toward them. "There you are," he said. "What have you been working on?"

There was a distinct whiff of anger in his voice and Maia had no idea why.

"We were at the power grid fixing a gear box," she said. "What's going on here?"

"You all get to go inside, and I'm assigned a task any two-year-old can do," Ren said in a strange distant way. His voice trembled and he seemed determined to not let it show. "You're all inner circle, I'm not. I'm kept out because I'm Xifarian. It doesn't matter what I've done with you . . . for you. I'll always be an outsider no matter what."

"I don't think it's like that, Ren." Maia placed a hand on his shoulder. "I think you're overthinking things. This is just the first day. You might be tasked with something else tomorrow."

Ren glared at her and Maia realized it was the first time she had seen him so angry.

"Don't lie, Maia," he hissed. "All of you know it. But none of you have thedare tot. It's the same way you think of Miir. No matter how good he's been to you, he'll always be a Xifarian first. Reason can go to hell, you'll hate him."

It was Maia's turn to be outraged. Perhaps there was some bias in the way the jobs were picked for them, but Ren did not have to compare himself to the backstabber Miir.

"Ren," she yelled. "For goodness sake, don't bring Miir into this. The stars know you've always been my friend first, always. I can't change the way other people think, but I know what I think of you. I think of a great friend. I don't think of you as a Xifarian. Never."

Ren crossed his arms and looked away, his nostrils flaring as he heaved. Maia wanted to stop right there but words kept slipping out of her mouth.

"Miir is different, Ren. I had faith in him, in his goodness, in his ability to do the right thing. But he let me down. He betrayed my trust. You're not him, and you never will be."

Ren whirled around, his eyes blazing. "Shut up, Maia," he screamed. She fell back at step or two at his vehemence, but Ren did not seem to want to control himself. He was fuming; his teeth gritted when he spoke again.

"People go against the interests of their families and their nation to keep you safe. They stand up for you and this is how you pay them back?"

Every word Ren spat out stung even though they did not make much sense to Maia. She had always held Ren dear; why would he think otherwise? Or was he talking about something else altogether?

As she stared wide-eyed, Ren fidgeted endlessly. He chewed his lip as if he wanted to hold back his words and his anger, but it came out anyway. "Never expected *you* to sink so low."

"Ren!" Dani cried out, rushing to wrap her arms around Maia's shoulders. But Ren had already stomped his way out of the courtyard.

***

They had crept back to their rooms in silence, and Maia stared listlessly at the gazing crystal she had set down at the center of her bed. It felt like a boulder had rolled over her, crushing every bone in her body. Maia could not think; every thought in her head was a gigantic pile of mush. Ren's words rang in her ears, but more than anything, his eyes filled with rage and disgust were forever burned in her memory. Ren had always been a close confidante; he had always been by her side when she needed him most. He had cared for her, for all of them. Yet, tonight, there was not a shred of affection in his eyes, and that thought made Maia's stomach churn.

Maia was cradling her throbbing forehead in her arms and gazing fixedly at the colorful lump at the center of the crystal when it happened. The colors started to separate and reform into a picture, like a puzzle taking shape in her mind's eye. The blues morphed into a sea of waves, and out of tha,t a tree sprouted, its green branches reaching upward until a wave of red fire swept across it. The tree recoiled and so did Maia. She fell backward in a heap as if the fire had leaped out at her. Her eyes burned, and through the blackness that poured over her, Maia found herself soaring . . .

She was at a clearing, surrounded by Darkwood trees, staring from high above at two people fighting a vicious battle below. They were young—a girl and a boy—and sparring endlessly. Coils of fiery light flew out of the girl's arms and struck her adversary. The boy retaliated, creating waves of energy that rippled through the air between them. The waves countered the girl's fire, but only for so long. Her weapon was clearly stronger, fiercer, and deadlier than anything the boy had to defend himself. He was at the edge of the clearing, pushed near the brink where the cliff fell in a sheer drop to the valley below. He pulled out a sword and hit the girl's fire. Something happened and she stopped. Then she let out a vicious wave that scooped up the boy and threw him against the embankment, the only barrier between the clearing and the precipice. For a moment, everything was still. Then the embankment gave way and the boy fell.

"No," Maia sat up screaming, gasping for breath. Her clothes were soaked and her fingers cold. She had seen a strange vision . . . or was it a memory?

It had to be a memory because Maia remembered that clearing. That was where Ren had found her after she had fought off Chairman Phocluus and his people. She remembered waking up in the middle of a ring of charred trees. She had been there.

Realization crashed through her exhausted mind like an avalanche. She had seen herself. But who was she fighting? Whoever it was, she had thrown him over the edge to his death. She had killed someone and she had no idea who it could have been.

Maia pulled her knees to her chest, gritted her teeth, and inhaled sharply. She knew. It was as clear as the cold, hard bed under her. She was fighting Miir. And she had killed him.

Had she really? Then why did no one tell her? Because they did not know? Didn't anyone know? How could they not know?

Maia parted the blanket and pulled herself under it. The cold did not stop coming. *This can't be true,* Maia kept telling herself. Someone should have known if Miir went missing. His father, the Xifarian Chancellor would have known. There would be a hue and cry over it.

No! What she saw could not have been real. It was no memory. It was probably just her imagination. For long she had planned how she would take her revenge on Miir and this was just a dream of that. It had to be, or someone would have known.

Chapter Sixteen

Into the Outlands

Maia woke up to a raging blizzard the next morning. A headache hung like a dull curtain over her senses. The vision from the previous night weighed heavily on her heart and made even the daily chores tedious. Making things worse, Miir's face—his intense gaze burned through her mind—kept flashing before her eyes every so often. It was impossible to accept that she could have so knowingly pushed a person to his death, but if that vision was to be believed, that was what it looked like.

And that was where Maia's heart stumbled every time. It was one thing to unwittingly unleash her powers on Chairman Phocluus and his minions, to defend herself. But if her vision was to be believed, she had fought long with Miir. Killing him did not seem like an accident or self-defense. It looked like cold, deliberate execution.

It can't be, she kept telling herself. She could not be a cold-blooded killer. She was simply imagining things. But hard as she tried, the weight on her heart refused to lift.

All she wanted to do was curl into her bed and sleep so she

would not have to think about it. But Maia knew well that was an unfulfillable wish. Whether she wanted to or not, she had to attend Tessio's session and Sottekaja's after that. She had to keep going for the team. So she dragged herself down to the refectory for breakfast only to be solemnly greeted by her teammates. Every face was drawn; not a smidgeon of cheer could be spotted on any. As usual, Ren was missing from their table and Maia located him sitting next to Vyessa at her table, laughing and chatting gleefully. Seeing him so happy should have frustrated her more, but instead, Maia felt relief. At least he was not staring at her with accusing eyes.

Like every other day, Everrol showed up just as they were finishing up with the food.

"It's quite a snowstorm out there," he said, grinning wide. Maia stifled a sigh and concentrated on the last bit of pottage in her bowl. It was weird that anyone could find anything exciting about a snowstorm. To her, it was dull, dreary, and downright boring. After the storm passed, depending on how big it had been, it usually took ThulaSu a few days to dig itself out. Until then, they could not even get to the power grid and help with the Damoclian Connector. No one else said a word either, so Everrol went on about the time when ThulaSu's power grid had broken down completely. He seemed thrilled that they had had to resort to burning firewood to keep the buildings warm.

"What if it happens again? Wouldn't that be some experience?" he said giddily. "Getting back in touch with our prehistoric roots would be awesome."

"I'm done," Maia declared, ignoring Everrol. "Can we go now?"

It was as if everyone was waiting for the cue. Kusha, Dani, and Nafi promptly deposited their empty bowls in the wash bin and headed toward the exit. Everrol followed, trying to initiate conversation, but no one took the bait on this gray morning.

Monk Tessio was hunched over a large bowl when they trooped into the Glass House.

"Come in, come in. Take your seats, please," he said, raising his arms in greeting. "It's a perfect day for our experiments to begin."

Experiments? Maia looked askance at her friends, but they seemed just as confused. She trudged over to her seat and waited quietly for Tessio to begin. Ren did not join them until the last moment, and he did not look at any of his teammates when he sat down at the table. Instead, he stared, tight jawed, at Tessio. Thankfully, Tessio did not take long to begin.

"Today's the day you've all been waiting for," he started. "The day we try a bit of calorfine. Today we get to see if it indeed miraculously shields us against the cold."

Someone cheered, a few even clapped, and a lot of whispers were exchanged, but the Core 21 table remained dead silent.

Tessio cleared his throat and went on. "Any ideas how we are going to test if it is indeed as miraculous as Monk Tessio suggests?"

Suddenly it clicked. Maia understood why Tessio had praised the weather. She looked at the scene outside the glass panes; there was nothing but a swiftly moving curtain of white.

"Anyone?" Tessio asked again, and Maia raised her arm hoping she would be wrong.

"Yes, Maia?" Tessio said.

"We're going out in the blizzard?" she said tentatively.

Tessio grinned and that said it all. They were indeed going out in this sightless snowstorm. Next to Maia, Nafi inhaled sharply.

"Don't tell me that's right," Maia muttered.

"You're absolutely correct, Maia," Tessio said, and Maia slumped. Murmurs rose in the air at once and at every table except Maia's. Tessio clapped his hands. "All right then, we're quite excited, aren't we? Now let's see what we have to do today."

Tessio unfurled a large map that was hanging from a hook in the ceiling, and with a long pointer stick, he jabbed at the long brown structure at the center of it.

"This is the western wing of the mountain city of ThulaSu. This is where we are now," he said. "Down at the bottom of the city, there are tunnels that lead out to the mountains outside." Tessio poked at the forested area to the west of ThulaSu. "This area is the western Outlands. It's mostly just forests, but there are a few scattered villages also. This is where you will go. Since today is your first day, you need not go too far. But starting tomorrow you will practice going farther and farther out into the Outlands."

Maia held her breath. The western forests brought back painful memories. During the journey from Nafi's home in the Third Continent to ThulaSu, they had trekked through the forests west of ThulaSu. That was where Miir's brother Remii and other agents of Chairman Phocluus had captured her and taken her to that clifftop. Tormented and threatened by Phocluus she had unleashed a power she had no idea existed within her. She had hurt Phocluus and all the Xifarians with him even unknowingly killing a few. Then she had fled into the forests and then . . .

"Now, you'll come up to me, one by one," Tessio said, "and take your dosage of calorfine. Come up now."

Karhann and his teammates lined up first. A few more joined in after them.

"There's no point standing there," Kusha said. "We can wait until the queue gets shorter."

As if to make a point to Kusha, Ren left the table without a word and joined Vyessa and her team in the line. Nafi scowled and Maia drifted back into her thoughts.

Miir was not with Phocluus when they took her there. She had expected him to be, but he was not. She remembered clearly — the only people she had recognized were Remii and Phocluus. Then how could Miir be in her vision? He could not. She had only imagined him.

"Maia," Dani called. Her bright blue eyes were shining with concern. "Why are you shaking your head like that?"

"I was?" Maia blurted.

"Yes, like crazy," Nafi replied. "Were you daydreaming?"

"What? No," Maia said vehemently, tucking her arms close to her body. For a moment, she thought of sharing what she had seen the night before but decided against it. Ren was already furious, and she did not want the rest of the team to fall apart also.

It was soon their turn for the calorfine. Tessio carefully extracted some of the liquid from the bowl with a long, thin glass dispenser and poured three drops into Maia's mouth. Maia had expected to feel warmer but nothing of that sort happened. In fact, she felt no different than she was feeling before she was given calorfine. She was still cold, tired, and dejected.

After all the contestants had received the calorfine, Tessio picked up his pointer stick again. "Each team will work in the area assigned to them," he said, jabbing the map with the stick. "I've divided the western Outlands into ten subsections. We need you to stay in your zone. We don't want anyone crossing over to another zone. If you do, you'll be penalized. Do you know why you need to stay in your own zone?"

Jiri's arm shot up. "Because you want us to be familiar with our area?"

"That's part of it. You should be able to navigate the zone assigned to you with your eyes closed. Trust me, you'll need that knowledge later. Drifting into someone else's territory won't serve you well. Besides, we don't want you pillaging another team's prize."

"What prize?" Karhann asked.

"Well, I heard you're not doing too well in Revsi Sottekaja's session. True?"

Almost everyone nodded. They were all doing quite horribly.

"I've decided to help you," Tessio said, breaking into chuckles when everyone in the room sat up straight. "Every zone has a plant we call the Yako. Its roots are said to aid in seeing auras. Interesting, right? Now, since it's winter, the leaves are all dead, so we do not know where they have been growing. Our task during our treks is to find out where their roots might be hiding, dig them up, and use them to enhance your mental powers. Doesn't that sound grand?"

"Yes, but how are we going to find the roots? They won't have flags sticking out of them," a freckled-face girl said.

Tessio broke into another bout of chuckles. After he had finished, he wiped the corners of his eyes and shook his head. "No, my dear. There won't be any flags. But there'll be other clues. You have to find the answer to your question and you can find it in these."

Tessio walked to one of the shelves that flanked the door and pulled out a large bound volume. "This is the *Encyclopedia Botanica*, and it has information on every plant that has grown on Tansi, including the answer to how you can locate Yako roots. I have one book for each table. Come up here and get yours."

As soon as she heard the announcement, Maia jumped off her chair to get the book. At the same moment, Ren stepped forward. Awkwardness followed. Ren bit his lip and sat back down while Maia mumbled "It's all right. You can go," and took her seat. Heavy, uncomfortable moments trickled by until Tessio shouted, "Core 21, you need to get your copy from me."

Nafi rolled her eyes. "Too much drama," she muttered loudly enough for everyone to hear before marching up to Tessio. She slammed the dusty book in the center of the table. Dani promptly flipped through a couple of pages while the group hovered over the book.

They did not get long to look at the book because Tessio waved soon after. "Pack up, people. Let's get going. Time to brave the storm."

***

It seemed like they were in the bowels of ThulaSu. Maia had lost count of how many stairs she had climbed down. The dark, cold stone staircase had felt endless. Her heart held no joy and the journey held no promise. She trudged forward simply because she had to.

Ren did not speak to anyone, but he had not left the group either. He simply walked ahead, never glancing at Maia and the rest, his fists clenched and jaws tight. No one else had talked either; Kusha and Nafi walked side by side behind Ren and Maia brought up the rear alongside Dani. Finally, after a lifetime of walking down the stairs, they reached a dimly lit gate of sorts. Maia could see the Darkwoods and guessed they had reached the foot of the mountain.

Tessio handed out orange coveralls with the sigil of the sun drawn on the chest to everyone. Then he walked over to a group of Kausakas who were guarding the gate. While they chatted, Maia walked closer to the gate and stared outside. Snow had already piled up, possibly knee deep. Curtains of white swayed across the forest, sometimes wiping out even the dim silhouettes of the gigantic trees from view. From time to time, the curtains seemed to part and the endless forest outside revealed itself like a dream. Then it vanished again. And so it went on and on.

"These coveralls are ugly but the calorfine sure is working," Nafi said and she sidled up next to Maia. When Maia did not reply, Nafi shrugged. "I'm not wearing my parka and I'm still not cold. That has to be because of the calorfine, right?"

"Yes, has to be," Maia replied distractedly.

A loud grating noise and Tessio's "move back from the gate" disturbed the little peace Maia had left. As the gates opened, the thick, tarnished metal structure protested with all its might. Creaks and groans filled the air.

"Maia, listen to me." Nafi tugged her elbow as they watched the gates rise. "Ren is nuts, all right. You shouldn't pay attention to what he said yesterday. He's just . . . I don't know . . . lost it."

Any other day it would have been reassuring to have Nafi's support, but at that moment, Maia could only flash an awkward smile. *If only you knew of the dream I had about Miir,* Maia thought. Nafi, forever a fan of Miir, would lose it also.

"Line up, everyone," Tessio yelled. "Teams together please. Then follow me out."

Maia trudged out, bracing her already leaden heart for a long and tiring trek through the unending whiteness. And they slogged, round and round through the forest, knee deep in the snow. The blizzard waned after a while and from time to time, the sun peeked out. The bright sunlight, while uplifting, made matters worse. The whiteness turned blinding and soon Maia was wishing the sun away.

She did not feel cold at all, calorfine made her immune to the freezing temperature. But calorfine did not give her unending strength. Hiking through snow was tiring and tedious and Maia's legs screamed for rest. There was no giving up though. Tessio would not let them a moment of slack. Ren had thrown a snowball at Karhann when Tessio's back was turned, but the teacher wagged a finger at Ren soon after.

"You're out here to learn," he said gravely. "Let's not have any silly snow chucking at each other."

He marched them around, shouting orders from time to time when their pace slowed. It was not until the skies had started to dim that Tessio herded them back inside.

"Good work today," he declared when they were back inside the gates. "From now on, we practice going out regularly. You have to build up strength in those legs. But for now, you're free to leave."

Maia, drenched in sweat and craving for long warm soak for her legs, had never been happier to hear a dismissal.

Chapter Seventeen

The Mausoleum of the Sun

O ver the next few weeks, contestants of the Alliance Initiative had grown used to the trek outside. Blizzards came and went, always leaving deep snow behind. The calorfine was truly miraculous. Maia and her friends spent up to a day out in the snow and never even shivered once. However, the calorfine did not add extra power to their muscles, which meant sore legs for everyone.

"I don't like this at all," Nafi declared one afternoon as they were slipping into the orange coveralls before the team began their trek outside. "No sign of the Yako roots and I have no idea what we're doing out there every day."

"We'll find them," Maia said reassuringly. "We just have to keep looking."

Nafi scowled. Maia understood her frustration. It was more than a month into the third phase of the Initiative and Maia had never felt so clueless. This was starting to look like an impossible quest; the Yako roots they were hoping to find were buried deep under the snow and the humongous tome on biology had not yielded much on ways to find the roots. The only substantial thing they knew was that Yako roots were known to attract ground-bugs, a purple-blue critter native to the First Continent. None of the teams had any luck spotting the elusive ground-bugs either.

Still, Tessio kept sending them out into the cold, every day, sometimes for almost half a day. All the teams did not trek at the same time anymore; instead, each was allotted a time of the week as well as shown their respective zones. While Maia and her teammates had developed an idea of their zone, they had not ventured too far from the walls of ThulaSu.

"We have to go farther out and look," Ren commented gruffly. While he kept to himself for the most part, he was not totally silent anymore, which was a good thing. However, he was far from the Ren Maia had known.

"Go farther out?" Nafi retorted. "We're in knee-deep snow five steps from the gate and you want to go farther out? How far? Until the snow gets neck deep?"

Ren shrugged. "As far as we have to go to get the Yako."

"He's right," Kusha said, adjusting his coveralls and boots. "We've been looking over and over around here and found nothing. We have to look in places we've not looked before."

Nafi groaned and shook her head at the sky. "It's getting so dark. I think it'll start snowing soon."

"Which direction should we go?" Maia asked, ignoring Nafi's complaints. They had to complete the task they had been assigned, blizzard or rain. "Should we head directly westward?"

Kusha pulled out the map Tessio had given them and everyone gathered around to look.

"There's a village here," Kusha said, jabbing the paper. "It's right in the middle of our zone. Perhaps we could trek there. That way we won't get lost in the forest."

"What's this?" Maia asked, pointing at a large circular structure drawn close to the walled village on the map.

Kusha shrugged. "Not sure. I haven't lived that much in ThulaSu to know half of the things around here," he said apologetically. "Guess we'll find out if we head that way."

They headed out soon after, following the markers that showed the road to the village. Since this road cut through the middle of their zone there was little worry about straying out of their territory. Hiking through knee-deep snow was another matter altogether. It did its best to slow them down and the group walked at a snail-like pace toward their destination, keeping their eyes sharp for any sign of ground-bugs.

The storm started right around the time the village came into view. Through drifts of snowflakes—small and sparse—Maia observed the quaint settlement. Appian was also a village, but it was ten times the size of this one. This was more like a homestead, a random gathering of a few families who then decided to continue living there. A log wall surrounded about twenty stone houses. Lights shone through the windows, but Maia saw no one walking around.

"Told you the sky was getting dark," Nafi grumbled. "How will we get back to ThulaSu now?"

"The same way we came," Ren replied casually, drawing a glare from Nafi and a chuckle from Maia.

"Where are *you* going?" Nafi yelled as Maia started walking again. "That's not the way back to ThulaSu."

Maia had no plans of returning to ThulaSu so soon. Since they had come so far, she was determined to check out the village and its surroundings.

"I'm going to the village," she said.

"You crazy?" Nafi said. "We should head back while the snow is still light and we can still see. Right, guys?"

"I think we should check out the village, Nafi," Dani said. Nafi crossed her arms and was about to give them a fight but the storm chose that moment to pick up the pace. The flakes were suddenly fatter and the wind grew blustery.

"We have to find shelter. Storms in ThulaSu can turn real nasty real quick," Kusha said urgently. "Let's go to the village. Hurry."

They must have been halfway to the village when Kusha, who was leading the way, stopped. "Can't see the markers anymore," he said. The markers that acted as the guiding paths within the area had vanished. Even if they were not all covered in snow, the flakes were coming down so fast that it was impossible to see even an arm's distance away.

"What do we do now?" Dani asked breathlessly.

"Told you this was a bad idea," Nafi grumbled.

One choice was to wait until the storm slowed a little. But who knew how long that would be? They were all fine at the moment, thanks to the calorfine, but the drug's effects did not last forever. Out in the wilderness, swamped by the swiftly falling snow, they could die when the calorfine's effects wore off.

Maia looked around hastily. Other than the bleak grayness, she could make out nothing of their surroundings. She looked back in the direction of the gates where they had started, but that too was cloaked by curtains of snow. They were farther away from the gates of ThulaSu than they were from the village, she reasoned. So, the only thing that made sense was forging on forward.

"Let's keep going," she suggested, partly expecting Nafi to vehemently oppose the idea. Oddly though, she did not.

Dani nodded. "I guess that's the best we can do," she said.

They had not taken more than a hundred steps forward when Maia thought she saw a shadow. It was a vague movement to their right, a blur through the drifts of snow. Maia grabbed Dani by the arm and whispered, "Wait. Stop! I think I see someone."

The team gathered around her swiftly.

"Where?" Nafi demanded.

Even as Maia pointed in the direction where she had noticed the movement, chilly fingers grabbed her heart. *What if Phocluus had sent someone? What if . . .*

Stop worrying, she chided herself. Maia's hand clutched her sword Bellator's hilt, and she breathed in deep. This was one good thing about ThulaSu. Unlike Xif where they could only have their weapons out with special permission and under special circumstances or Zagran where their weapons were confiscated on the second day, here they were free to hold on to their weapon of choice.

However, even if all of them carried weapons, they were nothing compared to the trained agents of the Xifarian Scientific Defense Services or the SDS. Maia knew she had to be prepared with more; she had to use the power of the light inside her to defend if it came to that.

Hastily Maia muttered the chant the Xinhagyi had taught her. *"Yoteh. Yoteh."*

It always felt foreign on her lips, and it always chilled her heart. She had used it before, but never in the presence of her friends. But she had to be prepared, she had to stay focused and ready.

"I think I see it too. We should follow," Ren said, taking a step forward to the right. He stopped right away and turned around to look. "Are you coming or what?"

It was possibly the most sensible thing to do. Chances were that the person out there was someone from the village they intended to visit. Following him was the only way to safety.

With a quick glance at the rest of her teammates, each of whom seemed eager to accept Ren's decision, Maia followed. The figure disappeared from time to time, barely a specter to which her eager eyes clung desperately. Thankfully, the path did not vanish on them or did not come to a dead end. It was not until the figure disappeared completely into a dome of darkness that the group came to stop.

"He's gone," Ren said, heaving to catch his breath. All that was left now were drifting walls of snow.

"Is that a building?" Kusha asked, pointing at the darkish outline beyond the snowy curtains.

Maia strained to see what looked like a large domed building not too far from where they stood. "Hey, I know," she blurted as recognition hit her suddenly. "That's the other round building we saw on the map, remember?"

Nafi's eyes sparkled. "That means we're close to the village, right?

Well, what are we waiting for? Let's get there quickly. I can't stand this white stuff."

Nafi started first, marching steadily ahead toward the shadowy outline. The rest followed on Nafi's heels. That Maia was right became clear in another hundred steps or so. They reached a clearing, at the center of which stood a large, domed building. Wide steps led up to the burnished door that stood closed, and Maia and her teammates sprinted eagerly up them, Ren leading the way.

The door fell open at the slightest push revealing a circular room basking in the warm glow of a fire. At the center of the room, a group of people sat in a circle around a small raised podium. As soon as Maia and her teammates walked inside, the lone man on the podium sprang to his feet and rushed toward them. He held a thick stick in his hand and Maia fell back a little seeing him swing it as he bridged the distance between them.

She did not have the time to pull Ren back quickly enough. The man, his dark eyes flashing dangerously, shoved Ren forcefully in the chest with his stick. He pushed so hard that Ren almost fell over.

Behind the man, a circle of people rose and followed.

"Xifarian intruder," the man growled. "How dare you walk in here?"

Maia threw herself between the man and Ren. "Stop," she shouted. "We're from the University of ThulaSu. We didn't mean to intrude."

The man's eyes flashed as his gaze moved from Ren's face to Maia's. "You look like one of ours," he said. His stare was so intense that Maia felt it was burning through her. "Why are you defending this scourge?"

His words, sharp and hurtful, made her guts tighten in anger. "He's no scourge. He's my friend," she hissed angrily at the man. "You better back off. Right now."

The man chuckled disbelievingly at first before he broke into garrulous laughter. "Your friend? Be careful who you call a friend, little girl. Their kind has a knack for stabbing people in the back."

"My kind?" Ren said from behind Maia.

"Yes, your kind," the man replied without hesitation. "Your kind has no business being here. You're not allowed to set your filthy feet in the Holy Mausoleum of the Sun." He tried to push Maia to the side and grab Ren. Behind him, the circle of people came closer together.

"Wait!" Maia held up her hands just as Kusha stepped next to her to form a barrier between the man and Ren.

"I'm sorry for intruding. Really, I am," Kusha said. "I should've known this is the Mausoleum. I should've stayed away. It's all my fault. And we'll leave."

"What do you mean, leave?" Nafi muttered angrily from behind. "It's snowing like crazy. Why can't they let us wait out the storm?"

Kusha shot a cautioning glare at Nafi before turning to the man again. "We'll leave. And we won't come back here again. Ever. You have my word."

The man did not seem the least bit impressed. He raised his stick again and pointed it at Kusha's chin. "Your word is supposed to mean something? How do I know you're not a double-crosser yourself?"

"My name is Kusha, I'm of the House of the Sun." Kusha then pushed the hood of his coveralls off his head. As he pointed at his ancestral headband, the anger ebbed away from the man's eyes and he slowly lowered his stick. The group of people behind the man whispered busily between themselves.

Kusha continued. "These are my friends and I trust them with my life. No one here means any harm or . . . disrespect. And we'll leave."

There was a moment of confusion and hesitation, and taking advantage of the respite, Maia fell back and grabbed Ren's arm.

"Let's get out of here," she muttered. Ren looked crushed and tired, but he nodded. They all walked briskly toward the door. Outside, the wind howled and curtains of white swept across the clearing.

"Can't believe this," Nafi kept muttering. "What a bunch of idiots."

"That's it, Nafi," Kusha said in a tight voice as he herded the group out. "You can't reason with idiots. That's why we're leaving."

"But look at that snow," Nafi protested.

"You've had calorfine," Maia reminded sternly. "You'll live."

Still, as she stood at the threshold of the stairs looking at the raging storm, Maia's legs almost buckled under her. They did not have a choice but to walk back into the snow.

"You guys should stay," Ren said suddenly, staring intently at the woods ahead. "I'll go find a place to hide until the storm subsides."

"No," Maia declared solemnly, tightening her grip on Ren's arm. "We all go."

"That's right. Come on," Kusha said. Taking a deep breath and pulling the hood low over his head, Kusha stepped forward into the swirling snowstorm. Maia followed, pulling Ren along with her, and Dani and Nafi shuffled close behind them. They had barely taken a few steps when Maia heard the rush of footsteps behind them. She turned around, her heart stilling for a moment with fear even as her fingers curled around Bellator's hilt. From her experience, people who were scared and irrational could not be trusted.

The man who had struck Ren charged toward them, the stick held menacingly in his hands. Behind him was his cohort, all wearing long, dark cloaks.

Maia took in a long, chilly breath. *This is it! War!*

She pulled out Bellator and stepped in front of Ren, and before she could blink, the rest of her teammates had whipped their weapons out as well.

Seeing their stance, the man slowed abruptly. He dropped his stick and raised his arms. "I mean no harm," he said, "to anyone."

Neither Maia nor any of her friends budged. They were ready to take on this man if he dared to take another step closer.

Only he did not. He simply turned toward Kusha and bowed low.

"My apologies, Sahiiraan Kusha," he said. "I didn't recognize you right away. For that I'm sorry."

Maia stole a glance at Kusha. He had not moved a bit, his stance resolute.

The man continued. "You have to understand. We've fallen prey to . . . devious schemes before. We've had to learn to keep outsiders away. But any friend of yours is a friend of our village." He placed a hand over his heart. "You have Ori Pistado's word, Sahiiraan. Each one of your friends will be welcome in the Mausoleum of the Sun."

Maia grimaced. How much did his word mean? They did not know who he was, and one thing they clearly knew was that he abhorred Xifarians and he did not hesitate to strike Ren without a single provocation. How could they trust him?

Kusha, however, slowly lowered his sword. "Ori Pistado?" he said haltingly. "You're Ori Pistado?"

The man bowed, quicker this time. "The same, yes." He held out his left hand to Kusha to show him the glistening red-jeweled ring on his pointer finger. Kusha nodded slowly.

"Please come in, Sahiiraan Kusha," Ori Pistado said, making a sweeping gesture at the Mausoleum with both arms.

Kusha nodded and then turned to his friends. "He's good. Let's go," he said.

"Are you sure?" Maia asked.

"Yes, absolutely," Kusha replied without hesitation.

They marched back up the stairs once more and walked into the inviting warmth of the circular room. Even as they settled down near the largest grate with blazing fire Maia had ever seen, she could not stop the worry from pecking her mind incessantly. Just then, she gasped, suddenly recognizing the cloaks Ori Pistado's men were wearing. They were the same kind—a silvery-gray skull etched on the black—she had seen on the man gliding through the snow-filled courtyard of the Sun Temple as well as on the group that had intrigued Mahswa Tabrin near the Gathering House.

Chapter Eighteen

The Rebel Chieftain

The warm fire crackled, throwing shadows across their faces. Maia and Dani were huddled up together under a blanket, while Kusha and Nafi sat opposite. Ren sat on Maia's other side and kept his head down.

"I saw his ring," Kusha whispered when Ori was busy arranging a hot meal for them. "He's Ori Pistado for sure. His family has been chieftains of three villages west of ThulaSu for ages now. They even have a sigil of their own—a three-headed wolf head. That's what was on the ring he showed me."

As it turned out, Ori Pistado was part of the Resistance, a rebel outfit that had opposed the Xifarian incursion into Tansi for years.

"What if he made himself a fake ring?" Maia asked.

"Why would he?" Nafi shot back. "It's not like he's out here waiting to trap kids from the university."

Maia would have argued some more and even brought up the mysterious man she had seen in the courtyard, but then Ori and two of his men handed out bowls of steaming soup. The broth was brimming with favor and the chunks of meat in it were tender as butter. Their bowls were empty within moments, and they were refilled with care immediately. When Ori and his followers handed out more blankets, Maia huddled closer to her friends.

"What do you think we should do?" she asked, particularly to Kusha.

"It's still snowing like crazy outside," Kusha replied. "We don't really have a choice."

Nafi nodded. "We should keep Ren in the middle though." Her eyebrows danced meaningfully. "You know . . . in case they get any ideas."

And that was how they spent the night—in a blanketed huddle next to the fire—taking turns to keep an eye on Ori Pistado's men. Maia barely had fits of sleep. When she opened her eyes for what seemed like the hundredth time that night, the doors leading to the outside were open and the pale light of the morning sneaked in. The room was empty, except for them.

Maia nudged the person closest to her, which turned out to be Kusha.

"What?" He opened a bleary eye. "Is it morning already?"

"Think so."

Kusha stretched and yawned. "I'll go check if the snow has stopped falling yet."

By the time Kusha came back, the rest of the group was wide awake. Kusha flashed a wide smile.

"It's stopped. There's a lot of fluff on the ground, but at least there isn't any more falling."

"Good," Nafi sprang up. "We need to get back. Tessio must be worried."

"Yes," Kusha said, nodding wisely. "Let's find Ori Pistado and get out of here."

As if by magic, Ori Pistado strolled in at that very moment.

"You're up," he said, grinning.

"And you're observant," Nafi muttered caustically under her breath.

"Yes, we are," Kusha replied. "We will leave now. Thank you for your hospitality last night."

Ori held up his arms, closed his eyes, and shook his head vehemently. "Oh, no, no, that's nothing. I'm ashamed of my behavior last night. And you cannot leave right now, Sahiiraan. The road's too dangerous. We've sent word to your teacher in ThulaSu. I'm sure they'll send someone to guide you back. If not, I'll escort you back myself."

"You need not—"

"Besides, we've prepared a meal for you and your friends. You have to accept that."

"Fresh food," Nafi whispered. "I'll accept that gladly."

"Please, sit down, make yourselves comfortable," Ori continued affably. "We didn't speak much last night, but what brings you here?"

Soon they were telling Ori all about the difficult task they had been assigned of finding the Yako roots.

"You're looking for Yako roots? Really?" Ori said incredulously.

"Yes, we are," Maia replied. "Do you know where we could find some?"

"Of course," Ori said, chuckling heartily as if she had asked the silliest of questions. "You've come to the right place. We have the largest patch of Yako growing right around our village."

"You don't say?" Nafi blurted. Ori nodded. Nafi thumped Maia with such gusto that Maia almost fell over. "All right, Maia," she chirped. "I forgive you for bringing us this way. It was a good choice after all."

"Maia?" Ori gasped. His eyes turned into bulging balls. "You're the Nosiifarus?"

Maia recoiled when she heard that word. Nosiifarus was a legend of Tansi, a supremely powerful being, a child of the stars who wielded the power of the stars. She was not one. The Xinhagyi had said even though her outburst against the Xifarians had the signs of a Nosiifarus surge, he did not think it really was. Besides, that title was like a black mark against her name, reminding her of the destruction she had once unleashed, although unwittingly, and the lives—Xifarian enemies or not—she had taken with impunity.

"N-no, I'm not, don't call me that," she stammered, red-faced.

"So you aren't the one who decimated the Xifarians on Devil's Ridge?"

Devil's Ridge? Was that what the mountain was called?

Kusha stepped closer and slipped an arm across her shoulders and suddenly Maia was thankful for the warmth and support. "Come on, Maia. Stop being so modest. You have to honestly answer the man who gave us food and shelter," Kusha said. He turned to Ori and nodded. "Yes, she's the one. She fought them off on Devil's Ridge. But the Xinhagyi said that she's not technically a Nosiifarus."

Ori shook his head as if he could not believe what he had just heard. "Pardon me," he said, rubbing his nose that had already turned a violent shade of red. "I behaved disgracefully with you, O Nosiifarus."

"Please, stop," Maia pleaded. "Don't call me that, please. I'm just Maia."

"Just Maia?" Ori laughed. "We've been rejoicing your arrival since that day Devil's Ridge flashed with the light of the stars. We've been worshipping you. You can't be just Maia, not to us. You're a legend, the champion we've been praying for."

Ori's eyes shone as he giddily described that morning they had seen the light on Devil's Ridge. Apparently, the ridge on the Eatambian Range was in direct line of sight of the village and they had curiously watched it all—spacecraft landing with the Xifarians, the destruction, and later the battered Xifarians leaving.

"Wh-where is the ridge?" Maia asked hesitantly. If she could just see it in person, then maybe she could remember what had happened. If she had indeed attacked Miir, she had to believe that he had somehow escaped. She had seen him fall, but maybe he had somehow found safety. She needed some hope otherwise she feared she would be consumed by the darkness forever.

But the moment Ori Pistado showed them the cliffs, she realized there was no room for hope. The cliffs of the Eatambian Range rose high up into the sky. She could see the ridge, but barely. A building with a hundred floors would probably be that high, Maia deduced. There was no way anyone could survive a fall from there.

Miir was dead. She *had* killed him—that was the simple truth.

Why did it make her feel so disgusted with herself? She had wanted revenge against Miir. This was the ultimate revenge. Yet—

"Hey, Maia"—Nafi nudged her—"what are you thinking?"

"You look pale," Dani commented.

"Of course. You need food," Ori shouted. "What a disgraceful host I've been. Pardon me, O Nosiifarus."

Once again, Maia cringed, but that had no effect on Ori who left for the village in haste with two of his men, arms flying as they rushed to arrange breakfast for the team.

"Nicely done, Maia. You're quite the goddess to them," Nafi said, winking.

"I don't like that, Nafi," Maia snapped.

Nafi waved her off. "Doesn't matter. What really matters is that we now have our hands on the elusive Yako root."

Maia forced a smile before turning away from Nafi's gleeful face, her gaze lingering on the distant rock face high above them. Any other time, she would have been as thrilled as Nafi was, but not now. Instead, her heart was leaden the way it had not been in a very long time.

Chapter Nineteen

The Yako Challenge

Not all hope was lost. When they got back from their weary, cold trip, the team bustled with excitement that they now possessed the Yako root. Not only would Tessio and Revsi Sottekaja be pleased, but they were the first and only team to have their hands on the prize, and that gave them a head start.

Ori Pistado had told them to look around the village. So before they headed back to the university, the team had worked long and hard until they spotted some ground-bugs. Then they moved piles of snow to dig out the Yako roots. They had collected a bagful, enough to last them through training.

Still, Maia felt subdued. She was happy for her team and overall pleased that things went so well with Ori Pistado, but she could not shake the image of Miir from her head. She could almost hear him scream.

A scared-looking Everrol greeted them when they returned. "Where have you been?" he chastised. "Monk Hilledunn has called a meeting for all teams." Then he raced down the corridor and disappeared.

"I don't like this," Maia grumbled as they marched toward the meeting room. "He had no plan or reason to gather us up. So why —"

"You're getting paranoid, Maia," Dani chided gently. "Perhaps he's going to announce the first challenge. We've been here for two months already, so it's almost time they gave us the details of the first challenge."

Nafi snorted in response, and Maia was happy to have her support. Hilledunn was weird and rather nasty. If this had been anyone else calling an assembly, she would have not given it a second thought. But with Hilledunn? Even thinking of him filled Maia with an odd sense of unease, as if evil was waiting to spring on them.

"We'll find out soon, won't we?" she said simply.

They trudged down toward the assembly hall in silence and Maia felt an increasing sense of dread as they drew near.

Hilledunn and the other trainers were already in the room when Core 21 entered. Most of the other teams were gathered, so Maia and her friends picked one of the last benches to sit on.

The mentors — all ten of them, including a panting Everrol — were huddled in the area to the side of the podium.

"They're going to announce the first challenge," Dani said in a confident voice. "That's the only reason for gathering everyone here."

"Well, not everyone," Maia said. "The Arbitration Committee isn't here."

And that was strange. Masters from the previous phases of the Alliance Initiative had been invited to watch over the final phase at ThulaSu, and they had been present during Hilledunn's welcome address, but not now. Kehorkjin, Aerika, and Mahswa Tabrin were nowhere to be seen.

Maia hardly trusted Hilledunn to be fair. He had called Maia out rather unkindly during the first address, embarrassing her in front of all the teams. Maia tried to justify his actions but failed. She knew deep down that he was not on her side. It almost seemed like he had a grudge against her, and she often wondered what was going to stop him from taking it out on her team. The presence of the arbitrators could have helped them, but now Maia could not find anything to pin her hopes on.

"Friends, so good to see you all again," Hilledunn's loud voice boomed. He smiled, his gaze sweeping the assembly. "I gathered everyone here to announce the first challenge of this phase. I'm sure you're all very excited to find out what it will be, aren't you?"

A few cheers and a lot of mutterings filled the air. Maia sat still, eager to hear the details, yet a part of her was rigid with fear and suspicion. There was something about Hilledunn—odd the way his eyes narrowed when he looked at them—that made her hold her breath.

"Today we begin to train for the Yako Challenge, which starts, of course, with the finding of Yako roots. I know both Monk Tessio and Revsi Sottekaja have tasked you with finding those roots you'll use to discern auras. On the day of the challenge, you'll be asked to track a mark through ThulaSu using only an identifiable aura. Easy, isn't it?"

Loud sighs followed Hilledunn's short pause. Next to Maia, Nafi giggled. "We're well ahead of the rest, so yes, let's have it."

Maia smirked. It had been an eventful trek to Ori Pistado's village.

"Now, I have another announcement to make," Hilledunn said. He raised his arm and beckoned. "Core 21, can you please join me at the front of the room?"

Maia could not believe her ears. Just like she had feared, Hilledunn had something planned against them. Her fists curled a little, and even as she forced herself to think of peaceful thoughts, anger spread inside her like a stubborn wisp of smoke. No one spoke, not even Nafi, as they walked to the front of the room. Maia could see her friends' anger in their pursed lips and their tight jaws and the stiffness of their backs as they marched up. Hilledunn smiled as they lined up next to him.

"So, Core 21, I hear you've located a sizeable amount of Yako root?"

Kusha nodded. Maia dug her fingernails into her palm. How did Hilledunn find out already? They had not told anyone yet. Had Everrol been spying on them somehow?

"And I hear you appropriated it from one of the villages?"

Maia balked. "Appropriated? That doesn't sound right."

It was not right at all. It meant they had taken the Yako by unfair means and that was not the truth.

"The villagers gifted it to you then, I suppose?" Hilledunn said, tapping his chin thoughtfully.

What is he getting at? Nothing good, Maia supposed.

"No, they didn't," Maia replied steadily. "They told us there was a Yako patch near the village so we went and searched the area. And we dug up a bunch of Yako root."

Hilledunn's face scrunched up in a teasing smile. He turned to Tessio and Revsi Sottekaja as if to make sure they were equally amused. Both masters, however, watched with placid faces. Hilledunn turned back and raised an eyebrow at the team.

"Really? Why do I keep hearing gossip about the villagers besotted about a visit from the Nosiifarus? That they swore to do anything to please *her*?"

Maia stiffened as Hilledunn fixed a wicked glare on her. Kusha threw a quick glance at her. Contestants from the other teams possibly did not understand what Nosiifarus meant and what Hilledunn was saying, but they quickly broke into agitated whispers.

"It wasn't anything like that," she snapped. They had worked hard to dig up those roots and she was not going to let Hilledunn taint their diligence. "We wouldn't have taken anything that we didn't win fair and square. We were simply told they grew around the village, that's all. We followed the clues and found them ourselves."

"That's right," Kusha added.

Hilledunn shook his head. "Liars! All of you," he snarled.

"We're not," Nafi protested. "We trekked through that deadly blizzard to find the roots. We deserve every bit of it."

"Of course," Hilledunn said with a snicker. "You deserve the best, why won't you? You're so used to being heroes. Don't worry. I won't take the roots away from you, even though I think that's what should be done. But since your means are suspect, you're going to share your spoils with all the other teams. You see, heroes often sacrifice for the less fortunate. I'm sure you won't mind."

"But why would we share?" Ren blurted. "This is a contest. We trekked through the blizzard, almost got beaten to death, dug through a mountain of snow to get the roots out. And now —"

"Wouldn't it be so much easier for me to disqualify you?" Hilledunn chuckled.

"No, we'll share," Maia jumped in, ignoring her teammates' frowns. She was seeing red, but she was not about to give this vile man a chance to throw them out of the contest, which she was sure was his real intent. They had plenty Yako to share, and if they worked hard enough, they would still be in the top five. She noted with glee how the glint in Hilledunn's eyes faded. None of her teammates looked happy, but Maia was sure she could make them understand.

"Very well then," Hilledunn said. "You'll hand over your collection of Yako to Revsi Sottekaja right away. He will then distribute it evenly among all teams. You can go back to your seats now."

They trooped back to their seat slowly and quietly. While Hilledunn went on to describe more about the Yako Challenge, Maia barely heard any more. She feared this was only the beginning of Hilledunn's plans to sabotage them.

***

The next day, Revsi Sottekaja greeted the teams with a pot full of a pasty beige cream.

"Come, come," he called as the contestants trickled into the room. "Today you learn to see."

Corin, one of Jiri's teammates, was the first to be smeared with the paste. The Revsi drew a line on Corin's forehead following the arch of the brows, slowing to make a circular dab at the center of the forehead, and then dabbed some along the lower rims of his eye. Corin's look drew quite a few giggles and some snorts.

"No need to laugh," Revsi said somberly. "You all follow. This is how you see."

The paste was made of Yako root. Apparently, it enhanced the optical nerves and stimulated brain functions which in turn helped discern auras. Maia liked how cool and tight it felt on her skin and its musty, earthy smell.

"Close eyes, focus thoughts, let Yako paste dry," Revsi instructed.

Maia tried. She closed her eyes quickly, but focusing her thoughts was easier said than done. Starting from Hilledunn's most recent torment, Maia's mind bounded far and away from the dark room she was in. In her thoughts, she had reached Appian and lain in the soft grass that bordered their pond when Revsi called again.

"Open eyes. Look at me."

Maia blinked, partly in disbelief and partly to let her eyes adjust to the spectacle. The Revsi was radiant, not merely with a dim glow but a dazzling golden like the midday sun. Maia stole a look at her friends; they were all wide-eyed and open-mouthed just like she was. But the most amusing part was seeing every one glowing a different color. Maia looked around, mesmerized. It was as if the room had been filled with colorful and exceptionally large fireflies.

"Anyone cannot see?" the Revsi asked.

No one uttered a sound. They were all busy staring at each other. For a few moments, Maia was light as a breeze, free of the humiliation pressing on her heart, until Nafi gave out a shaky yelp.

"But, Maia," she said, grasping Maia's arm, "why don't *you* have any colors?"

And just like that, the breezy, floaty feeling vanished and a weight filled Maia's insides. She looked down at herself and saw nothing. Once again, she was different. Once again, she would have to be the weird one.

***

The next few weeks flew by. The good part was volunteering at the Damoclian Connector. Work at the grid entrance was going on at a frenzied pace and everyone was excited to see the project near a successful completion. Being there meant getting to see Maks, Aman, and Nisa who otherwise remained buried under classwork. Every night after the work at the Connector was over, Maks showed Maia around ThulaSu. Maia cherished the walks and wished there could be more of those, but it was never easy to make time. Maks usually had a ton of assignments and Maia was not free of them either, especially after Hilledunn had handed out thick books with architectural details of ThulaSu to study and memorize.

On top of that, Maia — Dani accompanied her occasionally also — had to visit the Xinhagyi every other evening. The training to control her powers was progressing well and now the Xinhagyi let her practice using the light on targets.

"Focus, Maia," the Xinhagyi barked one evening when the ball of energy Maia threw out hit the ceiling instead of the pillar she was meant to shoot. "Calm your thoughts. You cannot think of anything else other than the light when you're wielding it. If you lose focus too many times, the light will take over. It will wield you. Remember that!"

If only it had been so easy to clear her thoughts. She gritted her teeth and continued practicing.

"*Yoteh!*"

She missed the pillar again.

"Attention," the Xinhagyi said.

"*Yoteh!*"

This time, half of the ball of energy slammed against the pillar. It was not perfect, but —

"Not good enough," the Xinhagyi said.

"*Yoteh!*"

It went on and on. Sometimes she landed a perfect shot, but most times she failed. But it was not until she had tried at least a hundred times that the Xinhagyi beckoned her.

"Something upsets you," he said, his face crinkling like a dried prune. "You are more uneven tonight than I have seen before. What is the matter?"

She could not tell him about her vision of Miir, but she decided to ask him why she did not have an aura.

"Oh, that," the Xinhagyi chuckled lightly. "It's because of the light that resides in you. It's too powerful an energy that absorbs everything else. That's why your own aura doesn't shine through."

"B-but that doesn't make sense," Maia countered. "This power I have . . . it's all light. At least that should show up, shouldn't it?"

The Xinhagyi gently patted her shoulder. "It is a dark energy, Maia," he said, and for some reason Maia's heart dropped to the pit of her stomach. "That is why no one is able to see the light of the Sedara glowing within you even with the Yako root paste. Also, the light still possesses you. You're improving, but you do not have full influence over it yet. The moment you could wield absolute power over the light inside you, your own aura will shine through."

Maia got the explanation she was seeking but she was not sure if it helped. Even though Dani linked her arm through Maia's as they walked back to the refectory that evening, Maia felt as much of an outcast as she had felt earlier.

***

For the contestants, there was much practicing to be done for the first challenge, which involved tracking a mark only by their aura. That meant entire days of following cloaked men or women through every nook and corner of ThulaSu, which left the Maia and her teammates with permanent blisters on their feet. None of the other teams seemed to fare any better either. Everyone was exhausted at the end of the day, every day.

On top of that, the Revsi asked for reports from each team. They had to study the aura of every member and explain what the colors meant. Maia had first thought of a person's aura to be of one color, which turned out to be false. They were predominantly one color, but there was more. The colors changed also depending on the mood of the subject.

Nafi was mostly a yellow-green, which signified a vocal and impassioned personality. But she also showed a lot of red when she was angry, and her yellow often turned a vivid golden like the Revsi's.

"Gold signifies wisdom," Nafi said proudly as they finalized their report. "None of you glows as golden as I do. You guys need to listen to me more. I'm the wise one."

"Shut up, Nafi," Kusha said for what seemed like the tenth time that day. "If you were really wise, you'd let us focus and finish this stupid assignment without mistakes. But you keep talking."

"Some assignment. A waste of time," Ren grumbled. "I still don't know what we're learning here. People have auras, so what? We're not going to wear this crazy paste and go analyze people all our life."

Ren had reason to be unhappy. He was flipping through crusty pages of a large book hoping to find why his aura—as well as every other Xifarian Maia encountered—always glowed around the edges with flecks of purplish-blue. The Xifarians had explained it as an effect of L'miere crystals, but the Revsi demanded they keep looking for more reasons.

Dani patted Ren on his shoulder and chuckled. "It's not that bad, Ren. Remember, auras are nothing but energy that a body emits. The point of this exercise is to learn to understand that energy. According to Revsi Sottekaja, the more we study each other's auras, the better we get at sensing the energy variations. Even without the Yako paste, we should be able to sense changes in people's moods."

"I don't need auras for that," Ren retorted. "I can see Nafi scowling and know right away she's not happy."

"I don't always scowl when I'm mad," Nafi protested. "Do I, Maia?"

Maia wished Nafi did not drag her into the conversation. She did not want to say anything. Since discovering she had no aura of her own, she felt like she did not belong in this challenge.

"What's up with you?" Dani asked.

Maia shrugged. They could not understand how out of place she felt. On top of that, she was struggling with the flashes of memory that kept coming. She still had not seen the face of the person she had thrown over the edge of the cliff, but she did not need to. She was quite sure it was Miir. She still could not explain why no one knew he was dead. It did not make sense. Yet the dread kept piling higher and higher each time she had a vision. Every vision slowly eroded her conviction that they were just a figment of her imagination. She had started to believe she had killed him. She wanted to tell someone about it, but she did not know how to share the horrific truth about being a murderer.

"You aren't thinking about not having an aura again, are you?" Dani slipped an arm over Maia's droopy shoulders. "Maia, the Xinhagyi explained to you.

"I know," she said in a tired voice.

Dani squeezed her shoulders. "Come on, Maia, don't be like that."

It was difficult to not be like *that*. Not only was she missing an aura, but she had yet another problem since using the Yako, something the Xinhagyi also chalked up to the light inside her. From time to time, even without the Yako paste on her forehead, Maia saw people's auras. It would have been a perfectly fun power to have had it not been so random. As it were, it was freakish—one moment she was looking at people the regular way and the next they would turn into pillars of color. It was weird and disruptive.

"I hate this Yako business," she muttered.

"See, this assignment is the worst thing ever," Ren declared.

Dani simply sighed and even Nafi did not retort. Maia already knew it was true: The first challenge of the Solianese phase was just not going the right way for the team.

CHAPTER TWENTY

THE CHASE

The first challenge began after two whole months of practice sessions. Everrol showed up donning an elaborate headdress embroidered with colorful beads in neat rows. He also sported the biggest grins Maia had seen on him yet.

"Happy morning," he greeted the team at breakfast, grinning from ear to ear. "Today is a very important day. I'm excited," he said, rubbing his hands together. "Are you?"

Nafi rolled her eyes and exhaled loudly, and Maia simply stared in disbelief at Everrol. Something was wrong with him to be chirping like a bird in spring. A challenge was exciting, but they all knew by now excitement only made them lose focus. To win, they had to be calm and pool every bit of energy inside them.

"What are you doing here, Everrol?" Maia asked.

"I'm here to escort you to the meeting room, of course."

"You needn't worry about us," Maia said. "We've been to that room many times now. We'll have no trouble getting there."

Everrol perched on the edge of the bench next to Maia and

flashed a sugary smile. "Have I ever left you on your own?" he asked. "Today's a big day. I *have* to be with you today."

Nafi grunted in displeasure, but Maia could not be as rude. As annoying as Everrol was, he had been with them all along. That he was not of much help was another matter altogether. But he did not lack intent. He was there to cheer the team up after Hilledunn had forced them to share the Yako. He had also given them tips about navigating the university buildings, including showing them various shortcuts and alleyways that connected them.

"It might come in handy when you follow your mark during the challenge," he had said.

Sure, he was not comparable to Miir when it came to knowledge or skills, but he was not as useless as Joolsae either. Maia acknowledged that she could not be totally unappreciative of their current mentor.

"All right, thanks," she said, even though she knew Nafi was glaring at her and none of the others looked particularly pleased.

They finished the rest of the breakfast hurriedly and reached Hilledunn's favorite room not too long after. Everrol sat with them, right in the middle of the row. Hilledunn and the ThulaSuian masters were already present, along with the Arbitration Committee. As soon as all the teams had assembled, Hilledunn pulled out a sheet of paper.

"It's a big day, yes?" he started, scanning the assembly. Maia thought his gaze rested on them longer. "We will now start what we have fondly named the Chase. Each team will be assigned a mark who will crisscross ThulaSu and make his way to a golden chest somewhere in this city. That chest holds an important clue to the next challenge. Your task is simple: tail him. If you lose sight of him, you won't find out where the golden chest is and you'll be disqualified."

Hilledunn paused and Jiri's lanky arm shot up. Hilledunn nodded at him. "So we get to the chest and the clue. What then?" Jiri asked.

"Then you come back here and report to us."

"What if all ten teams get to the chest? Do you keep all of us?"

Hilledunn chuckled as if he had just heard the silliest of jokes. "Of course not. We still have to eliminate five teams."

"How?" Jiri demanded.

"You are too impatient, Jiri," Kehorkjin growled from behind Hilledunn. "Can't you wait till the master explains?"

Jiri shriveled at Kehorkjin's chiding and it seemed that every other contestant shrunk a little as well. Kehorkjin had been a tough taskmaster and his reprimands from their time on Xif were still fresh.

Hilledunn waved gleefully. "It's all right. They're excited. Like wee little bees venturing out of their hive for the first time."

Maia thought she saw Kehorkjin grimace. Aerika definitely winced.

"Well, Jiri, we've thought of a simple arrangement. We will have a clock running on you. It'll start as soon as you begin tracking your mark and leave this room. We'll stop the clock when you return to this room after retrieving the clue from the chest. Now, can you tell me how we shall eliminate five teams?" Hilledunn said.

"The teams with the best times will get through," Jiri said.

"Exactly! The top five teams get to stay on with us, and the other five teams will have to leave ThulaSu." Hilledunn forced a sad smile and looked around the room. Once again, it seemed that he looked longer at Maia than anyone else in the room.

"I hope we don't get a day slot," Everrol muttered. Maia had been hoping the same. Getting a day slot meant being saddled with two disadvantages—discerning auras in bright daylight was difficult, and running around in the sun was tiring. They did not have a say in the matter anyway, so all Maia could do was hope for the best.

"Listen carefully, teams," Hilledunn called from the podium. "This is the order the teams will follow. From now until midday, it'll be Core 6 and Core 19 in that order. After a snack break, we shall have Core 53 and Core 2. We shall have lunch after that and begin again with Core 21 followed by Core 45. Then we squeeze in a small evening break and resume with Core 10 and then Core 34. Dinner will be served after that and we will end the challenge with Cores 7 and 13."

Hilledunn paused and Nafi leaned forward and looked at her

teammates. "Did we get a good slot? Please tell me we did. I can't think clearly at all."

"I don't think we did," Maia replied, calculating the time of day they had been allotted. They had received a slot near midday.

Everrol shook his head. "It's terrible," he whispered. "You almost got the worst time. Look at the sun outside now. With all that snow around it's gonna be so blinding at noon. You'll hardly be —"

"No slot is perfect," Dani whispered. "Even the night slots will have some handicap."

"Like what?" Ren asked, frowning. "They get to rest all day, learn from our experiences, and have beacon-like auras to follow?"

Dani's eyes dimmed and she looked away. Ren was correct; the teams that had been given night slots did have a clear advantage, there was no denying it. However, that did not mean they had to stop hoping. Maia was not about to give up without a fight.

"Come on, guys," she whispered. "We've dealt with plenty of challenges. We'll get this one done too."

No one even looked in her direction, not even Everrol. Maia slumped back into her seat and tried to think of the near-impossible task ahead of her: keeping her team's spirits up. They had to show Hilledunn how capable they were. Also, with the Xifarians gunning for her, the longer she stayed in the Initiative, the better. This time around, winning the challenge was far more important than it had been in the other phases.

Disaster did not take long to strike. The ruckus started unexpectedly with Everrol. The mentor had been fretting and fuming since Core 21 had been assigned a midday slot. He was even more upset than the team members, which Maia thought was weird.

"Unfair," he muttered as the first team left the room after their mark. "This is not right. I don't care, it's not right."

"It's all right, Everrol," Maia said, tired of all his grumbling. "We have to make the best out of what we've been handed. We've made it so far. And we didn't exactly come this far because we were given the best opportunities. We did because we kept going no matter what."

"And stood up for what's right," Ren added.

"That's my point. This isn't right," Everrol said angrily, flushing a bright red. He shook his head and jumped off the bench. "You won't understand," he declared before stomping away.

"What the heck was that?" Kusha said as Everrol left in a huff.

"Useless drama," Nafi said caustically, drawing Dani's frown.

Time passed slowly after that. The first team, Core 6, was back with a rolled-up parchment; they had successfully followed their mark to the golden chest. As soon as the masters recorded the time of return, the team was sent away.

Nafi let out a frustrated grunt as Core 6 left the room. "Thought we could talk to them and find out how things went."

"That'd make things easy," Kusha replied.

The frustration was not Nafi's alone. It rippled across every remaining team. A low impatient hum grew and hung in the air as the rest of the contestants stayed—fidgeting endlessly—in the assembly room and waited.

The second team seemed to take longer to return, but they did get back with the prize. As did the third. Just like Hilledunn had instructed the first team, the subsequent teams were also dismissed right after they reported back. Food was delivered to the room as the teams awaited their turns.

As the day grew brighter and warmer, the atmosphere in the waiting room seemed to tighten. Everrol returned, looking grouchier, just in time to see the fourth team being escorted back to the room. They had failed to reach the golden chest and looking at the downcast faces as they trudged in, Maia understood how much was at stake here. After dedicating nearly two years of her life to the Initiative, this was all she knew and all she had. This was her world. Where would she go if they lost and had to leave ThulaSu tomorrow?

"Core 21," Hilledunn called when they had barely finished with lunch. "Come over, please."

A chill invaded Maia's toes and fingertips as she walked over to the podium where Hilledunn stood with the other masters.

CHAPTER TWENTY-ONE

RACE TO THE BOTTOM

Revsi Sottekaja smeared their faces with Yako paste before Hilledunn parted the curtain that hung over a doorway behind the podium. A cloaked figure stood in the darkened alcove. Maia blinked a few times before she sensed the aura—it was a bright yellow with tinges of orange at the edges.

"Take your time, let the Yako settle in," Hilledunn said.

Maia nodded, breathing long and deep to calm her thudding heart. The cold was spreading within her, and failure was starting to seem inevitable. It was going to be close to impossible tracking someone with an aura that yellow in bright daylight.

Everrol nudged her elbow. "What color did you get?" he asked, his brows knit tight, his face puckered.

"It's yellow," Maia whispered.

Everrol's nostrils flared and his lips quivered. "You gave them a yellow?" he shouted at Hilledunn, his fists curling into balls. "You can't do that."

A stunned silence followed. Everyone, including Maia and her friends, simply stared at Everrol. Then as people stirred around them, Hilledunn's jaw tightened.

"Watch your mouth, Everrol," Hilledunn hissed, but Everrol kept his glare fixed on the master's face. Hilledunn stared back at him, and Maia almost braced for him to pounce on their mentor. Thankfully he did not. "The assignments are completely random. If your team has yellow, then they have to make do with it."

"You assigned yellow at noon on purpose," Everrol shouted. "You want them to lose. You've always wanted them to fail. You rigged the contest against this team."

"Be quiet, you brat," Hilledunn said. If his eyes could rain fire on Everrol, they would. "You forget your place. You forget you're an orphan who wouldn't have survived without our kindness. Now you dare bite the hand that feeds you?"

Everrol's face dimmed and a familiar scalding pain in her guts made Maia realize how angry she was. At the most unexpected of moments, Hilledunn's demeaning words had kindled the fire inside her instantly. Maia breathed, hard and fast, to calm the drone within. She could not let it get any stronger. She could not risk hurting everyone in the room. She wished Everrol would stop.

"Everyone else before them got colors that'd stand out in daylight. Why not them?" Everrol was not about to give up.

"Leave the room right now." Hilledunn pointed at the door and leaned forward to bore a murderous gaze into Everrol. "If you don't, I will have you thrown out of ThulaSu. This is your last chance to stop that from happening."

Maia turned away, willing herself to stop hearing Hilledunn's continuing rebukes. She heard nonetheless. Someone, Kehorkjin perhaps, tried to intervene. A cold hand clasped over her wrist and Dani whispered, "Maia, are you all right?"

"I'm trying," she replied, trying to find peace in Dani's deep blue eyes. She could not get mad at Hilledunn. Not here. Not now. She could not put innocent lives at risk. She had to get over her anger.

"We'll be fine," Dani's soft whisper floated over the simmering heat inside her. "Trust me. Have faith in yourself."

"Yes," Maia whispered back.

"Core 21." Hilledunn's sharp voice cut through the fragile layer of peace Maia had constructed. "Do you see him? All of you?" he asked.

Maia nodded, barely feeling her head on her shoulders.

"Good. Your time starts now."

Dani's grip on her wrist was still firm when Maia stumbled out of the assembly room with her friends.

***

Maia quickly realized that even after practicing chasing marks across ThulaSu for weeks, the actual challenge was something else. The man was fast and tricky to follow. The sun was burning a hole through her back. Beads of sweat trickled down her forehead; her hair was a wet mop on her head, her throat was parched, and her feet hurt as she sprinted down the staircase of the north annex of the university. None of her friends was faring any better. Their faces were drawn, gaze intent and focused on the mark they had been chasing for what seemed like an entire day.

"I lost him," Ren yelled, jumping over a charred piece of log on the road.

"I still see him," Dani reassured, rushing past a pair of students engrossed in conversation. "He ducked behind that girl in pigtails."

"All right, I see him now," Ren replied. And they hurried on again.

It was a crazy run—dodging, shoving, and stumbling—across the crowd of students and residents of ThulaSu. Everything around passed by Maia in a blur of bright colors, clothes, hats, shoes, and auras wanting to coalesce into a jumble in her head. Smells hit her nose, varying from sweet perfumes at times to a heady mix of sweat and dust.

It was strange that after having chased the man for quite a while, they had not been able to narrow the gap. He was like a specter, drifting through people, almost like water slipping through fingers. Maia was glad that they had not lost him altogether. And at least the fire inside her had died down.

Her thoughts swirled around Hilledunn from time to time, even when she did not want them to, even in the heat of the chase. Was Everrol right in his allegation? Did Hilledunn assign them a yellow aura on purpose? How could they be sure that Hilledunn did not simply send them out on a wild goose chase?

She blinked to drive away the thoughts and focus on the man once again. The yellow aura was big trouble indeed. It was one thing being indoors, but as soon as they were out in the open, their troubles multiplied many times over. The bright sunlight cast the golden haze over everything and Maia's focus invariably wavered.

"At least it's five of us," she muttered to herself. Even if one of them lost track momentarily, one of the other four kept him in sight. Thank goodness not every person in the crowd was yellow.

"I don't have him," Nafi shouted. "Tell me someone still has eyes on him."

"I do," Maia said. She had seen him enter a north-facing door. "In there," she said, leading the team into the narrow alleyway that cut through two buildings.

Kusha pointed at the distance as soon as they turned. "There he is. We're too far away. Run!"

They broke into a sprint. The man picked up pace as well.

"Faster, guys," Kusha yelled. "This corridor leads to the North Bazaar. It's too crowded in there. If we lose sight of him now, it'll be impossible to find him."

Maia tried to recall the map of the North Bazaar of ThulaSu. It was the largest marketplace in the city and was always crowded. Four roads led into this massive building-enclosed courtyard. A large fountain with a statue of the sun god in his seven-horse chariot was set in the center of it.

"Faster," Kusha yelled again.

The golden chest had to be somewhere in the Bazaar. It was the best place to hide such a thing.

"Hey, listen," Maia shouted. "I'm gonna take a shortcut into the bazaar, all right? Cut him off from the side if I can."

"Not a good idea, Maia," Nafi yelled back. "The more eyes we have on him, the better."

"Trust me, it'll be better if we can track him from two sides. And I know a shortcut through that door to the right," Maia said. "I'll see you out in the courtyard."

"I'm coming with you," Dani said, huffing laboriously as she sped next to Maia.

"I hope Everrol is right about this one," Maia said, swinging through the rust-colored door that led into the foyer of a house. A bunch of kids were playing in the middle of the floor and the girls had to hopscotch their way through the play zone.

"Through there," Maia exclaimed, pointing at a glass-paned door that stood open in the distance. A terrace with a bright orange floor lay on the other side. Clotheslines zigzagged the terrace, and rows of clothes — mostly drapery — hung swollen in the breeze like the colorful sails of a million ships. Maia slowed, mesmerized by the billowing spectacle, as did Dani next to her.

A moment later Maia remembered a staircase on the north end that led down to the bazaar. She pulled Dani's arm. "Come on. This way."

They ran again, through the maze of drapes that swayed like a vibrant dream around them, weaving through them and under them as fast as they could. It seemed as if there was no end to the field of sails. For an endless while, the girls twisted and turned and kept running.

It ended as unexpectedly as it could have. One moment Maia was staring at an unending wall of fabric and the next moment they were out in the open. Sheets billowed behind them in a massive, dreamy wave. A carved balustrade a few steps ahead announced the end of the terrace. Down below was the marketplace, a large courtyard ringed with colorful shops and humming with shoppers.

"That way!" Dani pointed excitedly at the steep staircase that led down from the terrace to the side of the bazaar. As she hurried after Dani, she scanned the crowd below, intent on locating the man they had been chasing.

The bazaar was a throng of auras—blues, greens, purples, and yellows mingling together in a blaze of dazzling colors. There was too much going on and the sun was shining bright. *It's no use*, Maia thought. Her plan to isolate the man from a higher viewpoint had failed. With a heavy heart, she started down the stairs.

A familiar movement caught the corner of her eye when she was halfway down. Maybe it was the way he moved. Maia noted his cloak first, then stopped and squinted to figure out the aura.

It is him!

"There he is," Maia shouted, and broke into a dash down the staircase.

From the height, she could see him clearly. Not his whole face though—the cowl was pulled forward too much—but she recognized his characteristic aura, a bright yellow with flecks of orange dotting the edges. For the first time since they had started after him, he had completely stopped. In fact, he was not even standing. He rested quite comfortably on a rectangular box and looked around leisurely at people. As if it was done, the chase was over.

"I spotted Kusha and the gang," Dani said as they weaved through the crowd. "They have him in sight as well."

"But where's the chest?" Maia said, scanning back and forth for telltale clues to the prize.

Her mind screeched to a stop on the third sweep. What was that rectangular box the man was sitting on? Could it be the golden chest?

"Come on," she shouted, and pulled Dani by her arm and ran across the courtyard toward their mark.

Someone crashed into her and sent her flying to the ground.

"Maia!" Dani's cry reached her ears along with other voices and sounds. Strange hands grabbed her arms and pulled her to her feet. Her knees stung and her right shoulder ached when Dani held her by the shoulders and peered at her.

"Are you all right?" Dani said.

"I'm so sorry," a burly man with a red face blurted. Maia assumed it was the man who had collided with her.

"It's fine. I'm fine." Maia flashed a smile.

The mark! They had to get to him. She spun around looking for the man but found no one.

"He's gone." The words trickled out of her mouth along with a deflating sigh. "We lost."

"Maybe Kusha and the others still have him," Dani said hopefully as the duo trudged toward the spot they had last seen the man. For a moment, Maia felt a little hopeful until she found Kusha, Ren, and Nafi and saw their bewildered faces.

"No, they lost him too."

Maia could barely feel her legs under her when they gathered around the spot where they had last seen the mark. She sucked in a mouthful of air but her lungs screamed for more. The weight of failure sat heavily on her heart. It was hard to look at her friends' wilted faces so she simply scanned the crowd, hoping by some miracle she could find the man again, but he was nowhere to be seen.

Kusha fell with a loud thump on the big box the man had been sitting on and let out a groan. "Can't believe we came so far and . . ."

Maia did not hear anymore. A forgotten thought came crashing through her mind.

The box . . . the chest . . .

"Get up, Kusha," she said, tugging at his arm frantically.

"What? Wait!"

"This might be the chest we were supposed to look for," Maia said, pulling at the heavy lid of the large wooden box. "You know the way he was relaxing here, it felt like this was the end of the chase."

For a moment or two they all stared at her, and then hands swooped in. Together they pulled and tugged until they got the lid open.

The box was empty.

Maia's sight blurred and a lump of hurt throbbed in her throat. She blinked with all her might to fight the stinging pain in her eyes.

Then Nafi shrieked. Her shaking hand was pointing at a dark corner of the cavernous box. Maia leaned forward and squinted. A tiny roll of parchment lay in one corner.

Kusha scooped it up as Ren whooped. Dani threw her arms around Maia. Nafi's fists shot up in the air.

"We did it," someone yelled.

For a few moments, they huddled together, breathing in unison, relishing the ecstasy of a hard-fought win. Then Nafi broke the silence.

"Come on, guys, let's go," she said. "We don't have time to waste."

"You have the paper, right?" Maia checked with Kusha as they turned to leave.

"Got it." Kusha nodded and showed the roll of parchment in his pocket.

They sprinted across the corridors and courtyards, pushing, shoving, bumping, and swerving as they ran. Maia could not feel her legs anymore. The side of her stomach burned, and her shirt clung to her like a second skin. Her heart thrashed against her chest like a wild animal intent on breaking out of its cage. Maia did not pay attention to any of it. She could not wait to see the smile fade from Hilledunn's face. When they reached the assembly room after having dodged and ducked and skidded and slid and apologized a hundred times, everyone was long out of breath.

"You're back," Hilledunn said, and Maia did not miss the flicker of surprise in his eyes. Hilledunn quickly forced a wide smile. "How wonderful. You found the golden chest I suppose?"

"Yes, we did," Kusha said, panting. He pulled out the rolled parchment and handed it to Hilledunn.

"That's good, that's good," Hilledunn said. "We'll record the time."

"I've recorded it already," Aerika said from behind him. She smiled at Maia and her friends reassuringly. "You're in good standing. You're at the top."

The smile died on Hilledunn's face. His neck snapped around toward Aerika so fast that Maia almost thought it would break. "You've added the penalty, I hope," he said icily.

A ripple of surprise widened Aerika's eyes before she frowned. "What penalty?" she asked.

"They will get ten points deducted because of their mentor's appalling conduct, of course."

Aerika's mouth fell open slowly and Maia could not believe her ears. There was no doubt that Hilledunn seemed intent on making them fail. Even though there was no proof that Hilledunn did it on purpose, there was no denying that Core 21 had received the most difficult assignment so far. Now that they had still managed to get through the challenge, Hilledunn simply threw a nonsensical charge at them.

"We didn't ask Everrol to say what he said," Nafi shrieked. "You can't penalize us."

"I can and I will," Hilledunn said through gritted teeth, waving the parchment at Nafi like a stick.

Maia grabbed Nafi by the arm just as the girl opened her mouth again. They could not give Hilledunn an excuse to deduct another ten points. "Nafi, don't," she said sternly.

"But, Maia," Nafi yelped.

Maia could not bear to look at her teary eyes, or the hopeless faces of her teammates. Yet, she knew no good could come from challenging Hilledunn at the moment.

"That's enough." Maia had not noticed when Kehorkjin had stepped forward. His gray-blue eyes scanned everyone before they came to rest on Nafi's downcast face. "You've done your part, Nafi. You did your best. Now, you should leave it to us. Go have some rest."

There was nothing to be said after that. Maia and her friends walked out of the assembly room with slow, lifeless steps. Even though bright sunshine streaked through the large windows of the corridor as they walked, Maia could see nothing but an endless ocean of gloom ahead.

CHAPTER TWENTY-TWO

THE WORST OF DAYS

Head hung, eyes skimming the patchwork of stones under her leaden feet, Maia reached the open courtyard of the university grounds after what seemed like a lifetime. No one spoke on the way, and Maia could not blame her friends for their long faces. There was nothing to talk about and the less that was said, the better.

"What do we do now?" Maia said after the five had sat quietly for a while on the stone balustrade.

Nafi simply shrugged but Ren jumped off his perch and dusted his shirt needlessly. "I'm gonna go check something on the Viperine. See you later."

He took off with not a second glance at the rest of the team. Maia suppressed the twinge in her heart forcefully. Ren had changed, and it was not a good feeling seeing him pulling away from the rest.

"I think I'll go see my father," Kusha announced, mostly to Dani who nodded and flashed him a smile.

Maia wished they could all stay together. It was always easier to carry the grief of defeat when they were together, and it would have especially helped when a defeat so unfair was handed out.

"Anyone else want to bail?" Nafi asked drily after Kusha had left.

"It's all right, Nafi," Dani said. There was no cheer in her voice. "Let them be. Everyone deals with things their own way."

Nafi crossed her arms and chewed on her lips for a moment. "I know. But if you can't stand with your comrades when you're down, I call you a traitor. That's my way of dealing with things."

Dani drew a sharp breath but thankfully did not reply. Maia felt for Nafi, but there was little she could do. She could not drag Ren or Kusha back. She did not want to either. Dani was right; people had to handle situations their own way. They were no longer little kids who could band together as easily as they did two years ago.

"Hey, I know what we can do now," Maia said cheerily as an idea trickled into her head. "Let's go and help with the Damoclian Connector."

Spare time had been hard to come by lately. With the first challenge hanging over their heads, they could not help with the Connector work as much as they wanted. Maia missed being there and she knew her friends did as well.

"That's a great idea," Dani said, her face lighting up like the sun at high noon. Even Nafi's eyes brightened.

They started off jubilantly and soon were busy helping the engineers in the control room. Time flew by and Maia had almost managed to shrug Hilledunn's unfair treatment off her mind. She even thought of walking to the rose garden to look at how the plants were coming along. It did not take too long for her plans to fall apart.

Around evening, Vyessa walked in with a couple of friends and headed toward Maia. "Hello," she said, smiling.

"Ren isn't here," Nafi announced. Maia forced a chuckle down.

Vyessa's face turned red and she shook her head violently. "I know," she said. "I can see. I just came over to tell you that I'm sorry. I hated the way Hilledunn treated you."

Nafi snorted. "That's all right. If we're lucky we'll still get through."

There was something about the way Vyessa pursed her lips at Nafi's comment. Maia was sure the girl knew more than she had said.

"What is it?" Maia asked. "Something happened after we left?"

Vyessa shifted on her feet and looked away for a bit before turning back to them. "Well . . ."

"Oh, come on," Nafi said impatiently. "Tell us. It's not like we'll die of heartbreak or something."

"Well, Jiri's been keeping time," Vyessa blurted. "He's doing it on his own. He has put together this little timekeeper thing."

Dani sat up straight and crossed her arms. "So?" she asked.

"With the penalty Hilledunn slapped on your team, there's no way you'll be in the top five. You're done. It's over." Vyessa said it in one breath as if she was in some rush to say it all.

Maia's head reeled. She had known they did not have a chance after Hilledunn's penalty. They all knew it. Yet Vyessa's words, particularly the way she spat them out, stung.

"Thank you for letting us know," Maia said. She sounded cold, distant, and unreal to her own ears.

Then guilt raised its head quickly enough and made Maia twitch. Perhaps she was overreacting. Vyessa could not have meant to hurt them.

"I didn't mean to . . ." Vyessa said. "But you wanted the truth. And that's what it is . . . you aren't getting in."

"It's all right, Vyessa," Dani chimed in, icicles dripping from her voice. "It's good that you told us. But you know what? It's not done until it's done. So, we'll wait to hear the final results from Hilledunn. Now if you don't mind, we have tasks to complete here."

Vyessa shrugged and walked away. Maia and her friends continued with their chores silently for some time until Nafi sighed loudly and set down the circuit cover she had been putting together.

"I don't feel like staying here anymore," she declared.

Maia did not either, and judging by Dani's gloomy face, she could not have had any interest in being here.

"Let's leave," Maia said. "We can sit in the garden and then meet the boys for dinner."

"Yes, let's," Dani said, jumping to her feet.

It did not take long to get out of the control room. Maia breathed a sigh of relief when they stepped out in the open. A moment later, her spirits dipped once more.

"Hello, hello," a boisterous voice assailed them before the girls had a chance to get to the ramparts for their walk back to the garden.

"No. Not that stupid Lex. Not today," Dani muttered. Maia could not help a wry chuckle. When Dani was upset enough to call people names, things were indeed bad. Today was definitely not going well for them.

"Heard you were kicked out." Lex and his barrel-chested lackeys blocked their way, cackling wildly. "It should've happened a long time ago, if you ask me."

"No one's asking you, Lex," Nafi snapped. "And don't count us out yet. The results are not in."

"You talk too much, shorty." Lex waved dismissively at Nafi. "The results are in, trust me."

"How do *you* know anyway?" Maia asked, crossing her arms and fixing a glare on Lex's face. "You're not even part of the Initiative. Who tells you such things?"

Lex's eyebrows danced. "I have my sources. I'm from a powerful family, not a bunch of no-names like you."

Maia breathed in a lungful of air. She was not about to fall into his trap.

"Well, your sources are no good," Nafi retorted. "We have a better chance than you. Oh, wait . . . how could I forget? You were kicked out in the first phase. Some good you were."

"My sources are the best," Lex roared.

"Yes, that two-timing Vyessa is just your kind of source," Nafi shouted just as loudly.

Maia threw a beseeching look at Dani. Dread had been steadily rising inside Maia. The outcome of this shouting match between Lex and Nafi could not be good. Even the Kausakas guarding the entrance of the control room had started to frown at them.

"Vyessa?" Lex bellowed. "Who's that?"

Nafi cocked an eyebrow. "Don't remember your girlfriend? Well, she told us all about the results too. But I wouldn't get my hopes up much based on what she says. Who's she to know anything anyway?"

"You think I'd call a worthless girl from the Initiative a source?" Lex said, lips curling in indignation. "Lex isn't that cheap. I get my information from the most important person in the Initiative: Monk Hilledunn."

For a moment or two that stretched endlessly, a deafening silence fell around them. Maia could hardly breathe, let alone think. Then, like water escaping from a crashed dam, a torrent of questions struck her mind. What did Lex mean? Was Hilledunn a friend of Lex's? Or was the monk working for Lex's father and Xifarian sympathizer, Sahiiraan Leeam?

"You must be joking," Maia blurted, breaking the silence.

Lex smirked. "Told you, I have powerful connections." He looked so smug that Maia wanted to slap the look off his face.

"You don't say." Dani's wide eyes sparkled as they gazed upon Lex's flushed arrogant face. If Maia did not know Dani any better, she could have mistaken that look as admiring. "Can't believe Hilledunn would tell you that."

"Of course he would," Lex said, puffing up his chest some more. "Hilledunn's father used to be my grandfather's advisor. His family has been loyal to the House of Broken Seas for generations. Why would it change now?"

Dani exchanged a quick glance with Maia and Nafi. Things were getting clear as daylight now. No wonder Hilledunn had been nipping at their heels since the first day of the Initiative. No wonder he had penalized Core 21. The House of Broken Seas had no love lost for Maia and her teammates. A year or so ago, Core 21 had brought down the vile schemes Leeam had hatched with the Xifarians. Now, obviously, it was time for payback.

It was also weird how vulnerable Maia felt. She had not wanted to participate in the Initiative, but it had become her identity. It was the one thing left in her life that she had known so closely.

It was also her defense against the Xifarians. Sure, she was not as helpless as she had been a couple of years ago, but still, the Initiative felt like a shield around her. With that gone . . .

"What a disgusting low-life you are, you and your worthless family," Nafi spat the words out as if they burned her mouth. "You couldn't beat us fair and square, so you had Hilledunn sabotage us. You want to win? Maybe you should arrange a slime-ball contest. There's no doubt your lot will be the winner of that one."

Lex pounced like a wounded tiger, grabbed Nafi by the throat, and they crashed to the ground in a heap.

Maia jumped after them, tugging Lex by his shirt as forcefully as she could. Someone pulled her arm, twisting it behind her. It was one of Lex's minions and he was strong. He pulled Maia's arm with one hand and grabbed her hair with another, trying to peel her off Lex's back who squeezed Nafi's throat as the girl struggled to free herself.

"Help," Dani screamed.

"Hey, break it up," someone, perhaps one of the guards, shouted.

Nafi groaned, her eyes bulging as Lex tightened his grip. Lex was going to kill Nafi. Time was running out. The boy holding her hair pulled and searing pain spread through Maia's scalp.

No time!

Maia let go of Lex and fell back against the boy who was pulling her hair. She crashed her elbow into his chest, getting him in the ribs. He yelped. The pain in Maia's head vanished and her arm came free. It was just the break she needed. She spun around and with every bit of strength she could find, kicked the boy in his shin. Clutching his leg, he collapsed like a sack of potatoes.

Heaving, Maia looked for Dani. She was fighting the other imp. One of the guards rushed to help her.

Nafi choked and coughed. Maia threw herself at Lex, trying to peel him off Nafi.

"Stop," Maia yelled, anger burning stronger inside her.

A woman's voice, one Maia had heard before rang in her ears. *He's going to kill your friend. Do something about it!*

Putting her fists together, she brought them down on Lex's back with all the force she could muster. And again. And again. Lex let out a loud howl and fell to the side. His hands around Nafi's neck came loose. Nafi rolled away, coughing and gasping for air.

Dani was beside Nafi in a heartbeat, wrapping her arms around her protectively. Lex showed no interest in attacking Nafi again. He simply lay on his back, whimpering and writhing.

How dare he hurt her? How dare he? The woman's voice echoed in Maia's ears.

Maia was not done with Lex. She was far from it. The world was on fire. Heat and smoke swirled around her. Before she realized it, she was on top of Lex, straddling his belly.

"Stay away from my friends," Maia shrieked. "You hear me, you scum? Don't you dare hurt my friends."

She landed a punch on his chin and then another. And another.

Someone screamed. Someone else yelled, asking her to stop. Hands grabbed her shoulders, peeling her off Lex.

Light as bright as the midday sun blinded her vision, searing heat burning her insides.

"Calm down, Maia," Dani wailed.

She wanted to calm down. But she could not. Instead, Maia punched and kicked. And punched and kicked. Even when all her arms and legs touched was air.

Someone pinned her down to the cold ground. It was soothing. Calming. The fire within ebbed a little.

Then the world turned black.

CHAPTER TWENTY-THREE

CHAINED AND BROKEN

Everything around Maia was utterly cold and damp. It was as if she was immersed in an icy bucket of water. Maia moved her head, trying to shake the wetness off her. It did not go away, only shifted a little. Far away, someone screamed. Maia's senses wanted to hang on to the sound, hoping it would pull her out of the darkness and cold.

What was the voice saying? She tried to listen. For a while, there was silence. And then it came in a rush, like a mountain crashing through her senses.

End this quickly! End this now!

She knew that voice. It was a strange woman's voice, but it came from within her.

Maia looked around. She had been here before. She was in the middle of a clearing. Tree stumps, charred and broken, surrounded her. The young man across from her was ashen, his face drawn as if he were staring at the face of death. She had fought him before.

A blast of light sped out of her open palms, breaking into a million tentacles that struck Miir from all sides.

Miir? Yes, it was him.

Maia tried to break free of the vision. Not a thing changed.

Miir struggled to fight off the synchronized attack. A long fiery streak smacked his wrist, making him drop his sword. He scrambled to pick it up. As his fingers wrapped around its hilt, the glowing beams swirled around Miir. They scooped him up in a blazing vortex and flung him against the trees. When his limp body fell to the ground, they struck him again. He rolled across the forest floor, crashing against the embankment behind him. Then the ridge collapsed.

He was gone.

A menacing cackle rang in her ears. *You did it. You've won.*

Noooo!

She jolted upright, blinking furiously to clear her mind and sight. The fiery fog in her mind refused to budge, but the darkness around her parted slowly.

She was in a dark, cold room. A small light—a stubby candle—burned in the far corner. Maia did not know where she was or how she got here, but one fact shone as clearly as that candle in the corner: she *had* killed Miir! There was no doubt left, not anymore. She had seen it all, his pallid, terror-stricken face, the fire from her arms hitting him, twisting his body like a little twig, and throwing him to his death.

A brutal, bloodthirsty murderer, that was what she was. How was she any better than the Xifarians who were hounding her?

Maia pulled her knees closer to her chest and held them tight as if she would fall to pieces if she let go. She wanted to scream. Rip the choking pain out of her throat. She found no voice. So she sobbed instead. Mists of fire swirled endlessly in her head.

Maia had sat at the edge of the rope-strung cot and sobbed for ages when she heard the noise. Footsteps, voices, keys clinking. They were near, somewhere close . . .

She looked up, trying to locate the source. Her blurry eyes swung to one corner of the room and stayed there until a rectangular piece of darkness fell away.

Maia blinked. That was a doorway. A man stood with a bright light in his hand. A girl—her hair a sheet of gold—stood next to him.

"Dani," Maia said in a broken whisper.

The girl squealed and ran inside. Warm hands cupped Maia's face. "Are you all right, Maia?"

She was not all right. She was never going to be all right. She had killed. In cold blood. Miir had once been a friend. He deserved better. A second chance, maybe.

"What is this place?"

"We had to bring you here to calm you down," the Xinhagyi said. "You were close to falling apart when the guards intervened."

She remembered now. Lex had attacked Nafi. She had fought to get him off. "What happened to Lex?" she asked.

"He's alive. Got some scars. You burned him in places." Dani did not sound sad or sorry.

The Initiative. Hilledunn. The results!

"How bad did we lose?"

"About that . . ." Dani paused to let out a long sigh. "Hilledunn withdrew the penalties. We got through with the second best time."

"What? Really?"

"Yes, really."

At least something was fair in this world. Maia held Dani's arm and sobbed.

"Maia, what's wrong? Why are you crying?"

She could not tell her why. She could not tell anyone. Miir had wronged her—that she believed. But had she given him a single chance to explain? No. And that was utterly and indefensibly wrong.

"I want to go outside." She craved sunlight. And air.

"You can't leave this room, Maia," the Xinhagyi said. "Not yet."

She was back in the cold again. Alone. Miserable.

***

Days passed, although Maia could not tell how many. The images in her mind grew steadier after that. As if someone had opened a door she had shut and locked since the faceoff with the Xifarians on Devil's Ridge.

Maia remembered the words she had spoken and the things she had heard. She remembered Chairman Phocluus, his jibes, and how she had blasted them away. She remembered stumbling away into the clearing and how Miir had come looking.

Had he come to kill her or did he try to help?

She did not know. She had not asked. She was in a hurry to get back at him, to flaunt her power. She had blasted him away also.

"I have no idea why Hilledunn decided to take our penalty off," Nafi's incredulous voice tore through Maia's thoughts. Nafi . . . all her teammates had come to visit her cold, damp prison. "Someone must've forced him to reconsider, don't you think?"

Kusha nodded. "Probably Kehorkjin. Remember how he said we should leave it to them?"

They were all seated around the room where Maia was being held captive since the incident with Lex. She was dangerous, Lex's father Leeam had proclaimed, too dangerous to be let to walk around freely. A council had been summoned to assess the situation, and for days they had been debating the threat Maia posed to people around her.

"Hilledunn couldn't have liked everyone finding out about how he was in Leeam's pocket," Dani added. "It's obvious he had a vendetta against us."

Ren stretched like a cat and chuckled heartily. "Stupid Lex. He said things he shouldn't have."

Days after the incident, Lex was still recovering from the burns Maia had unknowingly given him.

Nafi nudged her elbow. "Maia, don't tell me you feel sorry for Lex. He deserved that."

She was not feeling sorry for Lex. No doubt he deserved what came his way. If Maia had not intervened, he would have strangled

Nafi. She was not even thinking about how they had kept her captive. Her mind was stuck at Devil's Ridge.

"They'll let you go, Maia." Kusha leaned over to pat her shoulder reassuringly. "This is just a desperate stunt Leeam pulled, that's all. Everyone knows Lex started the whole thing and you had to intervene to save Nafi. Leeam has no case, but the council has to follow protocol and see this through. If they rush this, Leeam will create some other distraction to get back at you and us."

"It's still ridiculous," Dani said vehemently. "If Lex hadn't attacked Nafi like that none of this would've happened. Why isn't *he* considered dangerous then?"

"He should be banned from ThulaSu while the Initiative is on," Ren said.

Nafi scoffed. "I doubt they'll do that. The council doesn't have enough guts to shut Leeam out. I'll be happy if they let Maia free. Quickly."

Dani slipped an arm across Maia's shoulders. "They will. We didn't just make it through the first challenge, we came in second. They can't keep one of us locked in a room."

They had scored second best time. Yet, there was not a shred of happiness in Maia's heart.

"Come on, Maia. Cheer up," Ren said from across the room. Since the incident with Lex, Ren had come closest to normal. He resembled the Ren she had known before the Solianese phase started. Looking at his eager face filled Maia with dread. It also filled her with questions.

Ren's behavior made no sense. She had seen Miir topple over the ledge. He had to have fallen to his death. But why didn't Ren say Miir was dead? Did he not know? Wouldn't the untimely death of the Xifarian chancellor's son be big news?

Or maybe she was wrong. Maia came back to the one conclusion that made any sense: Miir had to have escaped. Somehow. Or maybe what she thought she remembered was just a figment of her imagination. It *had* to be her imagination.

Maia's fists tightened. She could not go about chasing a

hallucination. She was not going to.

"Won't you miss Vyessa?" Nafi asked, and Ren shook his head in a distracted sort of way. Vyessa's team, along with four other teams, had been eliminated in the last round.

"It wasn't working out between us anyway," Ren said. "She was too competitive. All she wanted to talk about was the Initiative and how to improve her skills and score better. I couldn't take it anymore."

"Did you break up before she left?" Kusha asked.

"We parted ways a week ago."

Dani slapped the side of Maia's cot. "Aha! Maybe that's why she couldn't wait to tell us we lost. She was mad at you." Ren shrugged.

Just then, the door fell open. Maia saw a flash of pink, a twinkle of blue eyes, and a swish of silky curls. Then arms wrapped around her.

"Sana," Maia shouted, the last traces of heaviness in her heart lifting like fog. Heavier footsteps drew near and Maia beamed on seeing the gaunt figure that had followed her cousin Sana inside. "Uncle Alasdair. You're here too."

As if by magic, the drab, damp room turned sunny. Maia's spirit soared, light as a feather, carefree as a bird. She did not even notice when a happy tear had coursed down her cheek.

"Wait, there's more." Sana released Maia and grabbed a covered basket from Uncle Alasdair's good hand. "Here's someone special," she crooned, pulling the woven top of the basket.

"Dusty?" Maia screamed. The calico cat from Appian who she never thought she would see again leaped out of the basket and into her arms. "How?"

"Moritz stopped by a month ago and delivered him at our house." Sana rolled her eyes. "Mother dear wasn't very pleased, of course, but I . . ."

Maia threw her arms around her cousin, thanking fate for the chance to see her uncle and cousin again. She had never had a chance to thank them after they had whisked her out of Miorie before Xifarian agents could catch her. She hugged her uncle tight and whispered a heartfelt "thank you" to him just like she did to Sana.

"Hey, Maia," Ren called just as she let go of Uncle Alasdair. "Don't forget to introduce us to your family."

She had forgotten all about that. Kusha and Nafi had met Sana and her uncle in Miorie, but Ren and Dani had not. A flurry of introductions ensued and it took a while for Maia to get to the question on the top of her mind.

"Why did you come to ThulaSu, Uncle Alasdair?" ThulaSu was a long way from Miorie. Since the Jjord-imposed sanctions on technology, the Solianese did not travel so far often or without reason. Besides, Maia knew her uncle was not one who liked to travel.

Uncle Alasdair had sat down during the introductions. He now gave Maia a meaningful smile. "We came for you. Two days ago an envoy from ThulaSu visited me in Miorie and told me they had confined you. He said I could plead for your release, vouch for your sanity. He said you had a lot of distinguished people vouching for you already, but as your guardian and a Parliamentarian, my word could carry enough weight to sway the council against the House of the Broken Seas."

"So, here we are," Sana said, tossing her headful of curls. Her vivacious smile never failed to lift Maia's spirits. "We also had to bring Dusty to you."

"Aunt Rowyena . . ." Uncle Alasdair's wife and Sana's mother did not favor Maia much, and Maia wondered how she would have reacted to her daughter's plan to travel to ThulaSu.

Sana waved dismissively and made a face. "At least we're getting Dusty out of her hair. The woman should be happy for that."

"Watch it, Sana. She's your mother," Uncle Alasdair cautioned.

Sana rolled her eyes. A year ago when Maia had stayed with her uncle's family for a few days, Sana and her parents fought all the time. Nothing much had changed on that front, Maia mused.

"Anyway, the good thing is, we'll be here for a while," Sana declared airily. "Father will facilitate conversation with the Jjord while the Connector is built. So . . ."

Maia laughed. She could hardly believe Sana's words. They were almost too good to be true, almost like a dream.

"You're staying too?" she asked Sana.

"Of course," Sana replied in a heartbeat. "Father thinks it's a good idea to give me a break from her ladyship."

"Sana!" Once again, Uncle Alasdair's sharp voice came not a moment after Sana's dig at her mother. Once again, Sana rolled her eyes. Maia could barely stifle the laughter. Some things never changed.

"If you don't mind my asking, sir, how did you get here so quickly?" Ren said.

In the rush of meeting her family, it had not struck Maia as odd, but Ren had pointed out the most curious thing. How could an envoy have traveled from ThulaSu to Miorie so fast?

"Oh, I don't mind at all, Ren. The envoy came in a Xifarian transport. In fact, he brought us back here in the same craft."

Kusha leaned forward and peered at Uncle Alasdair. "Who was he? What's the name of this envoy?"

"Monk Timmon, he's an assistant to Monk Hilledunn, the chief arbitrator of this phase. He said Hilledunn was the one who sent him."

Maia's mouth fell open and her teammates froze. Sana and Uncle Alasdair stared questioningly from face to face. Only Dusty did not care, he purred contentedly on Maia's lap.

"What's wrong?" Sana asked, running a hand through her shiny curls.

After Maia and her friends had told them everything about Hilledunn and the events leading up to Maia's being locked up, a frown formed on Uncle Alasdair's forehead.

Sana tapped her chin thoughtfully. "Interesting," she declared. "Strange that Hilledunn would have such a change of heart. I mean this is some change of heart, right? From trying to disqualify you guys by any means possible to trying to keep you in the contest even if that means being disloyal to the hand that feeds him."

Uncle Alasdair wagged a finger at Sana. "Let's not insinuate. Monk Hilledunn is his own person; there is no proof of anyone owning his loyalty."

Sana crossed her arms and raised a shapely brow at Uncle Alasdair. "Really, Father? After everything you've heard, is there any doubt?"

"There is, unfortunately, no proof," Uncle Alasdair said.

Sana sighed loudly.

"That's a good point, sir," Ren jumped in before Sana could retort. "But even if Hilledunn is acting on his own, his change of heart is remarkable."

Uncle Alasdair nodded. "Perhaps someone with a level head advised him."

"Or perhaps he was forced to reconcile," Nafi commented.

"Perhaps, Nafi, but again, it's conjecture," Uncle Alasdair said. "So let's not go sharing our opinions."

Uncle Alasdair was very particular about statements. Maybe that was what being a parliamentarian was like.

"Anyway, whatever the reason Hilledunn brought me here, the good news is my assertion of Maia's intelligence and wisdom worked. You, my dear child, are free to go."

"I am?" Maia blurted. She could not believe that freeing her from Leeam's clutches could be as easy as her uncle providing a statement to the council. "I can go about doing things just like before?"

"Well, there's one clause," Uncle Alasdair said.

Maia drew a deep breath. Knowing Leeam, it had to be one crooked clause.

"You cannot be in a public place on your own. You always have to be in the company of a person older than you."

Maia blinked in confusion. "What? That's it? That's all they want?"

Uncle Alasdair nodded. "You could even be with Sana since she's a bit older than you, and you'd be fine."

It was weird that they let her off so easy. It was almost as if someone high up in the rungs of power wanted her to continue her normal life more than anything else.

Maia did not understand why that would be, but the thought needled her endlessly. Even after Maia left the little damp room with her friends and family, and even after she had had a sumptuous dinner at the refectory, worries lingered.

CHAPTER TWENTY-FOUR

NEW BEGINNINGS

The next few days were totally and annoyingly tiring. Maia could not be on her own, not even in her room. Leeam's clause demanded that she be chaperoned, so someone always accompanied her. Friends—except Ren and Nafi who were both younger—took turns escorting her around ThulaSu, and to be extra safe, at night Rayan set up camp in Maia's room.

A week after the first challenge, Hilledunn called another assembly and Maia was more than eager for the usual routine to resume again. With nothing to do but be followed all over ThulaSu, with not even a moment to herself, she was exhausted.

On the day of the assembly, the team started early. Maia expected Everrol to show up at breakfast but the mentor was not there.

"Anyone else miss our mentor?" she asked.

"I don't miss him exactly," Nafi replied. "But it's weird that he hasn't been around since the first challenge. I mean, he wouldn't let us be on our own before. But now, he doesn't show up in seven days? It's just bizarre."

"I hope he didn't get into trouble for standing up for us during the challenge," Maia said. They did not like him much before, but since he fought Hilledunn's nasty putdown of the team, they had started to care a lot.

"He somehow suspected the truth about Hilledunn," Kusha said wryly.

"Suspected?" Maia scoffed. "I wouldn't be surprised if Hilledunn put him up to following us around like a sticky fly. I think Everrol did his bidding until he couldn't take the unfairness anymore."

No one disputed her theory. Hilledunn was as crooked as could be and there was no denying that Everrol could be in some kind of trouble. Maia only hoped it was not too bad.

The assembly room was almost empty except for Jiri and his team, Core 13. All of them waved. Anja, a girl from Shiloh, a town neighboring Appian, leaned over to talk to them. "Hey, guys! It's exciting, isn't it?"

"Sure is," Maia replied. "Great work! You deserved to come out on top."

Anja chatted eagerly but Maia could not shake away her nerves and speak freely to the girl for too long. Her mind kept drifting to Hilledunn and she constantly worried about what he would do next.

More people trickled in. The other three teams—Core 7, Core 34, and Core 10—that had won arrived before the masters. The room was barely filled since five teams had been eliminated. The masters arrived late, after the contestants had waited a while. Hilledunn led the party, and Sottekaja and Tessio followed. Kehorkjin and Aerika came in behind them. Mahswa Tabrin was absent again, Maia noted. The group of mentors entered the room when the masters and the Arbitration Committee had taken the podium.

"Everrol," Nafi whispered excitedly. She even waved. But Everrol scarcely noticed. He was the last of the procession and he refused to look up at anyone.

Nafi crossed her arms and snorted. "What's with him? Why wouldn't he even look at us?"

"Maybe that's what Hilledunn instructed him to do," Maia said.

Hilledunn took to the podium and cleared his throat. "Congratulations to all the teams that secured a position in the second Solianese phase of the Initiative," he said in a dull monotone, reading from a piece of paper. It almost felt like he had no interest in being there, that he had been forced to address the assembly. "The next challenge—I've named it the Roots—will begin with a clue, one you've retrieved from the golden chest during the last challenge. I'll hand them to your mentors now."

Hilledunn stopped and opened a box. One by one, the mentors walked to him and picked up a roll of parchment.

"You will have your own parchment to read the clues anytime you want, but I will read it out now so you all know what it says."

Hilledunn unrolled a parchment and read aloud:

"For nine hundred and fifty-six years the Ikarus flew,

From the mother to another mother, seeking life anew.

A century and ten or some later

Fifty-seven Nouvus were set to wander;

One brought us home and then lay in forever rest

In the land of the dead, sentinels watch over her crest."

Maia looked at her friends and furrowed her brow. They had been given clues before, but nothing as crazy as this. What did it mean?

Nafi's lower lip jutted out. Kusha sighed and whispered, "That's just totally a bunch of hamjibies."

Maia chuckled. She had not heard that word in a while, but when she was younger, she used it often to describe utter nonsense. Kusha was right; hamjibies was the perfect word.

Not just her teammates, but everyone in the assembly seemed just as flummoxed.

"Mentors, you can hand out the parchments to the teams now," Hilledunn announced.

All of the mentors, including a stony-faced Everrol, scuttled to their respective teams. Dani, who sat at the end of the row nearer to the mentors, gasped as soon as Everrol handed her the roll. The rest of the team leaned over to check.

"What happened to you?" Dani said. Her hand had flown up to her mouth. She was staring intently at the side of Everrol's face.

After having to crane her neck, Maia saw the right side of Everrol's face and gasped. From near the ear down to his neck was an unnatural patch of the deepest shade of purple.

"It's nothing. Please. It's nothing," Everrol said, shaking his head vehemently.

"How can that be nothing?" Dani whispered, but her tone was sharp. "Did someone hit you?"

"No. Why would anyone hit me?" Everrol protested in a fierce whisper. "I fell."

"There's no way you get a bruise like that from a fall," Dani said. She had learned enough of the healing arts to know what could have caused a bruise, that Maia was sure.

At that moment, Hilledunn clapped to draw attention. "All right, teams, now you have your clues. This is another treasure hunt. A much bigger . . . grander treasure hunt. Your task is to find out what the riddle means. Once you decipher the riddle, you'll have to find a way to the treasure."

Dani fixed a glare on Hilledunn's face, and Maia understood why. All fingers pointed at Hilledunn hurting Everrol. It was not too far-fetched a thought. The way Hilledunn had yelled at Everrol when he had protested the master's unfairness; it was he might have foundl punishment for their mentor.

At the podium, Hilledunn went on. "For this challenge, you'll have a lot of unique resources at your disposal. The library at the XDA and the research portals at UAAS are open for you."

"Really?" Jiri blurted.

Excited whispers floated across the room. The offer was indeed unbelievable. The riddle had to be particularly difficult for organizers to have granted access to both Xif and Zagran. It was particularly hard to believe that were allowed to visit Xif again.

"Yes, really," Hilledunn said in a mocking tone. "However, you should start your research with the library at ThulaSu. Your mentors will arrange for your entry passes. They will also arrange for your trips to Xif and Zagran. Please note, you can access our library here as many times as you want, but you can make only one trip each to Xif and Zagran. So make good use of your time there. Any questions?"

No one had any questions. The masters left and Everrol rushed out of the room as if he could not wait to get away from the team. Dani crossed her arms and shook her head at Everrol in a very un-Dani-like manner.

"I'm going to get to the bottom of this," she hissed, nostrils flaring. "And if Hilledunn is behind it, he's in for trouble."

***

The library at ThulaSu became the team's new home. Access to the Great Library was a privilege not everyone in ThulaSu could boast of. Apart from the monks, only the scholars of the highest grades were allowed to enter the premises. There were many other smaller, less impressive libraries scattered all over the place, and those were used by most. The Great Library, on the other hand, was sacred and out of reach of the masses.

The Great Library was divided into many sections, each section housed in a room. One of the first sections was the electronic archival center where a monk in a yellow robe greeted the team.

"Hello, you must be Core 21," he said with a wide smile that stretched from ear to ear. "I'm Monk Atriss. I'll be your guide. I'm always here at the archival center. Call me anytime you need."

Atriss seemed like a nice person, jovial, with kind eyes that always twinkled and a smile that perpetually turned his mouth upward. He gave each of them a badge that had to be worn when they needed entry.

"Now, let's take a tour of the Great Library," Atriss said. "This is the newest addition to the Great Library." He pointed at the long storage rows holding spools of electronic data. "Unfortunately, we didn't get to expand this section much. After the Solianese fall, we barely had access to technology to maintain what we had, and we certainly couldn't keep it growing. But we have old tomes, plenty of them. Come on, let's enter the vaults."

The vaults were a place to behold—high arched gates led into the dark, cavernous insides where shelves of crisp and ancient books rose from floor to ceiling. Paper books and their musty aroma filled the area. Chandeliers hanging from the ceiling cast a web of dim light and shade over the walls of books. The shelves, Maia noted, were arranged like spokes of a gigantic wheel, and the central hub was always a clearing scattered with tables and chairs for people to study the volumes.

"I'd recommend you start in the history section," Atriss said as they entered the third room. "I've said the same to the other teams who came before you. You cannot take many books out of the Great Library, so I'd advise you to take copious notes."

Nafi nodded wisely and pulled out a thick notebook from her satchel. "Yes, we plan on taking lots of those."

That evening they returned with notepads scribbled from top to bottom. They had found nothing that related to anything in the vague verse they had been handed. But at least it was a start.

***

Days flew past. Maia and her teammates made zero progress on the clues. Their only consolation was none of the other teams did much either.

Even though Maia and her friends knew there was time—the entire challenge would not be called before three months had elapsed — tempers had started to flare.

"I don't think we belong at this stage," Nafi declared morosely one day as they mulled over the verses for the millionth time during lunch. "I'd rather have lost it in the first challenge and left than get totally stumped now."

"We'll get to the bottom of it, I'm sure," Kusha said. His voice did not reflect any of the cheer the words were expected to convey.

"We have to." Ren sounded far more determined than the rest.

Dani ate quietly and Maia knew why she was distracted. She was thinking about Everrol again. Dani had had no luck in tracking down the mentor. Everrol did not miss any of his mentor duties — he left copious notes, tips, and instructions on the team's study table — but he never showed up in person.

"No news of Everrol, huh?" she asked Dani.

"I spotted him with Tessio once, but he slinked away before I could get to him," Dani replied with a sigh. "I'm telling you, Maia, that Hilledunn's up to something. He's been messing with Everrol. I'm sure."

Dani was hardly ever in a cranky mood, but since she discovered Everrol's bruises, she barely showed any interest in the Initiative or in unraveling the clues.

Maia tried to comfort her. "Perhaps he's just busy, Dani."

"Just like Hans is busy?" Dani said morosely.

The comment about Hans came out of nowhere and left Maia stunned. She knew Hans had not been messaging Dani since he left ThulaSu right before the Initiative resumed, but had things been as bad? How could she have missed it?

"What about Hans?" she asked guardedly, hoping Dani would not be terribly upset.

Dani jabbed her bowl with the spoon and her mouth twisted. "He hardly talks to me. It's always a 'yes,' 'no,' 'all right.' Something's not right, Maia."

"But Hans could really be busy," Maia ventured cautiously. "The Damoclian Connector is taking a lot of effort, isn't it?"

Dani made a face, dropped her spoon into the bowl, and stood to leave. "No, it can't. I'll see you later." With that, she stormed off.

"I'll catch you guys later," Kusha said suddenly and gathered his things. "My father wants to talk to me about some ThulaSu business."

"Good, I'll go and spend some joyful time at the library," Nafi declared. She looked around the table expectantly and Ren nodded.

"I'll come with you," he said.

And just like that everyone got busy with one thing or another. Maia did not want to follow Nafi and Ren into the dark library, but thanks to Leeam's clause, she could not walk about on her own either. She gathered her things and was just about to follow Ren and Nafi when she heard a familiar voice calling her name.

"Maks!" she yelled as Maks approached. Maia turned to Nafi and Ren. "Can you two go ahead without me?"

Ren's eyes narrowed.

"Of course," Nafi said.

Maks strode up to her quickly. Maia hoped she could spend some time with the boy from Appian. It had been a while since she had last seen him, and with all the other stuff going on with the Initiative, Maia looked eagerly to be with someone outside of the Initiative. Besides, he was a teeny bit older than her, so Hilledunn's clause would not be broken either.

"Been a while," Maks said, grinning wide, his sandy-blond hair a mop on his head. "Tell me what you've been up to."

"Don't you have classes?" Maia asked.

Maks shook his head. "No, I don't. We have midterm evaluations coming up soon, so we have a preparatory break now."

"That's nice."

"Yes, it is," Maks said with a large grin. "I had been wanting to talk to you. We've been hearing gossip about Hilledunn. Are they true?"

Maia chuckled. The story about Hilledunn treating them unfairly had spread far. Her heart sank a little as the thought settled into her brain. That meant the story of her bout with Lex had made rounds also.

"You want to walk to the gardens while you tell me all about it?" Maks asked.

"All right," Maia said. She did not mind spilling Hilledunn's secrets even though it meant admitting her own flaws.

They talked all the way to the bowers. They laughed and chatted until the afternoon sun started to slide down to the horizon. Maia told Maks about Hilledunn and how he had tried to sabotage her team. She also told him all about the fight with Lex and how Hilledunn had changed suddenly.

"I don't like that," Maks said worriedly as Maia concluded her tale. "Hilledunn is a two-faced monster; we've known that for years. He's super nice to anyone who is either rich or powerful, but we've seen him be so horrid to the kids from the orphanage. One day he had a girl stand out in the field for talking back at him or something. It was the middle of summer and the poor thing collapsed in the afternoon heat. I don't know why they still have him as the deputy of the orphanage."

Maia's heart raced. If Hilledunn had a history of cruelty then Dani was indeed correct. He must have been the one who gave Everrol the bruises. Everrol was also an orphan, Maia recalled. That could have given Hilledunn more reason to exact revenge on him.

"What are you thinking?" Maks asked.

"Umm . . . nothing," Maia lied. She did not want to spread rumors yet. She had to be sure about the crime before she went on and accused people.

"Keep an eye on him, Maia," Maks cautioned. "He's a snake."

Maia nodded. As she watched hues of orange take over the evening sky, her mind drifted. She suddenly remembered the fiery night sky when Appian burned. And just like that, her family was no more.

"Maia?"

Maia blinked. Maks was peering at her, his usually happy eyes dark with concern. Maia rose to her feet, hastily pushing away the distressing jumble of memories from her mind. She had work to do. She had to get back and tell Dani about Hilledunn. They had to find out about Everrol. Then they had to put a stop to whoever was responsible for his injuries.

"It's getting late. Let's get back," she said hastily.

Maia had taken a step or two when she noticed Maks was not next to her. She turned to look around. He stood at the spot they had been sitting, looking sheepishly at her.

"What is it?" she asked.

"Maia," Maks blurted. He looked away, twiddling the brass ring on his thumb awkwardly.

"Yes, Maks."

"Would you . . . would you absolutely hate me if I ask you out on a stroll?"

For a moment, Maia did not understand what he meant. Then it came crashing through her numbed brain like a wave. Then the world stilled.

Maks was courting her.

Maks was a perfectly wonderful boy. She liked him. She should have been happy. The sky should have looked rosier; the air should have turned fragrant.

None of that happened. And Maia could not bring herself to say yes to him. Yet she could not refuse him either. Maybe it was his flushed, anxious face that made her hesitate. Or maybe she wanted to be just another regular girl with a regular life.

"Maia, I really like you. A lot." Maks stepped closer. So close she caught the musky whiff of Hansa flowers on him. "I've liked you since I met you. And wanted to ask you out."

"But, Maks." Maia's words came out in a whisper. "You know the way I am. It's dangerous to be—"

"I don't care, Maia," Maks said vehemently. "Besides, I don't believe in the talk about you being dangerous."

Maia tried to think it through, but thoughts refused to cooperate. They kept spinning, like an endless, gigantic whirlpool in her mind.

The sky was dimming fast and Maia heard the distant gong announcing dinner.

"That's the dinner bell. We'll be late," she said, sounding almost frantic.

"You didn't answer me, Maia. Will you come on a stroll with me?"

There was no evading Maks or his question. And Maia was sure that she cared too much to refuse him and break his heart. A stroll did not mean they would be engaged to get married; they would simply get to know each other better. What could be wrong with that?

She nodded slowly. "Yes, Maks. I will."

Maks's eyes sparkled, and his face broke into an ecstatic grin. Looking at his happy face, Maia had no trouble believing that she had said the right thing.

CHAPTER TWENTY-FIVE

IN SEARCH OF ROOTS

Maia hardly expected things to go crazy so soon after the second challenge was announced, but they did. It was mostly because they were all too stressed about the challenge and the nearly indecipherable clues. They had found out about the Nouvus; it was a spacecraft that had brought the first settlers to Tansi hundreds of years ago. But that was all they knew, and the information took them nowhere. Tired of browsing dusty books that always ended fruitlessly, the team decided to visit Ori Pistado's village, Walenveil.

Two weeks had passed since Maks had proposed. Maia had no plans to tell her friends about Maks right away—she did not much fathom what she would tell them—but that day, as they were walking through the forest to the village, the team ran into Aman.

He rushed up, eyes sparkling. "Congratulations, Maia," he said, bubbling with excitement.

Before Maia could reply, Nafi raised a curious brow. "For what exactly?" she asked.

"About the thing with Maks, of course."

"What thing with Maks?" Ren demanded.

"Maks asked Maia out on a stroll," Aman said innocently.

Ren, who did not have a clue what asking a girl out on a stroll meant, looked at Maia questioningly. Maia's face burned, but thankfully, she did not have to answer because Kusha chimed in instead.

"On Tansi, asking someone out on a stroll is the first step of courtship," he said, succinct in his reply.

"You must be joking," Ren said. Although Maia knew the news was abrupt, she did not quite get why Ren's mouth curled, almost mockingly. "Really, Maia?"

"What do you mean?" she asked.

Ren stared at her for a moment or two, then shrugged. He flashed a careless smile. "Never mind."

Some more chitchat later, Aman went his way and Maia and her friends trekked down to the village. They met a few villagers on the way who were thrilled to see Maia. Ori Pistado must have already gotten news of them coming since he was waiting at the village gates to meet them.

"Welcome back," he greeted warmly. "And congratulations! I heard you made it to the next challenge. That Hilledunn couldn't stop you after all, huh?"

They had met a few times since Hilledunn confiscated the team's Yako stash and Ori Pistado had no love lost for the monk.

Ori led the team across the village to a dining hall. Villagers were busily piling plates of food on the table and Maia knew it was going to be a spectacular lunch for them. Cloaked men guarded the doors and walked around the room. Maia had learned that they were the Black Phantoms, members of the Resistance and the rebel chieftain's close aides who rarely showed their faces to outsiders.

"Your next challenge is pretty interesting, right?" Ori said.

"You heard about it already?" Maia asked.

"Of course," Ori replied with a sly smile. "We know everything.

Knowing is our job."

Kusha flipped his hands. "Well, we haven't made any progress. Hilledunn will be happy to hear that."

"I'm sure you'll find a way to crack the riddle. Me and my people have thought a lot about the riddle and we think it's about our roots," Ori said. "How we got started on Tansi and all that."

"You shouldn't probably tell us any more about it," Maia said hastily. "If Hilledunn gets wind of it, he'll devise a plan to kick us out."

Ori frowned and waved as if he were shooing a pesky fly. "How will that brainless Hilledunn find out?"

"You never know. He found out about the Yako," Maia said. "He has spies everywhere."

"Heard they're letting you go to Xif. Is that true?" Ori strayed to another topic.

"Yes," Nafi replied, smiling giddily as she plonked down on the bench. "I can't wait to see the XDA again. We had so much fun there."

Dani and Ren joined in animatedly. Very soon, they were deep in conversation talking about the XDA and about how they had once deciphered the clues of yet another puzzle a long time ago. The table was now laden with three types of bread, and Maia nibbled on the one with the golden brown crust as she listened to the conversation.

Her mind drifted soon. She thought of Maks and wondered if she had done the right thing by accepting his proposal of a stroll. It was odd that she did not feel any different about Maks than she did for any other of the friends. To be honest, it was actually worse. Since accepting Maks's proposal, she had started dreading being alone with him. That was not right, she knew. Perhaps, she needed time. Perhaps, eventually, she would grow a passion for him?

But Ren's reaction to it was weird. Why did he have to sound so sarcastic? It was not like Ren at all. Then again, he had been snippy lately, sometimes with little or no reason.

Maia had hoped that would conclude her worries about Maks, but it did not. Other worries took their place. She was still an enemy of the Xifarians and everyone she knew was at risk by extension. Was it wise then to agree to get closer to someone new? Was she knowingly endangering Maks?

"Now take your mind off work. Let's just eat." Ori's boisterous voice pulled Maia out of her thoughts.

They feasted on a large fish that had been smoked whole, a medley of roasted vegetables, and a pasty dip that had been made out of ground beans and tasted so wonderful that Maia could not stop gorging on generous dollops of it. Ori grabbed a seat next to her when they were almost through with the food.

"Something bothers the Nosiifarus?" he asked. His question was well intended, but Maia flinched at the name he used to address her. Ori Pistado and his villagers kept calling her "Nosiifarus" even though she insisted time and again that they did not. Convincing them to call her just Maia was a futile venture.

Maia sighed. "Nothing much. I'm just worried about the riddle, that's all. It isn't all about us winning, but I'd hate to see Hilledunn gloat."

Ori's lip jutted out and he nodded. "As I said, you should look into how we got started on Tansi. We don't have all the books they have at the university, so we can't be sure, but that's what the wise ones in the village seemed to think."

"We will," Maia replied. They had already been trying to find out more about the Nouvus, but there was little about it in the books . . . or at least in the books Maia and her friends had managed to dig up so far. But she did not want Ori Pistado saying too much about it. Not just because she worried Hilledunn would find out, but also because she wanted to figure it out on her own.

After the meal, and after profusely thanking Ori and his people for their hospitality and the much-needed break, the gang trooped out. They came across a group of Black Phantoms right outside the village gates. Some of them nodded while a few waved. The groups had almost passed each other when the last of the Black Phantom bumped into Maia. The unexpected collision would have sent her tumbling had it not been for a strong hand that grabbed her by the arm and held her until she steadied herself.

"Thank you," Maia muttered, looking up at the hooded face. The cowl was pulled so low that the face was not visible. He did not even nod, only waited for her to catch her breath before striding off behind his comrades.

"Are you all right, Maia?" Dani asked.

Maia nodded distractedly. The jolt had once again left her seeing auras and suddenly everyone around her flickered in a wave of hues. Maia stared dumbfounded at the man who had collided with her, blinking to keep her eyes from seeing auras, but the aural vision went away as unexpectedly as it had come.

"What's the matter?" Kusha nudged her elbow.

Maia shook her head. "Nothing." Her vision was back to normal now. But Maia was sure she had not just seen the man's indigo and gold aura but also the vivid specks of purple that was characteristic of Xifarians.

She had to have seen it wrong—there was no way Ori Pistado would have a Xifarian in his closest circle. She shook her head again, hoping to clear her memory. "Let's go. We're getting late. Stay here any longer and Hilledunn will send out a cavalry after us."

Ren chuckled loudly. "You got that right."

They set off across the Darkwoods with resolute steps and Maia found herself trailing the group as a thought gnawed her mind. Something was oddly familiar about the man who had bumped into her, only she could not figure out what, no matter how hard she tried.

***

Maia was among the Darkwoods. The air was icy, and she could feel every frozen particle of moisture in it. The silent, towering trees surrounded her with their grayness. For a few moments, she could not recall what she was doing there. Then it came to her in a flash: She was chasing a person cloaked in a Black Phantom cape. She saw him, a dash of darkness in the distance. Fists curled, Maia rushed forward.

Through the cold and misty Darkwoods, they played a game of cat and mouse in an endless and hazy loop. No matter how hard Maia tried, she could not reach him. One moment he was right behind the closest tree, the next he had darted away. Maia didn't give up though. Her feet longed for rest and her throat was parched, but she carried on her quest. She had to get to him. Somehow, anyhow.

She'd almost caught up. Then he vanished. Maia looked. And looked. Other than the thickening mist around her, she saw nothing else. Tired, lost, and hopeless, Maia roamed the bleak forest alone.

A steep ravine opened up under her feet before she knew. She clutched at the air. She screamed but no sound came out. She teetered toward the dark abyss.

An arm grabbed her and pulled her away from the chasm. Heart pounding, Maia turned. It was the person she had been chasing. The hood had fallen off his face and Maia saw him, as clear as daylight.

Miir?

Maia woke up with a start, clutching at the sides of her throbbing head and panting to fill her lungs.

For a while, she only felt relief that she was in the safety of her room and not lost in the Darkwoods. Then the questions streamed in.

Why in the stars did she see Miir? What did it mean? She had no idea. Rayan was sound asleep, and so was Dusty, so Maia lay in her bed, tossing and turning endlessly, dissecting and analyzing what she saw until the sun rays lit up the room.

One thing was clear: her mind was so stuck on thoughts of Miir that it had been cooking up dreams. Another idea, a suspicion rather, needled Maia more. Had the dream been triggered by that Black Phantom who had bumped into her near Ori Pistado's village? The one she thought had an aura with purple flecks? The one she thought was a Xifarian in hiding?

Something about the man had reminded her of Miir. Or perhaps she simply wanted the man to be him. If he were Miir, it would relieve her of the guilt of killing him.

Yes, that had to be it. But Maia also knew she could not be correct. Ori Pistado, of all people, would never have a Xifarian in his team. Therefore, no matter how badly her subconscious wanted Miir to be secretly lurking around, it was nothing but a senseless dream.

***

Maia discovered the note that evening. She would have missed it for a long time if it had not been for Maks who stopped by the study room the contestants had been assigned. Maia and her teammates were hunched around a table, thumbing through notes they had jotted down all day at the Great Library, trying to find any clues they might've missed.

Being up for a good part of the night left Maia groggy and miserable during the day. Since she could not share her thoughts with anyone, she spent the day in a dejected mood trying to forget the senseless dream. She was half-heartedly flipping through her notes when Maks walked in, smiling.

"Hello, guys," Maks said. He walked up to Maia and smiled nervously at everyone.

Nafi waved, Dani greeted him back, Kusha rose to offer his congratulations, but Ren scarcely even looked up at him. And Maia simply wanted to run away to her room and hide.

This was wrong. She was not supposed to feel this way. Maks was supposedly her beau, her heart was supposed to leap every time she saw him, yet her fingers were like icicles. Not too long ago, when they were just friends, seeing Maks always made her happy. But now . . .

Was she scared? Or was she sorry she agreed to be in this relationship?

"Hey, Maia, do you have time to look at something?" Maks said.

She did not have time. They had a lot of work to finish.

"It won't take long," Maks added.

Across the table, Nafi looked quizzically at her.

"All right," Maia said, closing her notebook and grabbing the jacket she had slung over her chair.

The multicolored jacket—a gift from Ori Pistado's elderly aunt—had become a favorite of hers. After the Xifarians murdered her family and destroyed her home in Appian, Maia had no possessions left other than Bellator and a broken pendant her mother had passed down to her. She treasured every little gift she received since then, and this hand-knit gift was particularly precious. She slipped her arms in, buttoned it up to the collar, and shoved her hands into the pockets. Something sharp poked her left hand as soon as she did.

"What in the stars—" Maia blurted.

Everyone looked up.

"What happened?" Maks said, rushing over to her side.

"Something pricked my hand. I don't know what," Maia replied distractedly as she pulled out the offending piece of paper that had been folded multiple times into a tight square with sharp edges. Maia frowned, unable to remember when she had put that in her pocket.

"What's that?" Ren demanded. He snatched it out of Maia's hand when she shrugged. Ren unfolded it and scanned it before closing it hastily.

"Where did you get this?" Ren asked.

Maia shook her head. She had no idea how it got there.

Nafi jumped up. "What does it say? Give it to me," she said.

Ren pulled his arm away from her. "I can't. We need to talk about this." He shot an uncomfortable glance at Maks. "In private."

It took a few moments for Maks to understand. He flushed like a carrot when he did. "I'm sorry. I—"

"Can we meet later, Maks?" Maia blurted. She cringed, immediately realizing it almost sounded like she was eager to get rid of him.

Maks grinned and nodded before walking away hurriedly. It was funny because even though Maia felt sorry for Maks, she was relieved to see him go.

"All right, you got rid of that poor boy. Now show us," Nafi demanded.

Ren did not dawdle. He spread the unfolded piece of paper on their table and read it out aloud. "Check the Origin Scrolls at the Chancery Archives."

Nafi crossed her arms and tapped her feet. "What in the world is that supposed to mean?"

Maia remembered hearing about the Origin Scrolls before. Karhann had mentioned it once to Loriine. But who had put that note in her pocket?

The dorers were always around and they pulled plenty of crazy antics — pushing flowers or candy into her hand, or a note or two saying how highly they thought of her — but Maia would have noticed if someone dropped a note into her pocket.

"Well, the Origin Scrolls are supposed to be the history of our people, the Xifarians," Ren explained. "Other than that, there's no recorded history of us which is . . . strange. Anyway, it's stored in the Chancery Archives."

Bewildered looks flew across the table.

"Maia, when was the last time you checked your pockets?" Kusha asked.

"I don't remember," Maia replied. "I had last put the jacket on yesterday when we visited the village. I don't think that paper was in there then."

"Wait!" Nafi raised a finger skyward. "Could Ori Pistado have slipped it in? He sure was eager to help us solve the riddle."

Maia had to shake her head at the theory even though it could have tied up the mystery neatly. She knew Ori could not have put it there. For one, she had asked him not to help them solve the riddle. Secondly, how could he know about the Origin Scrolls?

"That man," she muttered, and Nafi squinted at her.

"What man?" she demanded.

"The one who bumped into me when we were leaving the village," Maia explained. "He could've slipped something into my pocket when we collided."

"You're forgetting something though," Dani said. "No one but a

Xifarian could've known about the Origin Scrolls or its location. Certainly not Ori Pistado or one of his men."

"I-I . . ." Maia hesitated to tell them about his aura.

"What is it?" Dani asked, her eyes wide.

"The man who I bumped into . . . I saw his aura. I-I think it had purple flecks," Maia blurted. "It was just a flash, but . . ."

Kusha slipped an arm across her shoulder and gave her a squeeze. "Come on, Maia. You couldn't have seen that. There's no way Ori Pistado will have a Xifarian in his team of Black Phantoms. No way."

Maia let out a long sigh. "That's what I thought too. And that's why I didn't tell you guys earlier. I must've hallucinated or something." The thought of the dream she had had later about Miir crossed her mind, but she was not ready to tell them about her rollercoaster of emotions over thinking she had killed Miir, then not killed him, then thinking Miir was the man who had bumped into her. Kusha was correct; there could be no Xifarian among Ori Pistado's people.

"Never mind that," Nafi said. She pointed at the scrap of paper on the table. "The real question is: What does this mean?"

Tugging his hair, Ren bent over the paper. "It's simple really. It means the answers to the riddle will be in the Origin Scrolls."

"Great. How do we get to it?" Nafi asked.

"We have to break into the Chancery, of course." Ren was just as fast with his reply.

"Hold on a moment." Dani jumped to her feet, her hands up in the air. "How do we know the Origin Scrolls are the real thing? That we're not being set up? And even if this were true, following this would be cheating. Not to mention, breaking into the Xifarian Chancery would be a crime."

Looks flew around the table once again. Dani fell back into her chair. "I don't believe you guys. How can you even think of doing this?"

Nafi crossed her arms. "Do you think Hilledunn's fair? Don't you think he's cooking up a plan right now to throw us out of the Initiative?

"Knowing that, you're ready to give him a real cause to throw us out?" Dani countered. "Besides, the other participants had nothing to do with Hilledunn's plan. They don't deserve to be cheated."

Nafi was not about to give in without a fight. "I didn't hear any of them stand up for us or against Hilledunn. They happily took from our stash of Yako. They didn't say a word when Hilledunn penalized us for nothing."

"Wrong is wrong, Nafi," Dani said. "You can't justify your wrongs by quoting someone else's."

Nafi shook her head and turned away in a huff as Kusha, Ren, and Maia exchanged glances. Maia did not know what to do. Nafi was not entirely wrong. The whole Initiative was a sham the Xifarians created to get access to Tansian territories so they could look for the shards they had lost to her mother, Sophie. Did anyone really care about fairness?

Dani was right also. Following the note would count as cheating and Maia did not want to deceive other contestants like Jiri and Anja.

Just then, a thought hit her like a whip and made her stiffen. What if this was not about the riddle at all? What if this was about her? And Sophie? Someone could be trying to give her clues about the Sedara and the light inside her.

"Maia," Dani called, startling Maia. "What do you think?"

Maia did not want to say the words that had formed in her mind, least of all to Dani, but she had to. "Sorry, Dani. I have to see the Origin Scrolls. Not because I want to cheat though. But because I don't think this is about the riddle at all. I think it's about me . . . about my mother and my past."

"You know that . . . how?" Nafi asked.

"First, I told Ori a hundred times to not give us clues. And he happily agreed. I don't think his Black Phantoms would flout his directive," Maia explained. "And then, the note was in my pocket, not in any of yours. Why's that? Because it's for me, only me. This *has* to be about me."

Even though her friends did not look fully convinced, no one debated her points. Maia continued. "So, I have to go, Dani. I have to find a way to get into the Chancery Archives."

Silence crept in as everyone pondered Maia's words. Finally, Kusha spoke. "Maia, we haven't told you, but we're all worried about you going to Xif. You're a target for Phocluus and his cronies, remember? What if they attacked you there? Did you even think about it?"

Maia shrugged. She had thought about it, but briefly. "They won't hurt me while I'm part of the Initiative," she said, recalling the words of the Xifarian chancellor. "The chancellor gave his word to your father, remember? Besides, what can I do? Not go to Xif?"

"We're just worried, Maia," Nafi said. "We even spoke to Kehorkjin about it. He said the sanctity of the Initiative was supreme."

"There you go," Maia said. "That's exactly what the chancellor had told me. And Steward Lok. The sanctity of the Initiative is supreme."

"Well, all right," Nafi said, throwing up her hands in the air. "We trust Kehorkjin enough to stop fretting all the time, but you seriously can't be thinking of sneaking into the Chancery."

"This could very well be a trap," Dani said.

"So what do I do? Ignore it?" Maia asked. "Remember Bikele? He had contacted me in a similar way. If I had been too scared to take up on his invitation, I'd have never heard about my mother or known him."

Years ago during the second phase in Zagran, a stranger had passed a note to her and asked to meet. Even though she was scared, she—along with all her teammates—had gone to meet the weird stranger. It turned out that Bikele had been one of the closest friends of her mother Sophie. He had told Maia all about Sophie, her adventures, and Maia's birth in Zagran. He had told her how he had escorted a dying Sophie and the newborn Maia home to her grandfather. Maia's heart twisted thinking of what came after that, of how the Xifarians had later captured Bikele. She had fought to save him but failed.

"Things are worse now, Maia," Kusha said. "We . . . you can't be taking risks like that anymore."

"You're forgetting something, Kusha. I'm stronger now," Maia said. Even the Xinhagyi was happy with her progress. Lately, she had progressed from shooting measly balls of energy to making specific forms out of it. "I can protect myself."

Kusha sighed. Then he shook his head. "Don't underestimate your enemies, Maia. That's not wise."

Dani placed a hand on Kusha's shoulder and threw a meaningful glance at him. Maia looked away for a moment. She was probably being foolhardy. She thought through the situation one more time and came to the same conclusion as before. She was not about to give up the prospect of finding out more about a mother she never knew.

"Please understand, Kusha," she said, firm in her plea for understanding. "I have to find out everything I can about Sophie. About how she took the heart of the Sedara apart, who helped her, who betrayed her, and why? Anything really."

"Well, there's not a chance I'm letting you go alone," Ren declared. "Even if this has nothing to do with the riddle and everything to do with you, I'm coming."

"Ren, you can't risk your —"

"What I risk is up to me to decide, Maia." Ren snapped. He rapped the table and looked around. "So, who else is in?"

Three more hands shot up in the air in a heartbeat, even Dani's.

Ren got off his chair and handed the note to Maia. "There you go, you have a vote. Now if you'll excuse me, I have a break-in to plan. You can go back to attending to your boyfriend. Sorry I interrupted your grand plans."

Before Maia could even frown at his rather sharp words, Ren had sauntered away. But Maia's worries were far beyond Ren's surly attitude. Doubts had started raising their stubborn little heads already.

Was this the right thing to do? Breaking into the Xifarian

Chancery was an enormous risk, and probably the worst thing for her and the team under the current circumstances. And she had not only suggested risking her own neck but was dragging her friends along also.

Maia took a long breath and pulled the jacket tighter around her. Even then, the flutter of panic in her guts that sent waves of chill up her spine refused to go away.

CHAPTER TWENTY-SIX

RETURN TO XIF

The next few weeks, long and tedious as they were, passed quickly. Bad things happened, good plans were made, and Maia mostly spent them in a miserable state. The thought that her friends were risking their lives trying to break into the Chancery for her was a heavy burden to bear. One particularly foul day stood out.

Both Kusha and Ren had been missing since morning and no one seemed to know where they were. Kusha finally showed up in the evening, his face drawn and brows knit tightly.

"What's the matter?" Dani asked.

"There's bad news," he said, slumping into his chair morosely. "The energy curfews have been getting worse since last winter. The Xifarians hardly send us anything. And the Damoclian Connector isn't ready yet. Remote and smaller settlements have been suffering."

Maia's thoughts flew to Appian, the little village on the Second Continent where she had spent a good part of her life. A year ago, the curfews were bad enough. Even the windmills of Appian could not generate enough energy to make up for the shortfall. Winter had been particularly harsh and cold had been hard to stave off. Some days Maia almost thought Dada would die of the cold. And Appian was still better off than most villages. Most settlements did not even have windmills.

Nafi let out a heavy sigh. "I know," she said. "A village just north of Contes had no power to process drinking water. Many children died last summer."

Maia wondered how Appian was faring and made a mental note to ask Maks about it. "So, what happened, Kusha?" she asked.

"There are a couple of settlements north of ThulaSu. They're usually cut off during winter. Now that the roads are clear people went in to check on them." Kusha paused and rested his head on his palms. Maia waited patiently for him to speak again, bracing for the worst kind of news. "Three villages were frozen to death. All of them. Thirty families in all, including five infants."

There was little to say after that news. They simply sat, stupefied, shaken to the core.

"Who found them?" Maia asked, her voice barely audible.

"Ori Pistado and his Black Phantoms run food drives to the remote villages. This year the blizzards up north have been bad and the passes stayed blocked for longer than usual. The Phantoms couldn't reach them in time."

For a long, heart-wrenching moment, everyone held their breath. Then Nafi slammed the table with both fists. "These blasted Xifarians," she said through gritted teeth. "Haven't seen anyone worse. Who knows how many more are dead that we don't yet know about."

They spent the rest of the evening in a gloom, barely speaking to each other about anything other than Xifarian atrocities. Ren did not show up at all, which was a good thing. Maia was not looking forward to discussing his nation's barbarism with him.

***

The following morning Maia woke up to an envelope sitting on the floor. Someone had slipped it under her door, and it was not that unusual of a thing. Dorers did it all the time, slipping letters, notes, cards, and anything else they could fit through.

Maia poured some kibbles out for Dusty and opened the envelope. Turned out it was from Maks. It was a nice and simple letter that made Maia smile.

> *Maia,*
> *You're busy, I know. I'm not, since our exams just got over. I won't nag you every day, but can we meet once? There's a special rose in the gardens that blooms once in three years. Lucky us, it's blooming now. You might like seeing it.*
>
> *In the afternoon, then? I'll see you at your study.*
> *Maks*

That was an invitation Maia could not refuse. Maks was rather crafty to entice her with a rare bloom to lure her out on a date. She headed for breakfast with a light heart, looking forward to the afternoon's outing with Maks. She found Dani and Nafi at the table stirring bowls of pottage. Maia had just picked a bowl when Sana careened in.

Maia rushed to hug her cousin. As much as she would have enjoyed spending time with Sana, reality had kept them apart. It was not just Maia's engagement in the Initiative, but Sana too had been placed with a private tutor. Even though Sana did not take that happily, Uncle Alasdair was firm.

"If you want to stay for a while in ThulaSu, this is how it's going to be," he had declared.

The tutor kept Sana busy with assignments, and Maia did not see her cousin as much as she would have liked. Sudden visits like this was exciting.

"Sana, nice to see you," Maia said. She suddenly noticed Sana's grim face. "Is everything all right?"

Sana shook her head morosely before slumping into a chair. "A lot of people died this winter. We're getting news from all over Tansi," she said.

Maia balked. "All over Tansi?" Kusha had only told them about the settlements north of ThulaSu.

Sana nodded gravely; her usually vivacious presence was marred by gloom. "Well, they're now sending scout teams to the remote northern settlements in the Second Continent also, and the outlook isn't good. This winter was brutal."

"Why didn't your government ask for more this winter?" Dani said.

Sana scoffed. "It did. The Parliament sent in multiple pleas. They'd even appealed to the Xifarians for lifting the curfew for a few months, but they didn't respond. The curfew actually got worse over winter."

"They are truly a scourge," Maia said morosely. "I wish we could get the Damoclian Connector ready faster."

Work on the Damoclian Connector was going on at a steady pace, but it was not expected to finish until summer. It was too late for most who had to spend the winter with the nominal energy supplies.

Just then, Ren rushed in and the girls fell silent. They had all learned to avoid topics that could start a debate, particularly since Ren seemed to be in a perpetually foul mood.

This morning though he seemed happy. He flashed a bright smile at Sana before slipping into the chair next to her and Maia almost thought his eye twinkled.

"What are you doing here?" Ren asked Sana. "Brightening up our day?"

Sana giggled and her cheeks flushed a little. "You're funny."

"You have no idea," Ren replied with a cheeky smile. He turned to his teammates. "By the way, guys, I have a plan."

Maia held her breath. She had half-wished that Ren would not find a way to get into the Chancery, but knowing Ren, she also knew that possibility was remote.

"Spill," Nafi said, leaning across the table.

"Remember Adienos?" Ren asked.

The girls nodded. Maia remembered Adienos well. He was a business associate of Ren's and the man had helped the team sneak into the Sanctuary of the Stars on Xif years ago.

"Well, he has a good plan to get us in. Turns out, we've been allowed access to the XDA when the classes are off to celebrate Commemoration Week. That's also the time the Chancery hosts the Grand Gala. Remember that?"

Maia nodded. How could she forget? After their win during the Xifarian phase of the competition, the team had been invited to the Grand Gala, but they got involved in thwarting a bigger conspiracy. Maia and Ren barely survived Yoome, an assassin of the R'armimon, and, under the pretext of security, the Xifarian chancellor had revoked the invitation to the gala.

"So, are we going to pretend to be guests at the gala?" Dani asked. "Won't they run biometric security scans on the guests?"

"No, we won't pretend to be guests," Ren said. "We'll sneak in, plain and simple."

Sana had been listening quietly. Now she raised a cautioning hand. "Should I even be part of this conversation?" she asked. "I don't think I should know this."

Maia had expected Ren to shoo Sana off just the way he had Maks the other day, but he did not. Even after Sana's timely question, he waved her concern away.

"It's nothing," he said with a roguish smile. "We're just breaking into the Chancery on Xif, that's all."

"You are a little crazy too," Sana commented. "I have nothing against break-ins, but I think it's wise to keep it between you. I'm an outsider; I don't need to know."

"You're no outsider," Ren protested. "You're Maia's family. Which means you're family to all of us. Right, girls?"

Dani responded with a nod and a smile, but Nafi's eyes narrowed.

"Thank you for being so welcoming," Sana said. As she bowed her head in appreciation, silky curls tumbled around her flawless face.

Ren chuckled. "You get a welcome hug too," he said before pulling Sana into a quick embrace.

Maia's insides swelled, thankful that Ren was kind to her cousin and they could all be friends. Ren was correct—Sana was a spot of happiness in their day.

***

The day was turning cloudy when Maia and Maks walked along the ramparts to the bowers. As hard as Maia wished to keep the conversation light, it turned gloomy quickly when Maks shared news of more deaths reported from the Second Continent.

"You should be able to do something, Maia," Maks said as they walked down the stairs leading into the garden. "After all, they're afraid of you."

"How, Maks? They've left me alone for a bit, that's true. But what can I do to them? Nothing, really."

"Then who can? Aren't we supposed to fight back? There has to be a way to make them pay."

"The Damoclian Connector is our best way out of their clutches," Maia said. "And making them pay? Well, I don't see that happening."

"Not fair," Maks grumbled.

Maia did not reply. This was a lengthy discussion and one that had no promising conclusions. Every Solianese child had to learn to live with unfairness; Maia had as well. At least now, the Jjord were helping them rebuild the Connector. That was something.

"Where's that flower you spoke of, Maks?" Maia asked, hoping to divert the conversation.

"This way, come on."

He led her down a narrow path that weaved through the bowers, charming little nooks built out of vines and creepers. Girls and boys were scattered about, most of them chatting. Maia caught sight of a few holding hands as well. The bowers were indeed "the perfect stage for a lovefest," as Nafi had put it.

Maia's heart fluttered a little faster. What if Maks wanted to hold her hand?

"Watch your step, Maia," Maks called. The road was narrow and slippery along the hedges and the surface gravelly. Maia had to tread with care, balancing herself as she walked. At the second turn where the path descended steeply before opening up to a spectacular vista of the western Darkwoods, Maks held out a hand.

"Hold my hand, Maia. Might help," he said.

Maia's heart skipped a beat before annoyance made her flush crimson. Why did he think she needed to hold his hand? Was it because that was expected on a date? Or was it because he thought she needed protecting?

"What's wrong?" Maks asked, his hand still extended.

"Nothing." Maia bit the inside of her cheek and lied. She was overthinking it, she had to be. She placed her hand in Maks's and together they made down the incline to a little ledge. A medley of shrubs lined the backside but a plant with bright red foliage stood out among it. Scattered over it were buds, each as large as Maia's fist. A couple had bloomed already and Maia forgot about everything else as she stared in awe at them.

"That's the ThulaSuian Midnight Blaze rose," Maks whispered as if speaking any louder would offend the blooms. "Come on, look closer."

The petals were indeed the color of midnight, but what astonished Maia was the fine golden veins that spread like a web over their surface. She held her breath as she stared open-mouthed at the exquisite flower. She did not even notice when Maks slipped an arm over her shoulder and pulled her closer.

"There are lots of them in the mountains up north but only a few of these in ThulaSu. This one belongs to Nisa, Aman, and me. We discovered it. We kind of keep it a secret."

That explained why there was not a long line of people surrounding the rose bush.

"You brought me here, so it isn't a secret anymore," Maia said. She turned to look at Maks, suddenly realizing how close he was.

"You're special," he said.

Her heart did not do a somersault the way it was supposed to. Maia only wanted to peel Maks's arm off her shoulder and jump away. Something was not right, this could not be right, but she could not move . . . at all.

"You know what they say about the Midnight Blaze?" Maks asked.

Maia did not know. Even if she did know she could not have answered him, because she was numb, her mind frozen.

"If you kiss in front of it, your souls are matched forever."

Kiss? Maia wanted to run, but her feet did not budge. Maks leaned forward, his head wiping out the view of the reddish sun that had just peeked out of the cloud. Maia braced herself, watching helplessly as Maks leaned closer still . . .

***

Maia rushed into the study room a little after sundown to find all her teammates crowded around their table. Nafi raised a curious eyebrow as soon as Maia reached the table.

"Did you guys kiss?" she asked, the hint of a smile quivering at the corners of her lips.

Maia slumped into a chair before nodding. Ren smirked, barely able to stop laughing. "You don't seem impressed," he said. "He wasn't any good, was he?"

"I wouldn't know," Maia blurted. "I don't exactly go around kissing everyone I meet."

Ren broke into a throaty guffaw. "I knew he was useless."

"Ren, what a thing to say," Dani said. She stole a furtive look at

Kusha. "First kisses are always . . . not the greatest. You get better with . . . practice."

Nafi nudged Dani in the ribs and smiled evilly. "How many tries did it take you and Kusha to get better?"

"Shut up, Nafi," Kusha snapped. "And leave Maia alone, Ren. Maks is fine."

"I agree," Dani said, throwing a meaningful look at Ren. "Let's instead talk about what Kusha and I found today."

Kusha flashed a bright smile at Maia. "Yes, Maia, we found some important information. I think." He pushed a page of notes toward her. "Remember the Nouvus? That's what brought our ancestors, the first settlers, to Tansi. It's supposed to be this enormous craft, large enough to house a million people at least and provisions."

"That big?" Maia's eyes grew wider. "A million people?"

"Yes. They traveled in hibernation pods for hundreds of years before they reached their destination. One fine day, they woke up to find themselves on Tansi," Dani explained. "Anyway, the curious part is that no one seems to know what happened to that humongous craft. We don't see it on Tansi, do we? It's like our Nouvus simply vanished."

It suddenly started to make sense. That was what the verse said: *One brought us home, and then lay in forever rest . . .*

"It lay down for eternal rest, right?" Maia sat up, the wheels in her brain spinning in frenzy. "What if the first settlers buried it somewhere?"

Nafi shook her head. "I doubt that. Can you imagine how large the Nouvus must've been? They'd have to have dug extremely deep into the ground to fit it. You think they had the time to do all that when they had a new planet to settle?"

"Besides," Ren chimed in, tapping his chin thoughtfully, "you guys say you've never seen or heard of any memorials for the Nouvus. How could they hide it completely? And why would they want to hide such a marvelous thing anyway?"

Kusha fell back in his chair and stretched. "Well, that's what we need to figure out. I'm pretty sure we're supposed to find the final resting place of our Nouvus. That's the purpose of this challenge."

"Yes. And if you want my advice, less kissing and more studying would help," Nafi commented wisely.

Ren chuckled and Nafi joined in, even Dani's cautionary glare could not stop them. Maia flushed and thought of retorting but in the end, simply let them be. At least, she decided, it was nice having some silly laughter back in their lives.

CHAPTER TWENTY-SEVEN

AT THE CHANCERY

The trip to Xif started another week later in the early morning. A couple of days before that, Everrol had dropped off instructions for the trip. He took care to not see anyone and left them at the team's study table after they had retired for the night. That left Dani in a livid mood. However, making preparations for the trip did not allow anyone to brood over Everrol for too long.

On the day of the journey, all contestants assembled at the central courtyard near the Sun Temple. Master Kehorkjin was already waiting, his sharp eyes sweeping the gathering over and over again. Their transport Pod, an orb flown by the gray-skinned Tokii, had arrived before daybreak. It was weird how small the orb seemed now compared to two years ago when she had first seen them, Maia mused. Things had changed . . . a lot, and so had she.

The trip to the Xifarian spaceport of Arpasgula was just as exciting though, and everything felt new. It brought back many memories.

"Remember how we fought Lex here," Dani recalled, chuckling as they waited at one of the docks.

It seemed a lifetime away that they had flown into Xif for the first time. A gigantic spacecraft, a Fahrbot, had arrived to pick them up then. This time, a smaller craft, an Aroflot, came instead. Even though it was not as majestic as the Fahrbot, this craft was just as elegant and efficient. It passed through the airlocks that led into the belly of Xif and emerged from the *hole in the sky* just as gracefully.

The view of the Xifarian cities stretching from horizon to horizon under them, the buildings glittering in the early light of the Sedara, Xif's artificial sun, did not fail to take Maia's breath away. Just like the last time, the craft weaved through the buildings and landed on the perfectly manicured lawns of the XDA.

Maia took a deep long breath before stepping out on the grounds. Behind her, Nafi sighed.

"Here's hoping we have a safe stay," Nafi whispered.

Maia hoped the same, particularly since their plans involved breaking into one of the most secure buildings on Xif, the Chancery. Doubts she had always had, but now the question if this was the right thing to do loomed in her mind. She had learned to listen to her gut, and her initial gut feeling was that someone was trying to tell her something, and those answers would be found in the Chancery. But now that they were actually here, Maia wondered if she was being blinded by her thirst for wanting answers and ignoring the dangers.

Ren smiled brightly as they walked up the XDA stairs. "Why so glum?" he asked, his brows dancing. He placed his hand over his heart and gave a quick bow. "Have some faith in your friend. I'm good at this. And Adienos has it all figured out."

***

Ren herded the team out of the XDA grounds that evening through an unmanned side gate. While Ren sauntered out proudly, Maia's steps were slow. Even though she wanted to think she was tired from the day's work, she knew it was from fear.

The day had been truly long and tiring, as well as useless for the most part. Jiri and his team had found some information, but the other teams had a fruitless search at the library. When they had retired for the night, most faces were long. The plan was to leave early the following morning so the despair was not entirely misplaced.

Maia and her teammates were both worried and excited about their night trip, so they did not have time to wallow in misery for too long. There were plans to be gone over, communicators to be tested, and gear to be packed. Now, as the transporter shuttle drew closer to the Chancery, Maia's heart thudded like a war drum and her fingers grew icy. No one spoke. No one even looked at each other until the transporter left them among the thronging crowds near the Chancery.

The Xifarian Chancery was undoubtedly one of the grandest buildings Maia had ever seen. At the same time beautiful and formidable, the structure made of bright beige stone towered at one end of Boulevard Central that cut right through the heart of Armezai, the Xifarian capital. The night air was not warm, but a chill crept into Maia's heart as she stood staring at the massive structure.

"Let's keep moving. We have to leave here before the stardust falls," Ren said.

The shower of the stardust was a light show that happened only during Commemoration Week. It was quite a spectacle, with shooting stars coming out of the Sedara, Xif's artificial internal star. Xifarians gathered at the capital city from far and near to watch the falling of stardust. The wild frenzy of thousands of visitors was the perfect cover to sneak in or out of the Chancery.

Ren led the group toward the side of the Chancery, away from the enormous guarded gates. He tugged at the thick bars of the fence when they neared the middle of Chancery grounds. This side was some distance away from the main street and almost deserted. Ren went on tugging, one bar at a time, until one came loose. He threw a quick look around and pushed it up. Then he moved on to the bar next to it. Soon he had made an opening in the fence large enough for everyone to crawl through.

"Let's go. Get in," he said.

Once everyone was inside the Chancery grounds, Ren put the bars back in place.

"Stay behind me," Ren said. "I know the path through the guard zones and we have to keep within that. Don't stray. All right?"

He started across the gardens, leading them away from the building's main staircase that rose in an elegant curve to meet the tall front doors inlaid with metallic motifs. Across the darkened grounds crisscrossed by neat walkways and plentiful trees, Ren crept forward, aiming for the shaded rim below the windows lining the right wing of the house. He did know how to weave through the guard zones; stopping, sprinting, and tiptoeing through the garden and precisely avoiding the guards.

The façade of the Chancery followed a pattern, Maia noted—a set of ten windows clustered together followed by a large doorway that opened into a balcony that overlooked the grounds, and then another cluster of windows. And so it went on repeating about ten times until the end of the right wing.

A mellifluous note reached Maia's ears as soon as they had reached the first sprawling balcony. The doors might have been left ajar, she deduced. Instead of relishing the soft melody, Maia bristled with anger. While on the dusty planet next door, everyone was scrambling for survival, entire villages were freezing to death, the Xifarians were busy celebrating.

Callous, as always!

"The gala we never attended, huh?" Nafi whispered to Maia.

"We have to find the vent under the third balcony," Ren said in an admonishing tone. "It will be difficult to spot in the dark, so focus. We don't want to draw the attention of the guards with the chitchat."

"Yes, sir," Nafi muttered, sarcasm brimming in her voice.

Maia wanted to talk about the inappropriateness of the festivities herself, but they needed to focus to reach the archives in time. She moved along, picking up pace as they crossed under the brightly lit windows.

"Should be around here." Ren kneeled as the group gathered in the shadow of the third balcony, its bulbous form hanging over them like an oversized upside-down umbrella. They found the vent quickly—the rectangular grille that sat on the wall. Warmth from inside the building seeped out through it.

"Pull it," Ren said, gripping one end of the grille. "It's supposed to come off."

"You sure it won't set off alarms?" Nafi asked as she found a grip herself.

"I trust Adienos with my life. I've known him longer than I've known you," Ren snapped. Maia noted the grimness in his voice; it was hard to ignore how surly Ren had become of late. The Ren she had known all these years had vanished; suddenly, he had turned serious, inhospitable, and even a tad unkind. "You want to do this, or what?"

"We're doing exactly what you have asked of us, Ren," Dani said in a soft tone to calm the air.

No one spoke after that. All hands were on the grille, and just as Adienos had informed, it gave way easily, noiselessly, and without sounding any alarms. One by one, Maia and her friends descended through the opening and into the room inside. Maia felt the vibration as soon as she set foot on the darkened floor. It was an unnerving sensation, one that left her breathless for a moment or two.

"We're right above the shafts that lead into the exhausts," Ren said hastily. "The stairs are up on that side. Come on, follow me."

"What exhausts, Ren?" Nafi asked as they all followed Ren through the floor strewn with a multitude of machinery that generated a collective dull cacophony.

"They're air vents," Ren replied. "Remember, we're inside the crust of a planet and the air inside has to be continuously regulated and monitored. If that purification stops for a moment, the stale air could kill everyone. The shafts are constructed right under the surface at regular distances, and of course, every building has vents of its own."

"Yilosario does all the monitoring, right?" Maia asked, recalling the super powerful automaton that took care of maintaining the complex atmosphere inside Xif.

"Yes, Yilosario and Second," Ren replied, nodding. "They take care of the air systems. Without them, we'd suffocate and die."

"Scary," Kusha commented. "Don't say anymore, Ren, please. It's no fun imagining being trapped inside a box unable to breathe."

No one needed to discuss the unpleasant matter anymore as Ren found the door out of the room. They filed out of the dingy room that was filled with machines into a dimly lit corridor that stretched on both sides.

"The archives are on the top floor. Should we take those stairs?" Dani pointed at the staircase that peeked from about three doors away.

"Of course not," Ren replied, quickly looking over the map that Adienos had given him. "We can't be running up and down the Chancery stairs. We have to use a far more difficult route."

"Difficult? How?" Maia wondered what route Adienos has suggested. Difficult she could manage, but she was anxious to know how risky the path could be.

"We have to climb through the exhaust pipeline all the way up to the roof."

Maia's heart picked up the pace. *This isn't a good idea,* she thought. But then, this whole venture was probably their most perilous one ever.

"This one has a notice on it." Dani pointed at the door right next to where the group was standing. A large sign was stuck on the dark panel. "Keep Out: DANGER OF HIGH WINDS," it said.

Ren looked at his map again, then he looked up and nodded solemnly. "Yes, that should be it," he said before striding forward.

Nothing could have prepared Maia for the sight that lay on the other side of that ordinary-looking door. The carpeted floor under her feet had morphed into a mesh of dark metal that hung at the rim of a deep well. They had entered from the side of an endless cylindrical shaft, Maia realized quickly. It stretched from below the surface to the rooftop of the Chancery. She looked up; right above them was another door, likely an entrance into the ventilation shaft from the floor above. Maia craned her neck looking for more such doors, finding two more before the walls faded into the darkness above.

"We have to climb five floors," Ren announced, referencing his map once again. "See those rungs?"

He pointed at the wall next to them where there was a series of rungs enclosed inside the same metallic mesh that they were standing on. The series of rungs stretched upward toward the door above.

"What are we waiting for?" Nafi asked. "Let's climb."

"No, not yet," Ren said. "The fans will start any moment now. The turbulence will be too much to endure when the fans are on. We have to strap ourselves to the grill and wait it out when the fans start. Once the timer is clear, we will get back in and start climbing."

A zillion butterflies sprouted in Maia's stomach.

We have to strap ourselves to the grille while the exhaust is blowing? What if the belt snaps?

"And then wait it out again at the next level?" Kusha asked.

"Well, Adienos said we should be able to easily make it through three floors during one quiet cycle of the fans. We'll see. I'll have to time it first. There, the fans are starting up again."

Maia heard the low hum start somewhere far down in the darkness below. It was faint now, but the sound was growing stronger by the moment.

"Here, Maia." Ren held out a body harness; two belts hung from the middle of it, each with a sturdy buckle at its end. "Slip it on and hook the buckle onto the mesh of the floor," he instructed.

The hum was louder now, but that was not what unnerved Maia. It was instead the vibration. But this was nothing compared to what came next. Maia hunkered down on the floor, keeping her body as far away as possible from the path of the wind that roared through the confines of the channel, but it felt like she could be ripped out of the hold and tossed around like a twig had it not been for the anchors that secured her. She held her breath, praying to the stars that the harnesses Adienos provided were sturdy enough. And they were, unflappably withstanding the ferocity of the winds.

As soon the cycle ended and the hum died down, Maia took a long deep breath. Who knew it could be so hard to breathe with the fans blowing on them?

"Let's go, guys," Ren instructed. "We have to do this as quickly as we can."

Ren led the way, hoisting himself up into the tubular covering over the rungs and climbing forward. Nafi and Dani followed next; Maia and Kusha were at the end.

They climbed with all their strength and will, as quickly as they could. But the climb was tiring, and even with the rugged gloves she wore, Maia's palms burned from grabbing the coarse rungs and her arms hurt from the climb. It felt like an eternity had passed before Ren shouted from above them.

"Level three coming up, guys. The timer is almost at the end as well," he yelled. "We have to wait it out here."

Soon they had all reached the extension around the door at level three. Maia was halfway up and Kusha just below her at the second level. Maia was pushing forward hastily when Kusha groaned.

"My hook just broke," he said with a frustrated yell.

"Both?" Ren asked.

"One, the other is just fine."

Below them, a faint hum had come to life.

"You have to get out, Kusha," Ren said. "Can't be in here with just one strap working. You have to get into the passage outside and find a place to wait it out. Here, take the timer. When it's over, come back in. We will head up as soon as the quiet cycle begins."

The hum below was growing in strength.

"He has to go out there?" Maia asked, worried. "Alone?"

"These are the main levels, Maia," Ren replied. "It will be hard for all five of us to find a place to hide quickly enough."

"I'll be fine, Maia," Kusha had slipped the harness off, ready to walk out the door at the second level.

Maia glanced at Dani at the platform above; her face had paled. Maia knew Dani would be the last person to say anything. Only two days ago, Dani and Kusha had a huge argument about her worrying too much about everything. But even if Dani could not say anything did not mean that Maia had to stay silent.

This was the Chancery of Xif, the home of the supreme ruler of a ruthless and powerful nation. It was the night of the Grand Gala and chances were, most of the guards were in the room where the gala was in progress. But what if someone noticed Kusha? What chance did he stand alone? There was no way she was going to let him venture out on his own.

"I'll come with you," Maia declared, rushing down the rungs.

"But—" Kusha began protesting but the wind picked up just then. Maia grabbed his arm and pushed him out of the door and into a wide passageway wrapped in opulent red carpet.

All that red, the incredible softness that almost engulfed Maia's feet, distracted her for a bit. Then she remembered to look around. On their two sides, the corridor stretched to the distance. Luckily, there were no guards or people on this floor, on either side. It was likely that guards were by the entryways rather than the inner passages. Large, ornate doors, etched in red and gold, stood along the length of the corridor. Music and laughter drifted in from their right, and the music was extremely pleasing, Maia had to admit. Kusha stepped closer to the door next to the exhaust room, and Maia followed.

"It's just an empty storage room," Kusha whispered as he peeked inside cautiously. "We can use it to hide. Come on in."

The music ceased right about then.

"Thank you all for being here tonight," a voice rang out. It was the smooth, stony voice of the Xifarian chancellor, a voice that Maia would never forget. Years ago, it had coldly threatened her. "Tonight is very important for me and my family, and I am happy for this opportunity to share some special news with you."

Maia was sure Kusha's face mirrored her own curiosity. He

clearly hesitated at the door of the storage room, debating whether they should ignore the speech and step inside its safety.

"That's the chancellor," Maia said, watching Kusha's eyes grow wider. Maia waited. She knew it was risky for them to be standing there. But the temptation to watch the gala was too strong.

The chancellor's voice boomed again. "You already know the delightful news. I am a proud grandfather now."

Claps rose and reverberated through the building. Something inside Maia twisted painfully at the unfairness of it all. She remembered her grandfather's face, and she remembered how they had taken Dada away from her. She found herself walking, stepping forward in the direction of the sound.

"Today, I proudly share the name of my grandson, the firstborn of my son Remii and his wife, Lyssa. Please meet Koriin Alyss."

The clapping started again, and a wave of "oohs" and "aahs" rose immediately after.

Maia stepped forward with urgency. She *had* to see this; she had to find a place from where she could watch. Kusha was following her closely, guarding her back, but Maia would not have cared if he did not. She walked forward with the sole purpose of seeing the face of her tormentors, seeing their happiness, etching their laughter in her memory. Someday she was going to make them pay and this memory would help her along. Then she found it—a small nook between two columns that looked into the spellbinding ballroom below.

"Wow," Kusha whispered, and that was all he could say. Maia stared, her disbelieving eyes taking in the splendor of the magnificent scene that lay below.

The hall was huge, decorated in red and gold. Silvery white columns ran around the perimeter, their girths wrapped in wide ribbons of red. About twenty chandeliers hung from the tastefully frescoed ceiling, the crystals glittering in a daze-inducing beauty. The floor was a sea of color and sparkles, as men and women swirled around. Many of the men were wearing uniforms, and most women wore colorful gowns that swept across the floor. All their outfits were embellished with crystals and gems and encrusted with precious metals, and they caught the light and shimmered like a sea of sparkles.

Maia's gaze quickly moved to the people standing on the sizeable dais at one end of the room. The Xifarian chancellor was smiling. Next to him was his elder son Remii and a woman with pale gold hair who Maia deduced was Lyssa, Remii's wife. She was holding a fluffy bundle in her arms, the baby Koriin.

Maia's eyes scanned the crowd for Miir, desperately hoping she would find him. She did not. Fear that she had killed him at Devil's Ridge came surging back. She fought the thought back down with a forceful hand. The chancellor would not look so happy if his son was dead. He would be mourning. All of Xif would have known if Miir was dead. Ren would have known. Miir was alive. He had to be.

But why was he not here?

A new thought swirled in Maia's mind: *Where is the chancellor's wife?* Why were some of the chancellor's family missing on this momentous occasion?

Asiyaah, the chancellor's wife and Miir's mother had been Sophie's teacher and friend. According to Bikele, Asiyaah was the one who had led Sophie into destroying the heart of the Sedara, in turn stopping Xif from flying out of the Tansian system. Zaara had said even more: Asiyaah had betrayed Sophie.

A sharp nudge made Maia tumble out of her thoughts. "Maia, we need to leave now," Kusha said. Her eyes lingered on the assembly, on the chancellor and his family, looking, searching for a familiar face.

"Maia," Kusha muttered irritably, tugging her by the arm. "We have to go. Now!"

They had to go, and she left with even more questions. Kusha dragged her back to the door to the vent and pushed her back into the air duct, and all she could think about was Miir and Asiyaah.

Chapter Twenty-Eight

Old Scores, New Wounds

Soon they were all up on the expansive roof of the Xifarian Chancery. The nippy night air shook Maia a little and cleared her mind some. She looked around, scanning the view.

"So, where are the archives?" Maia asked. Her teammates were hunched around Ren's map. Dani held up a minuscule LumTorch that showered light on the paper.

"Right here." Ren jabbed a finger on the map, then looked up and pointed toward a darkened dome in the distance that rose skyward from the roof. "My guess would be that dome right there."

"Let's go then." Nafi rose to her feet almost immediately.

"We should split up," Ren said as he folded the map and placed it carefully inside his coat. "There's a stairwell entrance a few blocks away and I don't know . . . guards might come up to check it. Someone needs to be here, make sure that our path back to the exhaust shaft is clear."

"Why don't you stay here with Maia?" Nafi said, looking Kusha in the eye. "The rest of us can find the archives and do what needs to be done."

"You expect me to stay here?" Maia blurted. "This is my mission. You came here for *me*. I should get to the archives."

"You're the one with the bounty on her head, so to speak," Nafi retorted. "What do you think will happen if you get caught in there? Besides, you might get swept up in your sightseeing sprees and spend too much time enjoying the views."

Maia did not fail to detect the tone of reproach in Nafi's voice. She had a point; Maia had been distracted by the gala for a moment or two, but she was not about to take Nafi's rebuke quietly.

"I can't let you guys risk your lives while I save my skin out here."

"You don't have a choice," Ren declared. "You have to. That's the team's decision."

Maia was about to retort, but Dani slipped an arm around her. "Please, Maia. Let's not waste time arguing. Stay here. We'll be fine."

"All right," Maia said after a moment, letting out an enormous sigh. "I'll stay here, no big deal."

"Fine," Ren said and walked over to Dani and Nafi. "Let's go."

"Sorry, Kusha. I shouldn't have lingered near the balcony. But seeing them in the flesh . . . I forgot where I was," Maia said as soon as Ren and the girls had disappeared into the darkness.

A sliver of uncomfortable silence hung in the air before Kusha spoke. "Maia, we're past the 'sorrys' and 'thank-yous,' don't you think?"

"But, still — "

"I know what you've been through, Maia. We all do," Kusha interrupted. "You don't have to justify your actions, to me or any of your friends. We don't need any explanations. We feel your pain, but we don't want to see you in danger either."

"I endangered all of you, not just myself."

Kusha reached out to pat Maia's shoulder. "Don't kill yourself over that, Maia," he said. "Truth is, if we get caught here, you're the one who has the most to lose, not us. If they find you, they won't care about us. If Nafi is yelling at you, it's more because she is scared that she might not be able to get you back home safely, and less because she is afraid for herself."

He was right, Maia thought as the duo settled down near the vent. She had to take better care of herself. She had to be less impulsive, and she had to trust her friends more.

Not much time had passed when she heard the sound of footfalls pounding up the stairs. Maia froze, as did Kusha next to her. Maia's gaze scooted to the exhaust vent behind them—the cover lay open, and anyone coming out to check the roof would notice right away. But there was no time to put it back in place. It had taken a lot of pushing to get the grille open, and it had made some noise as well. If they tried closing it now, it would only draw more attention.

"We have to hide," Kusha whispered.

They rushed to the side of the stairwell, trying to find cover under the shadow of the eaves. The creak of the door opening stilled Maia's heart for a moment. She held her breath, hoping that whoever had come out onto the roof would not notice the open shaft or venture in the direction of the library.

It was a woman in a dark gown. She walked across the roof toward the edge beyond the open exhaust. As she strolled past the vent, Maia let out a sigh of relief, hoping that she would soon be gone and not notice. Maia stared at the woman's silhouette as she reached the wall that ran along the edge of the roof and sat down on it. The woman stared, in a melancholy sort of posture, across the grounds and up at the Sedara.

The sharp note of an air instrument wafted through the air and Maia let her mind drift for just a moment, a vision of the chancellor's family downstairs flashing across her mind. The pain in her heart grew again. This was so unfair. They did not deserve any happiness.

No! Stop! Maia chided herself. *Focus!*

She could not drift into thoughts of revenge again. The Xinhagyi had warned her enough.

Maia looked back at the woman. She was wearing a vivid green gown, her deep red hair swept up in an elaborate style. The Sedara flashed brightly for a moment, and in that instant, Maia recognized the woman. She was one of the fiends who had descended upon Appian to kill her family. A stinging dryness spread inside Maia like wildfire.

"Kusha, it's Amanii," she whispered in Kusha's ear, and she felt Kusha stiffen.

What was Amanii doing up here? Why was she alone? Amanii was engaged to Miir. Her place was among the chancellor's family, with Miir, not up here on the roof, and certainly not alone.

"Wait and watch," Kusha said.

Maia hoped she would leave soon. And she did . . . almost. Amanii started back across the roof. She had crossed the vent and was barely a few paces from the stairwell when she stopped suddenly. Maia clenched her teeth. Amanii had to have noticed the open vent, and that was not good news.

"What should we do?" Kusha muttered under his breath as Amanii took slow steps toward the open vent. Maia did not know what to do other than they had to stop her. Maia had fought Amanii before and she knew Amanii would give them a tough fight, but the options were clear: They had to stop her or risk getting caught. And the choice was obvious.

"Confront her?" she said, watching tensely as Amanii pulled out a lamp similar to a LumTorch from her pocket and placed it on the floor. Then she kneeled next to the open cover. Maia held her breath until Amanii pulled out a rectangular receptacle from her pocket. Maia and Kusha looked at each other, both realizing that it was a communicator. They had seen Miir use something similar once. They were done for!

"You stay hidden, all right?" Kusha whispered to Maia. Then he turned toward Amanii and shouted, "Hey!"

Maia did not miss the hint of a tremble in Kusha's voice. She held her breath and braced for the worst as Kusha stepped forward.

"Who's that?" Amanii rose to her feet in a flash, and she drew a sword out in the next instant. She stared, her luminous eyes fixed on the darkness that shielded Kusha and Maia.

"Hello, Amanii," Kusha stepped out.

"Aren't you . . . Kusha?" The surprise in her voice was clear. "What are you doing here?"

"Um . . . we needed to pick up something from here," Kusha said awkwardly. "We'll be gone soon."

"You what?" Amanii took a step forward, sheathing her sword. "You think you can just barge into the Chancery to pick up anything you want, just like that?"

Maia fidgeted. She knew she could not reveal herself. She knew Kusha had told her not to. It was not safe to face Amanii. She would lose control. Yet, the urge to confront Amanii was growing stronger with every passing moment.

Amanii kept talking. "Did you break in through there? What exactly are you trying to do? Kill someone?"

"Come on, Amanii." Kusha managed an awkward chuckle. "Why would we kill anyone? Why would you think that?"

"I didn't—"

"Because that's what they do, Kusha," Maia said, words slipping past her lips in a cold, endless stream. "They kill because they enjoy doing it. They kill because they can." Maia stepped out of the shadows.

Amanii stared. "Maia? Is it really you?"

"It *is* me. The same Maia whose family you murdered, remember?"

Amanii took a step forward, her gaze scanning Maia's face. "I can't believe you dared to set your filthy foot in Xif, and the Chancery no less."

Maia's insides twitched. Where was her remorse for killing Dada? For setting fire to Hen's Beak that wiped out five families in Appian?

"You think I should've asked for your blessing before I came here?"

Amanii let out a long, jeering laugh. "Aren't you arrogant? Have you any idea what we'll do to you when we throw you into prison? You should've asked your mother. Oh, wait, that stupid woman's dead. Dead because she messed with us."

"Don't fall for it, Maia," Kusha whispered. "She's only trying to provoke you."

Maia knew that. She was not going to go crazy and erupt into flames, but she also had to teach Amanii a lesson.

"Try throwing me into prison, Amanii. Let's see how far you go," Maia said with a chuckle. "Want to try now?"

Amanii did not reply. She did not even move.

Maia laughed. "I didn't think so."

"You think your creepy, glowy powers will save you, Maia?" Amanii retorted. "For how long?"

"It's saving me now," Maia said coldly. "You aren't in a hurry to attack me, are you? Oh, I forgot. You prefer attacking helpless people like my Dada."

Amanii's gaze wavered a tad and a merciless pain twisted Maia's insides. *Cowards!*

"You killed my old and sick grandfather. You and Remii and Miir. Dada had never hurt anyone." Words spewed out of Maia. She could barely see through the raging fire that clouded her mind. "You enjoyed taking his life, didn't you?"

"It had to be done," she yelled. "You needed to get the message loud and clear."

Maia scoffed. "Of course. Are you proud?"

"I asked you to surrender," she said, her voice loud. "Miir asked you to surrender. Did you? Well, you should have."

"I'll only surrender in your dreams," Maia snapped. The fire was searing her insides.

"Then you're responsible for your family's death. Not us. You should've known what was coming," she retorted. "You should've known we'd strike back."

"Yes, you're right. It was *my* mistake," Maia almost screamed. "I didn't think you and your beau would sink so low."

Amanii gave a wry chuckle. "You worry way too much about my beau."

"I don't care about him," Maia retorted. "All I know is that I'll make you pay. All of you. For murdering Dada and Herc and Emmy."

"I don't know where you'll find him, but you have me," Amanii said, spreading her arms to her sides in mock submission. "You should know, I suggested burning down that wretched house of yours."

The wave crashed, flowing up from the pit of her stomach to the tips of her fingers. It was not a calm, controlled stream, nothing like the ones she invoked during her training with the Xinhagyi. But it felt good nonetheless. Maia saw how Amanii's expression changed from a mocking smile to wide-eyed disbelief. And then the fear Maia was hoping to see. She tittered inside.

Amanii would know fear by the time she was done with her.

"Maia," Kusha yelled. "Stop. Don't fall for this."

She had to. She needed to show them her true power.

"Maia," Kusha shouted again. "It's not worth the risk. Don't."

She had to do it nice and slow. Tease her. Torture her. Make her feel helpless like Dada must've felt.

Blinding white light glowed around her hand, waiting to be unleashed. Amanii had pulled out her sword again, but before she could raise it, Maia said the word the Xinhagyi had taught her.

"*Yoteh!*"

Only, she did not utter it as softly as he had told her to, or as calmly. She spat it out, and along with it hatred.

The light tore through the darkness. It swung at Amanii. She fell back a step and raised her left hand trying to defend herself. The light rebounded in a fiery wave back into Maia's outstretched arms.

Amanii had formed a TEK shield, Maia realized, a crude and weak one. Maia calmed her thoughts, squinting to figure out the forms Amanii had conjured. She had formed a flimsy bubble around herself. Amanii had no idea of the power she was about to encounter.

Maia let out another blast of light. It hit Amanii's shield and carved an opening in it in an instant. Amanii fell back, her face pale with terror, as the light ripped her defense apart and flicked at her face.

Amanii raised her arms again, and this time she formed a wall. Maia could not stop laughing. *Really? A wall?*

"Maia, don't," Kusha yelled frantically behind her.

But Maia was too busy exacting revenge. She unleashed another wave, a special form that she had only been able to create recently. It coiled out of her hands and snaked toward Amanii at a slow and deliberate pace.

"Afraid of me now, Amanii?" Maia asked, chuckling. "Don't you wish you'd never crossed my path? Never hurt my family?"

Amanii's eyes widened, but Maia did not see the remorse she was hoping for. Instead, they were filled with derision.

"I wish Miir was here to see your real character. I was correct. I knew you were no better than anyone else. You're worse. You're a traitor, just like your mother. And a savage killer too."

The light leaped over the wall and jumped at Amanii. She tried to cut it with her sword, but the piece of metal was no match for the power of the light. It wound around Amanii, picked her up in the air, and tossed her to the ground.

Amanii yelped as she hit the floor. She rolled across the length of the roof, crashing against the wall. As Maia pulled apart the remnants of the formation back into her, Kusha rushed toward Amanii.

"She's breathing," Kusha said, his voice almost choking. "Barely. Have you lost your mind, Maia?"

An unforgiving silence fell as Maia stood there gazing at the unconscious Amanii and a nearly petrified Kusha.

The communicator hummed.

"Are we in the clear?" It was Ren's voice on the communicator. "We're done here and all set to get back."

Maia could not find her voice, but Kusha answered. "Ren, all's clear. Come back out. Fast as you can."

Maia stepped forward, her gaze fixed on Amanii's body. She did not feel her legs under her, her mind was blank, but she walked on regardless until she towered over the sprawled form of her enemy. The fire within her roared as Maia stared at the foe she had vanquished. She had stared for what felt like an eternity when the anger finally started to ebb.

CHAPTER TWENTY-NINE

YILOSARIO PRIME

Staring at Amanii's limp body, Maia grimaced. As the fire inside her diminished, she realized how bad a situation this was. What had the Xinhagyi said? *Do not give into thoughts of revenge.* And now she had done just that. At the moment, Maia wished she could just vanish into the night air and never come back.

"Maia," Kusha's sharp call dragged Maia back into reality. "Go stand at the stairwell. Make sure that area is clear."

Maia cast another glance at Amanii lying on the ground, her flaming red hair scruffy and singed in places, her gorgeous gown splayed out. Even in the dark, she could make out the burn marks around Amanii's wrist, the welt across her left cheek, and the trail of blood from her nose.

Panic tickled her spine. *I shouldn't have done this. This couldn't have been anything Dada would have liked me to do.*

"Maia," Kusha said again. "Just go, all right? She's breathing, she'll live."

Maia hurried, almost bounding across the roof until she reached the stairwell and took position.

"Coming out now," Ren's voice came over the wrist communicator.

"You're clear," Kusha replied.

The sound of footsteps came from the direction of the archives, and Maia could make out the silhouettes of her three teammates soon after. Ren was leading the way, followed by Nafi and Dani. They walked in a neat line, close together, their heads bowed. Maia fell in line when the trio crossed the stairwell, and Kusha stepped forward to meet them.

"We found out lots," Nafi whispered excitedly. "Not sure what all this has to do with you specifically, but there's tons of history about the R'armimon, as well as about the star hunting and the blood feud and—" She froze, staring through the darkness toward Kusha and Amanii. "Who's that? What happened?"

Kusha sighed. "It's Amanii," he said slowly.

"*The* Amanii?" Nafi said incredulously. "As in Miir's fiancée?"

"Yes, *that* Amanii," Kusha said.

Nafi shot a scathing look in Maia's direction. "You just *had* to teach her a lesson, didn't you?"

Kusha jumped in before Maia could defend her actions. "She spotted us first, then Maia fought her. Amanii lost. And now, she's unconscious."

Ren shook his head wearily. "This isn't good. Not good at all. As soon as she wakes up, she'll alert the guards. We have to tie her up."

"Tie her up?" Dani exclaimed. "We break in, we beat people unconscious, and now we tie them up? What else are we planning to do? Go on a murder spree?"

"Would you rather spend the rest of your life in a Gnelexian prison then?" Ren snapped. "There's no other way."

As Ren pulled a coil of rope from his backpack, Kusha and Nafi rushed to help. Facing the dreaded Gnelexians, mind readers and enforcers of the Xifarian penal system was not an option—Maia knew that well. The mind probes they had used on her mother Sophie destroyed her sanity. They had also taken Bikele. Thinking of the many times the Xifarians had threatened her with Gnelexian probes, she shuddered.

Ren and Kusha swiftly tied Amanii's arms behind her. Then they tied her feet together.

"This should do it," Ren muttered, testing the knots. He pulled out the timer from his pocket and checked it hastily. "It's almost time for a quiet cycle," he declared. He turned out Amanii's LumTorch. "Don't need anyone to find her too quickly and raise an alarm. Let's go now."

One by one, they lowered themselves into the vent, perching on the frail ledge that ran along the rim. Maia stifled a small sigh as they pulled the lid shut above them.

She placed her feet on the rungs that led her lower into the darkness, whispering to herself, solemnly repeating the pledge the Xinhagyi had taught her, "I will end this here, now. No more anger." Her heart was heavy with guilt, sadness, and regrets. Amanii's battered face flashed for a brief moment, making her wearier still. Another broken whisper escaped her parched lips, "I shall forget the scars of my past. If my path ever crosses an enemy's, I won't let memories cloud my judgment. We shall meet as strangers and I shall always give them a second chance."

They went down the same way as they had come and soon slipped out into the dark grounds of the Xifarian Chancery, Ren leading the way.

"Adienos will be waiting for us outside," Ren said as they walked. "He'll have a transporter waiting around the corner. It'll drop us off at the XDA."

The walk seemed long, the trek endless. Maia kept trying to make eye contact with Kusha but he was not having it. The alarm sounded when they were midway across the grounds, a howling siren that pierced Maia's ears and shattered the night's quiet.

"Stop." Ren held his arms out as he slowed and almost dived into the shadow of a tree. "We can't use the path we used coming in."

Everyone quickly followed Ren into the shadows.

"What now?" Maia asked anxiously.

The alarm wailed in a mournful, desperate sort of way. Guards rushed toward the entrance of the building; some were huddled along the serpentine drive. So far, there was no discernible activity along the fence, and Maia kept hoping it would stay that way until they were out safely.

Ren dropped to his knees and pulled a bunch of papers from his backpack, then spread them on the ground and shined a tiny flashlight.

"Adienos says we can't use the fence if the alarms go off. Anything that trips the alarms will also power the fence. We'll get knocked out if we touch it."

Everyone gathered around Ren. "What's our way out then?" Nafi blurted.

"One of the employee gates," Ren said. He tapped on the map and looked up. "There should be one about a hundred steps that way."

Maia squinted in the direction Ren was pointing. She could not see much other than the dark shadows of the trees. Ren packed his bag up and the group headed across the grounds toward the employee gate. The sound of footsteps hit their ears when they had barely taken ten steps.

"Someone's on to us," Nafi said in a panicked voice.

"Nafi, slow down," Ren hissed, slinking into the shadow of a tree. "We can't run. We don't even know for sure where we're running to."

"We'll be in huge trouble if they catch us, Ren," Nafi said, slowing a little.

They were already in huge trouble. If the security protocol dictated the deployment of guards along the periphery, their chances of getting out in time to find Adienos were as good as gone.

Kusha pointed ahead. "There! I see the gate. There are no guards. Let's go!"

Even before Maia could let out a sigh of relief, footsteps sounded again behind them. She strode faster, and within a couple more steps, she saw the outline of the gate. They gathered under the nearest tree for a few moments, anxiously listening for the footsteps. There were none.

"Go?" Nafi asked.

Ren gnawed on his lips, cast a nervous look around, and finally said, "Go!"

They dashed in a frantic, breathless rush to the thick metal frame of the gate. As soon as the team neared, a large screen mounted on the gate flickered to life.

"Enter credentials," big bold letters flashed.

Ren quickly looked at the paper in his hand and punched the keys at the bottom of the portal.

"Place palm on screen for verification," flashed on the screen along with an outline of a hand.

Ren placed his hand on the outline but the screen lit up a bright red as soon as he did.

"Lockdown in progress," the screen declared. "Try again later."

"No, please don't lock us in," Ren muttered.

Maia looked around in the darkness. She could not hear footsteps anymore, but whoever was pursuing them could not be far away. The longer they stood at the gate, the more the chances they would be caught.

Ren tried his handprint on the portal again, but the screen flashed red. "Let me try," Dani said.

Nothing changed. The same flashing red screen greeted them again.

"What's going on?" Kusha asked. "Is the code wrong?"

"I don't think so," Ren said, checking the paper again. "I think they've enforced a lockdown of all the gates because of the alarm. That's why it won't accept the code."

Maia rushed to the fore. "Can I try? If it doesn't work, we should find a place to hide."

"I agree," said Nafi, nodding vigorously.

"The code is 43XZ8," Ren dictated from the paper he held. "Punch that in."

Maia's fingers danced over the keys as she entered the code and then an outline of the hand flashed on the screen. Maia whispered a prayer before placing her shaking hand on the smooth, cold surface of the portal.

The screen melted at her touch. Then it swallowed her hand. Or at least it seemed like so at the moment that followed. Maia tried to pull her hand out, but the screen swelled around her hand.

The portal morphed like mud, enveloping Maia's hand in its cold embrace. Maia felt Dani's hand on her shoulder at the same time as Ren pounced on the keyboard and punched at the keys furiously.

"Let her go," Nafi hissed at the screen, pulling Maia's hand with all her might. The screen refused to yield.

Panic rose swiftly and Maia had to struggle to hold on to clarity. She breathed just the way the Xinhagyi had taught her to calm her mind. A moment or two later, a semblance of peace descended and let her ponder her choices. There was one way to get out of this: the light. She could use the light to blast the portal. Maia closed her eyes and concentrated, trying to kindle the fire she was quite used to handling now. Nothing stirred within her. Maia could not find a shred of the power she had used moments ago on Amanii.

Helplessness and dread weighed Maia's shoulders down. This was the end of her. All that smugness and all those words she had screamed at Amanii were useless. No creepy power could save her now. Maia clamped her free hand over her mouth to make sure the sob rising from her guts did not escape her throat.

Then she heard the sound of footsteps again.

"I think I see them!" said a familiar voice from somewhere behind them.

They were caught. Maia blinked as the man drew closer. His portly frame was silhouetted by the light of the Chancery building behind him. Maia thought she recognized the man's gait, but then she could not quite place him in that frenzied moment.

She tugged her hand frantically, but the screen held it tightly in place. The rotund figure tumbled toward them.

"He's alone," Kusha whispered. "We can take him down. That'd buy us a little time."

"Kusha!" Dani exclaimed, but Ren took the satchel off his back and swung it like a cudgel in his hands. Nafi did the same with her backpack.

"Aim at his face," Kusha instructed.

This was getting too far out of hand. Could there be another way? Perhaps not. But even if they took this man down, as long as she was trapped at the portal, the outcome would not change. Maia gritted her teeth as she tried to yank her hand free.

The man was close now. Still alone, he was speaking to someone over a communicator. "No, I can't get them out. A lockdown is in place. No one can get off the grounds. Not even me."

Wait! The wild flurry in Maia's mind screeched to a halt. What did the man say? Did he say something about trying to get them out? Did that mean he was on their side?

"Guys, stop!" she said, just as Ren took a ferocious swing at the man's head. "He's trying to help us."

Ren lowered his whirling satchel and shot an incredulous look at Maia. The man following them had ducked to avoid Ren's blow. Now he straightened into view, his portly face flecked by the dark and shade of the light filtering through the foliage.

"Principal Pomewege!" Maia and Nafi exclaimed in unison. It was indeed the principal of the XDA. He had come to recruit Maia at her home in Appian and later helped her cover up when she had accidentally absorbed a L'miere crystal. He had always been a friend. Perhaps there was a chance they would escape a lifetime in a Gnelexian prison after all.

"Yes, it's me. Good to see you all, but can't say I'm happy about this situation you've created," Pomewege said with a disappointed frown. His gaze came to rest on the satchels in their hands. "Were you planning to kill me?"

"Not sure," Kusha said and continued even as Pomewege's eyes widened. "We couldn't be caught here."

"You should've thought of that when you broke in," Pomewege said. "Now there's nothing I can do to save you. I can't get you out. Yilosario Prime has locked the gates. It'll stay that way until the alarm is cleared."

"We could hide somewhere," Dani suggested brightly. "Can you hide us somewhere?"

Pomewege scratched his chin. "They'll scan every nook and corner for intruders. I'm not sure where—"

"That's not an option anyway," Ren said. "Not when Maia is stuck at this portal."

That was true. Even if Pomewege could find a place to help them, Maia realized there was no escape for her. She was stuck, helplessly stuck. But that did not mean her friends could not get to safety.

"Never mind me," she said forcefully. "You guys should find a safe place if you can. I'll wait for whatever happens."

Her friends broke into an animated debate over her comment when Pomewege raised his arms and flapped them like a bird.

"Quiet," he said. "All of you, quiet. They're deploying guards around the grounds now so no need to attract them here with the screaming." Everyone hushed right away. Pomewege stepped closer. "Now what's this about Maia being stuck?"

They explained to him about the screen, which was still swirling around Maia's embedded hand.

"That's bizarre," Pomewege said, scratching his knobby chin again. He grabbed Maia's arm and tugged, to no better outcome. A bewildered expression on his face, he muttered under his breath and all Maia could catch were a few words. "Why would Yilosario do that? Unless . . ."

"It's not letting go, Principal," Maia said as calmly as she could. "Please, if you can, get my friends someplace safe."

"Perhaps that's the best way," Pomewege said. Even as Maia's heart crashed obstinately against her chest and fear numbed her limbs, she felt a wave of calm inside her. At least her friends would be safe.

"We're not leaving Maia here alone," Dani said, her voice cracking. "We just can't."

Pomewege sighed. "That's the best you can do for her now. She can resist with her . . . abilities, but you . . . you'll only be leverage for them against her. So, please, let's not waste time here."

Pulling a communicator from his pocket, Pomewege turned away. "Maia is stuck in a security portal." He paused while the communicator crackled on. "I do not know why, but I'll try to get the rest to a safe spot. With any luck, they can wait out the lockdown." He paused again, listening to the person on the other end. "Yes, please be around just in case."

Pomewege had herded the reluctant group together and was about to walk away when the portal flashed brightly. The screen spit out Maia's hand just as suddenly as it had swallowed it. As Maia cradled her hand and stood rubbing it, everyone huddled around.

"What does Yilosario say now?" Pomewege said breathlessly.

The screen had returned to normal, but instead of the red refusal Maia and her friends had seen three times, it now turned purple.

"Restricted override in progress," said the flashing letters.

"Why would Yilosario do this?" Pomewege muttered as he stared at the screen. Then he shook his head. "That can't be."

Slowly he turned to look at Maia, his gaze at once full of awe and worry. Whatever the screen meant could not be good, Maia realized. She was about to ask the principal when the gate beyond the portal slowly swung open.

Pomewege did not waste another moment. He grabbed Maia by the arm and pushed her out. Then he shoved the rest of the team through the gate.

"Walk toward the main gates," he instructed, pulling the gate closed after everyone had slipped out. "Kehorkjin will find you."

"Master Kehorkjin?" Nafi asked incredulously.

Maia kept her surprise contained with much difficulty. Master

Kehorkjin had always been tough on them, and she could not have expected him to defend their undoubtedly criminal enterprise.

"What about you, Principal Pomewege?" Maia asked. He had come to help them. What if the chancellor found out?

The gate shut with a mighty click.

"I can't leave through here. I'm on the guest list. I have to go out the main entrance so they record my leaving." He shooed them with an impatient wave. "Go now. Find Kehorkjin." Then he turned and started walking back in the direction of the Chancery.

With another look at the principal's disappearing form, Maia and her teammates strode toward the front gates. Maia's feet dragged under her. Too much had happened, much of it hardly made sense. Maia only hoped her friends had found enough in the Chancery Archives to make this adventure worth it.

CHAPTER THIRTY

HARD ESCAPE

Maia and her friends had barely stepped out from the quiet side street when someone called Ren's name. Startled at once, the gang huddled together until Ren realized it was Adienos. Maia recognized the burly man she had met a couple of years ago; he was still as stout and walked with the same lurching gait. Behind him was the familiar figure of Master Kehorkjin.

"I do not have words for you or your conduct tonight," Master Kehorkjin hurled the rebuke the cold and scathing way only he could. His glare soaked the team, and as Maia stood with her head hung in shame, she knew his reproach was more than deserved. They should not have done this.

Soon they were inside a transporter that Adienos had brought and some distance away from the Chancery. The master sat facing them, glowering at them and muttering to himself. He looked tired, and once again, Maia felt a sting of shame in her heart. He must've panicked on finding they were missing. How did he know they had sneaked out? Outside, the crowds kept growing denser and Maia realized it was nearly time for the showering of stardust. The transporter hardly made any progress through the swelling crowds and the silence inside was unbearable.

After quite a while, during which the transporter made across a street junction, Nafi shifted uneasily. Master Kehorkjin immediately looked up at her.

"We're sorry, Master Kehorkjin," Nafi blurted. It was so sudden and unexpected that even the master blinked. "This was a mistake. We shouldn't have. We never—"

"Now you think?" Kehorkjin growled. He closed his eyes and took a long breath before whispering angrily, "Do you realize what would've happened to you if you were caught in there? What can still happen to you when they find out you were inside the Chancery grounds?"

"It's my fault," Maia said, desperate to take responsibility for the night's fiasco. "They came here because of me. I should've known better."

"Yes, you should have," Kehorkjin said through gritted teeth. "After all you've been through, after how Monk Hilledunn treated you not too long ago, you dare to do this? Here? On Xif of all places? Do you understand what it means to have a price on your head?"

She did quite well, but it was also true that she had forgotten. No, that was not entirely true either. She had discussed this with her friends and weighed their options. In the end, the temptation of finding out about Sophie washed away the concerns.

"What exactly were you trying to do in there?" Master Kehorkjin demanded. "There have been reports of intruders attacking guests. Please tell me that had nothing to do with you."

Maia hung her head and so did everyone else. Master Kehorkjin looked up at the roof of the transporter and let out an enormous sigh.

"We had to defend ourselves," Kusha said finally, his voice hardly audible.

"Who did you fight? A guard?"

"Amanii," Maia replied.

Master Kehorkjin sat up straight. "Amanii? *Our* Amanii?"

Maia nodded. Kehorkjin blinked.

"How bad was she hurt? Is she dead?"

Everyone shook their heads vigorously. The master gave out another enormous sigh.

"Why were you there?" he asked after another long stifling silence.

Maia looked at her teammates before she started to explain. "I got an anonymous note that said I should check out the Origin Scrolls at the Chancery Archives." The master's eyes narrowed. "I-I thought it had something to do with my mother. You know my mother was —"

"I know about Sophie," Master Kehorkjin said. The way he jumped in, it almost felt like he wanted to stop Maia from discussing Sophie.

"So, I wanted to look at the Origin Scrolls."

"Did you?"

Maia shot Nafi a sidelong glance. "Nafi did."

Master Kehorkjin looked intently at Nafi. "Did you steal the book?"

"What?" Nafi started. She shook her head so hard that Maia thought it would fly off her neck. "No. Of course not. We . . . I made a copy of it."

"You didn't."

Nafi gulped noisily. "Why wouldn't I?"

"Because there'll be a record, that's why." The master dropped his head in his palms and sat quietly for a while. When he raised his head, he looked even more exhausted, if that was possible. Master Kehorkjin looked each of them in the eye.

"All right then, mission accomplished," he said in a scornful tone. "We shall go back to the XDA and retire for the night, or whatever is left of the night. We will not discuss this ever again. Understood?"

They sat in silence after that. Master Kehorkjin had leaned back into his seat, his eyes closed and head limp. The transporter crawled through the masses and almost ages later, it turned onto an uncrowded road and picked up the pace. Maia tried to relax, trying to focus her thoughts on anything other than their current situation.

"It's starting," Ren exclaimed, and everyone turned toward him. He was staring out of the side windows of the transporter as it climbed up an overpass, specifically at the Sedara as it bloomed in a shower of light. Maia remembered waiting for it during their stay on Xif for the first phase of the Initiative.

It felt like a distant memory now, almost like a previous life. What a night that had turned out to be. They had been invited to the Grand Gala to be presented with medals for winning the Xifarian leg but they had instead ended up in the Grotto and saved the Stabilator from the saboteurs. They had never seen the famed shower of the stardust; they had snuck away from an unsuspecting Miir long before it was time for the event.

"It's beautiful," Dani said, awestruck.

It was indeed a splendid sight. The artificial star at the center of the Xifarian settlement, the one made of innumerable L'miere crystals tied in a mesh of Calbion, the one with a dark secret of its own, was now emitting a deluge of sparkles. A stupendous mix of every color imaginable burst out in a never-ending torrent of illumination.

"Oh, no," Ren said.

"Not good," Master Kehorkjin's dismal voice came next.

"Yes, not good at all," Ren whispered.

"What?" Kusha was the first to pay heed to the two Xifarians' dismayed comments. "What do you mean 'not good'? It's brilliant. Ren?"

"It's misfiring. The colors are all wrong," Ren whispered, sounding fearful and confused. "It's supposed to be all red and gold followed by a rainbow pattern and then silver and blue. Now it's all jumbled up."

"Maybe they changed it this year," Nafi ventured, and Ren shook his head vigorously in response.

"No one changes the colors of the stardust," the master's voice boomed. "It has not changed in centuries. And there is no reason for it to change now. This is not good."

Maia stared wordlessly at the Sedara, still beautiful for all she could tell. She knew the Xifarians were not too enthusiastic about change. She had seen them react violently to new ideas before, so she understood the predicament . . . somewhat. Master Kehorkjin seemed to have lost the strength to even blink, and Ren sat motionless, almost catatonic.

"Not good," Master Kehorkjin said for the third time. He reached up and pushed a switch on a small panel embedded in the luxurious covering stretching across the roof of the transporter. There was a brief buzz before a voice, presumably the pilot's, crackled.

"Yes, Master Kehorkjin," it said expectantly.

"Take the Skyroute," Master Kehorkjin instructed. Maia could easily detect the tautness of his voice. "Need to reach the XDA the quickest way."

There was no reply. But there was no need for any. The vehicle had swerved and picked up speed even before the conversation was over, zooming forward through the lanes. They lost the view of the Sedara immediately, and before Maia could mourn the loss, they were zipping through a nondescript tunnel, climbing upward through its brightly lit interior. There was nothing of interest outside so she turned to her teammates.

Ren sat quietly, his eyes glued to the floor. He had not spoken since seeing the Sedara change colors. Kusha lay back, resting his head on the headrest, his eyes closed. Dani stared intently at the tunnel outside, her serene gaze skimming over the bowed lights that ringed the tunnel. Nafi, the youngest of their team, was sitting diagonally across from her, biting her fingernails like a hungry fish snapping at food. Maia stifled a sigh. They had made a spectacular mess of things. No, *she* had. She leaned back into her seat and decided to spend the rest of the trip thinking of Appian.

In a few more moments, the transporter came to a stop in front of the XDA and the doors opened. The master led them out and toward the entrance.

"Good night," he said at the door of the living quarters. "Just so you know, I won't lock you in as I should, but my eyes are on you. No one comes out of their rooms until I call you in the morning for our trip down-planet. Understood?"

Five heads nodded in unison. Maia crashed into her bed as soon as she got inside her room. Tiredness, fear, and shame swamped her in an instant. She dug under the sheets and pulled her knees to her chest.

Everything they did was wrong. They should not have broken into the Chancery, they should not have copied the Origin Scrolls, and she should not have attacked Amanii. Now all of them were in trouble — the team, Master Kehorkjin, Principal Pomewege. Eventually, the Xifarians would figure it out and then the chancellor would make all of them pay.

As Maia drifted between sleep and wakefulness, her mind kept going back to Amanii. Fighting her went against everything the Xinhagyi had taught her. The Xinhagyi had warned her, yet she had given into her urges, and let her anger take over.

The Xinhagyi often said, "Revenge is not a good friend. It makes you take to the skies when you have not mastered the art of flight. It makes you soar and lets go when you are the farthest from the ground. Then, you fall."

She had fallen. Very far. And very low.

Chapter Thirty-One

The Origin Scrolls

The gang returned to ThulaSu around mid-afternoon the following day and they had hardly spoken to each other. Even the talkative Nafi kept quiet for the most part. No one discussed anything—not the trip to Xif, not their findings in the library, and certainly not their night adventure. Maia was eager to learn about what was in the Origin Scrolls. She wanted some sort of justification for getting them all into this mess.

Even after they had safely reached ThulaSu, Maia and her teammates kept their heads down and went about the mundane tasks with exceptional zeal. They were the first team at Revsi Sottekaja's aural projection class, and they stayed the longest at Tessio's Pantheronicas training session.

That night, after an unusually quiet dinner, the team decided to sit down for a chat.

"We can't meet in the study area. Anyone can hear us there," Kusha said in a subdued voice as they walked the corridor. "Let's talk in one of our rooms."

They quickly decided on Nafi's room, since all the material she had gathered from the Chancery Archives was hidden under her mattress.

As soon as they had all gathered, Dani cleared her throat in an odd way. "Maia, before we get to the scrolls, we need to talk," she said in a rush, as she did not want to say what she was about to say. Kusha, who sat next to Dani, placed his hand on hers reassuringly, and immediately Maia knew. This had something to do with her fight with Amanii. She drew in a long breath as Dani started to speak.

"I wasn't in favor of breaking into the Chancery at all, you know that. But I agreed because I realized finding out about your mother is important to you. There were huge risks but I thought we'd do all right if we stuck together." Dani paused and Maia desperately looked for a place to fix her gaze. "But we didn't stick together, Maia. *You* didn't stick with us. First, you went out on the balcony to watch the gala. What if someone spotted you? And then, you engaged with Amanii more than what was needed. Maia . . ." Dani's words trailed off. Maia looked at her tired face and winced. Had Nafi said this, she would have much less trouble handling it. But even an unfinished rebuke from the kind and reserved Dani was the hardest thing to endure.

"I'm sorry," Maia blurted. "I made mistakes. I promise it won't happen again. Ever. I promise."

Dani turned away, refusing to meet her gaze. Kusha slipped an arm over Dani's shoulders. Ren and Nafi exchanged a look. Then Nafi pulled out a pile of sheets from under her bedding noisily.

"On to the scrolls then?" she asked, forcing fake cheer into her voice. As soon as Dani nodded, Nafi spread the papers out. Maia found a spot to the side, still nursing a mountain-sized guilt. She had selfishly risked her friends' lives. Not just once, but twice. A dread—more potent than the embarrassment and the guilt—ate away at her. It was fear: That she would lose her friends, their support, and their approval.

Since returning from Xif, Maia had decided to ask Ren about

Miir's whereabouts, to put her worries to rest once and for all. But now . . .

They'll be mad at me. They'll never forgive me. I'll lose my friends and they're all I have!

Hard as Maia tried, she could not find the courage to ask Ren about Miir.

"Are you listening, Maia?" Nafi's sharp voice jolted Maia out of her thoughts. She shook her head nervously. "Good," Nafi said. "So, as I was saying, a whole lot of the scrolls are written in ancient Xifarian script. Even the part that's not is cryptic. Not easily understandable."

"But we know for sure there's a lot of information there," Ren added. "A lot of it is about the R'armimon."

Maia sat up. For all these years, Maia and her friends had tried to dig up information about the R'armimon and failed. They knew Xif was once part of the R'armimon Empire. They also knew an age-old blood feud raged between the R'armimon and the Xifarians. But what the feud was and how it came to be, they had no idea. Recently, the R'armimon had arrived in the Tansian system and that had sent the Xifarians into a frenzy. They desperately wanted to get away from Tansi in their planet-spaceship, only they could not because the heart of the Sedara that powered Xif was broken.

"So . . . the first thing that caught our eye is the reference in here," Nafi said. She tapped on the paper and looked around at her teammates. "I think it also ties in into one of the lines in our riddle, the line about 'nine hundred fifty-six' or whatever. You read it, Ren."

As Ren took the piece of paper, Maia tried to recall the first line of the riddle: "For nine hundred and fifty-six years the Ikarus flew."

Ren took a deep breath and started. "This is how the scrolls describe the beginning of the R'armimon Empire," he said. "'Our roots are dead—cut and forgotten as we flee with the light for hundreds nine, half and six more of years. Old mother Terra, may your children live and prosper.'"

Maia tapped her chin thoughtfully. That was an odd way to say nine hundred fifty-six. The verse was indeed cryptic at best.

Kusha cleared his throat and hesitated before speaking. "All right, so this sort of says nine hundred and fifty-six years ago the R'armimon settled the galaxy. I don't understand how that connects to Maia."

"Who knows if it connects to her at all?" Nafi said. Frowning, she flipped a few pages of the scroll. "Let's read through a few things in this anyway," she said. "We might get an idea about why the R'armimon is after the Xifarians. That might help Maia understand where she stands in the feud, right?"

"Most of this is very, very cryptic, like Nafi said," Ren explained. "So it'll take time to decipher. But let me read one passage to you."

Ren thumbed through the pages before stopping at the middle of the stack. He read aloud:

"Sacred blood lost, an Empire crossed.

Ages will keep their ire alive.

Kind will pay for kind: the blood, the heir, the Nasfarii."

"The Empire?" Maia interrupted. "That must mean the R'armimon Empire, right?"

Ren shrugged. "Possibly. They lost sacred blood. Sacred could mean . . ."

"Royal blood is considered sacred," Kusha said.

"So the Xifarians killed a R'armimon royal?" Maia asked.

Ren shrugged again. "Must be. Why would it be in here otherwise? Perhaps that started the feud."

Nafi sighed noisily. "This whole book is a huge, big puzzle," she said.

Ren nodded and jumped to another page. "Listen to this . . ." He paused a moment before reading another verse. "'Death is on the hunt. Forever near. Like a shadow, never apart.'"

"That *has* to mean the R'armimon," Dani said, and Maia had to agree.

"'Stars change, the heavens soar, the Nasfarii in our heart thirsts more.'" Ren read another line.

"That has to mean the Xif's travel from one star system to another," Maia said. "What's the Nasfarii?"

Kusha looked sharply at her. His stare was a bit weird, so Maia raised an eyebrow. "What?"

"Don't get mad at me, but . . ."

"What is it?" Maia asked again.

"Nasfarii sounds almost like Nosiifarus to me. What if they mean the same?"

The idea, regardless of how suddenly Kusha said it, made sense. But if the two words were the same, it would mean Tansi had a strong connection to the R'armimon Empire as well as to the Xifarians. Stronger and more recent than they imagined. And if that was true, the reference to nine hundred and fifty-six could be the same as in the riddle.

"Could be," she said, keeping her thoughts to herself. They were too speculative to share right away. "Anyway, who is the Nasfarii in their heart?"

Once again, Ren shrugged. "Don't look at me. I have no clue."

That was the problem. No one—not even Xifarians—knew anything about their past other than what their higher-ups chose to disclose.

Maia stifled a sigh. "You know what? We should focus on the final challenge and the riddle now." She grabbed the papers from Ren and rolled them up. "I'll keep these papers with me. We'll get to it when we get to it. After the challenge is over."

It was as if everyone was waiting for her to say that. There were sighs of relief all around. Dani grinned and pulled out a piece of paper from her pocket.

"I've been working a different angle for a few days and I think it has merit," Dani announced triumphantly. "So, I thought . . . they want us to find the final resting place of our Nouvus, correct? We've never seen or heard of the Nouvus or known of a burial site for it. So, it's hidden and hidden very well. No one has accidentally dug up a honking spacecraft either, right? Not in hundreds of years, right? That means the place has to be remote, where no one ever visits."

Dani paused and looked at the faces surrounding her. "Now the only lands I can think of that have never been settled are the southern end of the First Continent, the middle of the Second, and the entire Fourth."

Kusha rubbed his nose with vigor. "Can't be the south end of the First. That peninsula has had a population of indigenous Palonkians; they've lived here from before our ancestors came. That's also a sanctuary."

"All right, scratch that," Dani said. "That brings us down to two."

"I doubt it's the middle of the Second," Maia added thoughtfully. "I've heard of those parts. There weren't any big settlements there because it has always been dry and dusty, but there were lots of smaller mining towns up until the Solianese Fall. If there were mines, they had to be digging. And . . ."

Nafi's eyes had grown as big as hen's eggs. She waved as if to swat a swarm of flies. "I know, I know," she said between gasps. "It's the Fourth Continent. It has to be that. Remember, no settlements were allowed on the Fourth. Why? That's why! Nafi paused. Her eyes still wide, she waved her hands as if casting a spell. "No settlements . . . ever!"

Dani chuckled loudly. "I think you're right, Nafi. I came to the same conclusion. And that might also be why it was never connected to any of the other continents."

It made sense. Hardly anyone even visited the Fourth; it was kept intentionally remote for a reason. "It was preserved as a memorial for the craft that had brought us home," Maia said. "As a homage."

"I think so," Dani said. "I haven't found any proof yet, but I think it's a path worth pursuing."

Maia had no doubt that it was. They were finally getting somewhere, and more importantly, without using any clues from the

CHAPTER THIRTY-ONE

Origin Scrolls.

"Let's start digging for information about the Fourth Continent," she said. "I'm sure we'll have more on that in the library here. If not, we have a trip to Zagran coming up."

Dani put the piece of paper back into her pocket. An evil smirk twisted her face. "Let's see how you can stop us now, Hilledunn," she said.

Seeing Dani's jubilant face brought a smile to Maia's lips. She had grown to love them all, and this is how she wanted to always see them—happy. As she watched her friends gleefully discuss the clues, Maia quietly vowed to never let them down again.

Chapter Thirty-Two

An Orphan's Tale

Maia always thought that nothing good could come from meddling in someone's private life, but Dani seemed determined to get to the bottom of what—or who—had caused Everrol's bruises. Sadly, Maia had forgotten about Everrol, as she had had her own problems to deal with, but Dani was insistent. Maia, already reeling from the guilt of having endangered her friends on Xif, decided to tag along with Dani on her Everrol-hunting sessions. Usually, their hunts yielded nothing, but one evening their luck changed.

They found Everrol at their study table after dinner, arranging books and paper. He noticed the two girls approaching when they were about five paces away from him. Maia could have sworn his face paled. The way he threw a furtive glance at the door, it seemed he was weighing running away.

"Everrol, we finally found you," Dani said. She was next to him in a heartbeat and quickly linked her arm through his. "Can we please, please, please sit down and talk for a bit?"

Everrol cast a glance at the door again, looked at Dani's resolute expression, and gave out a defeated sigh. He nodded slowly and sank into one of the chairs. Dani slipped into the nearest chair and faced Everrol.

"You can tell me the truth," she said, poring over Everrol's face.

The corners of Everrol's mouth drooped as his eyes scanned the table back and forth. He wrung his hands endlessly, his eyes darting between Dani and Maia.

"Why are you doing this, Dani? It isn't going to change anything," he said in a quiet voice.

His nervous gaze and his pale face tugged at Maia's heart. Dani was right; there was something evil afoot. But Maia was torn, just like Everrol, about how much good this conversation was going to do. What if Everrol said Hilledunn hurt him? What would Dani do then? What could any of them do to stop the abuse? They were just some random kids, and other than Kusha, no one held any power over anyone. Even Kusha had no authority over the monks at ThulaSu since the university was considered its own dominion.

"Maybe not," Dani said, placing a reassuring hand on Everrol's. "But maybe telling someone will help ease your pain a little."

Everrol chuckled. "I doubt that, Dani. But thank you. I'm grateful for your kindness." He looked up at Maia who had been standing on the other side of the table. "You better sit down because this will take a while."

Maia slid into a chair as Everrol started his tale. From when his parents died in a fishing-boat accident when he was six and he was placed in the ThulaSuian orphanage, up until the past week, Everrol's tale was one of endless cruelty Monk Hilledunn routinely unleashed on the residents of the orphanage.

"He's always been a strict warden," Everrol said. "And every punishment he doles out is for a reason. If there isn't a good enough reason, he makes up one. His assistants are always prepared to vouch for him, so even if anyone complained about him, it wouldn't go far. I mean, who would anyone believe, a wretched kid or a well-known master? Besides . . ."

Maia frowned when Everrol's words trailed off. "Besides?" she prompted.

Once again, Everrol cast a nervous glance at the door. "One time, there was this boy, Laman. He was about eight years old when I came here. Hilledunn was younger then and even fiercer than he is now. He beat Laman with a hot iron rod once. That boy had some nerve, went to the head monk, and showed his burns."

Maia shuddered, thinking of the vicious act. She thought of the warmth of her childhood bed, how loving Dada and Emmy and Herc had been, and she could not even imagine growing up alone and unloved. The more she looked at Everrol's ashen face, the more she had to struggle to bite back tears.

"Then what happened?" Maia choked.

Everrol gave a sad shake of his head. "We never saw him again."

"What?" Dani blurted.

Maia had held her breath and now it came out of her in a slow, painful lurch. "How can a boy just vanish?" she whispered.

Everrol gaze skimmed the floors. "A lot of things happen to people who no one cares about."

"What did they do to him?" Maia asked again, and Everrol shot a strange look.

"Sent him away somewhere. Somewhere he couldn't cause trouble to Hilledunn."

Dani let out a little gasp and her hand shot up to cover her mouth. "You don't mean he killed Laman, do you?"

Everrol did not reply. He sat there, his eyes fixed on the ground, a statue carved out of stone. Then he shrugged. "I don't know," he muttered. "A lot of rumors have floated around since then."

For a long time, they all sat, stunned and silent. Finally, a question croaked out of Maia. "The head monk knew this? You mean he's in with Hilledunn?"

Everrol tilted his head a little. "Maybe not. People thought Hilledunn got rid of Laman somehow. I don't know."

Maia did not know what to say after that. Did Hilledunn really kill the boy? What kind of evil could think of killing a child? What kind of monster could even think of beating a helpless eight-year-old with a hot iron rod?

"I realized there was no point fighting Hilledunn," Everrol continued in a dim voice, "so I tried to keep my distance, stay away from trouble. We all did. As much as we could."

Dani sat up and crossed her arms. "What exactly happened a few weeks back? What did you do to make him so angry? Was it because you protested the mark he chose for us?"

Everrol shifted in his chair and scratched the table. "He assigned me as your mentor because he wanted to keep a close eye on you. He said no good could come out of riling the Xifarians and you were doing just that. You were going to be the reason for Tansi's ruin, so I had to stick to you always. I did what he asked me to do but . . ." Everrol looked away, then turned to them and leaned forward. "But I didn't see you doing anything bad. You worked hard and it was unfair how he was always putting you at a disadvantage."

Maia's fists curled into balls. She had been right. Hilledunn *had* asked Everrol to shadow them, to keep an eye on them. Maia knew from the moment she had laid eyes on Hilledunn that he was up to no good.

"So you confronted him?" she asked.

Everrol nodded. "Yes. I couldn't take it anymore. That night I went to speak to him. I overheard him telling Leeam that he'd find a way to disqualify you."

Dani leaned forward. "And then?"

"As expected, things went badly for me," Everrol said, rushing through the words. He jumped to his feet the next moment. "I have to leave now. I have to prepare for an exam."

He hurried away from the table but turned around and scurried back to the girls after barely taking five steps.

"Please," he looked beseechingly at Dani as he pleaded, "I told you everything. But no one else can know this. Hilledunn and his assistants will kill me if they find out about this. Please."

He rushed away, leaving the two girls alone at the study table. They sat quietly for a while before Maia nudged Dani. The rest of the team was at the library, and they were all supposed to meet there.

"Let's go, Dani," she said. "The others will be missing us by now."

Dani nodded distractedly.

"What are you thinking, Dani?" Maia asked as they walked out of the study hall. "You heard Everrol. He asked you not to do anything about this."

Dani scoffed. "Come on, Maia. I can't *not* do anything. That man has been beating helpless kids for years. We have to stop it. I don't know how, but we have to."

Maia peered at Dani. "Dani, listen to me," she said. "You heard how vicious Hilledunn is. Everrol told you. He said even the university doesn't seem to care. We've seen ourselves how crooked Hilledunn can be. What if our meddling makes things worse for Everrol?"

Dani absentmindedly chewed her lip and shook her head. "I can't," she declared. "I can't let this go. I'll find a way to get Hilledunn."

"Have you considered that might actually hurt Everrol even more? Why can't you let this go?"

Dani's blue gaze held Maia's, piercing in its intensity. "Because I had let go once, Maia," she said in a quiet, broken voice. "I saw a friend being hurt and I didn't say a word because he asked me not to." Dani choked and stopped. She blinked furiously for a while before speaking again. "He died two months later from a fall that was never explained. I know what it was, and I know I could've done something."

Maia remembered Dani and her brother Hans had grown up as orphans too. Perhaps the friend she lost was from her orphanage, and perhaps that was why Everrol's situation had affected her as much.

Dani's jaw hardened and she looked Maia in the eye. Her usually soft gaze was steely. "I'm not going to let it go again, Maia. I agree we can't call Hilledunn out just like that, but I'll find a way to get him. I have to."

Looking at Dani's resolute face, Maia had no doubt that she would bring Hilledunn just desserts. And even though that'd be one risky enterprise, she was going to help her friend.

"I'm with you," she said, placing a hand on Dani's. "Whatever it takes."

CHAPTER THIRTY-THREE

A DEADLY TURN

As the two girls rushed back to the library to meet their teammates, they stumbled upon a group huddled near the entrance. Nafi and Kusha stood to one side, watching the huddle.

"What's going on?" Maia asked as soon as they reached Nafi and Kusha.

"Something's happened on Xif. Not sure what, but Karhann pulled Ren away for a chat." Kusha tilted his head toward the huddle of Xifarians, where Ren and all of Core 7 spoke in hushed voices.

"Where did you two disappear?" Nafi demanded. "What's going on?"

"Not much," Dani lied with ease. "I had to pick something up from the study room."

Nafi's eyes narrowed. "Like what?"

Maia looked away. She was going to let Dani do the explaining about Everrol, whatever way she saw fit.

"Why do you need to keep tabs on everyone? Let them be."

Kusha jumped in to defend Dani.

Nafi's nose crinkled. "Now you're going to do the 'protecting my girl' act? Really, Kusha?"

Kusha flushed a little. "It's not just about Dani. I'd say the same for—"

At that moment, the Xifarians concluded their meeting. Ren walked away and joined his teammates and Kusha promptly dropped the topic. Seeing how dark Ren's face was, Maia's heart filled with dread.

"Something's seriously wrong," Ren muttered. "We're not sure what, but some Xifarian envoys just arrived. Karhann saw them wearing mourning bands."

"What's a mourning band?" Maia asked.

"It's an armband Xifarians are required to wear when there's a national disaster or death of a prominent citizen."

Maia's blood froze. *Not Amanii . . .*

"Why are they here?" Kusha asked. "I would've heard if they came to meet my father."

"They're probably here to meet Kehorkjin or Mahswa Tabrin," Ren said. "I don't know."

Maia's gut clenched. Fear tapped the base of her spine with its icy fingers and goosebumps sprouted on her neck. Something was terribly wrong, she knew it. She also knew something ruthless and evil was coming to get her.

"Ren!" Karhann waved frantically from the entrance of the library, and Ren hurried over. Maia and the rest of the gang exchanged quick looks; no one was sure whether to follow Ren.

"Come on," Kusha said at last. "Let's find out."

Ren and Karhann were talking agitatedly when they approached. Karhann shook his head and Ren nervously licked his lips. The dread inside Maia grew tenfold on seeing their ashen faces.

"What happened?" Maia asked, her voice shaking. It was strange that she felt so sorry for whatever misfortune that had befallen the nation of Xif. The Xifarians were enemies of the Solianese; they always had been. They had murdered her family; they had tried to kill her. She had vowed to bring them to justice a thousand times over, and yet . . . seeing Karhann and Ren's wilted faces, she felt no joy.

"Can you tell us?" Nafi said. "Or is it a secret?"

Karhann looked sharply at Nafi but he did not snap as Maia feared. Instead, he let out a long sigh and shook his head. "We don't know for sure. But . . . something horrible must've happened because the Prime Directive is in force."

For a moment or two, Maia stared at Karhann and Ren, as did the rest of her teammates.

Maia found her voice first. "Prime Directive?" she said. "What's that?"

Karhann and Ren exchanged a quick glance before Ren started to explain. "Prime Directive is a rule that takes effect when the nation is in a state of maximum alert. It happens when the nation is under attack or there's a disaster or the sovereign has passed. It calls for all powers to be transferred to the royal heir who leads the nation until the state of alert is over."

Nafi tapped her chin thoughtfully. "But I thought the Xifarian royals like to keep their identity hidden. That no one knows who they are."

"Well, Prime Directive trumps personal preferences. It is called for only in times of national crisis," Karhann replied. "These are not normal times."

"The Prime Directive hasn't been called for in a very long time," Ren added in a morose voice.

There was not much to say after that. While Ren insisted his teammates go for dinner, Maia and her friends did not feel like deserting him when he was in obvious distress. So they lingered, lounging along the walkway as they awaited news.

They would have gone without dinner if Rayan had not come looking for Maia. Upon hearing about the situation, she soon disappeared only to reappear later with a large box filled with food. Maia and her friends jumped in eagerly, and even Karhann joined in.

It was not until they had collectively cleaned the box of every morsel that Loriine and Baecca—Karhann's teammates—streaked out of the library building. They looked worried, fearful almost, Maia noted. Loriine balked a little at seeing Karhann with the gang, but she quickly composed herself.

"Can you two come here?" She nodded meaningfully at Ren and Karhann from a few paces away. "I've got some information."

"You can say it here," Ren replied. "It's not a secret."

Baecca frowned, but Loriine snapped, "It's not exactly an announcement for the masses either."

Masses? The way Loriine dismissively threw the word out made Maia feel like she was a worthless peasant. Her thoughts tumbled into an angry ball and her fists curled, and she had to breathe in deep to calm her thoughts.

"Let's not fight over this. I thought saying it wouldn't matter since everyone will know it sooner or later anyway," Ren said.

Thankfully, Loriine seemed to think the same for a change. "The chancellor is critically ill," she blurted. "And . . ."

Fear turned Maia's hands icy. She had just seen the chancellor at the gala, happy and hearty.

"And?" Karhann prompted.

Loriine let out a long sigh. "And the Sedara is damaged and . . . dimming."

"What?" Karhann exclaimed. "How can that be? We just saw it a few days ago."

Loriine shrugged. "I don't know. That's all my father would tell me."

"Your father is here?" Nafi asked, her voice cold as ice. Maia recalled the tale Nafi had told about Loriine's father Ameron and how he had caused the death of Nafi's sister Sejya over a family feud.

Loriine cast a quarrelsome look at Nafi, her mouth pursed angrily. "Yes, he is. He's here as an envoy along with Statesman Orano Taillefei."

As Loriine and Nafi stared murderously at each other, Dani

linked her arm through Nafi's. "We should go now," Dani said, tugging Nafi's arm. She cast a pleading look at Maia and Kusha. "Don't we have some work to catch up on?"

"Yes, of course," Maia picked up the hint and quickly fell in line. Kusha nodded eagerly as well. The situation was pretty explosive already; they did not need any more arguments, particularly arguments that would resolve nothing.

Maia did not have much hope for Nafi listening to them, but it was an evening of surprises. Nafi tore her eyes away from Loriine's flushed face and muttered, "Let's go."

The three girls and Kusha left the group of Xifarians and started toward the living quarters. They had not taken ten steps away from where they had been standing when the door into the next block of buildings fell open and Kehorkjin walked out with a man with bright red hair. Maia and her friends slowed, squeezing into a single file to let the two men pass.

Maia stole a glance at the man and Kehorkjin. Both were wearing bands—black with red stripes—on their right arms, and both looked excessively glum. She tried to recall where she had seen the other man with a round nose that looked out of place on his otherwise bony face. It came to her quickly—he was the envoy who had spoken about renewing the promise on the Alliance Initiative. She did not know his name, but something about him seemed familiar. Maia and her teammates picked up pace as soon as Kehorkjin and the man passed their group without as much a glance.

"So that red-haired guy must be Taillefei," Kusha whispered as they walked away.

"Hey there, you," said an unfamiliar voice. Maia and her friends stopped and turned around. Xifarian envoy Taillefei, the red-haired man who had walked out with Kehorkjin, strode up. A deep frown etched on his forehead, he glared at Maia. "You're Maia, aren't you?" he asked in a glacial tone.

A sinister smile twisted his face as soon as Maia nodded. "I've never met you face to face," he said, "but I sure have heard a lot about you. You might know my daughter Amanii."

Maia was sure she saw an ominous gleam in his eye, and she felt the odd fear spread its icy veins through her heart. She nodded slowly, realizing this man knew they were at the Chancery the previous night because Amanii had to have told him. Statesman Taillefei took his cold gaze off her face and scanned her friends who stood behind her.

"You must know," he continued, "saboteurs have struck the Xif. They're trying to bring us down. You must know."

It was weird the way he kept on repeating that she had to know. What was he trying to imply? That she somehow caused the Sedara to break? That she was responsible for the chancellor being ill?

Before she could say a word, the man, Taillefei spoke again. His voice was barely a whisper, his words sharp. "You should know this: We don't give in so easily. You dared to strike at our heart and you dared to abuse the hospitality we extended you. If you think you'll get away with it, you're wrong. You shall pay for every wound you inflicted on us. I promise you that," Taillefei snarled, and every word clawed and tore at Maia's heart.

Any other time and Maia would have shouted in his face, but now she could not. He was right—she had sneaked into the Chancery when she was not supposed to and hurt Amanii in a fit of rage. She could not counter that, her actions were indefensible. So at that moment, her gaze dropped.

"What are you trying to say?" Nafi snapped. "We had nothing to do with what happened to your Sedara or your chancellor."

Kusha crossed his arms and met Taillefei's glare. "These are baseless allegations," he said, his voice stout and unwavering.

"Are they?" Taillefei said. "Sahiiraan Kusha, is it? You have gone against our interests time and again. You were supposedly at the XDA the night before these tragedies happened. Now explain to me, please, what inference am I to draw from these facts? And stars forbid, if we were to find that you had somehow wandered away from the XDA during your stay, what conclusions do you think would be drawn?"

Master Kehorkjin had walked over next to Taillefei. He did not speak a word, for or against either Taillefei or Maia and her friends. But his quiet presence seemed to unsettle the statesman who threw a sidelong glance at the master and grimaced.

"Make no mistake, we know and we won't forget," he hissed before turning on his heels and marching away. Master Kehorkjin lingered a fraction of a moment longer. Then he, too, turned and left.

Maia and her friends, shaken from the encounter, simply stood staring. Then Kusha cleared his throat. He looked worried and distracted.

"Why don't you guys go on without me? I need to go talk to my father," he said with a thoughtful look at the Xifarians. "I don't like this one bit."

Maia did not like it one bit either. The sharks were circling her again, hungry for her blood. And this time she hardly had the moral ground to defend herself.

CHAPTER THIRTY-FOUR

SANA AND THE BUZZERS

The next morning Maia barely had any interest in rolling out of bed. It was an off day with no scheduled classes, so she was in no rush to get to breakfast. In fact, she did not want to get anywhere outside her room at all. Dusty, however, needed attention and Maia realized it was better to tend to a stubborn cat than have it perching on her face.

After she had fed Dusty and washed up, she sat on her windowsill and watched ThulaSu come to life. She would have happily spent the rest of the day at her window but her growling stomach had other ideas. And then someone rapped on her door.

"Maia! Maia!" Nafi's yells, loud and strong, floated in. "Are you up yet?"

Just like there was no ignoring Dusty, there was no ignoring Nafi either. So, reluctantly, Maia left the windowsill. Nafi grinned toothily as soon as the door fell open. She was not alone; Dani and Sana were with her. They swarmed into Maia's room even before Maia could say hello.

"What's going on?" Nafi asked as she plopped down at the edge of Maia's bed. "Planning to take a break from eating today?"

"No, nothing like that," Maia replied as casually as she could. "Just tired, that's all."

Nafi squinted and Dani raised a brow. Maia knew there was no hiding the truth from them. They would know she was worried. Truth was, her heart weighed like a boulder and guilt made her sag. She should have never snuck into the Chancery. *Never!* She should have never risked her friends' lives. Now that Amanii knew she was at the Chancery, what would stop the Xifarians from arresting them? *Nothing!* It was just a matter of time before they struck.

"You worry too much, Maia." Sana threw her arms around Maia's neck and gave a light squeeze. A whiff of lemon blossoms, Sana's signature perfume, lifted Maia's spirits a little. Sana tinkled on. "There's nothing to break your head over yet. No one can just come and take you away. They can't take any of you away. You are not just random kids. You're at the center of everything. At least for as long as you're in the Alliance Initiative and at ThulaSu, all eyes are on you."

Sana was right. She was safe as long as she was part of the Initiative, but how long would that last?

"Come on, let's go eat," Dani suggested cheerily.

They marched down to the dining hall and Maia quietly worked on the regular serving of pottage as well as a generous helping of freshly chopped melons. Rayan appeared briefly during breakfast but took off soon.

"I'm taking combat lessons from Monk Konnae," she said before rushing away.

"Isn't that the teacher Maks and Aman spoke about the other day?" Nafi asked, chomping through a large piece of melon. "Which reminds me, where's Maks? We haven't seen him in a while."

"He's around," Maia replied tersely, hoping Nafi would not keep probing. Truth was, she had been avoiding Maks since the kiss.

"I'm surprised Monk Konnae is offering lessons to Rayan," Dani said, thankfully veering the conversation away from Maks and memories of their awkward last meeting.

"My father keeps telling me to take combat lessons," Sana said, studying her perfectly manicured nails.

"Why don't you?" Nafi asked. "I believe everyone should learn basic skills to defend oneself. You should too."

Sana rolled her eyes. "You sound just like my father. Can't make him understand that I don't like touching random people, let alone start grappling them."

Nafi's mouth fell open. "Say if someone attacks you, what are you gonna do? Scream for help and pray that someone comes to your aid?"

"Sure, I'd scream. That'd help."

"And then?" Nafi was not about to let the discussion end.

"Then what? As you said, there'd be someone to help," Sana replied nonchalantly.

Nafi shook her head vigorously. "No, Sana. You can't depend on others to help you. You have to learn to fight for yourself."

The tussle would have continued—Maia realized both girls were equally stubborn in their ways—had it not been for Kusha and Ren rushing to the table. Both looked glum, but Ren more so than Kusha. He was wearing an armband similar to the ones Kehorkjin and Taillefei were wearing the previous night.

"News?" Nafi asked when the boys had grabbed bowls of grub.

"Yes, plenty. And none of it's good," Ren replied. "Someone has broken the Sedara. Remember when we saw it misfiring on our way back from the Chancery? It must've been already broken then."

"But how?" The incredulous words barely escaped Maia's mouth. "Who can do that?"

Ren's face turned a shade darker. An unending pit opened up at the bottom of Maia's stomach. She had an idea how this could play out, and that alarming idea lurking at the back of her mind all along sprung forward. She sucked in as much air as she could, hoping that'd help her frame her next question.

"They suspect me, don't they? I'm a Shimugien, the obvious

culprit."

Ren held her gaze steadily for a moment and nodded. "Yes, they do. As you said, you're a Shimugien. You have absolute power over light and the L'miere crystals that make up the Sedara. You were on Xif the night this happened. And your family has a history of —"

"You must be joking," Nafi burst out. "Maia would never do anything like that. Besides, she was with us the whole time, don't you remember?"

Ren let out an exasperated sigh. "I've told them that, Nafi. Why do you think they aren't demanding that Maia submit to an interrogation? Because I vouched for her. I swore I was with her every moment we spent on Xif."

"Thanks, Ren," Maia said. Such suspicions and allegations were unavoidable. Ren was right and the Xifarians were right. She was the obvious suspect. But if she had not done it, then who did? "Can't someone fix the Sedara?" she asked.

Ren shoved a spoonful of lumpy pottage into his mouth and gulped it down. "They're trying. The Mahswa left for Xif last night. She's up there now trying to figure out what's wrong."

"So the Tierremorphes can fix this?"

"Well, if it's fixable. We don't know yet if it is. And then . . ." Ren stopped midway and gulped another spoonful. "We don't know how much the Mahswa alone will be able to help anyway."

"But there are other Tierremorphes, right?"

The Tierremorphes were people born with an innate ability to terraform or move land to their will. They had been fundamental in making the Xif of the present day possible. They had carved out the underground settlement with their power, a power that was said to have been bestowed by the magical L'miere crystals.

Ren gave a sad shake of his head. "The dimming of the Sedara has affected the Tierremorphes also. Most of them have lost their powers, either partially or fully."

Dani gasped and the others at the table sat with their mouths open. Maia could not believe this was happening. Years ago, the

Mahswa had told them of how the Tierremorphes were getting weaker over generations, of how they had to routinely travel to Xif's surface to rejuvenate and restore their abilities. The L'miere crystals had made them powerful. It made sense therefore that when the Sedara — basically a collection of millions of L'miere crystals — was endangered, so were the Tierremorphes.

Sana, sitting next to Ren, placed a hand on his shoulder. "I'm sorry, Ren," she whispered, speaking for everyone else gathered around the table.

A stifling silence settled until Ren dropped his spoon noisily into the bowl and pushed it away. "This tastes awful," he declared.

"What about the chancellor? How is he?" Dani asked.

Ren's face twisted. "Not well. He . . ." He threw a cautious look around before leaning forward to whisper, "he's infected with a bad virus. They suspect he was poisoned during the gala."

Poisoned? "What's going on? How can all this be happening at the same time? And don't tell me they suspect I did this as well?" Maia asked.

Ren shook his head. "No, they don't. But—"

"So that's why the Prime Directive was called for?" Nafi interrupted. "So now a Royal's in charge?"

"Yes. Rahina Quemiila is in charge. She's our queen."

Nafi gulped, her eyes turning wide and round. "Ooh, a real queen? I've never seen one. Does she wear a crown?"

Ren shot an annoyed look at her. "I don't know, Nafi. I've never seen a queen either."

"Sorry," Nafi said. "I didn't mean to—"

"It's all right," Ren said as he got to his feet. "I have to go. The envoys have asked us to see them before they leave."

"Guess it's an all-Xifarian meeting, huh?" Nafi asked when Ren had left the table.

"Should be," Kusha said. "My father has asked that everyone be extra cautious. We don't know how the Xifarians might react to this catastrophe."

Maia was sure of one way they would react—by attacking her. She was already in their crosshairs. She had made a mistake and dragged her friends into a silly plot, and attacking Amanii weighed on her heavily. But the thought of being blamed for the attempted murder of the chancellor was unfathomable.

"I'm gonna go follow Ren," Nafi declared, jumping to her feet. "I'd like to see what's going on."

"Nafi, I don't think that's a good idea," Kusha sounded a cautionary note. "Ameron will be there. And you—"

"I'll be just fine," Nafi said, waving dismissively at Kusha.

"Wait, I'll come with you." Dani ran after Nafi as she scooted away from the table.

For a moment or two, Maia hesitated, and then she got up as well. Kusha shook his head vehemently. "Maia, you shouldn't be anywhere near the Xifarians. That man practically threatened you last night."

"I won't go anywhere near them." Maia tried to reassure. "I'll just keep an eye on Nafi. Maybe you should come too."

Kusha exhaled loudly and shook his head in an exhausted sort of way. "I'll finish this mush and then come find you. But, please, Maia, don't get into another argument with those people."

With a quick nod at Kusha, Maia rushed off after Dani and Nafi. She had not reached the doorway of the dining hall when the sound of footsteps caught up to her. She turned to find Sana a pace behind her.

"I'm coming too," Sana said. "Can't sit out the main act."

Maia had to chuckle a little. If she had not known Sana any better she would have thought her cousin was just an airhead. But she knew this was simply Sana's way of talking through worrying situations.

They found Dani and Nafi huddled behind a large pillar near the walkway where the Xifarians had crowded the previous night. Nafi beckoned them over.

"They're in that room." She thumbed at the wall nearest to them. Then she pointed surreptitiously at a clerestory window that sat up high on the wall. It was covered by a thick metal grille. "We can hear them talk . . . but just a little. Kehorkjin's in there with the envoys now."

"What are you trying to do?" Maia whispered as Nafi tiptoed to the wall and pressed her ear on it.

"Trying to listen, of course."

Maia looked around quickly to make sure no one was watching them, as did Dani. Sana, on the other hand, chuckled.

Nafi frowned. "What's with you?" she demanded.

"You can't hear them through those walls by placing your ear on them," Sana replied, still chuckling.

Nafi crossed her arms and narrowed her eyes. "You got a better idea?"

"Yes, as a matter of fact, I do," Sana replied. She slipped a hand into her pocket and pulled out what looked like an egg. But it was not an egg; it was an exquisitely designed purse. Sana flicked the jeweled clasp and opened the top. She put her hand into the opening and yanked something out.

"What's that?" Maia asked, peering at the tiny object in Sana's hand that reminded her of a snail's shell.

Sana's brows danced. "Magic," she said mysteriously. She placed the snail shell on the wall, pulled out a conical object, and placed it on top of the shell. It reminded Maia of the megaphones the shopkeepers in Shiloh used to make announcements in the market, only they were twenty times larger. Sana was right. Just like magic, voices, clear and sharp, flowed out of the cone. Maia recognized Kehorkjin's voice.

"We have to be careful from now on. Whoever our enemy is, they could strike at you next."

"What did you do, Sana? What's this?" Nafi asked.

"Have you heard of buzzers?" Sana asked, then continued without waiting for a response. "Buzzers are tiny insects that are placed inside the walls to prevent eavesdropping. The bugs scramble the sounds and make them hard to decipher. Most old Solianese houses have them, and obviously ThulaSu as well. So if you placed your ear on the wall, you'd hear nothing but a muffled rumble."

"But this is just the opposite," Nafi said. "You can hear them clearly."

"Yes, and that's because of this instrument. It's called a de-buzzer. It not only clears the scrambling but also uses the buzzers in its path to amplify and transmit what they hear instead of scrambling it." Sana stroked the tiny equipment she held carefully on the wall. "De-buzzers are extremely hard to find and are very precious. Because as you can see, they are extremely effective."

"Where did you get this?" Maia asked, and immediately regretted asking. In some ways, Sana was like Ren. The less you knew about her means, the better.

"My mother might've misplaced a thing or two she inherited from my grandpa," Sana said casually. She pointed at the de-buzzer and raised her brow. "Wanna listen now?"

Maia nodded eagerly. "You can leave now," a man said; Maia guessed it was Ameron. "Stay near the door. Don't let anyone come in."

There was the sound of shuffling feet. A door opened and then closed. There was a moment of silence and then Ameron spoke again.

"Please keep watch on our children, Kehorkjin. If I could, I'd pull my daughter out of the Initiative, but a promise has been given and I have to abide by it. The stars know, I don't breathe in peace while they're on this god-forsaken planet. And now, after this—"

"I'll keep watch." Kehorkjin's short reply came quickly.

"You should also keep an eye on the traitor's spawn and her friends," Taillefei said. Maia stiffened, fists curling on hearing the offensive name they called her. "They're behind this dreadful situation, I know it."

Kehorkjin chuckled. "They are just kids, Taillefei. They could not possibly have done half of this. Besides, they were at the XDA the whole time. I told you so."

Maia's fingertips turned cold. How long could Kehorkjin's lies shield them? Lies always fell apart . . . always.

"You lie, Kehorkjin," Taillefei snarled, almost making Maia jump. "I know they were at the Chancery that night. I know it. Only I don't have proof. But I'll find it sooner or later."

Once again, Kehorkjin gave a wry chuckle. "You don't believe my word now?"

"No, I don't," Taillefei snapped. "I would've had you interrogated already, but Ameron here keeps stopping me. You're lucky to have him as a friend, Kehorkjin, but one of these days your luck will run out. I'd be careful if I were you."

Maia and her friends exchanged a quick glance, guilt surging in Maia's already heavy heart. Their actions—her need to find answers—had also landed Kehorkjin in trouble. If anything were to happen to him . . .

"You need not worry about me. You have plenty on your hands already," Kehorkjin replied coldly. "Please keep us updated on the chancellor's health."

"Yes, we will," Ameron replied.

"Any news of the younger one?" Kehorkjin asked. Maia did not quite understand what he meant, but she could hear the master's voice shake.

"No. Nothing at all," Ameron replied.

"I wouldn't be surprised if he were part of this," Taillefei said suddenly. "He mentored that team of rats, didn't he? Who knows what that traitor's spawn brainwashed him to do?"

Realization hit Maia squarely in the gut. They were speaking about Miir! She leaned closer to the de-buzzer as if that would transport her into the room. *Was Miir alive?*

"Taillefei!" Kehorkjin shouted. "I don't mind if you besmirch my name, but do not, in the name of the Sedara, dishonor that kid. That boy is one of the most trustworthy students I've ever come across in my entire life. He would not, no . . . not ever, even dream of treason like this. The Miir I know will die a thousand deaths to protect Xif, and I know people well. So, stop this vile accusation right here."

For a moment, there was quiet. As a heart-numbing rush of fear swept through her, Maia craved for air. Then Taillefei spoke again.

"All right. If Miir is such a loyal soldier, then why did he desert our greatest cause? Did you know the last time he was seen with his father, the chancellor, they had been arguing?"

"I know all that," Kehorkjin snapped. "That doesn't prove anything."

"Maybe not. But now that the chancellor's been poisoned, I don't see one reason to stop the Rahina from naming him a fugitive of the Xifarian nation."

"He hasn't been seen for months. And yet you accuse him of this?"

"He could've snuck back in easily to finish what he'd started. You know what? This is starting to make sense now. He came back to tie up every loose strand—attacked my daughter, poisoned his father, and destroyed the Sedara—all in one clean strike."

Miir hasn't been seen for months? By the time Kehorkjin's words sunk in, Maia's insides had turned to mush. Her legs almost buckled under her, and the world turned cold.

"Don't you dare, Taillefei," Kehorkjin said. "Don't bring your personal vendetta into this. Miir deserves better, particularly when he's not here to defend his name."

"Or what, Kehorkjin? What are you going to do?"

Maia had never heard a silence so deafening. She braced for the sound of Kehorkjin's fist crashing into Taillefei's jaw, or more angry words. Nothing of that sort happened.

"Have a safe journey. Prayers for our nation," Kehorkjin said.

There was a shuffle of feet, the sound of a door opening and closing. By the time Sana peeled her de-buzzer off the wall and slipped it into her purse, heavy footfalls were already drawing near.

And Maia stood there dumbfounded, heart pounding like a war-hammer and the world around her teetered precariously.

CHAPTER THIRTY-FIVE

ABOUT A BOY

Master Kehorkjin strode past the corner, his heavy treading echoing ominously across the corridors. He stepped off the paved walkway onto the yard separating the building they were in and the next residential block. As soon as Kehorkjin stepped on the grass, Nafi shot out of their hiding place.

"Come on, we have to catch him," she said, and then sprinted ahead.

"What is she trying to do?" Maia asked Dani, bewildered. She was still shaken up by what she had just heard about Miir, and she did not know what to think. In one moment, it sounded as if he was alive, and in the next moment, her hopes deflated like a balloon.

"Not sure," Dani replied as she and Maia headed after Nafi. "But I guess it has something to do with Miir."

"Miir?" Sana asked as she followed Dani while tugging Maia behind her by the arm. "That's the guy they were talking about? The chancellor's son who—"

"Yes," Dani replied.

"You knew him?" Sana asked.

Dani did not reply, so Maia felt obliged to satisfy her cousin's curiosity. Ahead of them, Nafi had already caught up with Master Kehorkjin.

"Yes, we did," Maia said. "He was our mentor during the Xifarian phase." As she summarized their interactions and encounters over the years, Sana's eyes grew wide.

"Oh, they were talking about you then," Sana said finally. She was about to say some more but Kehorkjin's sharp voice drew her attention.

"I do not think it is your place to meddle in these matters," he said. His voice had dropped when he spoke again. "You're lucky you got out that night. You're lucky Yilosario chose to cover your tracks. Do not squander away that blessing. The best . . . safest thing for you is to stay out of this."

"But—"

"Games are over, Miss Nafi," he said sternly. "A good use of your time right now would be to prepare for war."

"But—"

"I have a lot of work to do and I have to rush," he continued, ignoring Nafi's attempts to speak. "A word of advice, although knowing you, you'll have no use for it: It is better if you lie low for a while."

"I—"

"You were a plucky bunch," the master said, thoughtfully as he turned to Dani and Maia, "and a deserving team too. It's a shame. And who may you be?"

He was looking at Sana, and Maia was surprised that he had known right away that she was not part of the Initiative. All the time he seemed so disinterested, but he actually knew all of the participants.

"I'm Sana. Maia's cousin. I'm here, visiting."

The master grunted in response. This break in conversation was all Nafi seemed to have needed. She pounced in, eyes shining.

"It's about Miir. I have something to tell you about Miir," she almost threw out the words.

It came out so suddenly, so unexpectedly that Maia did not know what to think. What could Nafi know that'd help Miir?

The master frowned, and a pall of sadness quickly fell across his face. "What has that—"

"Will you listen to me? Please?" Nafi cried out. "He's not guilty of . . . anything that Taillefei said."

Kehorkjin stared at her and shook his head. "How do you know about . . . what Taillefei said?"

"We eavesdropped," Sana declared with a bright smile. Master Kehorkjin's eyes narrowed. Sana shrugged in response. "Well, don't look at me. Nafi said we had to listen in, so I just helped."

"I see," Kehorkjin's replied. He turned toward Nafi. "And what do you know about . . . this?"

"They are wrong to accuse him," Nafi said. "He couldn't have—"

"Calm down, Nafi. Tell me what you know."

Nafi threw a look at Maia and took a long breath. "All right. First of all, you know it was Maia who fought with Amanii that night. Miir was never there." She looked beseechingly at Maia. "Maia, tell him."

Maia swallowed the lump in her throat. "She's right. Amanii was about to call the guards on us, so I had to take care of her. Didn't want to hurt her much," she said.

"I know. You've told me that already," the master said. "Well, Amanii was hurt. She couldn't recall much of what happened to her that night, which is another lucky break for you. But the problem is that you can't vouch for Miir because then you'd be admitting your unlawful entry into the Chancery. And that's probably what Taillefei is counting on."

Taillefei's twisted plan made sense. Their words could never be used against his.

Kehorkjin continued in a sad voice, "Amanii is only part of the story though, the smallest part. The other accusation, of Miir poisoning his father, is truly grave."

"I know. And it's not true either," Nafi blurted.

"Nafi, I know you are upset," the master replied, sighing deeply. "I do not believe that Miir is capable of such an act. But his own brother Remii gave his sworn testimony that Miir had a fallout with the chancellor. And he's been missing. So, if you add up the two—"

"What was the fallout over?" Nafi jumped in.

The air was spinning around Maia fast. She sincerely hoped she was not the cause of Miir's troubles.

Kehorkjin avoided glancing at Maia. "The fallout between Miir and his father was about pursuing a certain person of interest to the Xifarian Republic."

Maia twitched. *A person of interest!* That was what she was to the Xifarian Republic, just a bunch of cold, lifeless words. Maia's thoughts flitted along and settled on the pricklier subject. Did Miir think she had been treated unfairly by the Xifarians? Would he go against his people to defend her? Could he have voiced his opinion against Chairman Phocluus? Nothing he said ever suggested that he could, yet . . .

"You have a funny way of talking, you know that?" Sana giggled, drawing a frown from the master. "You could just have said Maia instead of the person of interest of so-and-so, and—"

"Thank you for your observations," Master Kehorkjin snapped, glaring at Sana. "Now—"

"You have a temper too," Sana declared. "You will do well with a mix of Hortenso leaves and bark of Clovin. What do you think, Dani?"

Dani did not reply. She looked sheepishly at the master and then back at Sana and shook her head. Thankfully, Nafi jumped into the conversation.

"Master Kehorkjin, that couldn't have been something the chancellor and Miir disagreed on," she said in an insistent voice. "I know because I heard Remii talk to his father about it on the night of the gala, the same night when you came to help us out of the Chancery grounds."

Maia forgot to breathe. She could hardly even think. Why didn't

CHAPTER THIRTY-FIVE

Nafi tell them about this before?

"Hush, they're looking," Kehorkjin said, his sharp eyes scanning back and forth. "Come this way," he said, gesturing in the direction of a line of shrubbery a few paces away.

"But I heard, Master Kehorkjin," Nafi blurted once they were all safely clustered behind the shrubs. "You see, the archives are right above the chancellor's office."

Kehorkjin inhaled sharply. "What did you hear exactly?"

"Remii was mad at the chancellor for forgiving Miir."

The master's eyes lit up. "What?"

Nafi nodded vigorously.

"I was there, too, but I was looking for a book, so I didn't pay much attention," Dani added. "But I'm quite sure Remii and the chancellor were arguing."

"But . . ." Kehorkjin said, a look of disbelief rippled across his face. "But that's not—"

"Yes," Nafi interrupted. "Remii was mad, raving like a crazy guy. He said Miir was too soft and their father had spoiled him. He said no good would come out of this. Apparently, when Miir had planned to resign from his apprenticeship at the SDS because he did not approve of their ways of retaliation, the chancellor supported Miir."

Nafi paused a bit. Her gaze fell on Maia for a moment but she quickly looked away.

"And then?" Kehorkjin asked impatiently.

"The chancellor said he didn't care what came out of it. He would always support Miir's decision. He said he should have stood his ground, but his weakness came in the way. He wished he had courage like Miir and he wished Remii could be more like his brother."

"Oooh boy!" Sana's comment made everyone turn toward her. She made a face and wiggled her brows. "That couldn't have sat well with Remii. I'm guessing he would be in a murderous rage after that? That's your motive right there, Master K. I would look for that dastardly Remii if I were you."

"Thank you, dear, again," Master Kehorkjin replied, his tone surprisingly warm. He scanned their faces quickly and nodded. "Anything else? Nafi?"

"No, nothing else," Nafi said. "Remii left the room right after. The chancellor looked fine. After a while, we had located the book and we got out of there."

"Hmmm," the master said as he patted Nafi's shoulder absentmindedly. "Let me see what I can do. I just hope that the boy is safe, wherever he might be."

Chapter Thirty-Six

A Date with Disgrace

The girls lingered near the shrubbery after Master Kehorkjin left to speak with the Rahina immediately on the matter. There was very little to hope for anyway, even with Nafi's testimony because he could not reveal Nafi was in the Chancery that night.

Maia stole a quick glance at Nafi as they watched the master walk away. The girl looked sad, forlorn. A wave of emotions washed over Maia as she stood there, her limbs numb and tingling. She felt relieved and sad, but more frustrated and angry. Why hadn't Nafi disclosed what she had heard that night at the Chancery? Why didn't her friends share important details with her anymore? Was it because Maia was always so vehement about Miir and his actions?

The crux of Maia's problem lay deeper. Thoughts were coalescing fast and furious in her head, like long-missing pieces of a puzzle. She was not happy to find them though, because she did not want this puzzle completed. Yet they came anyway in an endless rush.

How long had Miir been missing? Had he been gone since

Chairman Phocluus had tried to kidnap her?

Maia's legs buckled under her as her mind frenziedly connected the dots. Gulping frantically to stop the dryness in her throat from swallowing her up from inside, she sank to the ground and slumped against the bushes.

Stop! She *had* to stop thinking she had killed him.

Maia turned away from her friends, angry at herself for encouraging imaginary guilt over a make-believe incident. In her mind, she repeated the lines she had been telling herself for months. That fight with Miir she had seen *had* to be a dream, nothing else. Miir was alive. He *had* to be alive. He had simply had a disagreement with his family and left home. People did that sometimes, especially idealistic young people like Miir. And now that had gotten him into trouble.

There! Simple as that!

But even if that were true, wasn't she responsible in a way? He had stood up for her, hadn't he? That was what they all said.

Maybe . . . or maybe not.

Surely she was guilty of having accused Miir of things when he had been defending her, but the mess he was in now could not have been Maia's fault. If anyone wanted to take a stand against anything, they had to first know what the outcome could be. And Miir had decided to go against his brother Remii and Chairman Phocluus. There had to be consequences, he had to know. If Miir did not think that through, how could it be her fault?

Dani's hand fell on her shoulder. "What's going on, Maia?"

Maia clutched at her mother's pendant, hoping to draw strength out of its broken shape. Tears threatened to burn her eyes. "I misunderstood him," Maia blurted, forgetting all her resolve to keep the gut-wrenching self-reproach away. "He'd been trying to help me all along."

"It's all right, Maia," Dani whispered. "I'm sure Miir will be fine."

How can he be fine when he's dead?

Maia cradled her head and shook it vigorously as if to fling the thought of Miir's death far and away.

Stop! You don't know if he's dead.

"Like she cares if Miir lives or dies." Nafi's sharp words were jolting. Every effort Maia had put in to keep her emotions in check faded away in an instant. The smothering mountain of guilt vanished with Nafi's bitter comment. Instead, an aching need to protect herself swamped over Maia.

"Tell me why I should care," Maia shot back.

"See?" Nafi tilted her head toward Maia as she glared at Dani. "I told you, didn't I? She doesn't give a hell's hoot about Miir. About what he did for us."

"Just tell me why," Maia shouted back. "All right, so he has done a few things for us. But he's also done me plenty bad. I don't understand why you always expect me to cry a river for him."

"Because he's a friend. That's why," Nafi yelled.

"Maia!" Sana tried to pull her out of it, but Maia nudged her away. She had to end this with Nafi, right here, right now.

"No," she screamed. "He is not my friend. He's your friend, and that's fine. But don't try to make me like him, because I won't, all right?"

"Oh, sure." Nafi's face burned red. "After all the time he helped you, why should you like him?"

"For the last time, Nafi," Maia hissed through gritted teeth, "he helped me once, with Yoome, just once."

"And if he hadn't, you wouldn't get to live on and be the queen of this wonderful drama, would you?"

"Nafi, stop this, please," Dani intervened.

Maia had the urge to smack Nafi. How dare she say such things! Center of attention? She did not give a hoot about attention.

Nafi showed no intention of stopping. "So now you know Miir went against Chairman Phocluus because he didn't like the way Phocluus was harassing you. Think any different now?"

Nafi's mocking smile stoked Maia's anger. "All right, let's say he did take a stand against Phocluus. It doesn't mean he did it for me. I think he stood up for his own beliefs. There's a difference."

Nafi rolled her eyes and scoffed. "Really, Maia? That's your excuse for not caring?"

Dani tugged Nafi's arm. "The boys will be looking for us. Let's go."

"No," Maia said with vehemence. "We're not going anywhere. Not until we're done with this."

"I agree," replied Nafi, crossing her arms as she locked stares with Maia. "Let's figure out who you really are."

Maia's fists curled and her spine stiffened, ready to deal with Nafi's scorn firmly.

"I'm thankful to Miir for saving me from Yoome, and I always will be. Maybe he took a stand against Phocluus because of me. If that's true, then I'm grateful. But I can *never* forget that he was responsible for Dada's death. And Herc's death. And Emmy's. That was my family, Nafi," Maia screamed. "You expect me to forget them? Have you forgotten your sister? You'll never forgive Loriine for things her father has done and yet you expect me to forgive Miir?" She paused, suddenly realizing she was trembling like a leaf.

Nafi's gaze wavered. For a moment, a conflicted, almost pained look glazed Nafi's eyes and she looked away. Then she sighed and turned back.

"Maia, I'm not saying what he did was always right. What I'm saying is that he's trying to make up for his mistakes. He really is. You know that, don't you?"

He was, Nafi. Not anymore. He's dead now. I killed him.

She was sure, more now than before that Miir tried to make amends. And he had chosen that path because of what he had brought upon her Dada, knowingly or not. Miir put himself in jeopardy because he had tried to make up for his wrong toward her. And that's why . . . she had to tell them everything. A dream or not, people had to know.

But they'll hate me. And they're all I have.

"Don't you want to give him a chance, Maia?" Nafi's pleading voice shook Maia out of her trance. "You know, not everyone asks for a second chance, and not many people have the courage to ask. So, when someone comes along trying to fix what he has broken, I think he at least deserves a kind thought, if not a helping hand."

The world, Nafi's blazing eyes, receded. All Maia was left with was shame and guilt. It was too late to give Miir the second chance he deserved. She should have given him a moment to plead his case. She did not. Instead, she blew him away to his . . . death.

Yes, I killed him.

Nobody knew where Miir was. That was because he was dead, his body rotting among the Darkwoods. She had to tell them the truth because until they knew, people like Taillefei would keep accusing him of crimes he did not commit, dragging his name through the mud. Miir did not deserve that. Kehorkjin was right, Miir deserved better. She had to clear his name. She owed him that much.

Maia collected her thoughts and calmed them as much as she could before speaking. Maia laid out each word carefully, knowing well there was no coming back after they had left her mouth.

"I know why Miir is missing," Maia said finally.

They turned to look at her . . . Dani's clear blue eyes wide and worried, an uncomprehending stare from Sana, Nafi's gaze narrow and questioning. Everything moved slowly, and Maia could see each blink, each twitch of brows, and every little curl of lips. The air felt thick, too warm for comfort. Yet an icy cold engulfed her insides and refused to budge.

Then a loud voice fell on her ears like a hammer, shaking her out of the tight moment and out of its discomfort.

"There you are," Kusha said. "We've been looking all over for you guys. What are you doing here?" He grinned.

Ren peeked from behind Kusha. "What's going on?" he asked.

Ren! He would never forgive her.

"Maia says she knows why Miir is missing," Nafi said.

"Wait. What?" Ren frowned and crossed his arms. "Miir is missing? Since when? And who told you that?"

"Kehorkjin said he's been missing for a while," Nafi replied. "And now Taillefei's accusing him of trying to poison his father."

Ren held his arms up. "Slow down. Taillefei did what? How do you know this? Even I don't know this."

Nafi gave a careless wave of her hand. "We eavesdropped. It's a long story. Sana has this thing . . . never mind all that. Taillefei thinks Miir had a fight with his father over how they were hunting Maia down and that's why he deserted the Xifarian cause and took off. Then he came back to take revenge on his father."

"That's not true," Ren said vehemently. "That's a filthy lie."

Nafi nodded. "I know. I told Kehorkjin that. I told him I heard Remii fight with the chancellor because the chancellor took Miir's side."

"Where did you hear that?" Ren asked.

Nafi cast a quick look around and whispered, "At the Chancery Archives. The far end of the archives I was searching in is right above the chancellor's office. That's where they were arguing. I heard them."

"Stop." Ren held up a hand. "You didn't tell us that before. Why not?"

Nafi exhaled noisily. She looked around at the ground, the shrubs, and the sky. Finally, she looked Ren in the eye. "Because some people around here don't exactly like Miir being mentioned," she said in an accusing voice. "I'm tired of fights over whether he's good or evil and whatnot. Besides, I didn't think knowing that would make a difference. No one cares anyway."

Ren jabbed his chest angrily. "I do. I care."

"Well, sorry. Anyway, I told Kehorkjin what I heard. He said he'll look into it. And now Maia says she knows why Miir's been missing."

They turned toward her once more, eyes blazing and brows scrunched. There was no way out of this other than through the fire. Maia knew she would have to walk through hell. And she would never be ready for it. She had to do it nonetheless.

"I think I killed him," she said.

It was a short sentence, but far from simple. Faces froze, twisted, and crumpled as the words sunk in. Ren teetered and dropped to the ground. There was silence—nervous, prickling, and suffocating silence. Maia knew this was the moment she would remember forever, the moment she lost the most treasured thing left in her life—her friends. Color seeped out of the bright golden sunshine bathing them. As Ren kneeled in front of her and looked into her eyes, his face turned ashen.

"You can't mean that," his voice barely a whisper.

Maia wished that were true. But it was not.

"I saw Miir after I escaped from Chairman Phocluus and his people. Sometime before you came and found me on the cliff," Maia said. Every word that escaped her mouth seemed to suck away a bit of her strength and left her hungry for air. Maia wheezed before she could speak again. "I fought him."

Ren's mottled eyes went blank as if someone had wiped every trace of emotion from them. His lips moved to make up words, but there was no life in them. Just sounds strung together to carry thoughts across.

"Why did you fight him? Did he attack you?"

Miir did not attack, but she had thought he meant to imprison her. She had done the only thing that made sense at that moment—fight for her freedom, her life.

"I thought he was with Phocluus."

"And?" Nafi's sharp voice tore through the gray around her like a flash of lightning and made Maia flinch.

"I fought him. He fought back. And . . . I think he fell off the cliff."

Even Dani did not slip an arm over her shoulders like she always did. A pallid world surrounded Maia and only her friends' eyes burned through it.

Ren scoffed. "You *think* he fell? You think? What does that even mean?"

A guttural sound escaped Maia's throat. "I don't remember clearly, Ren. I see flashes of scenes. I hear pieces of conversation. But that's all. I'm not sure what I did. I still don't know what exactly happened."

Ren fell back and ran his hands through his hair. "We need to tell Kehorkjin. We need to find out."

"Let's go," Nafi said. "Let's go find Kehorkjin."

Was that it? Wasn't anyone going to yell at her for what she did?

Ren jumped to his feet and looked at Kusha. "Are you coming? We need someone to guide us to the cliff."

Ren turned toward Dani when Kusha nodded. "What about you, Dani?"

"Yes, of course."

Wasn't anyone going to ask her to come? Maia scrambled to her feet and tried to peer at their faces. No one glanced back.

"Should I come with you?" Maia asked finally, and it took the last bit of strength she had left to get all the words out. A lump sat doggedly in her throat and grew bigger as she waited for someone— anyone—to answer.

Ren turned around. The edge of his mouth twisted cruelly before he replied, "I think you've done your part."

Sana had been listening quietly so far. Now she almost sprang forward to face Ren. "You know what? Enough's enough. Maia didn't purposely attack anyone. She thought he was going to drag her to prison so she defended herself. She has the right to defend herself, doesn't she?"

Ren's eyes had stilled. He had clearly not expected Sana to jump in. He quickly recovered and waved her away. "You should stay out of this, Sana. You don't know anything about this."

Sana tilted her head and chuckled. "Really? I don't, huh? Well, I know this. I know Phocluus and his cronies set Maia's family on fire and chased her halfway across the planet. I know for almost a whole year she went to bed at night not knowing if she would live to see the following day. I know Maia had friends die in her arms, and I know she heard Phocluus threaten everything she holds dear."

The more Sana defended her, the more Maia's eyes burned. A barrage of tears, hurt, and pain wanted to crash out of her. She did not let it. She was not going to show them how badly she was broken inside.

Sana had not finished yet. "The guy you cry for? Well, he was another of Phocluus's puppets. What was Maia supposed to do?"

Ren stared silently at Sana's flushed face. Then he shrugged. "She could've at least asked whose side he was on before driving him off that cliff."

"Yes, why not? And while she was at it, she could've blown him a kiss and hoped he'd turn into her knight in shining armor," Sana retorted. Frowning, she shook her head and shooed Ren away. "Go, Ren. Just go. Leave us alone."

Ren looked uncomfortable. Perhaps Sana's words—harsh but undoubtedly true—had stirred something in him. He nodded at Maia, his face twisting as if he was debating something.

"You know, Sana's right. You were . . . are in a situation that I can't even imagine. You didn't think, you reacted. I remember. I saw you right after you escaped Phocluus and you . . . you weren't yourself."

He paused and distractedly poked the ground with his feet. Maia wondered if that meant she was forgiven, but even if Ren looked a tad less furious, Nafi stood with her fists curled, glaring.

"You know why I'm upset though?" Ren asked, and Maia realized he was not done chastising her. "Not because of how you acted in the heat of the moment, but because how any time we talk about Miir you refuse to give him a second chance. As Nafi said, she didn't speak about what she heard because she was afraid of your rants. That's not fair, Maia. Sometimes, you have to see if someone is trying to make amends."

Ren had a point just like Nafi did, but how was she to know Miir was trying? He did not tell her anything, nor did his actions or words give a clue.

"I didn't see a change in him, Ren," she said. "Or I wouldn't—"

"You were blinded by rage, Maia. And you still are," Ren said. He turned away for a moment and when he looked back, his face had twisted with pain. "I had made a promise to never tell you, but . . ."

Ren paused for a moment, his eyes shining with tears. "Do you know how I made it to that cliff to rescue you from Phocluus that day?"

Maia blinked. The world had become a blur. Every part of her was numb and cold from fear of what Ren was going to say. She was sure she already knew. It had been Miir all along. The unknown friend who had helped Ren find her that fateful day was the one she had rewarded with death.

She held her breath, nails digging into her palms. The pain felt good. It was the only thing that felt real.

"I was there because Miir told me to. He had been preparing me for months so I could come to help you when they struck. While you were busy hating him and wishing the worst for him, he was risking his reputation and his life to save yours."

"I'm sorry," Maia blurted. She felt an arm circle around hers. A whiff of lemon blossoms nudged her dulled senses. "I'm so sorry."

"It's too late now," Ren said. "He's gone. You took care of that."

Sana's grip on her arm tightened and for that Maia was thankful. She could barely feel her legs under her. It was strange that even after dealing with a zillion hurtful words from her enemies, a few harsh ones from her friends left her so utterly drained. Or perhaps, that was how it was supposed to be.

"You've been blessed with an immense power, Maia," Ren continued in a sad yet scathing tone. "What you do with it is up to you. You choose. Just because you have this power doesn't mean you can blast anyone off this world. Just because you can doesn't mean you should."

Ren's wilted face turned away from Maia. Silent moments trickled past tediously until Nafi stomped forward and tugged Ren's arm. "We should talk to Kehorkjin now. Let's not waste any more time," she said.

Nafi glanced at Maia. Her face was carved out of stone, and anger blazed fiercely in her emerald eyes. Maia held her fiery gaze, feeling wretched as it pierced her soul, making her heart twist painfully with guilt and shame. Then Nafi shook her head, with slow and obvious deliberation.

There would be no fixing this. Her friends would not forgive so easily, particularly not Nafi. She would not betray Maia, but she would never forget what Maia had unleashed on Miir.

"I thought you could do better, Maia," Nafi said in a quiet, detached sort of way. "I thought you could choose better. Now I don't know what to think of you anymore."

With that, Nafi grabbed Ren's arm and walked away. Dani and Kusha wavered for a few moments. Then they left as well. Watching them hurry away, even with the bright and warm sunshine streaming over her, Maia felt utterly cold and miserable, as if she had been abandoned in the middle of a raging blizzard.

Chapter Thirty-Seven

The Search for Truth

After her teammates left in search of Master Kehorkjin, Maia stood near the shrubbery until Sana nudged her back to the living quarters. Maia spent the rest of the day simply staring out of her window. For the most part, she could not think of what to do next. She could not even fully fathom what the outcome of her revelation could be. Sana refused to leave her alone, scuttling back and forth between the kitchen and Maia's room, ferrying food supplies. In the afternoon, Maia's roommate and chaperone Rayan also joined forces.

Maia did not sleep a wink that night, her mind a messy swirl of thoughts that kept growing bigger as time passed. The more she thought, the more jumbled it became and kept Maia tossing and turning. But, by the time the skies caught the first blush of pink, Maia knew what she needed to do.

True to her promise, Sana arrived, cradling a basketful of fresh bread and a jar of mixed-berry jam before the sun peeked over the buildings.

Maia glanced into the basket and raised an eyebrow. "It's not breakfast time yet. How did you—"

"Since you've decided to spend the rest of your days cocooned in your room like a hermit, I had to bribe the kitchen staff to get stuff."

Maia let out a small laugh and Sana looked at her curiously. "You laughed. That's a change. You'll live after all." She placed the basket on a small table and pulled it to the middle of the room.

"I'll live, Sana," Maia said. "Don't worry, I'll be fine."

"She didn't sleep all night," Rayan informed Sana, somewhat reproachfully. How Rayan knew she had not slept, Maia had no clue. But she was not wrong. Maia had been tossing and turning through the night, fighting battles in her sleep. "Make sure she eats well," Rayan instructed. "I have to meet Monk Konnae, but I'll try to come back quickly. Don't leave her alone."

"Of course not," Sana replied. "I'll be her shadow."

The two girls ate in silence after Rayan left and it was not until Sana had wrapped up the remainder of the bread and tucked the basket away in a corner that Maia decided to tell her cousin of her plans.

"I need to see Master Kehorkjin," she declared. "I need to find out where his room is."

Sana shrugged. "What's to find out? I already know."

"You do?" Maia did not hide her surprise, but she did not ask Sana how she knew either. Sana had her ways, and sometimes it was best to not know how.

"Yes, I do," Sana said. She perched elegantly on the side of Rayan's cot, evened the shiny pleats of her bright purple frock, crossed her legs, and arched a perfect brow at Maia. "The question is though, why do you need to see him? What are you up to?"

"I have to help him find the spot where Miir went over the cliff," Maia said. There was no hesitation in her voice, no fear either.

Sana's forehead scrunched. "You do remember that Ren and the others refused your help yesterday. If you go there now, they might refuse again. I don't think they'll come around to forgiving you so quickly, Maia."

Sana was not one to mince her words. Her cousin was not as caustic as Nafi—who could match Nafi anyway—but she was not the dainty wallflower that she appeared to be at first glance.

"I don't expect them to forgive me, Sana," Maia said. A small sigh tried to escape her, but she forced it down. "They're mad at me for a reason. Miir was good for the team. It's understandable they're devastated. They'll need time to come around, if they do at all."

Maia walked over to the window and studied the carefree clouds sailing across a purplish sky. Stifling another sigh, she forced her eyes away from the achingly beautiful scene.

"Miir was honorable to a fault. You know . . . it's true that I owe my life to Miir. When he went against me—captured Bikele and then went after Dada and Herc and Emmy, I . . ." Maia paused to fill her lungs with the crisp morning air.

"Are you *sure* he had anything to do with Dada's death?" Sana asked, peering into her eyes.

Maia inhaled sharply, but her lungs screamed for more. She drew in a jagged breath, knowing even all the air in the world would not be enough to satisfy her.

"I don't know, Sana," she said, rubbing the bridge of her nose. "*Shadow*, his Raptor, was there when our house was set on fire. He'd never give *Shadow* to anyone else, so he *had* to be there."

"Being there doesn't mean—"

"I know," Maia interjected desperately. "I know it doesn't mean he actually had anything to do with it. But still . . . he was present. He could've done something to stop it."

Sana nodded thoughtfully. "Well, you were there on Xif when the Sedara broke. So, the Xifarians would be right in accusing you then? You were at the Chancery when the chancellor was poisoned. You wanted him dead. Does it follow—"

"I know, Sana, it doesn't," Maia said through gritted teeth. Sana did not have to tell her, she knew already. She had blamed Miir for Dada's death because she wanted to. There was no proof of anything, there was no justification for her reasoning. Ren was right, it was blind rage, nothing else.

"I was wrong to accuse him." The words came out in a torturous wave, but hard as they were to say, Maia felt relief when they were out of her mouth. "It had stung so much more because I didn't expect him to be there. I didn't think he was my friend, but I was sure he'd side with what was fair. When he didn't, it hurt like hell. And I leaped to conclusions."

Sana tilted her head. "So you're saying you'll grovel for your friends' forgiveness?"

Maia shook her head. She wished it were as easy as that. But it was not. Nothing about Miir was easy.

"I'm not saying that. If my teammates don't ever talk to me again, it's their choice and I'll respect whatever they choose. But their forgiveness isn't what I'm worried about."

Sana left her perch and walked over, her face tight with concern. Maia continued with a bracing breath. "I've wronged Miir, Sana. And even though I can't bring him back, I can make amends. Regardless of what happened between him and me, Miir doesn't deserve a nameless death. He certainly doesn't deserve being slandered for something he didn't do. I have to help them find him—his remains—so his soul can rest in peace."

Sana's eyes narrowed as she carefully scanned Maia's face. "That's all nice, Maia," she said, "but your teammates might still refuse. They might say things that—"

"Of course, they will. That's why I need to speak to Kehorkjin directly. I'll have to find a way to convince him so he lets me do my part."

"You're absolutely sure about this?"

"Yes. As sure as I'll ever be."

Sana shrugged. "All right then. Since you've made up your mind, let's go find the K."

"The K?"

Sana wiggled her brows. "What's wrong with that? His mighty

presence deserves a distinctive name, so . . ."

They left the room soon after and went looking for Master Kehorkjin. Sana led the way across the central courtyard to one of the buildings on the northern side of the university complex. They walked up to the third floor and along a long corridor to the last room at the eastern end where Sana stopped.

Sana gestured in a grandiose way at the door. "The K's abode. Do you want to knock or should I?"

Maia's knuckles had barely touched the door when it fell open. Master Kehorkjin looked tired. Dark circles had grown overnight under his eyes. Maia noticed he was not wearing the traditional Xifarian Gambrill but a casual long-sleeved vest and pants. He looked different . . . approachable and open. Maia had expected curtness, if not outright anger, but she found none of that.

"Come," he said. Kehorkjin had always been sharp, but the familiarity with which he ushered them in surprised Maia. The master gestured at a small couch on one side of the room. "Please sit."

"You were expecting me?" Maia asked as Kehorkjin pulled an armchair across from them.

"Obviously," the master replied. "I am a teacher, Maia. Do you know what a good teacher does?"

Sana's arm shot up. "I know. Can I?"

The master's eyes narrowed a tad before a smile tugged the corner of his mouth. "Yes, please do."

"A good teacher makes a difference. Am I right?"

Kehorkjin chuckled. "Yes, they do. But how do they do that?" He paused for a bit and continued when Maia and Sana stayed quiet. "A good teacher has eyes to see through his pupils. He has to be a good judge of character first and foremost. Only after he knows a student — their strengths and their weaknesses — really well can he try and make that difference."

His clear gray eyes came to rest on Maia's. They were tranquil and had no trace of judgment in them. Maia did not hesitate to tell him everything she thought she knew.

"I want to help you piece it together," Maia said. "That's why I'm here. I should've come yesterday, but I couldn't think straight."

Kehorkjin nodded. The clear gong of breakfast hours drifted in through the open windows.

"I'm glad you came, Maia. I do admire your courage." Kehorkjin shook his head morosely. "This is an unfortunate turn of events. Miir was a respectable young man who had a very bright future ahead of him. It grieves me to think that future won't come to pass." He paused for a moment as if mulling his next words. "When the Republic hears of this tragic incident there will be uproar. You are already at the center of this storm, and I'm not sure that you want to insert yourself into it anymore by taking personal responsibility. That's what I told your friends yesterday."

As Maia fathomed the meaning of Kehorkjin's words, Sana jumped into the conversation. "What are you going to say then? What will you say happened to Miir?"

"That he was a casualty of Chairman Phocluus's failed venture. That Miir came to back them up and died in the aftermath. We only just discovered his—"

"No," Maia interrupted. "I'm sorry, Master Kehorkjin, but I'm not going to hide behind lies. Certainly not when it would mean lying about someone I've already wronged so dreadfully."

"Maia, it may be the wise choice," Kehorkjin said. "He won't come back no matter what you do, so why not protect yourself? After all, that's what he wanted to do."

Kehorkjin had a good point. But even thinking of twisting facts to protect herself prickled Maia.

"That's true, Master Kehorkjin. But like you said, I'm already at the center of the storm, so they'll come after me no matter what. Miir took a stand. He didn't mean to hide it. I think we'd disrespect his wishes if we suppress it. The truth must come out."

Sana placed an arm on her shoulder and squeezed a little. "Think about it this way, Maia. Miir's reputation with the Xifarian leadership might be in much better stead if they don't know he came to help you."

That was another way to think about it, but not the right way, Maia was sure. She looked at the far corner of the room, desperate to hide the dampness that had crept to the edges of her eyes.

"Miir was never afraid to speak the truth, Sana. Never. Every time we met, he said things I didn't like. As a matter of fact, that was why I hated him. I wasn't strong enough to handle what he said, so I found a way to put everything back on him. From what I can recall of our fight on the cliff, he said some bitter things again and I wanted to shut him up. I wanted to show him that I could shut him up. So you see, in a way he died defending the truth." Maia paused to moisten her rapidly drying lips. "I can't bring him back even though I want to. The least I can do now is stand up for what he believed in."

For a while, there was only the sound of their breathing. Then Kehorkjin cleared his throat. "All right then. You'll come with us. Your friends should be here anytime now. Ren will fly us to Devil's Ridge—that is the name of that cliff." He rose to his feet and peeked at the brightening skies. "Now if you'll excuse me, I shall get dressed. You can wait right here."

He had barely taken a step away when Maia said, "Master Kehorkjin, I know it makes no difference, but I want you to know that I'm truly sorry. I'd give anything to change the past so Miir could live."

Kehorkjin sighed. He placed a reassuring hand on Maia's shoulder. "So would I, Maia," he said. "So would I."

After Kehorkjin disappeared into the washroom and Maia sat back down, Sana linked her arm through Maia's and leaned close. "I'm proud of you, Maia," she whispered. "The K just gave you a way out, yet you chose the hard path because it was the right thing to do. Even if your friends don't see that, you should know that you just fixed a bit of the wrong."

Maia did not reply, but she was grateful for Sana's comforting words. Just her steadfast presence was like a soothing balm on Maia's blistered spirit.

CHAPTER THIRTY-SEVEN

"I just wish . . ." Sana let her words drift away in an odd way.

"What?" Maia asked.

"I wish I had met him," Sana said wistfully. "Miir, I mean."

"You would've liked him," Maia said.

Sana waved her away. "Probably. But that's not what I'm getting at. I'm just blown away thinking how he has totally, completely transformed you. Right from the moment he spotted you flying that flyer in Shiloh, your life hasn't been the same." Sana sank back into the couch and scanned the joists, lost in thought. A moment or two later she sprang up, looked into Maia's eyes, and whispered, "It's almost like . . . destiny." Then she slumped backward again and let out an enormous sigh. "Too bad it ended this way."

Maia could not make heads or tails of Sana's statement. She would have surely demanded an explanation had it not been for a loud knock. Master Kehorkjin opened the door and Maia's teammates trooped in, slowing immediately on seeing her inside. And even though they glanced at her, no one as much ventured a smile.

Maia's insides crumbled at the willful slight but she held strong. She had made a grave mistake and she was willing to go to any lengths to make it right, but that did not mean she was going to keep begging for forgiveness. Her teammates did not seem to be in a generous mood either. So they waited in uncomfortable silence—Maia and Sana on the couch, the rest of the team huddled near the window—until Master Kehorkjin declared it was time to head out to Devil's Ridge.

CHAPTER THIRTY-EIGHT

A MATTER OF FAITH

That long and wearying day ended with a stroll along the ramparts with Maks late in the afternoon. The last rays of the setting sun warmed Maia's face as they walked. She had hoped being with Maks would keep her from moping over the recent developments, but it did not work. Maia's thoughts were somewhere else altogether, swirling endlessly around dismal memories.

Thankfully, Maks did not seem to notice. He chattered nonstop about the strict regimen Monk Konnae had imposed on his class.

"She has even ordered a new diet for us, can you believe it?" Maks said, indignant at the teacher's demands. "I don't know what good it could . . ."

Maia drifted in and out of thoughts, her companion's voice fading from time to time. She could not tell Maks all that had happened, but she had explained the part about Miir. Maks hardly seemed to care or was purposely trying to keep her distracted. His strategy clearly failed because all Maia could think about was the morning's trip to Devil's Ridge with Kehorkjin, Sana, and her teammates.

The trip had turned out to be useless. Ren had flown his Viperine to the clifftop where Chairman Phocluus had held Maia, and the entire group had scanned the place for proof of Miir's presence there months ago. Being back there was terrifying. Every insult Phocluus had hurled at her came rushing back. She persisted, even though she was shaken to the core. With Sana by her side, she had retraced her steps back to the clearing behind the ledge.

"Are you listening to me, Maia?" Maks asked. "Don't you think that's unnecessary?" As soon as Maia heartily agreed, Maks frowned at her.

"You weren't listening to me at all, were you?" he asked, shaking his head. "You're still thinking about that Xifarian guy you might have accidentally killed, aren't you?"

Maia gave in and nodded. There was no use trying to cover it up and no reason to do it either.

Maks wagged a wise finger at her. "Not good, Maia. You shouldn't think about it anymore," he said in a reproving tone. "You went out to Devil's Ridge today and you couldn't find any evidence of him being there. You don't even remember clearly what happened. Maybe you simply dreamed it up."

"I wish that were true, Maks," Maia said, "but there *was* a fight. I saw plenty of evidence of that. Charred trees, shrubs that had been burnt to stubs, the ground still black from the fire, sooty rock faces — all proof that I was there and I used my crazy, weird powers on someone."

Maks crossed his arms. "*Someone*, that's a key word here. It could've been anyone, not necessarily your mentor. Also . . . whoever you fought could've escaped for all you know. You didn't find his — "

"His remains. You can say it," Maia said. It hurt like hell to use that word, but she welcomed the hurt. It grounded her and kept her face-to-face with the monstrosity of her actions.

Maks let out a long breath. "Yes, his remains. You didn't find them, did you?"

They had not. After hours of searching, the group found nothing.

Maia had led them to the edge where she remembered seeing Miir last. Other than staring at a sharp incline that dropped into the forest of Darkwoods below, there was nothing to be seen. Kusha had even arranged a party of Kausakas to check the bottom of the incline but they had found nothing—no remains, no tattered clothes, or other signs of a man having fallen to his death.

"So?" Maks demanded. "What are you going to do? Keep thinking about him and wasting your time blaming yourself for nothing?"

Maia held up a hand. "Maks, stop. Miir is missing, there's no doubt about that fact. And I was the last person to see him alive, that's also true. He . . . his remains have to be out there somewhere. We just didn't find them today, that's all."

Maks's eyes narrowed. "All right. Then you're going to keep on searching for him until he shows up hale and hearty one day or until you come across a skeleton in the Darkwoods around Devil's Ridge. Is that the plan? Keep looking? Forever?"

Maia did not know how to answer that. She needed closure; all of her teammates, Kehorkjin, and anyone who cared about Miir needed closure. Until then, they would all be searching. Maks was not going to understand that, Maia was sure. He looked annoyed, his face scrunched and eyes narrowed.

"Have to find an answer, Maks," Maia said. "No one just vanishes into thin air."

"Let me tell you, Maia. That's insane," he said. He stopped a moment, his lips pursed. "And stupid, if you ask me."

A day ago, Maia would have been mad at that disdaining comment. But now she simply reined her thoughts and retorts in. There was no point in trying to make Maks understand. He was too far removed from her world even though they were right next to each other physically.

"All right, let's think of it another way," Maks said. "Maybe you did kill him, all right? But didn't he deserve that? He murdered your grandfather, Herecule, and Emmaline. That fire he started on Hen's

Beak took four other innocent families as well. How can you forget that? You make him seem like a saint, but he wasn't."

Maia shifted on her feet, seeking a spot to fix her gaze. Maks was wrong, just like she had been all along.

"No one is a saint, Maks," she said in an exhausted voice. "But the truth is: I don't know who killed my family. If Miir was there, so were others. Amanii, his fiancée, boasted that setting the fire was her idea. She would've bragged about Miir if he took part in the slaughter, wouldn't she? Yet she didn't. And I keep thinking . . . that was weird."

Maks rolled his eyes and shook his head. "You're determined to forgive him, aren't you?" he said in a mocking tone.

"It's not like that," Maia retorted. "It's . . . The more I think about it, the more I see the flaws in my reasoning. I was in a rush to hold him responsible, so I concluded what I wanted to conclude. Miir was there, no question about it. What I seriously doubt is the role he played in the killing."

Maks scoffed. "I don't know, Maia. Seems to me you're turning a blind eye to this guy because of your friends."

"No, Maks. For the first time, I'm looking at him clearly, without prejudice. I only wish I'd done it sooner."

Maks sighed and placed both hands on her shoulders. "Come on, Maia. Don't kill yourself over this."

She flashed a rueful smile at him. "I'll try not to think about it too much, all right?" Maia said, knowing fully well she would stay consumed by these thoughts for a long time, perhaps for the rest of her life. But Maks did not need to know that. Maia hopped on to the topic dear to Maks. "What's this diet Monk Konnae put you on? Maybe I should try it."

Maks laughed. He was sweet, Maia had to admit. Looking at his carefree face, sandy locks blowing across his tanned forehead and happy blue eyes, Maia could not stop a pang of jealousy from welling up in her heart.

What would her life have been had she not flown Kusha's glider all those years ago in Shiloh? Where would Miir be if he had not spotted her that day doing the Siroccan Spiral through the clouds?

Maia did not get to finish her thoughts. A dark blob—a mass of people in black—appeared to their right and pulled her attention away. For a moment she stiffened and then relaxed as she recognized Ori Pistado, the rebel chieftain. Ten of his Black Phantoms, an elite unit of the Solianese Resistance, followed him.

Maia scanned the men behind Ori. Could that man with the purple flecks in his aura be here? She blinked a few times, hoping her aural vision would kick in even though she knew those instances of random aural vision were getting fewer and fewer nowadays. As expected, she did not see any auras, and she could not tell one Black Phantom from another. Maia tore her eyes off them and pushed her disappointment away.

What was she hoping for anyway? That some kind of miracle had saved Miir and now would liberate her of the overwhelming guilt? She scoffed at herself. Miir was dead; there was no doubt about that. She had to live with remorse.

Yet . . . she could not stop hoping.

Ori Pistado stopped and bowed. "Good to see you, Maia," he said.

Maia was happy he did not call her Nosiifarus again. She quickly introduced Maks before returning a bow. "Good to see you too. What brings you here?"

Ori gave Maks a quick once-over and smiled. "The House steward summoned. Matters needed attention."

His reply seemed evasive and his voice distant. Perhaps he did not want to say much in front of Maks.

"People came to Devil's Ridge today," Ori said in a low voice. "Were you with them?"

Maia suddenly recalled that Ori Pistado's village had a direct line of sight to Devil's Ridge. He must have noticed the Viperine. A thought stirred in her mind.

"I was there," she said. "We were looking for something . . . someone."

"Someone?" Ori chuckled. "No one lives on Devil's Ridge. No one even visits anymore. It's hallowed ground and to step on that land is a bad omen."

"Hallowed? Why? Because of what I did?" Maia asked, hoping Ori would say no.

"Because the Nosiifarus displayed her true power there."

Maia stifled a sigh. To think that people considered her murderous rampage somehow sacred was unnerving. "Good that the place is pretty inaccessible," she said, eager to change the subject.

"Not inaccessible enough. We were quite offended that people went back there today," Ori informed gruffly.

"That's why you came?"

Ori nodded. "Reporting the incident was part of our plan. Then we found out you led them there. Which of course changed the situation."

"Maia went there to look for an old friend of hers," Maks jumped into the conversation. "She thinks she fought him and he fell off the cliff and died. So she went to look for his remains."

Maia gritted her teeth. She could not stand when people spoke of matters they knew nothing about. What did Maks think he was doing? Rescuing her from an unpleasant task? She did not need rescuing. Even if she had to struggle to tell the bitter truth about Miir's death, it was her bitter truth to tell.

Ori's eyes narrowed immediately. "A friend? Why would you fight a friend?"

Maia held his gaze. "I wasn't in my senses. I made a mistake . . . a terrible mistake."

"Come on, Maia," Maks chimed in. "We just talked about this. You don't even know if you pushed anyone off the cliff. It might just be your imagination."

Maia flashed a frustrated smile at Maks before taking a step closer to Ori. "Can I talk to you alone for a moment?" she asked. Ori immediately stepped away from his men and Maks.

The chieftain thumbed in Maks's direction as soon as they were a couple of paces away.

"Are you seeing the lad?" he asked, a curious smile on his lips. He chuckled when she flushed and nodded. "It shows. He's needlessly protective."

"Never mind Maks," Maia said. "I wanted to ask you something else. You can see Devil's Ridge from just outside your village, right? On the day the . . . thing happened on Devil's Ridge, did you notice someone fall off it?"

Ori shrugged. "We weren't watching it, you know. We hadn't expected an explosion in the mountains."

"Yes, but what about after the explosion? The person I'm talking about would've fallen afterward."

Ori exhaled rather noisily. Then he stuck his lip out and shrugged again. "It's not right next door, you know. It's too far to see if someone falls off."

"Are there any other villages close by? Could someone have helped him?"

Ori's eyes grew into perfect rounds. "You think someone could survive a fall from way up there?"

Maia knew it was a long shot, but she sure hoped that somehow, by some weird twist of fate, Miir survived.

"No, I guess not," she said.

"Sometimes it's best to let people go, Maia. Don't beat yourself up. Who knows, maybe you've done your friend a favor."

"I've done him a favor by killing him?"

Ori let out a chuckle. "You take things very literally sometimes." He smiled and bowed his head a little. "I'll take leave now. Please come to the village with your friends. People have been missing you."

"I will," Maia said, wondering when, if ever, things would become normal with her friends for them to visit the village together.

As Maia watched Ori Pistado and the Black Phantom march away, she realized that Ori had not answered any of her questions, just expertly skirted them.

"I want to go back to my room, Maks," she said, suddenly

exhausted.

Maks did not seem pleased with her decision, but he nodded nonetheless. Soon he walked Maia up the stairs and to her room. After a quick hug and a peck on Maia's cheek, Maks left and Maia entered her room.

She noticed the piece of paper as soon as she walked in. It was a bright spot of color on the dark floor, screaming for attention. Strange that the hawk-eyed Rayan had not noticed it already. Or perhaps not so strange at all. The dorers left notes all the time, so it was not unusual to have pieces of paper on the ground. Over the months, Rayan had learned to ignore them.

The older girl who had been curled up in bed—always exhausted from her training with Konnae—half-opened her eyes to watch Maia.

"You're back early," Rayan said as Maia picked up the paper.

"Yes, I'm tired," Maia whispered, her heart pounding like a hammer as she recognized the writing right away. It was from the same person who had sent the note about the Chancery Archives. This one was just as short as the first:

Mahswa can read the scrolls.

Maia read the note over and over again. She turned the paper over to see if there were any other marks or words. Nothing except for the short message.

"What's that?" Rayan had sat up, perhaps noting Maia's anxious face.

"Someone slipped in a note." Maia sat down at the edge of Rayan's cot and showed her the piece of paper.

"I must've dozed off," Rayan said. "Didn't hear a thing."

"Someone keeps sending me these," Maia said. "He knows my room and he also knows about the scrolls. And he knows about the Mahswa too."

"He? Who's he?" a bleary-eyed Rayan asked.

"Karhann?" Maia muttered. It had to be Karhann! He was the one who had mentioned the Origin Scrolls that day when he and Loriine were fighting. And he knew where her room was. Perhaps Karhann was too afraid to talk to her directly—understandable since Loriine was always hounding him—so he had found an indirect way to tell her something.

But Karhann was nowhere near when she had found the first note in her pocket. She had been at Ori Pistado's village then.

A loud rap on her door made Maia jump. *Must be Sana*, she thought. But she was surprised to find Kusha standing outside her door. "K-Kusha," Maia said, crumpling the note in her fist as she parted the door some more. "What is it?"

"Our trip to Zagran is coming up in a couple of days," Kusha explained, "so we're planning down in Dani's room. Want to come over?"

Maia wanted to join them like she wanted nothing else in the world. "I'd like that," she said, nodding eagerly.

Her steps were light, but her heart was lighter as she followed Kusha down the corridor.

Chapter Thirty-Nine

Back in Zagran

The days leading up to the trip to Zagran flew past. A semblance of normalcy had settled on Core 21, and Maia regularly joined the planning sessions. There were no flare-ups or fights, but tension simmered below the surface. Maia tried her best to ignore it.

The journey to Zagran began early one morning. The final five teams gathered in the central courtyard where the Holding Pod of the Tokii was waiting. Aerika, Kehorkjin, as well as a sour-faced Hilledunn were also present. Dani seethed on seeing Hilledunn, and Kusha tried fruitlessly to pacify her.

"It's no use, Dani," he said. "There's no proof. You can't simply accuse him when no one, not even Everrol, is willing to testify against him."

"We simply give up and let him carry on as usual then?" Dani retorted.

Maia wished she could intervene, but she decided to keep her mouth shut. She did not want to rock the boat any further. Thankfully,

Aerika addressed the teams soon after.

"Gather around, everyone," she called and waved. "You've all been to Zagran, so you know the basics already. We are going to spend two full days in Zagran. This time you shall board at the guest housing section of the university. That will give you easy access to the rest of the city. I'd advise that you do not roam around on your own. Zagran is a large place and we do not want you lost. Also, you do not want to lose valuable time that you could rather spend on deciphering clues to the final riddle."

Heads nodded solemnly. Maia felt Kehorkjin's keen gaze on her face. *Save your worries, Master K,* she thought. She was not going anywhere this time. She was not risking the team's safety or reputation ever again. From now on, she was on her own.

"All right then," Aerika said. "Get into the pod. Go on."

Soon they had all settled inside the pod. Aerika and Kehorkjin boarded the craft as well, but curiously enough, Hilledunn stayed behind.

"He's not coming?" Nafi muttered.

"Good riddance," Dani said.

"Well, Hilledunn didn't come to Xif either," Ren replied. "Neither did Aerika. I'm surprised Kehorkjin's visiting Zagran."

"I'm sure he wants to keep an eye on us," Kusha added, and Maia could not agree more. Kehorkjin's gaze lingered on them regularly since their visit to Xif and their trip to the Chancery.

The pod took off and before long they had flown down from the ThulaSuian ranges and skimmed past the bright blue waters over Coloni Primei. They went down the funnel and bobbed up in the brightly lit cove of the Jjordic settlement, a beautiful and majestic underwater colony.

Maia remembered the first time she had visited the undersea cove, how she had met Dani. Later she had come back to stay at Zagran for the second phase of the Initiative. That was just a year or so ago, but it felt like a whole lifetime had passed between then and now. So many things had changed. So many people she cared about were gone.

"Come on, Maia." Kusha nudged her gently. The steps were out for disembarking.

She followed the team down the silvery-white walkways to the inspection room where hawk-eyed women sat in booths and checked their credentials.

"Now for the heartwarming split-up," Nafi muttered as the teammates walked toward the door leading into the Aquiccela terminal.

Maia could not hold back the sigh. The last time they were here, the Jjord had segregated teammates based on their heritage. The Solianese children were made to board a separate section of the train while the Jjord and the Xifarians boarded another—seemingly favored—section. The policy had stunned and distressed Maia back then and she was cringing now. The rest of the team looked equally unhappy.

"Core 21!" Aerika's snappy voice shook Maia out of her cocoon of anxiety. "Hurry up, the train's waiting."

Maia looked around hastily. The other teams had already left the inspection chamber. Aerika stood at the doorway with her arms crossed and frowned at them. As soon as the team reached her, she practically pushed them into the terminal.

"What's the matter with you?" Aerika snapped. "Everyone else is on the train already."

A sleek but shorter version of the trains they rode the last time stood at the terminal. All the other contestants were inside the single-passenger compartment that made up this train.

"That's a really small train," Dani said. "I've never—"

"It's a special one sent just for you," Aerika said impatiently. "Now get in please."

As soon as they had stepped inside the carriage, the doors closed and the train took off. Maia found a window seat and stared out. The Aquiccela sped through the underwater tunnels, sparkling blue waters surrounding them on all sides. Where was the wonder she had felt seeing it for the first time? Her heart was leaden. Herc had wanted to visit Zagran. Someday, Dani had said, all of them could visit her. Herc would never see the beauty of Zagran. A tear trickled down her cheek and then another. Oh, how she missed Herc, his loud laughs and kind smile.

A sudden movement to her right made Maia tear her gaze from a large school of striped fish. Kusha slid into the seat across from her and flashed a sheepish smile. Maia ran a hand hastily over her eyes.

"Mind if I sit here?" he asked.

Maia forced a chuckle. "Mind? I wouldn't mind. But are you sure you want to be here talking to me?"

Kusha glanced at the rest of the team. They had settled down on the other side of the aisle. He shrugged. "It's fine. I don't think Nafi or Ren will like it much; they're still mad as hell. But Dani's fine, so I'm good."

It was not that Maia had expected Ren and Nafi to forgive her so quickly, but hearing about their anger still hurt.

"I'm sorry," she blurted. "I really am."

Kusha patted her knee. "It's all right. Don't be so hard on yourself. Sure, you made a mistake. But I'd have done the same if I were in your place. Miir sure didn't make things easy for you."

Miir had tried. It was so much clearer to see it now than it was then. She had run into him one evening, right after arriving at Zagran. He had worried about her safety. How did she not realize that he cared?

However, prickly questions still remained. There was no doubt Miir was there when they set her house on fire. If he was not involved, what was he doing there in the first place? The push-and-pull of emotions weighed on her.

"What are you thinking?" Kusha asked. His face was grim. "Don't, Maia. Don't punish yourself like this."

"Shouldn't I? He didn't deserve to die by my hand, Kusha. I used my powers without thinking. I have to make sure it doesn't happen again. I have to remember it's not my job to go about getting revenge, doling out punishment, even to people who are guilty and deserve it. I'm just another person, bound by the laws of the land."

"You will," Kusha said assertively.

His confidence made Maia smile. She hoped she could live up to his faith in her.

"There's Zagran," Nafi squealed from the other side.

Maia turned around to look and held her breath. The underwater capital of the Jjord had indeed revealed itself. There it was, the city right out of a dream. Zagran—a breathtaking arrangement of shimmering shapes, a composition of gigantic bubbles stacked and connected through a complex series of tunnels, passages, and corridors—towered ahead. Its transparent surface gleamed in the soft blue light filtering through the waters. The curves and the bulges that housed the city reflected the myriad of colorful sea creatures that swam all around it.

"Just as stunning as the first time we'd seen it, huh?" Kusha said.

The Aquiccela scuttled toward the superstructure and a few twists and turns of the tunnels later, it pulled into a sprawling platform. Aerika, who had been seated at the front of the compartment along with Kehorkjin, clapped her hands.

"We've arrived. Now let's speed up and get out of here, all right?" she barked.

"Always the warmest welcome from Aerika," Kusha muttered, and Maia could not help a chuckle. Although, Aerika of now was an angel compared to the snippy Aerika they had met on their first visit.

As soon as Aerika had herded the contestants out to the platform, a girl and a boy—both around seventeen or around eighteen—in the blue uniform of the UAAS rushed forward. The girl had short golden hair and bright hazel eyes waved. The dark-haired boy simply nodded.

"There you are," Aerika said on seeing the duo. She turned toward the group and gestured at the two UAAS students. "These are your guides, Aemmon and Rikka. They will help you around the library while you're here." She patted the girl on the shoulder. "Core

21, Core 7, and Core 13, you'll be with Rikka. The rest, follow Aemmon."

Everyone nodded.

"First, you'll be taken to the Guest House," Aerika explained. "After refreshments, we will visit the Grand Central Library. Your guides will find you later during the day and bring you back to the Guest House. Do not, I repeat, *do not* leave the library premises unless accompanied by your guides or me or Master Kehorkjin."

Solemn nods followed. The two guides led the groups up elevators and along corridors to a floor with a giant UAAS Guest House banner across its gigantic doorway. Rikka, who seemed a serious sort of person, showed everyone to their rooms one by one after the steward had checked them in. After a brief stop at the refreshment room, the two guides gathered them all for their trip to the Grand Central Library of Zagran.

Maia could not wait to get started. Zagran was special, the swirling water around had already calmed and soothed her frayed emotions. Zagran was special in other ways too. This is where she was born and Maia hoped she would make a new beginning here once more.

CHAPTER FORTY

THE GRAND CENTRAL

The Grand Central was a shining piece of modern art. Row after row of portals crisscrossed the floors, each of which was dedicated to a particular subject.

"You can look into any subject you want," Rikka explained after she had checked them in. "Just gather here at clock-out time. I'll wait for you here."

With that, Rikka left and Nafi looked questioningly at Dani. "What's clock-out time? How do we know it's clock-out time?"

"It's when the library closes to the general public," Dani explained. "Don't worry, there'll be chimes to announce the time."

Karhann and his buddies had already headed to the history floor. The other teams were also making a beeline to the same.

"Let's go dig into some history," Nafi announced, thumbing at the crowded staircase.

"Perhaps we should split up," Maia suggested. "Some can go to history and some others can look into other things."

Ren gave her a dour look. "What other things?"

"I was thinking of checking out the power grid layout," Maia replied hesitantly. Seeing the frowns, she explained, "The Nouvus were important to our ancestors, right? I figured, they couldn't have simply laid such an important relic in the ground to rot and disintegrate. They'd have to have created some sort of an underground receptacle for it and done some sort of upkeep on it. And for that, they'd have needed some—"

"Energy supplies, of course," Ren completed for her. For a brief moment, his eyes shone. Then the gloomy look fell over his face again. "Sounds like a good idea to me. You need any help?"

Even before Maia could nod, Kusha jumped in. "I'll go with her. You guys can go to the history section."

"Actually, I'll head to the geology section," Dani declared. "I know we have annual studies of Tansi's crust and topography. Who knows, I might find some clues in those studies."

They dispersed quickly and time flew by faster than Maia realized. She and Kusha had barely gone through a few old blueprints of Tansi's power grid when a tinkle echoed through the library.

"That could be the clock-out chime," Kusha said.

It was indeed. Dani came by to call them momentarily, and together they walked to the entrance where Aemmon and Rikka were waiting. They finished dinner quickly and gathered in Dani's room to go over the day's findings.

"We didn't find much," Nafi declared with a sad shake of her head. She pulled out her notebook and read a few lines from it. "There are three laws regarding Continent Four. There shall be no settlements, visitor permissions are to be strictly enforced, and this final one that stumped us . . . the Sursangei gates shall remain closed until the end of the Tansian Colony."

"Sursangei gates?" Maia asked. "What does that mean?"

Nafi shrugged. "Wish I knew," she replied snippily. "But sorry, I don't."

"All right, Nafi." Kusha stepped in determinedly. "Dani, anything from you?"

Dani did not reply. She sat on a small couch across from the rest of the team, absentmindedly tapping her chin. Her usually bright and happy face was dark with worry. Maia noted how she kept checking the Urso — the Jjordic messenger device — every few moments. And the more she checked it, the dimmer her face got. Maia could easily guess what it was — Hans. Or to be precise, his failure to show up until now.

Hans and Dani were close, and it was unlike Hans to take so long to visit his sister. Maia did not have to ask Dani to surmise that she had not been able to contact him on the Urso either.

"Dani," Kusha called once more.

Dani sat up with a start. "What?"

"Did you find anything in the geology section?"

Dani gave a half-hearted shake of her head. "Not really. Other than the fact that Four has a fat layer of soft chalkstone under the top which makes it an ideal place for digging and storing a large artifact . . . I have nothing."

"That's good though," Ren said. "It makes for a stronger case. The Nouvus must be in Continent Four then."

"Maybe so," Kusha said. "But if we don't find solid proof, we can't simply go on our assumptions. We have to rethink our findings soon. It may be that we're going in the wrong direction altogether."

"Hey, guys," Dani started hesitantly. "Do you mind carrying on? I need to go speak to someone."

"Who? Why?" Nafi demanded.

"It's a personal matter," Dani replied curtly. "I'll be back soon. You keep on going without me."

With that, she stormed out of the room, Kusha following. The rest of the teammates stayed there for a bit but dispersed soon after. Maia went to bed with dark thoughts clouding her mind. She was sure that Hans was in some kind of trouble.

***

The next morning all the teams gathered at the entrance of the Guest House but Dani was missing. Rikka had just raised a questioning brow at Maia and her teammates when Dani rushed in, looking exhausted.

Rikka crossed her arms. "You were outside?" she asked Dani pointedly.

"Yes, I went out for a bit."

"You're not supposed to," Rikka replied in an icy tone.

"I know. I asked Aerika. You can check."

Rikka stared at Dani for a bit, then she turned toward Aemmon. "Let's go then."

As soon as they reached the library, Nafi and Ren sped off to the history section again. Dani however, hesitated.

"You can come with us, Dani," Maia offered and Kusha nodded eagerly. "We could always use some help looking at the blueprints. There's too many of them to go through."

Dani flashed a grateful smile and nodded. They walked over to the blueprint section and had settled into a corner when Dani let out a huge sigh. "This isn't like Hans. Not like him at all," she almost wailed.

"Haven't you heard from him?" Maia asked.

"I have. But it's just a 'yes' or 'no' or 'I'm fine.'"

"Maybe he's busy," Kusha offered.

Dani shook her head. "It's hard sending messages to me when I'm at ThulaSu, so for the last six months I've scarcely heard from him." She cradled her face in her hands and breathed heavily. "He used to visit me in ThulaSu so often. That stopped. He said he'd visit when they had that huge meeting over the Connector. He didn't. I thought he was busy with work. But he doesn't even show up when I'm in Zagran? Something is wrong, Kusha. Very, very wrong."

Kusha walked over and slipped an arm over her shoulder. Dani leaned against him and sobbed softly.

Guilt made Maia's shoulders sag. About a year ago, Hans and his friend Jed had come to her aid when she was on the run from the

Xifarians. The Jjordic government had ordered Hans and Jed to stay away from matters of the Solianese and uphold the Covenants of Duality that enforced separation between the two nations. But they refused to abandon Maia. Much later, when the Xifarians cornered Jed and threatened him, Jed betrayed Maia and disappeared. Hans, however, had stayed until Maia was safe in ThulaSu.

Hans had defied a direct command of the Jjordic government to help her. He had taken an immense risk with his career. What if the Jjordic government was punishing him for that?

"He wouldn't miss this chance of seeing me," Dani said between sniffles. "He knows I'm here and he doesn't even send me a message? That's not like Hans at all."

Maia wished she could help her friend, but she was helpless. She could only hope Hans was well.

"Where did you go last night?" Kusha asked. "This morning?"

"Last night I spoke to a few of Hans's friends. They didn't know much, just that he hasn't been around for months," Dani said. "So this morning I spoke to Aerika. I requested permission to see the premier."

"Did they let you?" Maia asked.

Dani shook her head slowly. "No. Premier Oliena was unavailable to meet, but Aerika promised she'd try to get the message across." Dani broke into sobs. "What if they put him in prison?"

"Don't think like that, Dani," Maia said, even though she knew there was a good chance that Hans was being taken to task for flouting Jjordic directives. "You'd know if that happened. They'd let you know."

Kusha leaned forward and held Dani's hands. "Maia's right, Dani. I'm sure Aerika will find out. Nothing could've happened to Hans or you'd know."

Dani inhaled sharply and wiped away her tears. "You're right. I'm sure Aerika will get some news. Let's look at those blueprints now."

There were thousands of blueprints to go through. It was amazing how much information was stored in the library, but the amount of information also required a lot of time to look at it all. Every continent had its own stack of charts, and Maia even found the one that showed the grid under Shiloh and Appian. However, there was nothing at all listed under the Fourth Continent. The day passed swiftly as they looked for information that did not seem to exist.

Late in the evening, Maia closed her tired eyes and decided to rest a little. Dani had been distractedly checking her Urso, but Kusha soldiered on.

"Look at this one," Kusha, who had been poring over the charts for the First Continent, exclaimed suddenly. Dani and Maia scooted to his side. Kusha was pointing at a map of the Palonkian Peninsula. "Look at the power grid here. It gets sparse as it approaches the Palonkian Peninsula, see?"

That made sense. The Solianese never built in the Palonkian Sanctuary.

"It should be sparse, shouldn't it?" Maia said.

"It should," Kusha replied. "But look at this! One channel of the grid goes all the way down to the tip of the peninsula. The size of the channel is huge!"

Kusha was right, there was a long, thick line denoting a power grid right through the Palonkian Peninsula. That was weird indeed.

Dani tapped her chin. "I don't understand. This channel isn't feeding any settlements. Then where is it going?"

Kusha zoomed in on the tip of the peninsula where the power grid ended to enlarge the map. "I can't tell. It just ends at the tip."

"In the water?" Dani said. She shook her head. "This is useless. And I'm too tired to think anyway."

It was late, and everyone was exhausted. Not just Dani, Maia could not think clearly either. They had made a few copies of the map to study later and had stowed them away safely when the chimes sounded.

"We're going to stop briefly at the Guest House for refreshments and then head out to the Aquiccela Terminal," Aemmon said. "I hope you've got the information you came seeking."

The other teams did not look happy, Maia noted. And even though that was a sad turn of things, Maia felt a bit more hopeful of their chances. If no one else had cracked the clues yet, there was still a possibility they could catch up.

The walk to the Guest House was long and tiring. Aerika was waiting at the entrance hall and she strode up to the group as soon as they walked in.

"You're back, and you're running late," she said, frowning generously. "Go on, eat up quickly. We'll have to leave for ThulaSu soon." She turned toward Dani. "Dani, come this way."

"Have you heard something?" Dani blurted.

"Of course," Aerika said. "I found Hans and brought him to meet you. Now don't waste time talking to me."

"Oh, thank you!" Dani squealed. She rushed off after Aerika toward a room on the other side of the hall. Along with the rest of the team, Maia headed into the refreshment room. She was halfway through the rolled-bread sandwich when Aerika marched into the room with Master Kehorkjin and walked over to where Maia and her teammates were seated.

"Hans wants to see you all," she said in a low voice. "If you're done with the food, you can go visit."

Maia dropped the half-eaten sandwich right away and jumped out of her chair. She could go hungry for a night if it meant seeing Hans. Her teammates seemed to think the same way. They rushed across the hallway into the room where Aerika had taken Dani.

It was sort of a waiting room. Plush, color-coordinated couches of various sizes were placed all around. Hans—gloomy-faced, tired-looking, and so unlike the vibrant young man Maia knew—sat with Dani on one end of the room. Two men—rigid, stern, and in sharp gray uniforms—sat at the opposite end. Hans smiled at the group as soon as they entered.

"There you are," he said. "Look at you all. Kusha, you're almost as tall as me."

"Are you all right?" Maia asked, worrying about Hans's slightly sunken eyes and bony face. "Please tell me you didn't get into trouble because of me."

Hans smiled ruefully and shrugged. "I might've gotten into a bit of trouble," he said, and Maia's heart sank. "But it's not because of you. It's because of the choices I made. And I'd make the same choices if I were to choose again. So, Maia, don't think you're responsible for this, all right?"

Sure, that sounded good, but it did nothing to lift Maia's spirits. If something were to happen to Hans, she could never forgive herself.

"What happened exactly?" Kusha asked. "Did Jed snitch on you?"

Hans let out a sigh. "Something like that. Apparently, I willfully disregarded the Covenants of Duality and forced him to do the same."

"That sneaky two-faced rat," Nafi hissed.

"But Premier Oliena must know what is at stake, what you were trying to protect," Kusha said. "You were trying to save Tansi's future. How can they—"

"The premier knows, Kusha," Hans interrupted. "But there are people in the Council who didn't like that I intervened. They wanted the Xifarians to capture Maia and I didn't let that happen. So now, they're trying to get even. And they're making my interrogation unduly long."

"Aloysus?" Maia asked. She remembered the portly Jjord who was against helping the Solianese. He had openly sided with the Xifarians as well as Leeam and his dastardly allies.

Hans nodded. "He's not alone."

"How can we help?" Maia asked. "Is there any way at all that we could—"

"Keep my sister cheered up," Hans said, pulling Dani close. "There's nothing to worry about at the moment. Oliena knows the truth and she's on my side. But Aloysus and his friends want to stretch this as long as they can. While this interrogation is on, I'm pretty much in detention."

"They put you in prison?" Ren blurted.

"Well, no," Hans replied, chuckling under his breath. "It's not that bad. But my movements are restricted." He paused and nodded at the uniformed men at the far end. "I'm escorted like a celebrity. Even my correspondence is limited."

"That's why he couldn't message me," Dani explained.

"I'm sorry," Hans said, squeezing Dani's shoulder. "I couldn't even let you know what was going on. They'd confiscate all my letters."

Nafi stomped her feet. "Stupid, stupid, stupid . . . people."

Hans patted Nafi's arm. "Calm down, Nafi. Anger won't help anyone."

Right then, the door opened behind them and Aerika walked in. "We have to leave now, kids," she announced from the door.

Dani hugged Hans tightly and sobbed.

"I'll be fine, Dani," Hans said. "I'll be fine."

When Dani let go, Hans looked at each of them in turn. "Now listen up. I'll be fine. There are laws here that'll protect me. But out there in ThulaSu, there are few laws, so you need to be careful and stay safe." He paused to take a long breath. "If people are so angry at me, imagine how unforgiving they might be to you."

It was indeed a sobering thought. All the way to ThulaSu, Maia and her teammates huddled supportively around Dani. Fear swirled ceaselessly inside Maia. She was sure, now more than ever, that evil was lurking out there, waiting for the perfect moment to strike.

CHAPTER FORTY-ONE

BACK TO THE WALL

I t was curious that Rayan was still around when Maia woke up the next morning. Usually the girl left for her morning session with Konnae before sunrise.

"Good trip?" she asked in her usual succinct manner.

"I saw him," Maia blurted. "I saw Hans."

Rayan's eyes brightened for a moment before they turned aloof in a calculated sort of way.

"He is well, I hope," she said, gaze flitting over Maia's face.

"No, he isn't."

Rayan's face turned rigid. "What is wrong?" she said in a slow, halting way, as if she were too afraid to hear the answer.

Maia explained, as reassuringly as she could, of Hans's situation. Rayan stayed characteristically passive, but Maia did not miss how the girl's fingers clenched the edge of her bed from time to time. There was no doubt she cared—a whole lot more than she let on—about Hans.

A soft rap sounded on the door and a wilted-looking Dani

sauntered in. She flashed a halfhearted smile.

"Did you tell Rayan about Hans?" she asked Maia.

She sat down facing Rayan as Maia nodded. "Hans sent you this." She held out something, possibly a note, for Rayan. "All his communication is being stopped, but he managed to sneak this out to me."

Maia did not want to intrude on the girls' conversation, so she dressed quickly, picked up her satchel, and peeked outside. For a moment, she hesitated—she was alone, and per Leeam's mandate she could not go about on her own. But the corridor was deserted and her stomach was growling, so Maia stealthily headed for breakfast.

She was late and the refectory was almost closed. Maia grabbed a piece of bread and went looking for a nook to study the blueprint they had brought back from the Grand Central. She climbed up the ramparts and was headed toward the groves but stopped midway when she spotted a pair of familiar figures further east on the rampart.

Maia squinted and realized it was Mahswa Tabrin and . . . Ren. She remembered the anonymous note about the Mahswa and the Origin Scrolls, yet she hesitated to bound up to the woman. She did not want to talk about it in front of Ren who continued to be cold and dismissive for the most part. But Mahswa Tabrin was hard to find, if not impossible. So, bracing herself for a frosty Ren, Maia marched forward.

"Maia, good to see you," Mahswa Tabrin greeted warmly. Maia noticed her face was pale and her eyes sunken. The smile on her face was just as calming as always.

Maia bowed to show her respects. "How are you, Mahswa?"

"Not as well as I hope to be," the Mahswa said. "You know of the situation on Xif, I presume?"

"I do," Maia replied. "Any good news with the Sedara?"

Mahswa shook her head sadly. "I'm afraid not. We tried to fix it but something is broken at its core. We don't know what or how yet. The chancellor is not doing very well either. Things are rather precarious up there."

"We heard the queen is in charge now," Maia said.

"Ah, Rahina Quemiila, yes, but . . ." Her words trailed off and her gaze drifted. "But there are challenges to her powers," she finished.

Maia balked. "Challenges? But I thought the Royals were held in the highest esteem. Why would anyone challenge her?"

"There are a lot of people who don't want a Royal in charge," Ren blurted. "They want a chancellor at the top."

"But this is only provisional," Maia said. "Your chancellor could get better, right?"

The Mahswa closed her eyes and whispered a prayer. "By the power of the Sedara, I hope he does." She gave Maia a sad smile. "For certain agitators, even interim situations are unbearable."

"Oh, I see." Who knew there could be a power struggle on Xif? Such things only seemed possible in Tansian politics. Xif, on the other hand, seemed disciplined and efficient and above such pettiness. Maia could not voice her thoughts in front of the Mahswa and Ren, so she asked about another matter. "How are the Tierremorphes? Did they get any of their powers back?"

Mahswa's face tightened and her gaze drooped some more. "The damage to the Sedara has affected them immensely. They are slowly dying."

"Oh no!" Maia cried. "Why can't you bring them out to Tansi? Maybe they'd heal here?"

"No, Maia. They're all in bad shape. If we try to move them, their condition gets worse. We've already lost a few trying to get them to the Seliban Temple."

Icy fingers of fear gripped Maia's heart at a sudden thought. "Mahswa, are you all right?"

Mahswa Tabrin smiled. "I'm fine. I happened to be here in ThulaSu when the Sedara was damaged. That stroke of luck possibly saved me, or I'd be withering away now."

A heavy hush descended on the conversation and lingered for what felt like forever. Mahswa Tabrin broke the oppressive silence. "It's not much use pondering things we cannot change," she said.

CHAPTER FORTY-ONE

"What else? How is your riddle solving coming along?"

"We're stuck," Ren said gruffly. "It's the vaguest riddle I've ever seen in my life. Tough as hell."

"You're in the final stage of a grand competition, Ren," the Mahswa said. "You can't expect things to be easy. Besides, if you could win the Seliban Challenge when you were so young and inexperienced, there's no reason you can't solve this one. All you have to do is put your heads together."

Maia and Ren stole a glance at each other and quickly looked away. The Mahswa frowned. "Working together is a cornerstone of success in these missions. I don't have to remind you, do I?" she said, chuckling.

Maia flushed. The Mahswa was always observant, and nothing escaped her eyes.

"We'll solve it, Mahswa," she said, forcing that elusive confidence into her voice. "I wanted to talk to you about another matter though."

"Yes, Maia. Go on, ask!"

Maia hesitated. She had not told anyone about the anonymous note she had found in her room, and now Ren would find out. A moment later, she decided to press on regardless. "Can you read the Origin Scrolls?"

The Mahswa stared incredulously. "Not many can read Cahryllic. That's the script used in most of the scrolls."

"But you can, right?" Maia asked.

"She said not many can read that script," Ren said irritably.

"I heard that," Maia replied in a snappier tone than she intended. "But she didn't say *she* can't."

"All right, stop. I hate to see you bicker even when I know you have reason to," the Mahswa said. "So please don't. Not in my presence if you can help it." Her voice was still calm and soft, but somewhere in it was a hard edge that made Maia and Ren nod right away. The Mahswa let out a long, tortured sigh. "I can read Cahryllic. How did you know, Maia?"

She was not going to try lying to the Tierremorphe. "Someone left a note in my room. It said you can read the scroll."

The Mahswa's mouth crinkled. "Really? Hmm . . ."

Maia could not be sure, but it almost seemed like the Mahswa had expected that answer from her, as if she knew someone would give Maia that note. It was weird, the knowing way the Mahswa smiled. Even stranger was the fact that the Mahswa did not ask how Maia got the Origin Scrolls.

However, Maia did not want to waste time questioning the Mahswa about it. She dug out the copy of the Origin Scrolls from inside her satchel and held out the roll of paper for the Mahswa. "Can you read it for me then?"

The Mahswa's fingers shook as she reached for the stack. "Let's sit down somewhere. This might take a while since my Cahryllic's quite rusty."

Maia had hoped Ren would leave her alone with the Mahswa, but he followed with a grim face to the Mahswa's chambers. Mahswa Tabrin evened the pages out on a table and flipped through them slowly. About midway through it, she shut it abruptly, closed her eyes, and heaved.

Maia did not know what to say, and she was not looking to get snubbed by Ren, so she simply held her breath and waited.

"This is a sad tale," the Mahswa said finally. "No one is supposed to know this, not even I."

"This explains the feud between the R'armimon and us, doesn't it?" Ren asked. "But I don't understand what's there to hide. I mean, conflicts happen between nations, but they're not kept hidden like this. Causes of conflict go into history books for later generations to study and understand and learn from."

The Mahswa took a deep breath. She had paled considerably, and her gaze flitted back and forth across the table nervously. "It is kept hidden for a reason, Ren. Because this is a shameful secret we don't want to know. And I don't know if I should tell you this."

"Please, Mahswa Tabrin, tell me," Maia pleaded. She searched frantically for the right words to sway the woman. She had to know what was in the Origin Scrolls. "I need to know why the R'armimon is here. I really need to know where I fit in."

The Mahswa's intense gaze bore into Maia for an uncomfortably long time, but Maia held it bravely. In the end, the woman rose to her feet and strode to the darkened far corner of the room. She came back holding something Maia had seen before: Seigvard, the dazzling sword of the Xifarian queen, Ataii. The Mahswa placed Seigvard on the table and took a slow step backward.

"This is as much a tale of this sword as it is of our people," she said in a morose voice. "And you must promise me to not reveal a word of what I'm about to tell you to anyone without my permission." She tilted her head toward Seigvard. "Place your hand on the sword and give me your word."

"I promise," Maia said.

Ren took a moment or two before he, too, touched the sword and muttered," I swear, I won't reveal what I hear about the Origin Scrolls without your permission."

The Mahswa nodded solemnly and another sharp breath later, she began to read from the scrolls.

CHAPTER FORTY-TWO

A HAPPILY NEVER AFTER

Sunlight was rippling over Ataii's magnificent sword when Mahswa Tabrin read the Origin Scrolls. She translated as she read, in a voice soft and mournful and soothing, all at the same time. Maia listened intently as the Mahswa read word for word from the ancient scrolls . . .

> *The Xifarian nation was born a renegade. Even though its twin planet Ara grudgingly accepted the nation of Xif, the neighbors never went beyond an uneasy peace. Xif's plentiful Calbion deposits were the real reason this upstart new nation was tolerated at all. But it was barely tolerated, never treated as an equal. The R'armimon Empire was huge, spread across a massive spiral galaxy. Its reach was far and wide. The planetary systems that made up the Empire were ancient, rich, and bound to archaic traditions as old as the Empire itself. The newborn Xif and its leaders found themselves on unwelcoming turf.*

Calbion was a miracle metal. It was essential in the building of spaceships, particularly long-range, deep-space freighters. Trade was the key source of revenue in the Empire, and trade was almost entirely regulated by the Tokii. After Calbion was discovered, the Tokii formed an alliance with Xif. A few years later when the Tokii sprung a new trade pact on the Empire, Xif turned out to be its biggest ally. That did not sit well with the Empire and its most prominent members. Xif's neighbor Ara, led by King Arihan, did its best to lobby against Xif. Elaborate court intrigues in the R'armimon capital of Ragamallor followed.

The Empire eventually negotiated a new trade deal with the Tokii, the terms severely demolishing its profits and standing, seen as a necessity to keep the lifeblood of trade flowing. For a while, tensions eased and all seemed well on the surface, although it was anything but. Xif was branded a traitor, a demarcation King Arihan was determined to wield as a weapon to its fullest extent.

King Arihan's opportunity came soon after at the Centennial Gala at Ragamallor. Xif's emissaries were the royal children, King Arka's sons: Crown Prince Afriel, and his twin brothers, Minhaas and Lenetto. The geologist, Veiles, who had become fast friends with Afriel, also accompanied the Royals along with his young son, Castien. Unknown to Xif's Royals, a conspiracy of the foulest kind was waiting to greet them at Ragamallor.

On the third day of the Centennial Gala, on the pretext of enforcing security, Minhaas, Lenetto, and Veiles's son were held hostage at the capital. The R'armimon demanded a larger tax on Xif's Calbion sales in exchange for the safe return of the two princes.

The R'armimon did not foresee the biggest twist of fate. Crown Prince Afriel had met the R'armimon princess Ataii during one of the numerous balls and it was love at first sight. It is said that Princess Ataii devised Afriel's escape out of the R'armimon capital, and together with Veiles, the couple reached Xif soon after. Minhaas, Lenetto, and Veiles's son Castien remained in Ragamallor as hostages.

However, Arka himself welcomed Ataii at Xif. The R'armimon was furious. They called this act an abduction and an affront to the Crown. Princess Ataii's elder brother, Emperor Ondeiir, demanded that the princess be returned to Ragamallor and the Crown's honor be restored. The Empire had not accounted for Princess Ataii's boldness. She refused to return to Ragamallor unless the young hostages were promptly freed. The R'armimon declined to release the captives. Ataii married Afriel and became Consort to the Crown Prince.

The Mahswa paused and took a long, deep breath. Then, smiling a little, she began once more.

A few years passed and the standoff continued. Prince Afriel and Princess Ataii became parents to twin boys and their love for each other became fabled. Arka, however, died with a broken heart, never seeing his younger sons, Minhaas and Lenetto, again.

While Afriel and Ataii became good monarchs to the Xifarians, Veiles drifted away from his friend into a world of plots and vengeance against the R'armimon. He secretly hatched plans to free his son from the Empire's clutches. He turned into a mad scientist, obsessed with finding a way to get the R'armimon to bow to Xif. One day, he stumbled upon a powerful secret.

Veiles discovered a secret about Princess Ataii, now the Queen of Xif. She had a terrible power; she could absorb the L'miere crystals. Veiles, and all of Xif, worshipped the L'miere crystals as their life-giver, so the thought of anyone harming them was terrifying. A shocked Veiles gave the young queen a name: the Cursed One, a Shimugien. That was how the word Shimugien was born.

Veiles held Queen Ataii's secret close to his heart and asked the queen to submit to a few experiments. He wanted to make sure he understood her ailment. He wanted to cure her of it. Queen Ataii feared that the people of Xif would consider her a threat to the nation, so she obliged.

Veiles discovered more about Queen Ataii in the days and months that followed. She had more than just the ability to affect the L'miere crystals; she had the power to assimilate the energy of the light within her and wield it when she pleased. She was what the legends called a "star child," a "Nasfarii."

Maia's heart wrenched and she was happy when Mahswa Tabrin stopped for a moment or two to catch her breath. Something told her that this was not a story with a happy ending, and her insides clenched when the Tierremorphe began reading once more.

Realizing he could use Queen Ataii's powers as a weapon, Veiles tinkered on. Queen Ataii on the other hand had been trying to free the R'armimon hostages, and during her correspondence, she came to know that her powers had been long known to the Empire. She was a child of destiny, she was told. Her brother, Emperor Ondeiir urged her to return to the Empire yet again. This time Queen Ataii considered the invitation. Unknown to her, Veiles had spies watching the Royal household. Queen Ataii's indecision tipped him into a far more aggressive course of action. He had a chance to get his son, Castien, back, and that chance was slipping out of his hands quickly. He had to act.

Veiles trapped Queen Ataii in a Calbion cage of a superweapon he had built into the heart of Xif. He claimed that his weapon could harness the power of the stars and destroy anything in its way. He demanded that the R'armimon return the hostages or they would face Xif's wrath.

The R'armimon cautioned him. He was dishonoring a Nasfarii and unleashing doom over the known universe. They cautioned against spilling the sacred blood of a R'armimon Royal, an act that would surely be followed by equal retaliation.

King Afriel begged that Veiles release his beloved wife. He appealed to the friend he had once known and trusted, but Veiles was too far gone by then. He had descended into madness, his mind orbiting thoughts of revenge. He struck King Afriel down in a fit of rage.

With King Afriel dead, Xif was leaderless. It was just what its enemies were waiting for. As Xif plunged into political chaos, King Arihan of Ara struck.

King Arihan's plots were far more vicious than a simple attack on Xif. Intent on wiping out Xif, he hired assassins.

The plot to kill the two infant princes was narrowly foiled and Afriel's mother went into hiding with the twins to keep them out of harm's way. A new political structure was hurriedly put in place of the monarchy to fight the dual threats: the attack of Ara's army and the mutinous Veiles who was holding Queen Ataii captive in his Calbion cage.

While Xif rallied back against Ara's armies, King Arihan's agents incited the old vanguard of the Imperial Court against Xif. These were representatives of the old planetarchies, steadfast in their support of the Empire, whom King Arihan incited into taking a final stand against Xif. In a bloody move, the R'armimon Emperor Ondeiir, with the support of the Court, publicly executed Minhaas, Lenetto, and Veiles's son, Castien, for treason.

If Veiles was broken before, now he turned into a raging demon with nothing but vengeance in his heart. He unleashed the superweapon he had built, one seated within the reinforced chambers that fed starlight into the Sedara.

Veiles's weapon sucked starlight into the Calbion cage, impinging on Queen Ataii. The Nasfarii absorbed the light, turning incandescent as she bathed in its power, until she unleashed a spectacular explosion of light. The star, drained of its energy, was pushed to the brink of collapse. Veiles used the energy of an entire star contained in the Calbion cage to propel Xif out of orbit.

The Nasfarii became one with the light. Ara turned into ashes along with its star. Xif became a fugitive of the R'armimon.

An incredulous silence fell after Mahswa Tabrin finished. Maia felt dizzy. She could not believe the story she had just heard.

"What happened after that? Where did Xif go from there?" Ren asked finally.

"Veiles set out to punish all the planetarchies that had aided the R'armimon in the wrongful execution of Minhaas, Lenetto, and Castien. He was going to make them all pay for their sins."

"Tansi was one of the planetarchies at the R'armimon court, wasn't it?" Maia asked breathlessly.

The Mahswa nodded slowly. "Seems like so."

"And the R'armimon followed?"

"Sacred blood of a Nasfarii had been spilled. It was a crime that could not be forgiven."

"So . . . they've been following Xif ever since," Maia said.

"And now they've finally caught up with us," Ren said. "They're here to punish us all."

There was no doubt about that. The R'armimon was here to make the Xifarians pay for their centuries of crime against millions of people all over the galaxy, as well as avenge their princess.

Ren looked tired and worried. Maia's heart twitched. This was not his fault, but he, too, would pay for the sins of Veiles. But then . . . it was not just Veiles, was it? There were people after him who carried on his legacy.

"Why didn't someone stop the killing?" Maia blurted. "I mean, Veiles has been dead for a while, right? Yet, Xif has been destroying stars and wiping out civilizations up until now. Someone could've stopped it. Why didn't they?"

Mahswa Tabrin shook her head. "I have no idea," she said. "The Origin Scrolls don't say anymore." She slowly rolled up the papers and held them out for Maia. "Did you get the answers you were looking for?"

Maia nodded half-heartedly. Looking at the Mahswa's drawn face, she did not have the heart to tell her the truth: She had more questions now than she had before. And the biggest of them was where she fit in.

CHAPTER FORTY-THREE

HUNT FOR THE NOUVUS

Maia had often had miserable days, but nothing compared to the days following Mahswa Tabrin's reading of the Origin Scrolls. Millions of questions crammed her mind incessantly and she found no answers to most of them. Worse was the fact that she could not speak to anyone about it because of her pledge to the Mahswa. The only person she could discuss it with was Ren, and Ren remained frigid to her at the best of times. So, Maia bore the weight of her thoughts solemnly.

Questions were numerous, but they always came down to one thing: What did the anonymous note-writer want her to decode from the Origin Scrolls? It had to be something since the person had wanted her to get the scrolls out of the Chancery vaults, which obviously was a risky enterprise. Then there was the specific instruction about Mahswa Tabrin. Whoever her unknown benefactor was, knew about the content of the Origin Scrolls and her friendly relationship with the Mahswa.

The burden of Ataii's story was not the only thing keeping Maia miserable. The effort to decipher the riddle for the Roots Challenge had gone nowhere either. More than a week had passed since they returned from Zagran. A tired and bored Maia sat with her equally bored teammates one evening with a copy of the blueprint in her hand. Kusha sat next to her poring over another copy. Dani was missing from the study table, an absence the team had come to expect nowadays. Nafi and Ren were both taking copious notes from thick books.

"Maia, look at this." Kusha sat up suddenly and spread the map on the table. Maia tried not to set her expectations up. They had been jumping at the sign of the slightest hope, only to be dashed the next moment.

Kusha tapped at a small network of lines. "These lines are the power grid near ThulaSu. Now, look at this thin one. What do you think is different about it?"

Maia squinted hard. The copies were a tad faded and difficult to make out. She traced the single power grid tunnel that stretched to the tip of the First Continent back up to near ThulaSu and then further to the west. "There's one branch of the grid that breaks off from the main network and goes west," she said.

Kusha's eyes sparkled. "Yes, that's right," he said in a low but excited voice. "Since the main entrance to the power grid is blocked by the engineers and scientists working on the Damoclian Connector, we can hardly investigate the grid through there. But if we can find this other entry, and if it is still usable, we can hike into it as see if it leads anywhere."

That was a good idea. Good ideas however, always came with a few "buts," and this particular idea came with a big one. "Even if we get in, Kusha, it's a long . . . very long way to the tip of the First. It's almost half of the continent, if not more."

Kusha fell back in his seat. "I know. It's going to be hard getting there."

"But we can try," Maia said. "We *have* to try." As she stared at the drawing, a tiny design caught her eye. She bent over the map and tapped the end of the power grid at the tip of the First. "What is this?"

Kusha's head shot forward. "The runes? I've noticed those. All I can say is they are ancient symbols . . . I have no idea what it means."

"They must mean something," Maia said thoughtfully.

Kusha sat back in his chair and exhaled slowly. "First step is finding where that other smaller grid ends."

Ren leaned across the table and tapped on the end of the small line. "I think this is near Ori Pistado's village," he said. "Look at this circle right next to it. That reminds me of the building we were in, the Mausoleum of the Sun."

Nafi shut her book with a loud clap and almost hurled herself over the map. "Maybe there's a secret entrance into the power grid from within the mausoleum. Remember how protective Ori Pistado was of that place?" Nafi said, her eyes large. "There has to be reason to protect it so."

"Maybe, we can find out for sure," Ren said, scratching the tip of his nose vigorously. "Nafi, remember that book we found about the heritage buildings around ThulaSu? That had information on the mausoleum. We skipped right over it because we didn't think it was important enough, but—"

"Let's go," Nafi said, jumping to her feet even before Ren finished.

"Go where?" Ren asked. "The library's closed now."

"I got the book for my own reading," Nafi declared. "It's in my room. Let's go now."

Kusha sighed loudly after Nafi had marched out, Ren in tow. "You're right, Maia. Even if we find the entrance, that's going to be one super-long . . . no, an impossible trip to the edge of the continent. I don't think they'd make us trek that far, do you? I mean, this will take days."

"Maybe there's something else we don't know yet," Maia said. "Maybe we'll find out something on the way. Maybe there's a secret system or a different means to get there."

"Or maybe . . ." Kusha paused and let out a long sigh. "Maybe we're chasing down the wrong path entirely."

That was also possible. But with no other way in sight, they did not have a choice but to follow this lead down to whatever end it took them.

***

The mausoleum was built to honor the deceased of the House of the Sun. It was also referred as homage to "the memory of things held most sacred on Tansi." Because of that, everyone on the team was sure that implied — although quite obliquely — the Nouvus that had brought Tansians home.

However, as Maia and her teammates stood in front of the mausoleum on a beautiful warm day, Ori Pistado frowned and shook his head vehemently when Kusha asked him about the power grid.

"Wherever did you get the idea that this is an entrance to the power grid?" he said, waving at the domed building behind him. "This is a sacred place, yes. But the rest is . . . your imagination. I've never heard of anything so wild."

"Would you mind if we look around the mausoleum a little?" Maia asked. "Just want to make sure we haven't missed anything."

Ori crossed his arms and his eyes narrowed. "My word isn't good enough for you?"

Her teammates' faces deflated instantly, but Maia was not about to let Ori Pistado browbeat them away. "What have you got to lose by letting us check this area out? There's nothing to find anyway, right? We'll be out of here before you know it."

Ori tapped his cheek before giving a half-hearted nod. "All right, you can look around," he said.

"You're most kind, Chief Ori Pistado," Maia said, bowing low. Ori Pistado bowed back, but his face stayed grim.

Maia and her teammates decided to look around the periphery of the building as well as its interior. Maia elected to start indoors; Kusha was by her side in an instant.

"I'll come with you," Ori said grumpily.

Except for a few of the Black Phantoms who hung in groups along the edges of the central hall, the room was empty. Maia and Kusha studied the large room at the center of the mausoleum. It had only one door leading inside and opposite to it was a massive fireplace. The weather had warmed up since the last time she had seen it, so there was no blazing fire in the dark grates at the moment. But Maia smiled recalling the night of the blizzard they had spent warmed by its fire.

They looked around. They checked every corner, door, and window. They scrutinized the floor. There was no sign of an entrance, hidden or otherwise, in the building. The rest of the team reported from time to time, their faces always dour. They had not found anything worthwhile in the near vicinity either.

"Told you there was nothing," Ori said, flashing an all-knowing look at Kusha and Maia.

"All right, All right! We will leave," Maia said. "We followed the wrong path after all."

She cast a last look around the mausoleum. Walking up to the looming fireplace behind them, she playfully tapped its massive mantel. Her fingertips promptly turned black with centuries-old soot. Kusha chortled when she made a face and blew on her fingers to rid the dust, only to have more soot fly from the mantel and to her face. Maia stepped back, coughing.

"Stay away from that place," Ori yelled. "Are you planning to kill yourself or something?"

"I'm fine, Ori," Maia said as calmly as she could. "It's just soot. I'll wash it off."

Ori however, was far from calm. Red in the face, he herded Maia away from the fireplace and instructed some of his people to fetch water so she could wash her face. Maia thought she understood Ori's frustration: the last thing he could have wanted was the Nosiifarus to get sick inhaling centuries-old soot in a building he was responsible for upkeep.

"You don't understand," Ori grumbled. "You're important. You should be more careful with things."

Maia was about to say something to reassure the chieftain when she noticed Kusha waving wildly at her, his eyes sparkling like gems.

"M-maia," he stuttered. "Come see this."

"There's nothing to see," Ori said.

But Maia was already next to Kusha and staring in the direction he was pointing. Soot had come off the mantel at the spot she had touched. A design peeked out from underneath a layer of grime. Even though Maia could not see all of it, she knew what she was looking at. It was part of a rune, just like one of those she had seen on the blueprint of the power grid.

Maia spun around. Ori stared at the floorboards, a look of feigned disinterest etched on his face. "Ori, you knew about this," she said. "There's a path from here to the power grid, isn't there? I think it's right through this fireplace."

Ori looked at her for a moment before hastily turning away. "Don't poke that fireplace, all right? You kids need to get out of here. There's no path . . . to anywhere." He waved at the Black Phantom who surrounded them. "Escort them out. Now."

"Come on, Ori," Maia pleaded. "We've been looking for clues for weeks now. You can't simply throw us out when we're so close."

"I can't have you endanger yourself," Ori declared. He snapped his fingers and Maia felt the Black Phantom close in behind her. Kusha looked utterly hopeless, but Maia had not given up yet. She had a plan. She let a smirk tug the corner of her mouth.

"I thought a request from the Nosiifarus would be a command to you," Maia said slowly. "And here you are, throwing me out like a piece of garbage."

Ori blinked. Then, slowly, he raised his arms. "Stop," he said to his men.

The Black Phantom fell back immediately. Ori shifted on his feet, his gaze scooting off to the distance. "I was told you're stubborn, but I didn't expect you to be manipulative as well," he said.

"I'm sorry," Maia said earnestly. "But you didn't leave me an option. We're trying to win this thing and I couldn't let you put up a wall like that. Now please tell us how to get into the power grid."

Ori gave a resigned sigh. "But you don't understand. This is the path to the catacombs. It's dangerous. No place for little kids."

"We'll be fine, Chief," Kusha said. "We're not little kids. We've dealt with dangers before. And anyway, we're not going anywhere right now. Today we just need to check out the entrance. Make sure it's in good condition."

***

The fireplace groaned and screeched and wheezed as it rotated on ancient gears, revealing a long flight of stairs down into Tansi's bowels. Maia and her teammates, along with Ori and a handful of his men, walked down the endless stairs, flashlights in hand. At the end of the descent was a large door and beyond it, lay Tansi's forgotten power grid.

The heavy, cloying air inside the tunnel brought back terrible memories and Maia reeled. She tried to hold strong, fighting back thoughts of fear and hopelessness, and followed her teammates as they examined the power grid. Ori looked curiously at her face when Maia leaned on a column and breathed heavily.

"I told you. This is *not* a place you should be in," he commented grumpily.

Kusha fell back a little and peered at her face. "What's wrong, Maia?"

"It's nothing. Just . . ." Maia let her words trail away. Just thinking about the trek from Shiloh to Appian through the power grid made her insides crumble and she hardly felt like speaking about it. But Ori Pistado's face grew grimmer by the moment, so Maia had to explain lest he forced them out of the tunnel. "Being in this tunnel reminded me of the last time I'd been inside one. It wasn't a good time, so—"

"The tunnel saved your life though," Kusha said, patting her shoulder. "Or you'd have drowned in Lupitiali."

Maia nodded. By the time Kusha had related Maia's story starting from her fall into Lupitiali and her journey through the tunnel to Appian to Ori Pistado and his men, the weight on Maia's heart eased a little. Nafi, Ren, and Dani had marched ahead and now they stood in a tight huddle, debating. They broke up as soon as Maia and Kusha neared.

"The tunnel is in pretty good shape," Dani said, shining a torch at the walls around them. "The issue is how to get all the way down to the Fourth. We can't simply walk the distance."

"We should use jetpacks," Ren said. "Strap them to our backs and we'll be there in no time."

Dani shook her head. "We can't do that. We have no idea what kind of explosive gasses have formed inside a tunnel that has been closed for a hundred years or more."

Nafi scoffed. "Are you crazy, Ren? You don't carry an open flame inside a bomb. Everyone knows that. Using a jetpack inside that tunnel is like a death wish."

Ren gestured at the dark endless tunnel ahead. "Walk then. Maybe in a year or so you'll reach the Fourth."

Nafi turned away in a huff. Dani tried to mediate. Maia strode ahead of the warring duo, trying to look further down the tunnel. Kusha fell in stride behind her, Ori Pistado and his men followed. About twenty steps down the tunnel widened some, and Maia slowed. The darkness in the bloated area seemed thicker and it took Maia another step or two to discern the massive shapes looming ahead. A muted yell—it was Kusha, most likely—echoed across the vaulted roof of the tunnel. Someone grabbed her arm and pulled her backward.

"Step away," Ori yelled, raising his staff at the massive shapes ahead.

One of the Black Phantoms held her tightly by the arm so Maia could hardly move, but her mind spun endlessly until recognition dawned. She knew—her heart leaping with joy at the finding—what she was looking at.

"Ori, I know what it is," Maia screamed. The man's grip on her arm loosened a little and she tore away from him and bounded toward the hulking shapes. "Come on, guys," she shrieked with joy. "Come meet the Crawlers."

Simply speaking, a Crawler was a basic craft the maintenance crew used to travel short distances along the power grid. They were massive, sixteen-wheeled monsters with a flatbed. A simple seating area and some driving gear sat on top. Here, three of them were lined up, side by side. Perhaps this area in the tunnel was for storing Crawlers, Maia deduced.

Maia excitedly told the group how she had found the Crawler in the tunnel near Shiloh that fateful night when Appian burned.

"That Crawler saved my life," she gushed. "I'd be buried alive in that tunnel somewhere without it. They are nothing to be afraid of, they're friends."

"So wait!" Ren cocked his head. "You drove one of these things from Shiloh to your village? You mean these things could still have working engines on them?"

"Well, no. The motor didn't work," Maia said, "but they have a pedaling mechanism that can be used to drive them once the motor is bypassed."

"So, we could use them to go all the way to the tip of the grid?" Kusha asked.

Maia shrugged. "Well, we could, but pedaling a Crawler all the way would still take a lot of time."

"Unless we fix the motor and make it drivable again," Ren said. "We could find a book on Crawler construction from the library, right?"

"Of course, we could," Nafi replied. "We will. We have to."

Things were starting to look good again. Staring at the huge, dusty shapes of the Crawlers, Maia felt happy and hopeful. She was sure they had a great chance to find the Nouvus

CHAPTER FORTY-FOUR

BROKEN PROMISES

Finding the hidden entrance to the power grid had brought spring back to Maia's steps. Everything—even Monk Tessio's laboratory sessions with the snippy Pantheronicas—looked rosier than they usually were. The aural projection training with Revsi Sottekaja was not half as successful as taming the Pantheronicas, but according to the Revsi, Maia was finally able to push her consciousness around a bit.

The day was sweltering. Maia was hoping for something cool, but as soon as she and Dani walked into the large dining hall, Maia could barely stop from breaking into a dance. Rows of glass pitchers were lined up on the tables. They were filled with chilled water in which colorful pieces of fruits floated like icebergs.

"That's just what I was praying for," Dani said, and Maia couldn't agree more. They poured themselves cups of the soothing beverage and were enjoying sipping the sweet concoction when Kusha rushed to their side, bobbing excitedly.

"The Damoclian Connector is about ready to launch," he

whispered. "There's going to be a celebration tonight."

Finally! Maia's heart did a flip. The people of Tansi would finally be free of Xifarians.

"It's a good day," Maia said, taking a long swig at her cup.

"What kind of celebration?" Dani asked.

"Well, I wish we could have a big one with a cookout and a bonfire, but my father thinks it's not wise to draw too much attention," Kusha said. "He wants to keep it low, so there'll be a quiet feast at the refectories. We'll hold off the bigger celebrations for a few more months."

That was not such great news, but Maia understood the wisdom of the decision. Xifarians were not happy with the Damoclian Connector at all. They did not like it when the project was resuscitated, thanks to Kusha's stand at Zagran, and they certainly did not enjoy seeing it progress so well over the past year. And seeing the history of Xifarian sabotage of the Connector, it was a good idea to keep the jubilation under wraps.

The day passed by happily. Maia, Dani, and Kusha visited the control room where work on the Damoclian Connector was being wrapped up. The workers and the volunteers were all in a cheery mood. Maia and her friends lingered in the room, enjoying the vibrant atmosphere. It was not until late in the evening that they trooped back to their rooms and left for the feast at the refectory soon after.

If this was meant to be a quiet affair, someone had clearly gotten the wrong instructions. The appetizing whiff of food made Maia's stomach growl even before she had sighted the entrance of the dining hall. Maks was goofing off with his friends at the far end of the walkway and he waved upon seeing Maia. Thankfully, he stayed with his friends and didn't run over to her.

"Look at this," Dani exclaimed when they were at the door. Maia blinked in disbelief. The worn-out wooden tables had been draped with red covers and the most succulent food was placed in eye-catching bowls and plates.

Maia's stomach growled again at the sight of large chunks of roasted meat placed in an artistic mound over a bed of colorful vegetables. Loaves of bread, still steaming, sat next to the plates of meat. Bowls filled with gravy and laden with the puffiest rice grains Maia had ever seen made up the rest of the arrangement.

Kusha gulped noisily next to her. "My mouth is watering," he muttered. "How long do we have to wait now?"

Maia and Dani chuckled. Waiting was going to be difficult for sure.

"Hey, guys," Ren shouted as he rushed toward them. Nafi trailed behind him. They both wore wide grins, which could only mean one thing: they had uncovered information on the Crawlers.

"We found out lots," Ren started. "You were right, Maia. The engines can be easily bypassed on all Crawler models. And the pedaling system is a simple tandem coupling, so it'd be pretty easy to do rotations and drive all the way to the tip of the First."

"But . . . now listen to this," Nafi chimed in, her eyes sparkling. "We studied the engine design and Ren thinks he can tinker with it and fix it easily.

Ren nodded. "I can get a spare L'miere crystal and put it in a modified combustion chamber. That should get the engine going," he said.

"We could even use a cell from my LumTorch if that makes things easier," Dani suggested.

Ren ran a hand through his hair and chuckled. "There you go. We've plenty of ideas. I'm sure one of them will work out."

The dinner chime sounded and Maia and her teammates filed into the refectory along with the rest of the students of ThulaSu. Rayan joined them at the table, and Everrol stopped by to say hello. The room was full and buzzing like a garden in summer.

"Where's Sana?" Ren asked as they were filling up their plates.

"Dining with Uncle Alasdair, I suppose," Maia said. More often than not, Sana dined with them. But once in a while, she stayed back to accompany her father and Maia assumed today she had done the same.

"You suppose?" Nafi said in a rough voice. "Isn't Sana your family?"

Maia's hand stilled over her plate and for a moment she could not think straight, let alone retort. But even before she could recover, Dani jumped in.

"Stop it, Nafi," she snapped. "Family or not, no one can keep track of another person all day. And then, how is what Maia does with her cousin any of your concern?"

Dani's reply was not any more caustic than Nafi's question, but it quietened the table immediately because such a scathing rebuttal was utterly unexpected from Dani. Nafi pursed her lips and started twiddling with her food. Maia also decided to drop the issue. That Nafi was still angry with her over Miir was as clear as daylight.

They ate in silence after that. It was funny how food that looked so perfect could taste so chalky. Maia ate only because Emmy had imposed a habit of cleaning her plate since she was a child and she could not simply leave the table until that was done.

Maia had planned to skip the desserts but seeing the silvery trays with the flakiest of pastries topped with nuts, jelly, and cream made her cave. Their table had not yet been served when Sana rushed in and plopped down between Maia and Dani. She looked a little pale.

"Sana, what took you so long?" Maia said.

"I got stuck," Sana replied. "It was —"

A server had placed a plateful of pastries on the table and Sana lunged for it, leaving her sentence unfinished. She took a large bite of a gooey red tart, closed her eyes, and munched while everyone else at the table stared at her. Quite a while had passed before Sana opened her eyes again. She sighed heavily and shook her head.

"Something bad has happened, guys," she announced. "Some Xifarian envoys just arrived at ThulaSu. My father got called to a council to discuss some urgent matter. And looking at them . . ." Sana's voice faded away.

Ren leaned across the table, frowning. "What? What about them?"

Sana held Ren's pensive gaze. "Whatever they've come to say

isn't good."

"And you know that . . . how exactly?" Ren asked.

"I heard." Sana stayed quiet for a while again. "Your chancellor is dead."

Silence, heavy and heart numbing, descended on the conversation. It lingered like a blanket determined to snuff out life. Then Kusha jumped to his feet.

"Excuse me. I need to see my father right away," he said. With a curt nod, he left.

Ren got to his feet soon after. He seemed to have trouble standing, his gaze was unfocused and his face ashen. "I . . . I have to leave. I'm sorry," he mumbled before rushing away to the table where Karhann was seated. It did not take long for all the Xifarians to storm out of the refectory after that.

Maia and the others finished their dinner in silence. A feast that had started with so much hope ended in a lurch. They waited past midnight for Kusha and Ren to return, but neither showed up. Maia went to bed that night with a heart heavy with worries and an unnamed fear.

***

"It's a horrible situation," Sana declared. She had caught up with the girls at the ramparts after breakfast the following morning. Sana did not have to tell them about the awfulness of the situation. They could sense it already. Kusha had been missing from the breakfast table as were all the Xifarian contestants, including Ren. Things were clearly not all right. "They've been having meetings all night. And they're nowhere close to an agreement."

"Agreement about what exactly?" Dani asked.

"About every other treaty we had in place during the chancellor's time," Sana replied. "As in providing us with energy—"

"We don't need energy," Nafi interrupted. "The Damoclian

Connector is ready now."

"Yes, that's true," Sana said. "They're also calling off the Initiative."

Maia gasped. *Not again!* This was the second time it had come to that. The first was after the big fallout in Zagran. It was not a huge thing in the big scheme of things, but Maia wished they could finish the contest. They were close to the end anyway. Besides . . .

Maia's heart pounded faster as she remembered the other benefit of the Initiative—a sanctuary for the participants. If it was called off, there would be nothing to shield her from the Xifarians. She was undoubtedly stronger now, but still . . .

"They're also going back on their bigger promise—returning the miners on Ti . . . what few is left of them anyway," Sana said.

Maia sat up and frowned. "Now they won't?"

Sana shrugged. "They're saying all this is our doing."

"Ugh . . . not again!" Nafi sighed.

"We didn't do anything," Maia said. "Why would we hurt the chancellor or destroy the Sedara? We have no idea how to do such things anyway."

Sana looked up sharply. She hesitated for a second before whispering, "You can't prove otherwise, can you? They have a witness who puts you at the Chancery the night all the sabotage happened."

Maia drew a breath and held it. Amanii must've gotten better and given a statement. Dani and Nafi looked at her with fearful eyes. A shiver sped up Maia's spine. With the Initiative gone, what would stop the Xifarians from interrogating her now?

"That new Xifarian queen is one hard nut," Nafi declared. "Loopy, if you ask me."

Loopy or not, Queen Quemiila was indeed a hardliner compared to the old chancellor. An image of a stony-faced, bitter old woman flashed in Maia's mind for a brief moment. For some reason, even in her imagined picture of Quemiila, Maia felt a wave of intense hatred oozing out of the woman.

"There they are," Nafi said suddenly, and not a moment too soon. She pointed excitedly toward the courtyard. Three people clad in white stood on one side of the courtyard. Maia spotted Ren talking with them. Karhann and his teammates were there as well. They spoke for a while, then the three men wearing white and Ren took off across the courtyard.

"Let's find out what happened in the end," Sana said.

"Yes, let's," Nafi said. She turned toward Maia and Dani. "You coming?"

While Dani nodded eagerly, Maia shook her head. She did not feel like listening to more bad news. She would know it sooner or later anyway. Right now, she yearned to be alone with her fears.

"You'd need to find someone to be with then," Nafi said.

Of course, the chaperone! Maia seethed. The way Leeam had snatched away her right to peace and privacy was not fair.

"It's all right," she said and got to her feet grudgingly. She did not want Dani or Sana to have to change their plans. "I'll come with you."

They were halfway down the stairs when Maia noticed Rayan walking toward the ramparts. "I'll be with Rayan," she said to the girls.

Maia's feet dragged as she walked, her heart crushed by the weight of a mountain. Things were falling apart quickly around her, and Maia could not see a way out of the mess.

CHAPTER FORTY-FIVE

A SEED OF DOUBT

Maia caught up with Rayan at the ramparts. While Rayan practiced her combat moves, Maia walked over along the promenade and looked at the vista. Regret kept surging inside her. She should not have gone into the Chancery. The Xifarians could not have put the blame for destroying the Sedara on her if Amanii had not seen her that night. And then the Xifarians would have let the miners return. This mess was all her fault.

If she could, she would run away, burrow into the ground somewhere, and stay there until the world ceased to exist. But Maia knew that was an impossible wish. So she did nothing but stared ahead. And after a while, her insides went numb, her mind a void.

The sun rays on her face were soft; the gentle winds caressed her wayward locks. People walked up and down the rampart, their feet pattering on the paved surface of the walkway. A few paces away, Rayan practiced. All was quiet; nothing was out of place. Yet there was no peace in the moment, only the knowledge of being wrong, so terribly wrong.

"Hey," a voice made her stir. "Lousy situation for such a beautiful day, huh?" Karhann asked.

Maia smiled and nodded. Karhann was a nice boy, no matter what Nafi chose to think of him. First impressions tended to be stubborn things, she mused; once an imprint formed on the heart it refused to give up and go away.

It was not often that she and Karhann could talk to each other directly, so Maia considered asking the question burning in her mind. Did he send the notes about the Origin Scrolls? Then she resisted. What if he did not send them? Then she would only end up exposing her interest in the Origin Scrolls. Amanii had probably implicated her already and the last thing Maia needed was to hand the Xifarians a confession.

"All this for nothing," Karhann said, his voice sad. He meant the Initiative, Maia deduced. He followed Maia as she stepped toward the south end of the sprawling rampart. Maia did not mind his presence; she found it comforting in an unexplainable way. "I mean, we did work a lot on this Initiative. And for quite a while too. I wanted some good to come out of it, you know?"

Maia nodded again.

"My father didn't like it one bit either," Karhann said with a bit of hesitation. "But he said he didn't have a choice but to carry out the Rahina's orders."

Maia forced herself to speak. "Your father is an aide to the queen?"

"No, Ameron Jarkko is an aide. Well . . . he was an aide to our late chancellor. You know he's Loriine's father, right?" Maia nodded once again. "My father is an advisor to Her Highness, Rahina Quemiila, just like Ren's father, Lowanabe."

"L-like . . . whom?" Maia stuttered. Did Karhann just say that Ren's father was an advisor to Quemiila? But that was not possible. Ren would have told them.

"Ren's father," Karhann repeated. "You met him, right? When he was here this morning?"

"No, but . . ." Maia's words trailed away. She had no idea what this meant, why Ren had kept this a secret, whether he had meant to keep it secret. *Maybe his father is a recent appointee. Maybe Ren just did not find the right moment to break the news.*

"You didn't know," Karhann said, studying Maia's face.

"I didn't," Maia confessed.

Karhann chuckled. "Ren must have avoided the details of his father's accomplishments. He can be sort of humble about certain things."

"You're right," Maia replied. She desperately searched for the right words to make Karhann go on. She needed to find out more about Ren and his father without making Karhann suspicious of her eagerness. "He's funny sometimes. He never told us that . . ."

"His father has always been one of the top advisors to the supreme ruler. That meant the chancellor before all these terrible things happened, and now that Rahina Quemiila is acting as supreme ruler, all the previous advisors support her functions."

Maia gawked. So, this was nothing new. Ren's father had been close to the chancellor all these years, yet he had not mentioned this, ever. It was strange . . . and worrisome.

"My father is a brand-new appointee actually," Karhann continued. "He didn't serve the last chancellor. He couldn't since we're related."

Maia remembered suddenly — Miir and Karhann were cousins. She could not recall clearly, perhaps their mothers were sisters?

"I'm sorry for your loss," Maia blurted.

"It's a loss for all of us," Karhann replied. "My uncle was a good man. He could be harsh but he was a man of his word. Things were quiet and stable with him at the helm."

Karhann paused abruptly and scanned the dark stones under their feet. Maia squinted at his hesitant face. "Rahina Quemiila isn't . . . as good?"

He drew a long breath and pursing his lips, looked up at the Darkwoods for a bit. "She's all right," he said in the end. "A bit eccentric maybe."

No wonder there were challenges to her. With the R'armimon closing in and the Sedara broken so badly, the Xifarians could not be happy with a crazy leader on top. Not that she cared one bit.

Karhann continued in a low voice. "My father joined the queen's panel to help things settle down but he doesn't have much clout yet. He said he wanted to keep the Initiative going, but he didn't have many voting on his side."

"Ren's father must have voted for it also?" Maia ventured, still not knowing how to proceed or if it was the right thing to ask Karhann.

Maybe, I should talk to Ren directly. Maybe, asking Karhann behind his back is wrong.

"Oh, no," Karhann said with a loud chuckle. "Advisor Lowanabe was never a fan of the Initiative. If it were up to him, he would never have started this in the first place, but the chancellor acted on the advice of Chairman Phocluus. There was a huge brouhaha at the Senate over this."

"I see," Maia replied. "Wonder how Ren managed to join the Initiative if his father was so opposed to it."

Karhann did not reply. Maia stopped walking and turned to face him. His warm brown eyes sparkled as they caught the sunlight.

Karhann shrugged. "I have thought about that myself, asked him about it too. Never got a straight answer from him though. He's a bit guarded when it comes to his family."

Maybe that was it. Maybe Ren was a private person, just like Nafi? Nafi had not told any of them about her family until just a few months ago. There was nothing sinister about that. It was simply because she felt strongly about her family, strongly enough to keep it away from anyone's questions. Ren must have felt the same way. That was it. Maia was sure. She breathed in a lungful of air. Breathing felt good again.

"Knowing Ren"—Maia giggled as she thought of the roguish Ren—"maybe he joined in secret and never told his father. He would totally do such a thing and get away with it."

"That's true," Karhann laughed. "But—"

"What?"

"You're forgetting his father."

"What do you mean?"

"You don't know?"

"What?" Maia could barely get the word out. Truth was, she almost did not want to know.

"His father would find out, of course, given what he is," Karhann said so matter-of-factly that Maia did not have the spirit to reply. As she stood staring at Karhann, knowing he was about to say something terrible, she realized one thing: a lot of things in her life were a mirage, and it had been that way all along.

Karhann's voice rang clearly in her ears, refusing to fade away. "His father is a Gnelexian. From one of the most powerful families too."

A Gnelexian!

So many times she had heard of them. The dreaded mind readers of the Xifarian penal system. The ones that had turned Sophie's mind into mush. The ones that killed Bikele. The ones she had to be wary about, always.

The sunlight felt cold. Maia closed her eyes and shuddered. One of her greatest foes suddenly had a face—the face of her best friend.

Chapter Forty-Six

The Seer

The days after Maia had that conversation with Karhann were a living nightmare. Suspicion, she realized, was a terrible thing. It ate into her soul; every waking moment was a constant reminder of the possible web of deceit around her. She did not dare confront Ren. Aside from the fact that they were hardly on friendly terms, Maia was scared. She had made far too many mistakes judging people and she was not about to take a chance on Ren. She mulled over speaking about it to her other teammates but in the end ,decided against it. Ren had been feeling like an outcast lately and it would not be wise to push him away even farther.

Nafi continued to be less than cordial; Dani had gotten busy studying remedial medicines with Sana. A day after the Xifarian envoys visited, the Initiative was called off. The return of the miners was voided and a band of Tansian leaders had turned up at ThulaSu. There were conferences and talks around the clock to try to mitigate the fallout. Kusha, freed of his role in the Initiative, eagerly jumped in to observe. Soon, he was running back and forth between endless sessions of meetings.

Every day, mostly while Rayan practiced Monk Konnae's assignments on the ramparts, Maia strolled about nearby, in and around the herb gardens on the lower walkways. She tried to be more cautious now that the Initiative was called off. She worked harder and longer on controlling her powers, and the Xinhagyi was pleased.

"You are approaching total control, Maia," he said one morning as she conjured a complex formation of intersecting spirals with the light. "Keep your mind at peace and your heart above trivial pursuits."

Dani, who had watched the session, patted her back later. "I'm proud of you, Maia," she said. "You've come so far. I don't think anyone stands a chance against you now."

Maia hoped Dani was right. She doubted the Xifarians would try capturing her again, but it was good to be ready to defend in case they did. Now, finally, Maia was sure she could fight them back.

***

A few days after the annulment, Maia grabbed a book on ThulaSuian crafts and found an empty bower in the rose garden to spend some time reading it. She had barely been through twenty pages when she heard twigs crackling somewhere behind her. She stiffened and turned around to look, her hand instinctively clasping Bellator.

Maia caught a faint flapping of wings. Then she noticed a flash of white through the shrubbery and heard footfalls. It was not just a bird, someone was walking down the pathway. Maia sat up, dropped her book on the bench, and grabbed Bellator's hilt tighter.

"Ruche?" she exclaimed when the tall man--his silver-gray hair long and flowing, his gray-white cape loose over his shoulders—came into view. He stopped and turned around.

"Maia," he said smiling.

Maia remembered the warmth of his smile and its power to

entice. A wave of happiness crept along the edges of her heart, the way it always did when she saw him. However, she also realized, this meeting was very odd indeed. This man had no business being in ThulaSu, none at all. Yet, he was here. He seemed to show up at the right times and the right places, every time. He had helped her and had never been unkind, but his interest was too convenient, too contrived. It could not be a simple coincidence that he always stopped by when she was at her most vulnerable.

Was he R'armimon as her friends suspected? Maia wanted to ask him right away, but she stopped. *Let's not rush to conclusions,* she told herself. She was going to let him come to her.

"A cool head serves well in combat," Miir had said. It was weird that she remembered that now. But perhaps, now was the perfect time to remember it. This was quickly becoming a war.

"Maia, so wonderful to meet you again." His gentle voice soothed as always. He took a seat next to her on the bench.

Maia nodded. She chose to stay silent and let him make conversation.

"I am here for the summit," Ruche offered, tilting his head in the direction of ThulaSu. "I have been observing the proceedings."

A silence fell. It was an uncomfortable hush, one brimming with distrust. Maia felt a chill course up her spine and realized something—the man in white was not happy with her silence; he was instead frustrated.

"You have grown," he said at last, breaking the quiet, "much stronger." As Maia frowned, he hastened to add, "That's a good thing. I am glad."

As another patch of silence threatened to swoop in on them, Maia decided to speak. "Who are you, Ruche? And why do we keep bumping into each other like this?"

"What do you mean?"

"Please. The truth?" she asked in a cold voice that sounded unreal to her own ears.

He hesitated for a moment, but just a moment. As he leaned

toward Maia, his eyes softened and shone in an aura of honesty.

"All right, then. I am a Seer, Maia," he replied, his gaze steady and unwavering. "I can see things, future events, fates, and fortunes. I shape destinies. That's my job. And we keep bumping into each other because I have been trying to influence yours. You have a grand destiny, but it needs some guidance once in a while."

It was funny that she did not feel much at this revelation. No surprise, no anger, no fear. As if this was a long time coming.

"Your job?" she asked simply. "Who gave you that job?"

"The R'armimon Empire."

Maia's heart skipped a beat. Obviously. That made sense. His shifting presence, his almost apparition-like movements—he did not belong in this world. She should have known.

"I am not your enemy, Maia," Ruche said. "Nor the enemy of the people on Tansi. I arrived here to help Tansi because Tansi has always been an ally of the Empire."

"So . . . Xif is an enemy then?" Maia asked, her mind racing to put the missing pieces together. "A common enemy?"

"Yes, that is true. They have been destroying all our allies. We finally caught up with them here. And now I am going to help you beat that enemy."

"Wait. Help me or help Tansi?"

"It is one and the same, Maia. You are the only way to help save Tansi. You are the Shimugien we had been waiting for. You are the one who had been promised, the one who could break the cycle of darkness."

"No, that must have been my mother. You came a little too late to know her."

Ruche chuckled heartily. "I knew her just fine, Maia. But back to the matter of Tansi. I suppose you want to get those miners back from Ti, don't you?"

"Of course I do," Maia said, suppressing a sigh. "We all do."

"You could still get them back," Ruche said, his eyes boring into hers. "If you wanted."

"If *I* wanted?" Maia asked, frowning. It could not be as easy as her simply wanting something. There was a catch, there had to be one. "All those leaders are trying their best to get the Xifarians to change their mind, and you say it's just up to me?"

"Those leaders don't matter much, Maia," Ruche replied, his face turning hard. "You and I do. You have to remember that. Remember the power you have inside you."

She rose to her feet. An image, a vivid one, flashed in front of her eyes. Miir lay on the ground, hurt, helpless. His face was singed in places. He had fought the best he could to protect himself from her. He failed.

No one stood a chance against her, Maia knew that. But . . . just because she could, did not mean that she should.

"I won't," Maia replied with conviction. "I will never use those powers you speak of. Not as a weapon to get people to bow down to me."

"No, no, no." Ruche took a few steps after her as Maia strode toward the upper rampart where Rayan practiced. "That is not what I am talking about, Maia. I confess that I helped release the fire inside you, but that was so you could protect yourself. I do not wish for you to use it as a weapon of aggression."

"So you did help release it?" Maia stopped and turned around to face Ruche. "It was when we met on the Dorgashians, wasn't it?"

Ruche nodded. "It was trying to find a way out, Maia. Had I not helped you then, it would have made you very unstable."

One more piece fits in. But Maia still could not figure out what Ruche wanted from her.

"I guess I should thank you then," she said. "But if not use that power, then how?"

"You don't have to worry about a thing. I will negotiate with the Xifarians. I simply need a few promises from you in return."

"Promises? What promises?"

"First, I wish for you to acquire the sword Seigvard."

Mahswa Tabrin's sword? That was a weird request. How would she get it? And how would that solve anything for the R'armimon?

"Second," Ruche went on, "you'll try and restore that pendant you are wearing."

Maia's hand reached for Sophie's broken pendant.

"This? But—"

"You only possess half of it. You realize that, don't you? Now you have to find a way to the missing half."

Her fingers curled possessively around the filigreed ornament. Why was the R'armimon interested in it?

"And the third?"

"You will help me get back home."

"Home?"

"Back to the system of the R'armimon. You know, I have never seen the place, only heard of its splendor. If you don't help me, I won't see it in my lifetime."

"But, I don't kn—"

"Ah . . . we'll talk about the details later."

"That's all?" Maia had to ask. Although strange, his list of demands was suspiciously modest on the surface. It was also lacking something . . . the desire for vengeance. And that was a red flag.

Ruche smiled. "That's all."

"All this to keep Tansi safe?" Maia asked. "You followed Xif here, after watching them destroy so many planets, killing so many people, and you still do not want to avenge those murders?"

"I do," Ruche replied in a heartbeat. "I very much do. But stripping the Xifarians of their power to fly is punishment enough for them, and that is revenge enough for me."

Maia stopped a frown with the utmost difficulty. Although what Ruche just said was hard to believe, she did not want to let him in on her doubts. She quickly brought up another question.

"You asked me to acquire Seigvard. It belongs to a Xifarian now."

Ruche smiled. "I know."

Of course, he knew. Hiding her impatience, Maia continued, "With the Initiative called off, I won't see her around often, if at all.

It'll be impossible to see that sword, let alone get near it. I'm not exactly welcome on Xif, you know."

"I know," Ruche said again with an annoying, smug smile. "But the Initiative won't be hard to restart, would it?"

Maia could not stop frowning this time. "You will make them start the Initiative again? How?"

"I'll ask them nicely. If they do not comply, I will have to show them what I can do."

"What is that?"

"Their Sedara isn't working that well anymore, is it?"

For a moment, Maia did not know what to say. Then she blurted, "You destroyed the Sedara?"

"Just tweaked it a bit."

"People died because of that. Tierremorphes, innocent people . . ." Words stuck in her parched throat, refusing to come out.

Ruche looked away for a bit. His gaze was resolute when he turned back. "I had to take care of that. For you."

"For me? How so?"

Ruche shook his head. "It's complicated. I will explain when we have more time."

"You poisoned the chancellor also?" Maia blurted.

Ruche held up his hands and shook his head. "No, absolutely not. I . . . the R'armimon have nothing to do with that."

"Who then?" Maia muttered to herself.

"That's not important, Maia," Ruche said. "The crux of the matter now is this: I can make the Xifarians change their mind about the miners and the Initiative."

Maia took a long, deep breath. "What if they still don't agree?"

"We shall see when we get to that."

"No, Ruche," Maia countered. "You're the seer; you have to see now. I need to know what I'm agreeing to. I need to know that your negotiations do not involve hurting any more innocent people. It doesn't matter if they are Xifarian. If they're innocent, they *are* innocent."

CHAPTER FORTY-SIX

"I will keep that in mind."

"That's the best you can do?"

"Yes," Ruche replied. "You have to trust me on that, Maia."

Maia scoffed. "Trust you? You've been using me as a pawn for years. And I should suddenly trust you now?" She watched Ruche's lips thin and his eyes narrow to slits. "You even sent an assassin after me," Maia added, recalling Yoome's vicious attack. She had escaped only because of Miir. "I was so . . . little then. Didn't bother you to send an assassin after a defenseless child? And now you expect that child to trust you?"

"I did not send the assassin, Maia," Ruche said. His eyes shone with earnestness and . . . pain. "She was a mistake. I would . . . I could never hurt you. And yes, I was less than forthcoming with you. But what choice did I have? I couldn't just walk into your home and announce who I was." He looked away to the distance for a moment, slowly shaking his head as he did. "Have you thought what would have happened to you if I had not unlocked your powers? Where would you be now?"

Maia shifted uncomfortably on her feet. Ruche had saved her life, Maia had no doubt. Without her powers, she would be in a Gnelexian prison now, her brain turned into mush from their mind probes.

She looked at Ruche's remorseful face. "Give me something more," she insisted. "Something I can use to keep my faith."

"You have known me for a while. Isn't that—"

"No, it isn't. As you said, you haven't exactly been forthcoming, Ruche." Maia knew it was time to walk away. The leaders of Tansi would have to find a way out, another way to bring the miners back. She was not going to insert herself into this blood feud between the R'armimon and the Xif. That would be reckless, to say the least.

Maia turned away. "I can't agree, Ruche. I'm sorry."

"I would make up my mind quickly if I were you," Ruche said. "Before it's too late."

Was that a threat? Fist curling, she turned around slowly. "Too late? For what?"

"For the people on this planet. The Xifarians won't give up so easy, they will strike back."

"And do what? The Sedara is broken, so they can't hurt us anymore."

"They will find a way. They tried to capture you, didn't they? That time you got lucky, but what about the next?"

"I'll think about it."

"Yes, do think, Maia. You have the power to make a difference. You can change the fate of your people. All you have to do is help me change mine."

Maia strode forward. She did not feel good about it—something was odd, something did not fit. She was not about to make a deal with Ruche.

"Summon me when you make up your mind," Ruche shouted. "It would be easy if you wore my ring."

That ring? Years ago, she had picked up a ring Ruche had dropped. She had kept it with her, hoping to give it back to Ruche when she met him again. But the next time they met at the Dorgashians, Ruche did not want it back. So she had worn it, until when her friends suspected Ruche was R'armimon, Ren had taken it away to keep her safe from its influence.

Maia smiled to herself as she walked up the stairs. Ren was correct about the ring after all.

CHAPTER FORTY-SEVEN

TO THE EDGE OF THE WORLD

Maia kept her meeting with Ruche to herself, but not without feeling a tad guilty about it. It had taken long to share all her secrets with her teammates and now she was clamming up again. But there was no other way. All her friends were already distraught with the goings-on, and she did not want to add to their worries.

She did mull over Ruche's offer for the longest time. Why did he need those promises from her? What would he do with Seigvard and Sophie's locket? Was he lying when he said he would get the miners back? Maia did not know the answers to any of those questions, but they clouded her thoughts endlessly.

A week after the Initiative was called off, Hilledunn called an assembly. He gave them five days to wrap up everything before finally going home. Maia did not know where to go after this, and even though Sana and her uncle had insisted she come with them, Maia was not so sure about taking the offer. One, her presence near them would endanger her family even more. And then, it would be difficult to endure Aunt Rowyena's open disapproval of her for too long. Perhaps, Maia thought, she was fated to join ThulaSu's orphanage.

A few days before they were set to leave, Ren proposed they check out the power grid tunnel to the edge of the First, just for the fun of it. Maia eagerly agreed, hoping it would keep her distracted from worrisome thoughts that had no resolution.

"What's the point?" Nafi said, frowning. "We're never going to need to find the Nouvus. Why even bother?"

"It's better than waiting around for the ride to take us home, isn't it?" Ren argued. "It'll give us something to do. We can tweak the Crawlers, see if our plans work."

"I'm in," Kusha said. He had been attending too many meetings of the Solianese and that took a toll on him. It was hard, he admitted, hearing how almost everyone—incited by Sahiiraan Leeam—accused his teammates for this fallout with the Xifarians. "I need a diversion. Anything to keep me away from this nonsense."

Dani agreed also, and Nafi grudgingly gave in after that. The same day, the team trooped toward Ori Pistado's village, Ren leading the way. Along with packets of food in their satchels, they also carried equipment that was needed to tinker with the Crawlers. Kusha slowed abruptly when the village came into view, making Nafi grunt in annoyance as she bumped into him. Maia walked up to Kusha and followed his gaze. He was staring at the black flag fluttering above the village. Maia knew what that flag meant—death of a dear one.

"What's wrong?" Ren asked.

"Someone has died," Kusha said before sighing noisily. "I doubt Ori Pistado would be welcoming."

"Guess we'll find out soon," Nafi said. "Coming here wasn't my idea in the first place, but it looks like I'm the one who'll lead you into battle," she added. She strode forward without another look back.

Ori Pistado was not in a foul mood at all. He greeted them like always, raising a curious brow when they asked permission to enter the power grid.

"The stupid contest is over anyway," he said. "What's the use of going down there now?"

"Tell me about it," Nafi said. "They dragged me along. I'd have much preferred some sleep."

"It's just too much depressing stuff floating around," Kusha explained, ignoring Nafi's eye roll. "We thought this could keep us distracted for a bit."

Ori Pistado shrugged. "Yes, I get it. Come along then."

"There's a mourning flag in your village," Maia said, pointing at the big black mark against the sky above them. "We would like to pay our condolences." It was a common Solianese practice to visit the family in mourning and offer prayers for the departed.

"Oh, that, yes," Ori said, nodding in a distracted sort of way. "I'll carry your words to the family." He waved at the group and gestured at the mausoleum. "Come along now."

It seemed to Maia that he was too keen on veering them away from the village and the topic of the flag. No one else seemed to mind though. They followed Ori into the mausoleum, through the fireplace, and down the stairs to the power grid. "I'll have a few men watching over you," Ori said before leaving.

"There's no need," Ren protested, but Ori waved his protests away.

"There's always a need," he declared. "No matter how tall you are, you're little kids to me."

Nafi seemed violently opposed to being called a little kid but before she could object, Ori had walked away. Two of his men remained, stony and distant presences in a shadowy corner as they observed. The teammates were soon too busy figuring out the workings of the Crawler and making changes to its mechanics to be bothered with the watchmen. It took long, almost the entire afternoon, to get the mechanical drive system partially automated with a L'miere crystal and a LumTorch.

"Let's give it a try," Ren suggested brightly, wiping the dust and sweat off his brows.

"As in . . . you're going to drive this?" Nafi asked. "To where?"

Ren gave her a disbelieving look. "What else are we going to do with it if not drive? We'll see how far it goes on the rails."

"You don't know the condition of these tunnels, Ren," Nafi yelled, her voice echoing across the vaulted roof. "We can't just take off like that."

Maia shined the light of a LumTorch into the dark side of the tunnel. Nafi had a point: no one knew the condition of these centuries-old tunnels. They could have caved in somewhere, or be on the verge of crumbling someplace else. They could end up buried inside it.

"Come on, Nafi," Ren argued. "This was going to be our final challenge for a reason. They wanted us to find a way to the Fourth through these tunnels. They would know if these were unsafe."

Ren also had a point. They were expected to find a way into an underground chamber in the Fourth Continent and the only feasible way to reach it was through a tunnel . . . these tunnels. Maia took a few steps into the darkness, studying the walls and the roof. They seemed to be in pretty good shape. She pointed her torch toward the floor and across the rails. These looked fine as well, the walls were sturdy and the rails shiny.

Shiny? Maia's heart skipped a beat. How could the rails be so shiny if they had not been used for centuries? She remembered seeing rails just as polished in the power grid under Appian, but they were being used by tree poachers. Here though . . .

Maia's thoughts were scattered by Ren's loud voice. "All right, just a few paces, that's all," he said.

Nafi stood with her arms crossed, a frown deep on her forehead as Ren and Dani gave the engine a try. For a few moments, nothing happened. Then with a loud creak, the massive Crawler lurched forward.

"Yes," Ren yelled, his fist shooting up in the air. His jubilation was short-lived. The Crawler truly crawled, moving barely faster than Kusha who strode alongside the rails. Ren stopped the Crawler and scrambled down, shaking his head at the behemoth. "This won't work," he said.

"Good. Now let's leave," Nafi said. Maia could not help but notice how eager Nafi was to leave the place.

Ren held up his hand. "Not yet," he said. "I have just the thing to get this monster going." Ren seemed just as eager to continue his experiments, as Nafi was to leave. He rushed to his satchel and carefully pulled out a well-wrapped package.

"What is it?" Kusha asked, kneeling next to Ren.

"A couple of modified jetpacks," Ren said. He peeled off the wrapping and placed two gray boxes with pipes sticking out from one end on the floor. "We'll stick these to the Crawler. They'll force compressed air out and propel the Crawler forward."

While her teammates were excited about their progress, Maia found herself receding, worries and questions pulling her away from the excitement of the moment. She could not shake off thoughts about Ren. Why was he so interested in making the Crawler work? Was it a simple curiosity or was something else at work here? Shame came swinging at her right after. Ren was a friend who had stood by her time and again. How could she even think so poorly of him?

"What are you kids up to now?" Ori Pistado's thundering voice ripped Maia's tortuous thoughts. He threw a questioning look at Maia before striding up to the Crawler where the rest of the group had just finished attaching the second jetpack. "My men said you're planning to sneak into the tunnel."

"Sneak? Um . . . no, not sneak," Ren stammered. "We were going to test how far the Crawler goes, that's all."

Ori stared at him for a while and Maia thought he was going to hurl them out of the tunnel. But he did nothing of the sort. "I'm coming with you then," he simply declared.

"All right," Ren said with a loud chuckle. "That's even better. Hop on, everyone." He looked inquiringly at Maia who stood a few steps away. "You coming, Maia?"

They were all aboard in a heartbeat, Ori Pistado and a bunch of his Black Phantoms as well. Ren tinkered with the engine controls, muttering endlessly as he worked. Finally, he sat back and took a long breath. "All right, this better work." He pressed the biggest button on the controller.

It felt like the atmosphere tightened with anxiety around the Crawler. Ren had always been good with machines, but this was something else. The Crawler was ancient, the jetpacks utterly foreign, and the tunnels dangerously unpredictable. Maia held her breath, her fingers curling around the guardrails.

CHAPTER FORTY-EIGHT

DEAD ENDS

Maia did not have to hold that breath for long. Nothing weird happened; the Crawler did not fly off the rails or crash into the walls. It moved, at a breakneck speed, but quite stably forward into the darkness. Dani had attached three LumTorches at the front end of the Crawler and their light gave a dim but reasonable view of the path ahead.

"We should slow down, Ren," Kusha sounded the caution, but Ren was hardly hearing it. He had pulled out another gizmo from his pack — a display unit of sorts — and was hunched over it.

"What's that?" Nafi demanded, kneeling next to him.

"It's a locator device that shows where we are relative to ThulaSu," Ren explained. "It'll tell us where we are and how close we're getting to the Fourth."

Curious, Maia inched closer to take a look. Sure enough, there was a steady green dot on one side, which possibly indicated ThulaSu, and a flashing red dot that likely signified their Crawler was on the display. It was curious how well Ren had prepared for this trip.

Suppressing a sigh and a plethora of suspicion, Maia stepped away from her teammates to the back end of the Crawler where Ori Pistado stood with two of the Black Phantom.

"You're not very excited by the adventure," Ori noted.

Her aloofness had not gone unnoticed, Maia mused. She tried to be careful with her response. "I am, but I'm more worried about other things. I thought this would be a distraction, but—"

"Nothing you can do by worrying," Ori said glumly. "Fates of those poor miners have been written already. You can do nothing to change that."

Couldn't she? What if she let Ruche negotiate . . . force the Xifarians' hand?

But Ruche was a ruthless R'armimon bent on revenge. No matter how nice and reasonable he seemed, he was, after all, a R'armimon whose sole purpose in life was pursuing Xif. He had pretended to be her friend, yet only used her like a pawn and had not thought twice about killing the innocent Tierremorphes. How could she buy into his offer and give him a free hand knowing that?

Dark walls flew past. Shapes, strange and grotesque, came to view and disappeared just as quickly. The Crawler rumbled on, the ride unusually smooth as it hurtled into the unknown.

"Have you been this way before?" she asked Ori, recalling how shiny the rails had been.

The chieftain's face froze. Maia could tell he had not expected that question. And he did not know how to answer it either.

"Why do you ask?" he said after a telling pause.

He had been here, Maia knew already. He or his men or someone else he knew. She was not going to call him out though, so she kept up the pretense. "The rails are very smooth, almost like they've been used quite regularly. When I rode the Crawler from Shiloh to Appian, the ride was hardly like this."

Ori shrugged. "Who would come here? For what?"

It was interesting how he was avoiding answering the question. That told Maia enough. She decided to leave it alone.

"You're right," she said. "Who would come here? It's not like you have business on the Fourth."

Ori nodded. "Anyway, we're not even allowed on there. I wouldn't set foot on the Fourth unless it was a matter of life or death."

Maia did not reply. There was no need to. Ori was lying. Not lying exactly, but being rather shifty. Instead of conversing with anyone, Maia mulled her exchange with Ruche once again. Time must've flown because Ren's jubilant cry pulled her out of her thoughts.

"Dani, brakes! Slow the Crawler down," he shouted. "We're nearing some sort of end."

"What end?" Maia asked. They could not have crossed the entire continent so quickly.

Ren shrugged. "Don't know. Something's changing."

Maia peeked over his shoulder. The display now showed a lighter band of color ahead. Ren tapped the band excitedly. "That shows a change in terrain. Must be the water."

"What happens when we reach the water?" Maia asked.

No one answered. No one knew.

The blinking dot on the display that was their Crawler was approaching the edge of the band.

"Stop," Nafi shrieked. Dani braked hard. Maia almost flew forward and hit the guardrails in the front. Kusha slipped and fell, then sat up cursing.

"What in hell's name are those?" Ren blurted, staring into the giant forms that littered the dimly lit tunnel ahead. Maia blinked, trying fruitlessly to clear her vision and mind.

"Pantheronicas," Ori said calmly.

"That can't be." Disbelieving words trembled out of Maia's mouth. "T-these are giants."

As her sight adjusted slowly to the dimness, comprehension chilled her heart. These were nothing like the tiny plants they studied at Monk Tessio's sessions. These were easily twenty times larger, their tops reaching the roof of the tunnel as they hovered ominously above the Crawler. Their branches were thick, and their leaves shiny and red with long, serrated edges that reminded Maia of the teeth of prehistoric predators.

"We should get away," Ori said, and not a moment too soon. A breeze wafted through and Maia realized the plants were starting to sway.

They *had* to get away. If the bite of the puny Pantheronicas in Tessio's session could send people to the sanatorium, Maia was sure the tiniest scratch from these giants could leave them dead.

"Quick, Dani!" Ren lunged at the nearest jetpack. "Get the other one out. We need to fit them on the other side to make the Crawler go back."

"We can't wait for the jetpacks," Maia yelled, seeing a massive head close to them swoop downward. Its powerful jaws snapped shut merely a whisker away from the Crawler. They were plants still, not walking monsters. So, if this was the closest the Pantheronicas could get, the Crawler was safe. But Maia was not about to trust some overgrown carnivorous monstrosities. While Ren, Dani, and Nafi turned the jetpacks around, and Ori led a few of his staff-wielding men to the fore of the Crawler, Maia frenziedly worked the manual gears, fitting the locks and setting the pedals to the correct mode.

"Kusha, help me," she called.

Kusha dropped to his knees next to her, but he seemed frozen. Clearly, he did not know how to assist and Maia did not have time to explain to him. She pulled and pushed the locks desperately, but there were far too many to change.

A Pantheronicas snapped, its jaw grazing the rails that surrounded the Crawler's platform with a gut-wrenching clang but still missing the central section. Another swung over them right after. Ori swung his staff at its ginormous head, landing a thudding blow. It shrunk back, but the rush of air chilled Maia's heart. *We're running out of time*, she thought, panicking when her fingers slipped on a badly jammed latch.

"Come on, come on," she muttered fitfully at the obstinate latch that refused to budge.

A cloaked Black Phantom strode up. His long, gloved fingers yanked the stuck lock open in an instant. He did not step away but continued unlatching the next. Pantheronicas kept snapping at the Crawler, and the air slowly filled with a thick, wild stench.

Along with the Black Phantom, Maia tugged, wrenched, fitted, and rearranged the links. There was no time to marvel at her partner's expertise, but Maia stole a glance at him anyway. As expected, his cowl was too low over his face so looking at him was useless. Nevertheless, Maia could not stop smiling at the ease and smoothness with which the man changed the gears and the wonderfully satisfying synchrony of her movements with his. It was as if they had known each other, worked side by side many times before. And for some reason, even in the heat of the moment, with the terrifying Pantheronicas nipping at their heads, Maia felt an odd yearning inside her. There was no time to indulge in emotions, so Maia pushed herself.

Harder! Faster!

As soon as the last latch was in place, the man who was helping stepped away. He mingled into the rest of the Phantoms, indistinguishable from the others in the blink of an eye.

Running an arm over her forehead to clear the sweat off her brows, Maia rushed to the driver's seat. "Kusha, pedals!"

This time around, Kusha did not dither. Together they pressed on the pedals and slowly the Crawler lumbered backward. By the time they had put some distance between the Pantheronicas and the Crawler, the jetpacks were ready. Everyone breathed in relief as the wall of Pantheronicas receded, so much so that no one spoke a word on the way back.

"Scared?" Ori asked as the group trooped out of the power grid late that afternoon. He did not wait for an answer. "That's why I didn't want you to go in there."

"So you knew about the Pantheronicas already?" Maia asked sharply.

Once again Ori Pistado froze. However, this time he recovered quicker. "I knew there could be dangerous things lurking down there."

"Well, at least we know we were on the right track," Ren said cheerily. "There was a reason we were taught to wrangle Pantheronicas since this phase began. It was because we would come up against them on our final quest."

Ren had a good point. They had found the way indeed. It was a pity that with the Initiative nullified, their efforts would not come to a fruitful conclusion.

Nafi shuddered. "Now I'm glad that the Initiative was called off. I wouldn't battle those monsters even if my life depended on it."

Maia was sure Nafi would fight bigger monsters if need be. She let the comment slide though, her mind bounding off as she looked at the Black Phantoms behind them. She wanted to thank the man who had helped her change the latching apparatus. If he had not helped, they could have been in trouble. Maia quickened her pace to get alongside Ori Pistado, but before she could voice her request, a villager shot through the door of the mausoleum and rushed up to them.

"They're sending back the miners. Sending them back dead," he wailed. "Lasha, Momon, and Midori . . . all of them . . . all dead."

Ori seemed to have lost the ability to reply. He simply shook his head, over and over. "No," he said finally in a broken voice. "Not all of them."

The villager dabbed the corner of his eye. "They've laid at least a hundred down at the temple in ThulaSu."

Ori closed his eyes and took a breath before looking at Maia. "I have to get to my village. You should go back to ThulaSu now." He turned and nodded curtly at the Black Phantoms following them. "Escort them back safely."

Maia wanted to assure him that they would do fine on their own, but words had dried up inside her. Everyone else seemed to feel the same way. Maia's steps were heavy and fear barely let her breathe.

CHAPTER FORTY-EIGHT

They made it to ThulaSu safely and in dreadful silence.

Sana was waiting for them at the gates, the sight of her pale tear-stricken face making Maia's heart sink to the deepest depths. Sana rushed over and grabbed Maia's hand. "Have you heard?" she said, wheezing. Maia did not even know if she nodded. Tears trickled down Sana's cheeks in an endless stream. "It's horrible," she said, choking on her words.

Horrible was not a word grim enough to describe the sight they saw. The central courtyard around the Sun Temple was green no more. Instead, gleaming in the newly risen moon's pallid light, it was a checkerboard of black and white formed by shrouded bodies laid in endless rows. The Xifarians had returned the Solianese miners after all . . . after they had been killed.

Maia numbed from head to toe—wordless, unfeeling, and disoriented. Nafi let out a pitiful cry as she fell to her knees. Kusha mumbled something before rushing away. Maia's insides twisted and crumbled, pain clawing at her throat and wanting to make her scream. Yet, she could not scream. She only stared at the devastating scene that she believed was her own making.

CHAPTER FORTY-NINE

A DEAL WITH THE DEVIL

The dead blankness that had fallen over Maia's senses lingered for quite a while. She stood mutely with her friends in the courtyard. She would never forget this scene, Maia knew. Just like the blazing hillside in Appian, this too would be forever etched in her memory. Along with the guilt. She could have prevented this. Yet, she had failed to act.

Not anymore, she pledged. At that thought, a semblance of clarity returned to her mind. She could feel those frozen fingers once again. She could suddenly hear the wails and the sobs and the hushed whispers. She could see the slow removal of the shrouded bodies from the courtyard. She could think.

She had to speak to Ruche. She had to stop this madness.

"Ren," she called, her voice breaking the surrounding hush in an instant. Ren took time to turn, his face pale and drawn.

"I need my ring back," Maia said, deliberate and succinct in her demand.

"Ring? What ring?"

It took a moment or two for him to remember the ring. A frown came to life on his forehead as soon as he did. "Why do you need it? That's not a good—"

"I need it, Ren. Now," Maia said. Ren's face paled another notch, but Maia did not care. She had to call Ruche and stop the killing of innocent miners as quickly as she could. It did not matter if a few feelings were hurt in the process.

Ren nodded curtly. "It's in my room," he said and took off toward the living quarters, Maia following behind him.

Ren did not stop or slow down even once, nor did he speak to Maia until he reached his room. "Wait here," he said at the door. "I'll get it for you." He was back quickly and placing the jeweled ring on Maia's outstretched palm, he strode off.

Maia could not stop the sigh that coursed out of her, leaving her empty inside. Ren had been angry at her about Miir, and now she had angered him further. But there was no other way. She did not have time to explain everything to him or debate the consequences of calling Ruche. Besides, didn't Ren keep his father's identity from them for years? What moral grounds did he have left to lecture her?

Gritting her teeth, she tore her eyes off Ren's disappearing form and scanned the ring—crudely carved of dull gray metal, with twelve white stones surrounding a round black one at the center.

Taking a long, bracing breath, Maia slipped the ring on her finger. She had to act decisively, and now. She took the side exit out of the building and walked up the stairs to the ramparts. On a moonlit evening like this, the ramparts were usually full of strollers of all ages. Tonight, though, the place was deserted. Maia cast a quick look around and headed to the entrance of the rose garden. She was not going to get inside alone, but she needed some privacy. The shadow of the gates would do fine.

Maia slid into the cover of the shadows and looked down at the ring on her finger, suddenly realizing she had no idea how to make it work. "Just call him," she muttered to herself. Closing her eyes and focusing on the ring, Maia did just that. "Ruche, I need to speak to you," she said over and over again.

Moments trickled past tediously. Nothing happened. Ruche did not appear magically, and Maia did not feel a presence in her mind. Frustration made its way in, then anger coiled at the pit of her stomach. Ruche must've bluffed. He had tricked her again, used her as a pawn. A fire simmered around the edges of her brain, rage surging up her spine and spreading to the tips of her fingers. Somewhere in the distance, a bird cawed, as if mocking her.

No! She could not let anger take over. She had to control the fire within. Maia closed her eyes and thought of the exercises the Xinhagyi had taught her, drawing the cool air in and letting her senses soak up the calm around her. Slowly she pulled the fire back in, all the way from the tips of her fingers and toes, to the core of her being. Slowly, she lulled it to sleep.

There! She had done it. She had handled the seething bundle of energy with poise. The Xinhagyi would be proud!

"You have grown quite used to your power."

Maia whirled around, her eyes flying open. Ruche stood on the darker side of the gates, smiling.

"It took you a while."

Ruche stepped nearer, his calm eyes flicked from Maia's face to the ramparts and back.

"I wish I could come faster, but . . ." He paused, almost stumbling over his words. He shook his head and fixed a clear gaze on her face. "What did you want of me?"

"Don't you know already?" Maia asked irritably. He was a seer; he was supposed to know everything before it even happened. Why the pretense?

"I know a lot of things," he said in an infuriating tone.

"They sent some of the miners back," Maia snapped. "Dead."

Ruche nodded. "Yes, I know."

"I don't want the rest of them to die."

"They don't have to. You just need to ask me to stop it."

In one way, she was more than sure she wanted to ask. She had to save the rest of those poor Solianese miners. They had suffered enough already. But then . . .

Ruche chuckled. "Still don't trust me?"

She did not. He had used her. Played with her, tinkered with her. How could she trust him?

"Tell you what . . . I'll get the Xifarians to make amends," Ruche offered. Maia scanned his face for anger, but found none. "Will you trust me then?"

"What amends?"

"What if I get them to release the rest of the miners? Alive this time."

"But I haven't accepted your offer yet, so why would you —"

"Consider it a show of my good faith." Ruche smiled. "Just like you wanted."

Something did not ring true. Maia pressed on. "You've got the Xifarians cornered. You've got what you wanted. Why do you care if I got Seigvard back? Or fix the pendant?"

"I really shouldn't care about this dusty, broken planet," Ruche said glibly. Maia frowned. She could not believe that she had once thought of this man as a friend. Ruche seemed to sense her thoughts. "Yet, I do care, Maia. When I see the utter and complete destruction of Tansi, it pains me somehow." He paused and took a long breath. "I can't look past it. I can't ignore the millions of lives at stake. I can't ignore the doomed future of Tansi."

Maia mulled Ruche's words, her heart starting to pound in a frenzy as they sunk in. "What exactly is going on, Ruche?"

Ruche did not reply. He simply studied the stone wall of the ramparts for a while. "The Empire wants Xif destroyed."

"Destroyed? How?"

"Blown to pieces."

"But . . . most of the Xifarians are innocent. They don't even know about the feud with the R'armimon. They shouldn't be punished for what a few have been doing. That's not fair."

Ruche waited until Maia had run out of words. He smiled.

"You're very kind, but it gets worse. It's more than just the Xifarians. Tansi is right next to Xif. Do you think your planet will escape unscathed if Xif is blown to pieces?"

Maia forgot to breathe. A whole planet exploding right next to Tansi? Ruche was right. Chances were that Tansi would be destroyed as well.

"You can't do that," she blurted. "You can't."

"I don't want to," Ruche said. "I've been trying not to."

He did not sound hopeful at all. Something was dreadfully, terribly wrong.

"But?"

Ruche let out an enormous sigh. "But the Empire wants a bloody revenge more than anything else. It wants a spectacle, one that people will talk about for ages. It doesn't care what that spectacle could cost."

"There must be another way," Maia said desperately.

"Yes, there is. I am trying to find that way. You need to acquire Seigvard and restore that broken pendant. That's needed."

Questions, too many of them cluttered her mind. Maia only managed to get a few words out. "How will I?"

"You have to find a way, Maia. Both of these are mystical artifacts. No one can steal them for you. They have to be bequeathed to you. You have to earn them from their current keepers. That's the only way you can stop the Empire."

Maia felt frantic. "I don't understand."

"You don't have to. You have to have faith in me." Ruche cast a quick look around and edged closer to the gate. Voices, quite a few of them, drifted in. People were coming this way. "I have to take leave now, Maia," Ruche whispered, bowing hurriedly. "You have my promise: I will stop this senseless slaughter of the miners. But if you want to help Tansi, you have to get me what I ask for. Think about it."

The Seer of the R'armimon vanished in the darkness of the garden. Maia started walking back toward the refectory, clouds of worry thick in her mind. She did not pay much attention to the group of ThulaSuian students walking toward her, or notice Maks among them, waving at her.

"Maia!" he called. Maia looked, but she was so caught up in her thoughts, it took her a moment to react. "Oh, hey!"

Maks glanced back and forth across the rampart. "What are you doing here all alone? You're not supposed to be walking about on your own. If someone reports to Leeam . . ." Maks left the sentence unfinished, but Maia understood it just the same. In the heat of the moment, she had forgotten all about the condition Sahiiraan Leeam had placed on her. Maks continued, "Besides, it's not safe. You know about the miners, right?"

He meant well, and he cared about her. Perhaps it was unfair, but Maia did not have patience for Maks. She needed time to think; she needed some time to herself.

His fingers curled through hers. "You look distracted. What is it?"

"Nothing," Maia said, desperate to get away.

His face drooped. But as much as her heart twitched, Maia could not make herself say a word to cheer him up. He could not fathom how much danger Tansi was in, and how much burden was on her shoulders. She could not tell him. Could she tell anyone?

"I have to go, Maks," she said. "We'll talk later."

"Come on, Maia, tell me now," Maks insisted.

Standing right next to each other, their hands touching, it was odd that Maks seemed so distant. Unreachable rather. He would not understand, Maia kept thinking. He could not handle the insurmountable doom hanging over them. Even if he did grasp the impossible odds they were facing, there was little he could do to help. It was far better to let him stay in his cocoon of peace. Maia could not bring herself to tell him anything. "Later," she said simply.

Maia snatched her fingers out of his grip and turned away.

"Maia, wait," Maks called and ran up to her side. "I'll walk you to your room," he said. Together they walked, side by side, yet all alone in their thoughts until they reached the refectory and found Rayan. Then, with a curt nod, Maks left.

CHAPTER FIFTY

THE QUEEN'S HONOR

An enormous cloud always hung over Tansi. Whenever Maia thought their planet was out of danger, something new always appeared. Some inconceivable threat always lurked behind the peace.

Maia could have spent the next day cooped up in her room, pacing endlessly and stewing in her murky thoughts, but hunger had different plans. Her stomach started growling before long so she grabbed a couple of cookies from the jar Sana had installed in one corner of the room, perched on the windowsill, and nibbled.

Overnight, the courtyard had returned to normal. Looking at it now, no one could guess the bone-chilling scene of the previous evening. But memories did not clear so easily. Or ever. Maia realized she was never going to un-see the evening's sight and never going to have a happy memory of the courtyard.

Her thoughts strayed to Ruche. Had he been able to do what he promised? Or would it take long and sacrifice of more innocents? It sounded like he had damaged the Sedara. Was that true or just a bluff? Either way, he was a cunning soul. Could he be trusted? Maia leaned against the window frame and filled her lungs with the rapidly warming air. She did not have a choice but to depend on Ruche. No one else she knew had the power to make the Xifarians bend over. No one else could stop the slaughter.

A thunderous rapping on the door almost made Maia topple off the windowsill. Heart thudding madly, she stumbled off her perch. The rapping was far too raucous to be her teammates, and there were many chattering voices along with the knocks.

Maia fell back in surprise as soon as she opened the door. About ten kids, all students of ThulaSu, stood there. What were her dorers doing here? She knew they idolized her, but thankfully, always from a distance. Maia recognized a few faces, among them the boy with curly hair and freckles who stood at the center.

"Merin?" she asked, and the boy's face lit up with a smile that could rival the sun.

"You know my name," he said, flushing vividly. He flashed a proud look at the bevy of friends and muttered, "She knows my name."

Some of his friends simply smiled, but some looked positively jealous. Even though Maia was taken aback by the unexpected show of emotions, Merin continued nonchalantly.

"Didn't bother you, I hope," he said. "We want to take a photograph with you before you leave ThulaSu."

"Oh!" was all Maia said. She wanted to tell them that she was going nowhere, but before she could, a gut-wrenching noise drew her eyes to the open window.

"What in the stars is that?" a girl in the group said loudly.

Maia could not tell what it was, but something huge and red was descending from the sky. She rushed to the window, the pack of dorers at her heels.

"It's an airship," a boy shouted.

He was correct. It was an airship, a humongous one to be exact. It was red and gold all over, and very shiny. Not as big as a Fahrbot, but still big enough to swallow up nearly half of the temple courtyard. It was undoubtedly Xifarian. Maia recognized the Royal Crest of Xif — a dragon-like creature entwined a faceted shield of red, black, and gold protectively, fangs bared and eyes glinting with unveiled menace — on its flaring tail.

But why was this ship here? Ruche had to have done something!

"Maia, have you seen it?" Kusha rushed into the room, his eyes as big as headlamps. Seeing the crowd already present around Maia, he slowed and collected himself. "The Xifarians are here again," he said, almost calmly. "But why? Why after what they did yesterday?"

"We shouldn't even let them land on the temple grounds," one of the smallest girls with long twin braids said. "Can't you do something, Maia? Stop them?"

She sure wished to. If yelling from the rooftops of ThulaSu, threatening the Xifarians with fire and blood could resolve everything, the world would have been a simpler place. But the world did not work like that. There were protocols to be followed, diplomacy pursued.

"I'm sure they have a reason to visit," she said calmly. "We'll find out soon. Let's watch and see."

Hearing footsteps in the corridor, she turned. Ren peeked through the door, his eyes sparkling. "Hey, guys, the *Queen's Honor* just landed. I'm going down there to check it out. Want to come?"

Kusha raised an eyebrow. "*Queen's Honor?*"

"It's a special ship in the fleet reserved for the supreme ruler," Ren explained. "Coming?"

"Do you mean Rahina Quemiila is here?" Kusha asked.

"I don't know. Perhaps," Ren said, gesturing impatiently to follow. "Come on."

There could be no harm in looking. The dorers were definitely up for it, even the tiny girl who had voiced annoyance at the Xifarians moments ago.

"We can take our photograph with Maia there," Merin suggested brightly and the excited horde readily agreed. They trooped out happily, Ren leading the way.

"Quite a group you have here," Kusha commented, and Maia had to agree.

"I feel ancient when I see them," she confessed. "They're so . . . bouncy, innocent. I can't . . . I don't think I'll ever be half as happy again."

Kusha slipped an arm across her shoulder. "You've been through hell, Maia. It'll take a bit to get over all that. But you'll see; things will get better with time. They always do."

She could surely hope. By the time the group approached the magnificent ship, a small crowd had already gathered around it, mostly students. Dani and Nafi appeared, likely from the refectory, and joined the group. Karhann was at the entrance of the ship and he waved at Ren excitedly.

"Come on, everyone," Merin yelled, pulling out a well-worn boxy device from his pocket. "Line up. Let's take our photograph."

By the time Merin and his friends had photographed with Maia to their heart's content, Ren rejoined the group.

"The Rahina's not here," he informed. "She has sent her top regent to talk to your leadership."

"About what?" Nafi demanded. "How many people to kill every day?"

Ren sighed, his face wilting momentarily. Since seeing the dead arrive the previous day, Ren had been in a particularly depressed mood. "I hope there's good in all this," he said. "She wouldn't send out the *Queen's Honor* unless there was good intent."

There better be, Maia thought. *Ruche better keep his promise.*

"Good, my foot!" Nafi scrunched her nose up at Ren. "I don't think your queen knows the meaning of good. Someone should teach her that first."

"I'm going to get something to eat," Maia declared. She was hungry, but more than that, she was not interested in a useless war of words. Kusha and Maia walked back to the refectory.

She had not cleared half her plate of stuffed bread when Sana rushed in, dropped into the seat next to her, and sighed noisily. "Now they say it was a terrible accident. Like anyone's buying that. They killed those poor people on purpose, I'm sure."

More like executed them. Anger, frustration, and helplessness swirled in a tumultuous wave inside Maia, making her grit her teeth. She had thought of the old chancellor as cruel, but this new queen was an epitome of evil.

"What a charade," Kusha said, nose scrunching with derision. He left the table to find out more about the regent and the council.

"Why the sudden apology? What do they want?" Maia asked Sana after Kusha had left, even though she was sure it was because Ruche had somehow sent a message across. He had possibly made a threat forceful enough to make the Xifarians bend their knee.

"They want the Initiative resumed, as if anyone cares about that stupid contest anymore," Sana grumbled. "And they're going to return the miners. Alive this time."

"I'll believe it when I see it," Maia said, and Sana gave a knowing look.

The two girls sat in the refectory for a very long time, chatting about everything from the Xifarians to their childhood in Miorie. The sun was almost starting to set when Maia and Sana finally ambled out. The *Queen's Honor* still sat on the temple grounds, but the crowds around it had now vanished. Karhann and his team were lounging at the entrance of the airship. Maia's teammates sat on one of the benches near the covered walkway opposite to the ship and argued.

"Why do your friends always fight?" Sana asked, her lips curling in annoyance. "What is it now?"

Maia had no idea what they could be arguing about, but the issue became clear as soon as they approached. Apparently, Karhann had been giving tours of the airship to anyone interested. Ren and Dani wanted to take the tour, but Nafi was hell-bent against it.

"I'm *not* going," Nafi said in a huff. "This is infantile."

Kusha crossed his arms and gave a solemn nod. "I agree. Karhann is acting like a carnival's come to town. It's not. This is a serious matter."

Dani chuckled. "You're making too big of a deal out of this. Karhann doesn't mean anything by it. The kids wanted to look inside and he offered them a peek. And these kids have never seen an airship before so you can't blame them for their excitement. Even I want to see what the supreme ruler's ride looks like inside."

Dani had good points, Maia had to admit. Regardless, she did not want to venture inside, mostly out of pride.

"Well, I haven't ever seen it either," Ren said. "So I'm going to have a look. I'll be back soon."

They watched Ren walk away. Maia was trying to think of something to do when Everrol streaked in. His face was flushed and a mad grin stretched his face.

"It's called the *Queen's Honor*," he said giddily, pointing at the red-and-gold craft. "They're letting people get inside too."

Nafi rolled her eyes and Sana chuckled. "It's quite fascinating," Dani said with a smile. "That's one good-looking ship."

"Have you been inside?" Everrol asked. He was rocking back and forth on his toes with the excitement of a two-year-old.

"We don't want to," Nafi said caustically. "We're not going sightseeing to the murderer's ship."

"The ship didn't murder anyone," Everrol said. He cast a longing look at the craft. "My friends all went in. I was stuck with an assignment with Monk Hilledunn." Everrol's face twisted when he mentioned Hilledunn's name and Dani sat up like she had been struck with a whip.

"Did he hurt you again?"

"No. Not at all," Everrol said hastily. He gazed at the *Queen's Honor* with lustrous eyes for a while. Then he cast a piteous look at the bunch. "Let's go, guys. It's just a quick visit. I hate to go alone."

Dani could not refuse that, she jumped to her feet. "Come on, let's go," she urged her teammates.

Poor Everrol deserved a break, and Maia did not mind visiting a murderer's ship just to grant the boy his measly wish. Still, she hesitated for a moment. Was it safe to walk into a Xifarian ship? With the Initiative voided, there was no sacrosanct shield around them anymore. And knowing the Xifarians . . .

They would not dare! It will not just be audacious if they struck at her here in broad daylight, it would be foolhardy. And Xifarians were anything but fools. Besides, Ruche was on her side and the Xifarians would not risk enraging the R'armimon Seer.

"Are you coming, Maia?" Dani called. She was already on her way to the Queen's Honor.

"Yes," Maia said, striding forward with resolute steps.

CHAPTER FIFTY-ONE

A GILDED CAGE

Ren noticed them coming. He was near the golden staircase that led up to the gilded entrance of the massive spacecraft that was the *Queen's Honor* and chortled as they approached.

"Couldn't resist after all, huh?" he said.

Next to Maia, Sana slowed abruptly. "You know what, I need to go. I just remembered something I have to do," she said.

Ren frowned when Sana strode away. "What's with her?"

Maia did not know. It was strange how Sana rushed away, her face puckered. Almost, as if she was offended. No, hurt almost.

Was it Ren's words? Or how he said it?

Karhann and his teammates, who were still lounging at the entrance, sat up on seeing the group. Baecca smirked. "Here comes the hero brigade," she jeered, and Loriine immediately broke into chuckles.

"Don't you have anything better to do than gatekeeping?" Nafi snapped.

Loriine was about to reply but Karhann grabbed her arm. "Actually, that reminded me. We have to check out those books, remember? Come on, let's go. We've wasted enough time here."

Loriine and Baecca did not seem half as interested in finding the book Karhann referred to, but they grudgingly followed.

"Good riddance," Nafi muttered, and Maia could not help but feel the same way. Karhann's team—Loriine and Baecca in particular— were always a pain.

The golden staircase led into the plush red-carpeted interior of the ship. Maia had seen quite a few spacecraft during her few years in the Initiative, but this one was different. It was eye-popping fancy. Rich fabrics draped aesthetically contoured furniture; jewel-toned curios shone pleasantly in the soft light. Everyone seemed frozen in awe. Everrol, who had never been exposed to anything beyond ThulaSu, was affected the most. His eyes were bigger than ever, and his mouth opened and closed like a fish gasping to breathe.

They would have stood there forever, simply staring in amazement, had it not been for the two uniformed employees who came forward to greet them. "Welcome aboard the *Queen's Honor,*" the red-haired man said. It was weird how his eyes lingered on Maia's face longer than anyone else's, but Maia chalked it up to her jittery nerves. "The tours have ended," the man said, chuckling. "We had too many visitors for a day. The ship has to recover, and so do we."

Everrol let out a loud despairing groan and Maia worried he was going to burst into tears. The other man with a pale skeletal face quickly came forward. "That's all right," he said with an admonishing look at his partner. "We can have one last walk," he said, smiling reassuringly at Everrol.

The red-haired man did not seem very pleased, but he shrugged and made way for the group. The skeletal-faced man waved at the room they were standing in. "This is the grand foyer of the *Queen's Honor,*" he started. "As you know, this ship is the official transport of our supreme ruler. It has been for hundreds of years. This craft is ancient, so be gentle while you're in it, all right?"

He gestured the group to follow him toward a door to the left that was decorated all over with ornate carvings of leaves and flowers. "Not much of this craft is open for viewing, but you're free to enter the main chamber."

The man parted the door of the main chamber and invited them in with a sweeping flourish of his arms. Ren led the way, Everrol following right behind. Kusha and Nafi went next. Maia was at the far end of the group along with Dani. While the room beyond beckoned her endlessly, Maia hesitated at the threshold.

Something odd . . . dark stirred in her mind. A guttural squawk reached her ears, a flutter of wings . . . the Ravenold?

She had not had visions of the Ravenold in a while. The legendary bird — Maia still remembered its shiny coat with a purplish tint, the crescent of the moon over its eye, its large and stout beak, the wedge-like tail, the eyes that glowed red sometimes, its croaking, screeching call, and its thick, bumpy talons — often came to her dreams while she was on the run from the Xifarians. Mostly it came to warn her of impending danger.

"Are you coming, Maia?" Dani asked. Her touch was light on Maia's arm, but it still helped clear Maia's thoughts a little.

"Is something wrong?" the red-haired man asked from behind. The Ravenold fluttered some more. Maia blinked, struggling to understand what the Ravenold was trying to say.

"You have to move on," the man said impatiently. "I told you we were closing up."

Maia ignored him and tried to focus on the dimness covering the Ravenold. Was it asking her to stop?

"Let's keep moving," the Xifarian man snapped.

Dani tugged her arm. "Come on in, Maia," she whispered. "We'll be out of here quickly."

The tenuous link that Maia had to the Ravenold faded and she stumbled into the sparkling, intimidating room.

"Have you met the Rahina Quemiila?" the skeletal man was asking the rest of the group, raising his hands respectfully at a wall-high painting of a woman at the far end of the room.

It took Maia a moment to see her features clearly. The Xifarian queen wore a Gambrill in Royal colors. Her silver hair was swept up in a severe style, her hazel eyes sharp as they gazed forward. She had a cruel mouth and angry wrinkles around her eyes. Looking at the Rahina left a shadow over Maia's heart. Yet, there was something about the queen, something Maia could not put a finger on, that made her want to keep looking.

"Come, come," the skeletal man called. "You have to see the Rahina up close."

Maia had no interest in seeing the heartless queen up close, so she hesitated. Dani seemed undecided as well, but the red-haired man behind them goaded them on.

"You will not find a more lifelike portrait anywhere. Why do you hesitate?" he asked, clearly perplexed.

Maia did not care how lifelike it was, but she wanted to get done with the tour quickly. So with a listless shrug, she stepped forward, Dani following.

"She looks like she could eat us alive," Maia whispered. Dani had barely chuckled in response when the floor swayed under their feet.

Before Maia could fathom what was happening, an ear-splitting boom made Maia teeter. In the next instant, a wave of cold swept over her, numbing her. Maia could see and hear, but only in abrupt chunks. Her heart pounded. Dani's fingers curled around her arm. The plush ground rushed up and closed around them. Someone screamed; someone else called her name.

When the fogginess lifted and Maia saw in a normal way again, the two men who were showing them around darted out the door. And around Maia and Dani, a golden cage shimmered into existence.

Chapter Fifty-Two

Blood and Fire

I t happened all too suddenly. By the time Maia realized what exactly took place, it was too late to think of a way out. She and Dani were imprisoned in a circular cage made with solid metallic bars, separated from the rest of the group. Her teammates and Everrol had pounced on the cage and they tugged and pushed and pulled . . . pointlessly. The bars, Maia deduced quickly, were stronger than anything they would be able to take apart with bare hands.

And then the most chilling realization of all dawned: this was no accident. It was a trap, a well-laid one to get to the one thing the Xifarians wanted . . . needed to survive. It was a trap to get *her*.

"Dani!" Kusha's gut-wrenching yell tore through the room. He pounded the bars in a manic frenzy but they did not budge.

"Help," Nafi yelled at the door that had now closed.

No one came.

Maia did not expect anyone to come. Although she still did not understand the point of putting her in a cage. It was weird how calm her thoughts were, how fearless.

"Someone get help," Nafi yelled again. Kusha, who had been uselessly pummeling at a bar, let go with a start and fell away.

"I'm going to find help." Kusha rushed to the door and tried the handle. "They've locked it!"

"Maia, what's happening?" Dani's anguished whisper floated to Maia's ears.

Maia did not know the answer to that, but she wished Dani could be free. This was not Dani's fight, and she did not deserve to be locked in here. She had to get Dani out . . . somehow. The gears in Maia's brain spun wildly and screeched to a sudden halt.

There was a way out, perhaps a risky one, but a way nonetheless. She had to use her powers, but carefully. Gripping the bars tightly, Maia looked within. She willed her consciousness to her core, pulling out the immense strength that slept there and forcing it out to her fingers. It flowed, quiet and controlled, down her arms, rippling over her fingers, dancing around the bars. Maia compelled them to tear the cage apart, one rod at a time.

They tried. Swirling, pulling, and pushing. Nothing changed, not the tiniest bit. Whatever this cage was made of was impervious to the light. Maia's mind raced. Maybe she could let more of the light out? More power could do the trick. *No!* Dani was near, far too near. She could not risk eviscerating her friend.

Truth stared Maia in the face: there was no escaping this impossible barrier. Suddenly exhausted, she let her mind off the light and leaned against the cage. Her head felt like a boulder on her neck; her limbs weighed down on her like a cumbersome load.

A distance away, Kusha pounded the door frantically. "Open up! Open up, you filthy rats!"

As if in response to his shouts, the panel slid aside. For a moment, Maia's heart leaped. Then the pit of her stomach dropped as she saw the scene outside the door.

"Kusha, get away from the door," she yelled. Kusha had already stumbled back a few steps as an army from their worst nightmares made its way in.

"That's right, boy," the man leading the way said. "Run. Find a corner to hide. You just might survive my grand experiment."

Chairman Phocluus!

The scheming scoundrel had not only survived, but he was well enough to plot this attack. He looked different. A huge bandage covered almost half his face, but it was surely him. He did not walk but floated into the room like a ghost gliding through the mist. There was something odd about him. Maia squinted hard, and soon she figured it out. This was not the real chairman, but likely a projection of the man.

"Hello there, Maia," the ghostly Phocluus bared his teeth as he approached the golden cage. "We meet again."

A group of whip-wielding, masked and caped thugs, ones from the Order of the Fyrstell, marched in behind Phocluus. Kusha, thankfully, did not try to stop them and fell back with the rest. Not only were they outnumbered, but their weapons were hardly any match for those fierce whips in such close quarters.

"What do you want, Phocluus?" Maia asked. Even though her heart had started to thrash wildly, her voice sounded surprisingly steady to her own ears.

"You know what I want," he said. "I want what was taken from us by your treacherous mother. And now I've found a way to get it back."

"The Sedara is broken, Phocluus," Maia said. "The light is gone. The shards are gone. You can't get them back because it's in me."

The ghost of Phocluus cackled, his wild laughter making Maia's spine tingle. Dani's cold fingers on her arm tightened. At the side of the room, Ren, Kusha, Nafi, and Everrol cowered as the Order's thugs flicked their whips menacingly at them.

"Yes, you're correct," Phocluus said. "You hold the light now. That's really unfortunate. For you." He paused and laughed some more. "Do you know how the heart of the Sedara came to be?"

She did. She vividly remembered the Mahswa reading the Origin Scrolls. Ataii, the R'armimon princess was trapped in a Calbion cage .

. .

As her thudding heart sank to the pit of her stomach, Maia reached for the golden bars around her and felt their cold smoothness against her palms. Were these Calbion too?

"You know already," Phocluus said, studying Maia's face and tittering. "So you can imagine what I plan to do to you."

She could well imagine. He was going to turn her into light, back into the heart of the Sedara.

Maia's heart stopped its frenzied thrashing. Every word Phocluus uttered came to her as clearly as the air that surrounded her. Her mind bounded—thinking, analyzing, and connecting dots.

The Origin Scrolls! This had to be the reason her secret benefactor asked her to read the ancient tome . . . to warn her of a terrible possibility. She should have read between the lines, she should have understood the threat to her. She grasped the connection now, but it was already too late!

"Do what you want to do with me, but let my friends go," she said, holding the hazy gaze of the chairman. "Your war is with me, Phocluus. Don't punish them."

Phocluus burst into wild laughter and circled the rim of the cage. "Just like your mother. Your friends are not going anywhere, dear girl. I can't let them go and call for help. But don't worry, the ones outside will live. But that girl with you . . . ah well, it's a small sacrifice for a great cause."

"Maia, use your powers," Nafi shouted from her corner. "Break that cage."

Hadn't she already? It did not work. She knew now that there was no breaking a cage made of Calbion. It was the only thing strong enough to hold the light.

Dani clutched at the bars, fear shining in her eyes.

"It's a Calbion cage, silly girl," the chairman said with a chortle. "Your all-powerful friend is as useless as a mouse inside it."

Maia bristled at his words but swallowed her anger. She had to persuade Phocluus to let Dani out.

CHAPTER FIFTY-TWO

"Please," Maia said. "Let Dani go, please."

"Too late for that. The encapsulation has already begun. Have you checked on your friend lately?"

Maia turned to Dani and screamed. Dani had turned deathly pale and clutched at her throat as if she was having difficulty breathing. Maia did not feel anything, but whatever it was that Phocluus had set in motion was clearly having a devastating effect on Dani.

"Dani!" Kusha shouted, his face crumpling with pain. He turned toward Phocluus, glaring through tears. "No, stop," he yelled. He pulled out his sword and leaped forward, but the Order of the Fyrstell was ready. A whip licked the air and jumped at Kusha's face. He tried to jump away, but the whip caught his arm and he toppled backward. Blood trickled down from a newly formed gash on his hand.

Phocluus laughed again. "Foolish kids," he said. "They think they can fight the Order of the Fyrstell. They'll all die."

"Let them go," Maia screamed, wrapping her arms around Dani who had sunk to her knees. "Let them go."

"You'll all die," Phocluus said, his voice hammering against Maia's ears. "Every one of you . . . unless you stand down right now."

Someone screamed. Someone—Everrol perhaps—hurled himself into the group of masked men. Nafi ran, swiping her knives at anyone who came near, dodging, weaving, and making a mad dash for the door. Kusha was right behind her and Ren at the end. They swirled in a blurred rush of limbs, screams, and flashing metal.

In Maia's arms, Dani paled even more, her breaths coming in short, tortured gasps. A chill sped up Maia's spine and spread across her limbs. It was a weird, bone-numbing chill that had no place in the warm room.

Phocluus laughed. It had begun.

Something sticky and warm splattered across Maia's arm.

Blood!

Where did so much blood come from? Maia could not cling to the question for too long, let alone find an answer to it. The cold in her veins spread, rushing in to capture her heart which felt as heavy as a mountain in her chest.

Phocluus's wild cackle rang above the dull racket and the dimness.

CHAPTER FIFTY-THREE

RETURN OF THE FACELESS

The door fell open with a loud bang and people rushed in. Maia blinked furiously to clear her vision, but it hardly helped. Voices reached her, but she could not make much sense out of them. All she heard was a muffled ruckus. Then someone darted to the front of the cage and peered at her.

"Maia, can you hear me?" the woman said.

"Mahswa Tabrin?" Maia muttered, wondering how the Tierremorphe had found her way here.

"Yes, Maia. Listen to me now. Go back to the center of the cage, do you understand? Take Dani with you," Mahswa Tabrin said. "I'll try to break this. But you need to stay away from the edge."

Maia nodded and wrapped her arms around Dani's waist, then dragged Dani's limp body as far as she could from where the Mahswa stood. The chairman's yell rang out before she caught her breath.

"No, Mahswa," Phocluus screamed, his shrill voice clearing the fog that had enveloped Maia. "You cannot break this cage. We'll never make another. This is our only chance out of this system. Our final chance perhaps."

Mahswa Tabrin shot a glare at the chairman's projection. "Shame on you, Phocluus. You used every Tierremorphe and played us like fools. You tricked us into making this, made each of us build parts of it so we wouldn't realize what we were actually building. If I knew you were planning this, I'd have never touched that Calbion," the Mahswa hissed. "Now that I know, you think I'm going to stand by and watch it kill two innocent kids?"

"Innocent?" Phocluus shouted. "That's the spawn of the traitor who broke the heart of the Sedara. Don't you remember?"

"You cannot punish someone for what their mother did," the Mahswa snapped back. "And for what it's worth, I'm not sure what her mother did was a crime at all."

"So you support the traitor's actions now? Of course. That's why you went and sided with the filthy R'armimon," Phocluus spat. "You betrayed your people to the enemy that's sworn to destroy us."

The Mahswa and the R'armimon? Together?

Phocluus continued. "They killed your kind, do you understand? They murdered every Tierremorphe. Those R'armimon did."

Maia's vision blurred some more, voices dribbled into her ear at a slow, lethargic pace.

"I had to stop you from trying this," thundered a familiar voice. "But I underestimated you, Phocluus. You got this despicable contraption built before I could take your weapons out."

Ruche? Could it really be him?

"You hear that, Mahswa? He killed them," Phocluus shrieked. "That's who you call a friend? One who took out your own?"

Mahswa Tabrin shot another glare at the projection of Phocluus. "Will helping you bring my own back, Phocluus?" she asked. Phocluus did not reply. "If not, stop talking to me."

"You are a traitor to our nation, Mahswa Tabrin," Phocluus raged. "Your name will be written in dark ink in the history of our glorious nation. You remember that!"

The Mahswa ignored the jibes and moved closer to the cage, and grabbing two of the bars, she started to chant. Her long fingers danced along the length of the bars in an entrancing rhythm. The more she chanted, the clearer Maia could think and see. Maia could not be sure, but it seemed like Dani's ragged breathing slowly grew steady and less tortured.

Maia tried to make out the scene outside. Blood was the first thing she noticed. It was all over the floor and the walls and splattered across half of the cage.

"Everrol!" the scream sprung from her guts and tore through her throat. Everrol lay in the middle of the room, face down in a pool of blood. The way his body was slumped on the floor, Maia was sure he was dead. And she had done nothing to help him.

They called her the Nosiifarus? For this? Phocluus was right; she was as useless as a mouse.

Through blurred eyes, Maia scanned the room, her heart thumping fearfully with worry for her friends.

A battle raged—a dark swirl of capes, arms, swords—in the room and outside the door. Kusha, Ren, and Nafi were in the middle, fighting the Order's thugs in black capes.

There were more people in silvery-white bodysuits, ghostly figures that swirled like a silvery mist around the caped thugs. Maia blinked. The ghosts did not have faces. The Faceless Ones, she remembered. Ruche had brought with him the fearsome assassins of the R'armimon.

The projection of Phocluus looked livid. Perhaps the Mahswa had made some progress. She must have. The suffocating weight that had sat on Maia's chest had lifted a bit. The Mahswa looked exhausted though—her eyes seemed sunken and her cheekbones sharper—but she carried on regardless.

"Dani! Dani, wake up," Maia whispered, patting her friend's cheek. She did not stir.

Maia looked around, the frenzy of action making her head spin. A blob of capes, limbs, and weapons whirled near the door like a twister. Metal clashed against metal, whips slashed through the air, and people crashed to the ground and against the furniture and walls. Screams, yells, and grunts filled the air.

Ruche rushed into the middle of the battle, shouting at Kusha. "Get out of here. Call your people. Get your father."

Kusha fell away and the man he was fighting immediately jumped forward, slamming the hilt of his whip sword against Kusha's neck. Kusha frantically swung at his opponent as he teetered and fell to the floor. Ruche threw himself on the Order's thug, grabbing him from behind and wrapping him in a headlock. "Go," he shouted at Kusha again. "Take your friends and go."

Panting, blood trickling down from the corner of his mouth, Kusha nodded. He cast a fearful look back at the cage. "And Dani? Maia?"

"I'll take care of them," Ruche shouted. "Go now."

As soon as Ren and Nafi, both bruised and bleeding, disengaged, the ghostly Faceless took their place. Kusha pulled Ren and Nafi out of the room and together they dashed away.

The Order was no match for trained assassins of the R'armimon. They were soon pushed back and corralled to a side.

"Maia," Ruche called. "Hold your focus. Don't fade or fall asleep. The Mahswa has stopped the encapsulation and she will get you out of this cage. Have faith. I have to go . . . need to take care of something else."

He pointed at the door, and Maia could guess his intentions. The projection of Phocluus was headed out the door and Ruche was following him . . . it. To what end, she was not sure.

The Mahswa's fingers danced along the bars, her prune-dry lips moved endlessly in a silent chant, and Dani lay comatose in Maia's lap. The fight, now down to a few of the Order fighting an uneven and hopeless battle against the Faceless, had moved to the grand foyer and Maia was left staring at the gruesome remnants of the fight. A hum descended around Maia, trying to lull her into sleep that she refused to yield to.

She hung on to the thinnest shreds of consciousness, looking from

Dani's pale face to the Mahswa's crumbling form, and finally at the portrait of the Xifarian queen Quemiila who showered a murderous glare at her. Defying the Rahina's fierce stare was the one thing that kept Maia awake until the front bars of the gilded cage fell apart in pieces.

CHAPTER FIFTY-FOUR

BEGINNING OF THE END

Hooking her arms through Dani's, Maia pulled the girl out through the opening in the cage Mahswa Tabrin had carved out. Dani did not stir when Maia laid her down on the ground outside, but she was breathing. The Mahswa, on the other hand, was clearly in bad shape. Tearing the Calbion sheath apart had taken the life force out of the woman. Her face was blue, and dark veins had formed on her face and arms, crisscrossing her like a deadly web. Blood had collected at the corners of her mouth and now it trickled past her lips. Maia had barely put Dani down when Mahswa Tabrin collapsed in a heap on the floor.

"Mahswa," Maia shrieked and ran to her side. The woman's arms were cold as ice and she barely breathed. "Help!" Maia shouted, but there was no one in the room left to help.

She had to get out and find help before it was too late. Maia bounded to the door and pushed it open, her heart sinking like a boulder to the pit of her stomach at the sight outside. There was no way out of the ship through there. A fierce battle still raged in the grand foyer—the silvery-bodysuit-clad faceless assassins Ruche had brought with him seemed to have an edge over the whip-wielding thugs from the Order of Fyrstell whom Phocluus commanded.

Ruche was not there, Maia realized. Could he be dead? Or did he abandon her? A shudder threatened to rush up her spine but Maia pushed it down. Debris, blood, body parts, and dead people were strewn across the floor, and the sight made Maia's insides reel.

She fell back, gritted her teeth, and collected her thoughts. First things first. She needed to get help. Even though the thugs from the Order were cornered, there was no clear path to the exit of the ship from where Maia stood. She had to fight the Order to get out and that would take time. The best thing, Maia reasoned quickly, was to use her wristband to call her friends.

Only the communicator had not worked for her in a long while. Still, she had to try! Grabbing the communicator, Maia focused her thoughts. "Dani, Dani, Dani," she muttered.

Just like the last time, there was nothing but silence in her mind. Maia's eyes burned and frustration simmered in her guts. "Please, please work," she sobbed.

Clear your mind, calm your thoughts, the Xinhagyi's words tinkled in her ears. Fingers curling around the communicator, Maia breathed the way the Xinhagyi had taught her. Slowly, her senses settled. Once again, she focused her thoughts.

"Dani, Dani!" Maia muttered.

"Maia!" Kusha's voice streamed into her mind. "We're on our way. Is Dani all right?"

"We got out of the cage," Maia replied. An endless stream of tears flowed down her cheeks. "Mahswa Tabrin got us out. But both the Mahswa and Dani need help. Hurry."

"We're coming. We've got help. You stay safe. Take care of Dani."

Kusha's voice broke and faded. Dabbing her eyes, Maia inhaled sharply. Help was coming. Dani was going to get better. Mahswa was going to make it.

She turned to study the scene in the foyer again. A huddle of flying limbs and whips squarely blocked the only exit of the ship. Four of the Faceless fought the Order near the exit, blow against blow, strike against strike. They were quite evenly matched. As a Faceless toppled to the ground screaming, struck by a ferocious blow of a whip, Maia winced. Two more Faceless jumped in and tackled the Order's thug to the ground. More whips flew in, tearing at clothes, flesh, and anything else that stood in the way.

Just looking at the endless struggle exhausted Maia. She mulled her options. She could simply wait and watch the Order and the Faceless fight it out, or she could join the fight. Standing there and watching was not an option at all, she concluded right away. She *had* to help. Maia grabbed Bellator's hilt and pulled it out, then she summoned the light.

The warmth surged out of her, tingling her spine as it flowed to her fingertips in a vivid swirl of light. The stream was so controlled this time, every swell measured and every ebb planned. Maia could not stop a smile from flooding her face. She was getting the hang of this after all. For the first time, the light twirling all around her hand and trickling down to Bellator's tip looked and felt soothing.

Maia was still smiling as she willed the light into a whip. It only was fitting that she used that form to fight the whip-wielding thugs of the Order. Concentrating her thoughts on the shining wave of energy, Maia whispered, "*Yoteh.*"

The word came out just as softly as the Xinhagyi had taught her. The light dancing around her hands looked its vivid best. Smiling some more, Maia flicked it toward the center of the battleground.

It was sharp and precise. The long wave of light—dazzling and beautiful, vigorous and accurate—lashed out and impinged on the fighters. It wrapped around the waist of the nearest thug and picked him off the floor. Maia pulled, twirling the man in the air for a moment before tossing him away and flinging him against the wall. He crashed with the sound of crunching bones and rattling walls, finally slumping on the floor in a bloody, unconscious heap.

Maia drew a long breath and took another step closer to the fight.

She was sure she could win this, possibly quicker than it would take the Faceless. She curled the light into a ball in her left hand and weaved it around Bellator in her right. Slowly but surely she advanced on the warzone.

"Maia! Stop." Ruche's voice, loud and clear, struck like a whip in Maia's ears. She pulled the light in and stepped back instantly. Ruche had not deserted her after all. But where in the world was he?

She spotted him seated in the darkest corner. He seemed to be casually lounging on a sumptuous couch, staring intently at the empty chair across from him. Maia took a few rushed steps toward him, carefully avoiding the death match near the exit.

"Ruche," Maia called. "Mahswa Tabrin needs help."

Ruche threw a quick glance at her. "No matter what happens, stay away from the fight. Do *not* engage," he said calmly, and then curiously enough, turned back to the lushly upholstered chair. It was about then that Maia noticed. A dim form, the specter of Chairman Phocluus, hovered over the chair.

It was odd, almost comical, that while a fierce battle raged on one side of the room, Ruche was having a quiet conversation with Phocluus on the other. Whatever Ruche was doing had to be important. Since she could not fight or help Dani and the Mahswa, Maia decided to find out what the seer was up to.

Ruche was speaking in a low voice, but Maia picked up a few words as she approached. "You'll stop your despicable attacks or I promise that you'll regret that you ever lived," Ruche said to the projection of Phocluus. His voice was cold and almost sent a shiver down Maia's spine, but it hardly had any effect on Phocluus, who simply smirked.

"You're going to kill us anyway," Phocluus said. "Why would I fear any of your threats?"

Ruche closed his eyes and breathed as if he was trying hard to hold his temper. "You stay away from her and I'll spare you. I'll even put in a good word for you with the Empire," he said. "But if not—"

"You make me laugh, stooge," Phocluus said, jeering. Ruche's face turned a bright shade of crimson and his lips thinned to lines.

"Don't worry, Ruche," Maia could not stop from interjecting. "He can't get me. I've slipped through his fingers every time. Isn't that true, Chairman Phocluus? I have friends, Phocluus, and truth on my side. Together, we will win, as we've always won."

The projection stilled for a moment, then its lips curled. "You have won nothing, girl," the chairman said. "Maybe you've earned yourself a few days at most, but your future is sealed. Your sun will soon explode on you, and you can't stop it even if you tried."

"You're bluffing," Maia said. "The Sedara is broken. You can't hurt our sun."

The projection broke into loud cackles. "Sure we can. We have already. Your beautiful little sun will start falling apart soon." He raised his arms and waved them over his head. "Ah . . . when a star explodes, they say it's one gorgeous spectacle."

Phocluus was a madman, Maia did not doubt that.

"The explosion won't spare you either," she shot back. "Don't you get that? This time you can't run."

Phocluus scoffed. The corners of his mouth twisted cruelly when he spoke. "We'll see about that. Anyway, Xifarians would rather embrace death than be tried by zealots of the Empire."

"Do your people know?" Maia shouted. "Do they know you've chosen death for them?"

Phocluus raised a jeering eyebrow. "People? What people? Who cares about useless, commonplace people? I decide their fates. I decide when and how their pitiful, ordinary lives end."

"You can't do that to them. They aren't things, they're people." Maia could not believe how cruel the chairman was, but she should not have been surprised. After all, he had destroyed her mother and her family. But she was not going to let him destroy her.

"Idealist to the end," Phocluus said, chuckling. "Just like your parents." Then he winked and waved. "See you later, traitor-spawn," Phocluus said, and in an instant, the projection started to crumble. Soon it vanished completely but Maia continued to stare blankly at the empty chair. She stirred when Ruche rose to his feet.

"Was he saying the truth?" Maia asked Ruche. "About the sun exploding? Or was he bluffing?"

Ruche returned an indecisive nod. "I don't know. I have no idea how the Heart of the Sedara works."

"There has to be someone who does," Maia said. "If it's true, we have to stop it . . . somehow."

Ruche nodded again, in a vague, distracted sort of way. "I have to leave now, Maia," he said abruptly. "Your friends are returning with more people and I'd rather not be seen here."

"But they're still fighting and—" Maia turned to point at the struggle near the door but stopped as soon as she did. The Faceless had disappeared, and so had the Order's thugs. "They're gone."

"Yes, they have," Ruche said. He cast a quick look at the Mahswa and Dani and sighed. "I hope they fare well. You'll need good friends by your side to face what's coming."

His words chilled Maia's heart. "W-what do you mean? What's coming?"

"I couldn't stop the Empire, Maia," Ruche said in a low, broken voice. "They're on the way to Tansi."

"But you said if I could get the sword and the . . ." Maia's words caught at her throat and it took a lot of effort to find them again. "Is it too late already?"

"No, it isn't," Ruche said, and Maia breathed a sigh of relief. There was a chance that Tansi could still be saved. Ruche continued in a solemn voice, "You need to get them as quickly as you can. There's no hope for Tansi otherwise."

"I will, Ruche," Maia said, fists curling with determination. "I promise, I will."

Ruche reached out and patted her shoulder. "I know you will. Keep safe, Maia."

He rushed out of the door and in the blink of an eye, vanished into the darkness.

Left alone in the once-opulent room, Maia looked around at the devastation. Blood was everywhere, bodies too. Some of them were devoid of faces, but more wore the capes and masks of the Order of the Fyrstell. In the inner room, Dani and the Mahswa still lay on the floor, unconscious. At the center of the room, Everrol's lifeless body was hunched over. Maia tried to gulp the pain away but failed. Everrol . . . the poor boy had tried to defend them and paid the biggest price. It should not have been this way. It was not fair.

Voices drifted in, and Maia heard her uncle clearly above the din. How was she going to explain all the mayhem?

They barged in—Ren, Nafi, Kusha, Sana, and Uncle Alasdair. Behind them were the envoys of the Xifarian queen and the Solianese leaders. Kusha's father, Steward Lok, was among them, as were Hilledunn, Sahiiraan Leeam, and Sahiiraan Tsininio. After them came the healer monks.

"They need help in there." Maia pointed at the inner room with the cage. While the healer monks rushed away, Uncle Alasdair dashed to Maia's side. He patted her cheeks and shoulders, his teary gaze skimmed all over her.

"Are you all right?" he said in a broken voice.

Maia nodded, resting her head on his shoulder. Even though her sight had turned blurry, she could see the Xifarian envoys throw fiery glares in her direction. They were going to accuse her of everything, Maia was sure.

It did not take long to prove her suspicion correct.

One of the Xifarians strode up to her. "How did this happen?" he demanded, eyes flashing.

Uncle Alasdair's arm tightened around Maia's shoulder. He did not just speak; he roared like Maia had never heard before. "You tell us. How could this happen? We welcomed you to discuss terms of peace, and you came here with a plan to kill our children. How dare you?"

Kusha's father stepped to Uncle Alasdair's side and nodded fiercely. "This is unthinkable. We will not tolerate such treachery."

Another Xifarian envoy, a woman, jumped to the fore. "This is a terrible, terrible misunderstanding. I assure you, the Rahina only wants peace. I think a rogue power is behind this and we shall do everything we can to bring those rogues to justice," she said. She flashed a charming but rather shaky smile at Maia. "We're just glad you're all right." She turned toward Uncle Alasdair. "Perhaps she needs some medical attention as well."

"Perhaps," Uncle Alasdair said gruffly. "But we need answers. Unless we have answers, there'll be no peace talks."

Uncle Alasdair and Sana led Maia out of the airship and soon handed her over to the monks at the sanatorium.

"Get some rest, Maia," Uncle Alasdair said before leaving. "I need to speak with the Xifarians and get to the bottom of this. We can't have them attacking you right here in ThulaSu. We can't have them here at all."

"I don't think they'll attack me again anytime soon," Maia said. "They have no one left to make another Calbion cage for them."

"Maybe not, but you'll be careful. Yes?"

"Yes, I will," Maia said.

"Don't worry, Father. I won't leave her alone," Sana reassured.

He left right after and Maia surrendered herself to the incessant questioning and elaborate examination routine of the ThulaSuian healers.

CHAPTER FIFTY-FIVE

THE LOST . . .

Maia's teammates, except for Dani, were waiting a distance away from the entrance of the sanatorium. As soon as Maia exited the building with Sana late that night, Ren broke away from the group and rushed up to her, eyes blazing. The rest watched quietly, their faces stony, their eyes questioning. While Ren planted his foot in front of her and cocked his head angrily, Kusha and Nafi hung a few steps behind. Maia braced herself. This was not normal. This was not looking good.

"How are they?" Ren demanded.

"Dani is better, but the Mahswa's not too well," Maia replied truthfully. "She's drifting in and out of consciousness."

Ren shook his head and sighed. "She's the last of our Tierremorphes," he said. "And now we'll lose her also."

"You don't know that yet," Maia said, trying to bring some hope into the conversation.

"But you do?"

Maia drew a breath. "What do you mean?"

"Your friend, the R'armimon . . . he must know." Ren's words were sharp, and they were meant to be. There was no hint of friendliness in his narrowed eyes and tight lips.

Maia could hardly believe her ears. Phocluus had killed Everrol and almost killed Dani as well. He had tried to encapsulate her in that Calbion cage. Even the Mahswa had gone against Phocluus. And yet Ren was raging against her over taking help from Ruche?

She took a long breath and forced her thoughts to calm down. She could not push Ren away. She had to hold on to him . . . at least try.

"He's not my friend, Ren," Maia replied with as much deliberation as she could. "He's the means to an end. Hopefully a peaceful end."

Ren scoffed. "And for us? Have you planned to slaughter every Xifarian on the way to your peaceful end?"

"Of course not," Maia said vehemently. "How could you even think that?"

Ren's eyes widened. A mocking expression stretched his lips into a false smile. "You're in with the R'armimon, Maia. These are the same people who've been hunting us down for centuries, trying to blow us out of this universe. What else am I going to think?"

Maia bristled inside. She had thought of calming Ren down, explaining to him that she was not going to buy into any plan of hurting innocents, Xifarians or not. But seeing the scornful expression on his face, her urge to pacify vanished in a heartbeat. If Ren was not going to give her the benefit of the doubt, let alone trust her, she was not going to try to cajole him either.

"You know, the R'armimon have reason to want to blow you away. You people aren't exactly the paragon of peace. You've killed millions in those centuries you speak of, and you would've killed millions more on Tansi if you had your way." Maia paused to rein in her rising voice. "Don't pretend to be what you're not, Ren. You're not the victim here. You're the perpetrators of unthinkable crimes. Why do you think you should go unpunished?"

Ren crossed his arms and smirked. "So . . . you're our self-appointed judge and jury now?"

The harshness of his tone made Maia flinch. Sana's grip tightened on her arm, but Maia was not going to back off. She hurtled on, like a sightless boulder, smashing everything in its way. Crossing her arms, she looked Ren squarely in the eye.

"What if I am? What are you going to do about it?"

For a moment, Maia thought she saw hurt darken those mottled eyes, but then they flashed with rage and Maia forgot the guilty twitch in her heart.

"I thought of you as a friend, and look at you now," Ren said, the corner of his lips curling with contempt.

"A friend, really?" Maia had nothing short of contempt either. "That's why you never told me about your father? You know, the advisor to the supreme ruler who also happens to be a Gnelexian?"

Her words had the effect she intended. His face dimmed instantly and his gaze faltered. A few steps away, Kusha and Nafi frowned upon hearing her words.

"I was never much of a friend, was I?" Maia said. She nodded at Kusha and Nafi. "What about them? Do *they* know? Any of them?"

Nafi walked over, Kusha following. Ren shook his head a little. "You don't understand," he muttered.

"What's this all about?" Nafi demanded.

"Ask your friend," Maia replied, her voice scathing. "Ask him about his father . . . who he is, what he does —"

"It's not how you think," Ren shouted. "I can explain."

"Well, I could explain about Ruche too," Maia shot back. "But did you let me? You started calling me names, accusing me. Why should I treat you any different?"

Ren looked away at the wall, but Nafi threw a fierce look at Maia. "At least he didn't murder a friend in cold blood," she said, almost spitting the words at Maia.

Nafi just *had* to bring up Miir again!

Maia's fists curled. They had said it enough times. She had killed herself over it enough. She was going to blame herself for the rest of her life, there was no changing that. But nothing she did was going to bring Miir back, so she had to end this cycle of humiliation. Maybe she was going to lose all her friends, but if they could not see how much she had been grieving, what sort of friends were they anyway?

Nafi was about to say more, but Maia held up her hand. "You've said enough, Nafi," she said in a quiet but resolute tone. "I have to say some things now. First of all, it was not cold-blooded at all. I don't care if you refuse to believe me, but the truth is, I couldn't even recall the moment I struck Miir down. I was not myself."

Maia paused to collect her thoughts, making sure she was not saying anything she did not mean. "I've said I'm sorry. You have no idea how bad I feel about what I did. Nothing I do is ever going to change the fact that I killed someone who stood up for me against all odds. And nothing I say is going to make you change your mind about me." Her voice caught for a bit, her throat parched and jammed with lumps of pain. "So I'm going to stop explaining myself. I don't need your judgment or seek your forgiveness because neither will bring Miir back. I'll hold on to my grief. And my guilt. I'm strong enough to bear them alone."

Tired and out of breath, Maia stopped. Silence fell. For a moment or two, she could hear nothing but a few broken breaths. Nafi looked away, her face flushed.

"Now if you don't mind, I need some time for myself," Maia said. "I think I've been through enough in a day."

No one stopped her. No one even said a word. Maia's guts roiled, her eyes burned, but she forced herself away from her teammates. All she wanted to do was curl up in her bed and cry, but that had to wait. She had to stay strong and soldier on. Alone. She had to stop the R'armimon Empire. Somehow.

The courtyard was a blur as Maia strode across it, but her steps never slowed. She knew of Sana's silent but unwavering presence a few steps behind. She also noted the presence of the Kausakas and the Black Phantoms at every strategic location. But other than that, all seemed as usual, so Maia marched on steadily until she reached the mouth of the main staircase to the higher floors. Very few people walked about, and thankfully, she came across no one she knew. Her luck ran out as soon as she turned into the corridor leading to her room.

"Maia," someone called.

"Maks? What are you doing here?"

"Been looking for you," he said, pulling her into a tight embrace. "Heard about the ambush. And . . . Everrol."

Everrol . . . they had shredded the poor boy into pieces. His life did not matter to Phocluus. No one mattered. Anyone was dispensable. "Necessary sacrifice," he called them. All he wanted was to get to her, at any cost. Poor Everrol, innocent and unprepared, had no idea what was coming.

"You shouldn't be here, Maks," Maia said. "You shouldn't be anywhere near me."

Maks chuckled, almost disbelievingly. "What are you talking about?"

Next to Maia, Sana shifted uneasily before blurting, "I'll let you two talk. Will check on you in the morning?"

Maia waited until Sana had vanished from sight before turning to Maks again. "I'm a dangerous person to be around, Maks," she said in an unflinching voice. "Everrol died because of me. I can't let anyone else get hurt, especially not someone like you."

"Someone like me? What do you mean? That I can't take care of myself?" Maks sounded hurt. That was expected. But Maia was not about to relent.

"You are no match for the evil that's out there to get me," Maia said. "Mahswa Tabrin is barely alive. She almost died trying to save me. I couldn't get out of that cage, even with all my so-called powers."

Maks shook his head stubbornly. "I'm *not* a child, Maia," he said. "I may not be like one of you but —"

"I cannot be with you, Maks," Maia said, watching his face wilt. "I won't be able to live with myself if something were to happen to you because of me. Why don't you understand?"

CHAPTER FIFTY-FIVE

His lips trembled. Slowly he pulled his hand away from hers.

"I'm sorry, Maks," Maia said. She felt truly bad for him, but there was no other way. She had to push people away. Things were going to get far worse and anyone close to her was automatically in her enemies' crosshairs. She could not let that happen anymore than was necessary.

Maks scanned the floor and nodded distractedly. "I don't understand. But . . . but if that's what you want . . ."

His voice faded and it hurt to look at his crumpled form. Maia steeled herself regardless. "That is what I want, Maks," she said.

Maia stood rooted as Maks walked away until the blurred, dimly lit corridor was all that remained. Then she turned away, exhausted. Even while she had fought the hordes of the whip-wielding Xifarians, she had not felt half as tired.

There was little to hope for, nothing to look forward to. Tansi was staring death in the face, and it was only a matter of when the time would run out. Either the chairman's plan would come to fruition or the Empire's forces would arrive, and there was a scant chance they could dodge both threats.

Ruche had asked for things and she would try to get them, but what was her likelihood of succeeding alone?

Friends . . . Dani was fighting death and she did not even know if she could call Ren a friend. Nafi was still barely even talking to her. That left Kusha. Only Kusha. How far could the two of them go?

Maia stumbled along, heaving when she finally reached her room. She pushed the door open, eager to throw herself down in her bed. An unexpectedly cold breeze hit her face as soon as she entered. Rayan was missing, as was Dusty. But there was something else different about the room.

She saw the silhouette at the window and froze, her heart thrashing against her ribs like a war hammer intent on breaking her apart. Her fingers curled around Bellator's hilt instinctively as her weary eyes struggled to focus on the dark figure sitting on the windowsill.

CHAPTER FIFTY-SIX

. . . AND THE FOUND

Maia blinked. Then she blinked again. She knew that person. She knew him well. But he was from a long time ago, seemed like another lifetime almost.

It could not be *him*. Or could it?

"Miir?" she called, the name quivering out of the painful lump in her throat. She took one step forward. Then another.

It *was* him. How he got here, Maia did not know, but she did not care either. Not at the moment. All she felt was relief surging out of every pore in her body. She muttered a prayer of thanks to the stars, thankful that he was alive, that he had come back to her for whatever reason, thankful that fate had not turned her into a cold-blooded executioner.

"You're alive," she whispered, not caring if he noticed that her voice was breaking up.

He did not reply. Maia suppressed a chuckle. Some things never changed. She took a step closer. One more step and she would see him clearly.

He had been sitting on the windowsill, a dark cape draped across his shoulders. Now he stood, the hood slipping off his head, and in the pale light, he looked paler than usual.

Overall, he looked strange, almost like he was a different person.

His cheekbones were sharper than she remembered; his dark gaze just as intense but somehow far calmer than before.

"You're all right."

"Yes, I am." His voice—so familiar yet so different—melted Maia's insides and coursed through her soul like a river, soothing and healing.

Maia did not know what took over her at that moment. The Miir she knew would not approve, but she did not care. All she felt was a severe need to know he was real, that she was not in some dream. There was no hesitation in the step that bridged the distance between them, or when she threw her arms around him and held him. Maia did not pull away even after feeling him flinch at her embrace. She was not letting go, not until his presence had filled her consciousness to the brim. Maia did not know how long she held him, but she stirred when he lightly touched her arm.

"There is not much time," he whispered, his voice soft but rippling with urgency.

Time for what? What did he mean?

Maia let go and looked up at him. His face was still half hidden by the shadows, but that did not stop Maia from seeing. He was only half-a-head taller than she was now and looking into his eyes was so much easier.

Something was missing. It was his neurogenic interface. He looked different without the metal patch—a device containing memories across generations—over his left eye.

Where did it go? Did he lose it? Or take it off for some reason?

They stared at each other, wordless again, Maia's mind swimming with questions.

How did he survive that fall from Devil's Ridge?

She recognized the cape he was wearing, the kind Ori Pistado's

Black Phantoms wore. Had he been with Ori Pistado all these days? Could he have been the one whose aura caught her eye? He *had* to be.

A thought—sudden but satisfying—came to her mind. He was the one who had passed her the notes about the Origin Scrolls, and he was the one who had helped her with the Crawler. He *had* to be.

"I need your help," Miir said, peering into her eyes.

Help? What help did he need? Miir never needed help. The least of all from her. And yet, he was here. So badly Maia wanted to ask, but she did not let the questions come out. She would not. Not this time. This time, for the first time since they had known each other, Maia decided to trust him blindly.

"How can I help? Tell me."

His eyes narrowed, his keen gaze scanning Maia's face over and over. Maia almost let a smile slip out. Miir probably could not believe her eager words. How could he? She had not given him any reason to.

But he took it in stride, just like he always did. "I need you to come with me."

Go with him? But where? Besides, there were guards everywhere. How could they go anywhere past the Kausakas?

Maia silenced the questions in her head. "When?" she asked.

"Right now."

"Sure. Let's go."

Her hand felt Bellator. All she needed was her sword.

"Put this on," he said, holding out a dark cape similar to his.

"Is this a Black Phantom cape?"

"Yes."

As Maia slipped the cape over her shoulders, Miir walked over to the door and looked back and forth across the dimly lit corridor. His eyes were sharp, his posture stiff and alert like a soldier at war. Like always. Maia smiled to herself, cherishing the familiarity. It felt good, almost comforting to have him back. A sigh, abrupt and deep, tore through her, along with an unexpected realization—she had missed him.

She also realized, since seeing him, her worries had vanished. As if . . . with him by her side, she could take on anything. A pang . . . an indescribable emptiness, sudden and strong, filled her guts at the thought. Maia could not fathom why she felt that way. She was supposed to be happy seeing Miir alive and she was. Yet . . .

Fear?

Maia had no doubt this was fear. But fear of what?

It hit her like a splash of ice-cold water, forceful but bracing at the same time. She was afraid of losing him again.

"Ready?" Miir's gaze turned curious when it fell on her fretful face.

Maia jolted to a start, fumbling with the last button of the cape as she hastened to his side.

"What is the matter?" he asked.

Maia could recall every instance over the years when Miir had asked her something and she had avoided answering. Sometimes she had felt too awkward or scared to reply, and at others, she had willfully snubbed him. Each time she had seen his face darken and his eyes dim. She was not going to do it to him again, she decided, no matter how much embarrassment the answer might cause her.

Breathing in deep, she looked up at him. "I have missed you," she said, holding his gaze steadily.

For a moment, Miir's eyes stilled. Then he gave a nod so subtle she could have missed it if she blinked. There was no ridicule in that response and no show of delight either, just a quiet acknowledgment of her confession.

Maia did not want awkwardness to encroach on them. "Shall we go now?" she said.

"Do you want to know where I am taking you?"

Of course, she wanted to know. She also wanted to simply follow him for a change. It was weird doing that, but she stuck to her decision.

"No," Maia replied forcefully. "You've always known what to do. If you think I need to go with you, then I'll trust your judgment."

His gaze burned her face. "All right then. Let us go."

Together, side by side, they stepped out into the darkness. Maia could not find a shred of fear inside her, only an unexpected tingle of excitement.

That was surprising. Or was it?

Maia picked up the pace. She was sure this would be a journey worth remembering.

— THE END —

APPENDIX

THE SOLIANESE

In order of appearance

Maia – girl from Appian, Core 21

The Xinhagyi – Chief of the Kausakas

Nafi – girl from the Third Continent, Core 21

Maks – boy from Appian, student at ThulaSu

Kusha – boy from the First Continent, Core 21

Steward Lok – steward of the House of the Sun, Kusha's father

Sahiiraan Leeam – leader of the House of the Broken Seas, Lex's father

Rayan – member of the Desert's Watch

Aman – boy from Appian, student at ThulaSu

Nisa – girl from Appian, student at ThulaSu

Lex – boy from the Third Continent

Aihnswothe Feirah – Chief of the Eliregen, House of the Sands, Nafi's father

Jiri – boy from the Second Continent, Core 13

Anja – girl from Shiloh, Core 13

Everrol – student at ThulaSu, mentor for Core 21

Monk Hilledunn – teacher at ThulaSu

THE SOLIANESE (CONTD.)

Monk Tessio – teacher at ThulaSu

Revsi Sottekaja – teacher at ThulaSu

Ori Pistado – village chieftain, member of the Resistance

Sana – Maia's cousin

Alasdair – Maia's uncle

Monk Atriss – librarian at ThulaSu

Merin – student at ThulaSu

THE JJORD

In order of appearance

Dani – girl from T'ra (Coloni Centrei), Core 21
Hans – Dani's older brother
Oliena – Premier, Jjordic Council
Aloysus – Member, Jjordic Council
Aerika – Training Supervisor, UAAS
Vyessa – girl from Zagran, Core 45
Rudi – engineer in charge, Damoclian Connector
Aemmon – student at UAAS
Rikka – student at UAAS

THE XIFARIANS

In order of appearance

Phocluus – Emeritus Master of XDA, Chairman of the SDS

Statesman Orano Taillefei – Xifarian statesman, Amanii's father

Lady Druuna – Xifarian woman

Ren – boy from Ixiil, Core 21

Karhann – boy from Armezai, Core 7

Mahswa Tabrin – Advisor to the Principal, XDA

Loriine – girl from Armezai, Core 7

Baecca – girl from Armezai, Core 7

Kehorkjin – Resident Master at the XDA

The Chancellor – Chancellor of the Xifarian Republic

Amanii – apprentice at the SDS

Pomewege – Principal of the XDA

Adienos – Ren's friend

Miir – apprentice at the SDS, son of Xifarian Chancellor

THE R'ARMIMON

In order of appearance

Ruche — Seer of the R'armimon
Aekken – Crown Prince, heir-in-waiting of the R'armimon Throne

About the Author

S. G. Basu is a telecommunications professional with a passion for writing. The first ideas for this story came to her on a blustery winter's evening while watching the setting sun and realizing how vital it is to our existence. As she dwelled on the central premise, characters joined the fray, each with a voice that would not be denied. Therefore, their stories grew, unfolding over several episodes. Their adventures continue as they mature and flourish.

Ms. Basu resides in Maryland with her husband and daughter.

Maia's adventures continue in the following books:
Maia and the Blades of ThulaSu
Maia and the Legend of Tansi

There's more to come. Find out about upcoming books at www.sgbasu.com.

www.ingramcontent.com/pod-product-compliance
Lightning Source LLC
Chambersburg PA
CBHW030538260626
47157CB00006B/2083